THE SHAPING OF MIDDLE-EARTH

THE HISTORY OF MIDDLE-EARTH

ᚱ ᚠ ᚠ ᚠᚱᚠᚠ ᚠᚠᚠᚠᚠᚠ ᚠ ᚠᚠᚠᚠ ᚠ ᚠᚠᚠᚠ ᚠ ᚠᚠ
ᚠᚠ ᚠ ᚠᚠ ᚠ ᚠᚠᚠᚠ ᚠᚠ ᚠᚠᚠ ᚠ ᚠᚠᚠ ᚠ ᚠᚠᚠᚠᚠ ᚠ ᚠ

J. R. R. TOLKIEN

THE SHAPING OF
MIDDLE-EARTH

THE QUENTA, THE AMBARKANTA
AND THE ANNALS

together with
the earliest 'Silmarillion' and the first Map

Edited by Christopher Tolkien

BOSTON
HOUGHTON MIFFLIN COMPANY

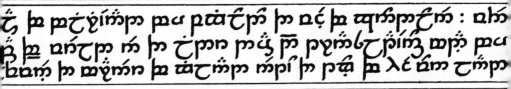

Copyright © 1986 by
Frank Richard Williamson and Christopher Reuel Tolkien
as Executors of the Estate of J.R.R. Tolkien

For information about permission to reproduce selections
from this book, write to Permissions, Houghton Mifflin
Company, 2 Park Street, Boston, Massachusetts 02108.

Library of Congress Cataloging in Publication Data

Tolkien, J.R.R. (John Ronald Reuel), 1892–1973.
The shaping of Middle-earth.

(The History of Middle-earth; 4)
Includes index.
1. Middle Earth (Imaginary place)—Literary
collections. 2. Fantastic literature, English.
I. Tolkien, Christopher. II. Title. III. Series:
Tolkien, J.R.R. (John Ronald Reuel), 1892–1973.
History of Middle-earth; 4.
PR6039.032S46   1986   823'.912   86-10338
ISBN 0-395-42501-8

Printed in the United States of America

FFG 11 10 9 8 7 6 5 4

TM

CONTENTS

PREFACE

This book brings the 'History of Middle-earth' to some time in the 1930s: the cosmographical work *Ambarkanta* and the earliest *Annals of Valinor* and *Annals of Beleriand*, while later than the *Quenta Noldorinwa* – the 'Silmarillion' version that was written, as I believe, in 1930 – cannot themselves be more precisely dated.

This is the stage at which my father had arrived when *The Hobbit* was written. Comparison of the *Quenta* with the published *Silmarillion* will show that the essential character of the work was now fully in being; in the shape and fall of sentences, even of whole passages, the one is constantly echoed in the other; and yet the published *Silmarillion* is between three and four times as long.

After the hasty 'Sketch of the Mythology' (chapter II in this book), the *Quenta Noldorinwa* was in fact the only complete version of 'The Silmarillion' that my father ever made. Towards the end of 1937 he interrupted work on a new version, *Quenta Silmarillion*, which extended to part way through the story of Túrin Turambar, and began *The Lord of the Rings* (see *The Lays of Beleriand* pp. 364–7). When after many years he returned to the First Age, the vast extension of the world that had now come into being meant that the *Quenta Silmarillion*, which had been stopped in full flight, could not be taken up from where it fell; and though he undertook exceedingly complex revisions and enlargements of the earlier parts during the following years, he never achieved again a complete and coherent structure. Especially in its concluding chapters the *Quenta Noldorinwa* is thus one of the primary elements in the study of the work as a whole.

In the *Annals of Valinor* and the *Annals of Beleriand* are seen the beginnings of the chronological structure which was to become a central preoccupation. The Annals would develop into a separate 'tradition', parallel to and overlapping but distinct from 'The Silmarillion' proper, and (after intervening versions) emerging in the years following the completion of *The Lord of the Rings* in two chief works of the Matter of Middle-earth, the *Annals of Aman* and the *Grey Annals of Beleriand* (see pp. 262, 294). With the *Quenta* and with these earliest versions of the *Annals* I give the brief texts in Anglo-Saxon feigned to have been made by Ælfwine (Eriol) from the works that he studied in Tol Eressëa, the Lonely Isle.

The commentaries are largely concerned to relate geography, names, events, relationships and motives to what preceded and what followed; inevitably this entails a great deal of reference back to the previous books, and the text of the commentaries is hardly enticing (though being in smaller print they can be readily distinguished from the original works). My object is to try to show, and not merely impressionistically, how Middle-earth and its history was built up gradually and delicately, and how a long series of small shifts or combinations would often lead to the emergence of new and unforeseen structures – as for example in the story of Gwindor of Nargothrond (p. 180).

The arrangement of the texts of the 'Sketch of the Mythology' and the *Quenta*, split into numbered sections comparable from one text to the other, is explained on p. 11. The earlier volumes in the series are referred to as I (*The Book of Lost Tales Part I*), II (*The Book of Lost Tales Part II*), and III (*The Lays of Beleriand*).

The maps and diagrams in the book are reproduced with the permission of the Bodleian Library, Oxford, and I thank the staff of the Department of Western Manuscripts at the Bodleian for their assistance.

The fifth volume will contain my father's unfinished 'time-travel' story, *The Lost Road*, together with the earliest forms of the legend of Númenor, which were closely related to it; the *Lhammas* or Account of Tongues, *Etymologies*; and all the writings concerned with the First Age up to the time when *The Lord of the Rings* was begun.

I
PROSE FRAGMENTS FOLLOWING
THE LOST TALES

Before giving the 'Sketch of the Mythology', the earliest form of the prose 'Silmarillion', there are some brief prose texts that can be conveniently collected here.

(i)

Among loose papers there is an early piece, soon abandoned, entitled *Turlin and the Exiles of Gondolin*. It will be seen that it relates closely to the beginning of the tale of *The Fall of Gondolin* (II. 149) but at the same time contains much that is new. That it was the beginning of a later version of the tale is clear at once from the name *Mithrim*, for this only replaced *Asgon* by emendation in the final text of *The Fall of Gondolin* (II.202). This brief text reads as follows. At the first three occurrences of the name *Turlin* in the narrative (but not in the title) it was emended to *Turgon*; at the fourth and fifth *Turgon* was so written from the first. I give *Turgon* throughout.

'Then' said Ilfiniol son of Bronweg 'know that Ulmo Lord of Waters forgot never the sorrows of the Elfin kindreds beneath the power of Melko, but he might do little because of the anger of the other Gods who shut their hearts against the race of the Gnomes, and dwelt behind the veiled hills of Valinor heedless of the Outer World, so deep was their ruth and regret for the death of the Two Trees. Nor did any save Ulmo only dread the power of Melko that wrought ruin and sorrow over all the Earth; but Ulmo desired that Valinor should gather all its might to quench his evil ere it be too late, and him seemed that both purposes might perchance be achieved if messengers from the Gnomes should win to Valinor and plead for pardon and for pity upon the Earth; for the love of Palúrien and Oromë her son for those wide realms did but slumber still. Yet hard and evil was the road from the Outer Earth to Valinor, and the Gods themselves had meshed the ways with magic and veiled the encircling hills. Thus did Ulmo seek unceasingly to stir the Gnomes to send messengers unto Valinor, but Melko was cunning and very deep in wisdom, and unsleeping was his wariness in all things that touched the Elfin kindreds, and their messengers overcame not the perils and temptations of that longest and most evil of all roads, and many that dared to set forth were lost for ever.

Now tells the tale how Ulmo despaired that any of the Elfin race should surpass the dangers of the way, and of the deepest and the latest design that he then fashioned, and of those things which came of it.

In those days the greater part of the kindreds of Men dwelt after the Battle of Unnumbered Tears in that land of the North that has many names, but which the Elves of Kôr have named Hisilómë which is the Twilit Mist, and the Gnomes, who of the Elf-kin know it best, Dor-Lómin the Land of Shadows. A people mighty in numbers were there, dwelling about the wide pale waters of Mithrim the great lake that lies in those regions, and other folk named them Tunglin or folk of the Harp, for their joy was in the wild music and minstrelsy of the fells and woodlands, but they knew not and sang not of the sea. Now this folk came into those places after the dread battle, being too late summoned thither from afar, and they bore no stain of treachery against the Elfin kin; but indeed many among them clung to such friendship with the hidden Gnomes of the mountains and Dark Elves as might be still for the sorrow and mistrust born of those ruinous deeds in the Vale of Niniach. Turgon was a man of that folk, son of Peleg, son of Indor, son of [Ear >] Fengel who was their chief and hearing the summons had marched out of the deeps of the East with all his folk. But Turgon dwelt not much with his kindred, and loved rather solitude and the friendship of the Elves whose tongues he knew, and he wandered alone about the long shores of Mithrim, now hunting in its woods, now making sudden music in the rocks upon his rugged harp of wood strung with the sinews of bears. But he sang not for the ears of Men, and many hearing the power of his rough songs came from afar to hearken to his harping; [?but] Turgon left his singing and departed to lonely places in the mountains.

Many strange things he learned there, broken tidings of far off things, and longing came upon him for deeper lore, but as yet his heart turned not from the long shores, and the pale waters of Mithrim in the mists. Yet was he not fated to dwell for ever in those places, for 'tis said that magic and destiny led him on a day to a cavernous opening in the rocks down which a hidden river flowed from Mithrim. And Turgon entered that cavern seeking to learn its secret, but having entered the waters of Mithrim drave

him forward into the heart of the rock and he might not win back into the light. This men have said was not without the will of Ulmo, at whose prompting may be the Gnomes had fashioned that deep and hidden way. Then came the Gnomes to Turgon and guided him along the dark passages amid the mountains until he came out once more into the light.

The text ends here (though manuscript pages written at the same time continue on another subject, see (ii) below).

Turlin must have been a passing shift from *Tuor* (cf. the form *Tûr* that appears in texts of *The Fall of Gondolin*, II. 148), and *Turgon* likewise; in the Tale *Turgon* is of course the name of the King of Gondolin. This curious passing transference of a primary name in the legends may be compared with the brief substitution of *Celegorm* for *Thingol* and *Maglor* for *Beren* in the *Lay of Leithian* (III. 159).

Particularly interesting is the account here of the origins of Tuor's people: they came out of the East to the Battle of Unnumbered Tears, but they came too late. This can hardly be wholly unconnected with the coming of the Easterlings before the battle in the later story. The genealogy of Tuor (Turlin, Turgon) is here 'son of Peleg son of Indor son of Fengel'. In *The Fall of Gondolin* he is 'son of Peleg son of Indor' (II. 160); in the fragment of the *Lay of the Fall of Gondolin* he is the son of Fengel, and in associated notes Tuor is himself called *Fengel* (III. 145). His people are here the *Tunglin*, the folk of the Harp, whereas in *The Fall of Gondolin* (*ibid.*) he belongs to 'the house of the Swan of the sons of the Men of the North'.

Also noteworthy is the opening of the present text where Ulmo's desires and devisings are described: his unceasing attempts to persuade the Gnomes to send messengers to Valinor, his isolation from the other Valar, his wish that the power of Valinor should go against Melko in time. There does not appear to be any other mention of Ulmo's attempting to arouse the Gnomes to send messages to Valinor; and though his isolation in his pity for the Gnomes in the Great Lands appears strongly at the beginning of the tale of *The Hiding of Valinor* (I. 209), there Manwë and Varda beside Ulmo were opposed to the withdrawal of Valinor from the fate of 'the world'.

Lastly, 'the Vale of Niniach' must be the site of the Battle of Unnumbered Tears; cf. 'the Vale (Valley) of Weeping Waters' in the outlines for *Gilfanon's Tale* (I. 239–40). *Niniach* never occurs again in this application, though the way by which Tuor went down to the sea came to be called *Cirith Ninniach*, the Rainbow Cleft.

(ii)

The manuscript *Turlin and the Exiles of Gondolin* continues (the paper and the handwriting are identical, and all were placed together)

with a further text of great interest, since it represents the first step towards the later story of the coming of the Noldor to Middle-earth since the outlines for *Gilfanon's Tale* (I. 237ff.). This was hastily pencilled and is in places difficult to make out.

Then Gelmir king of the Gnomes marshalled his unhappy folk and he said to them: 'We are come at last to the Great Lands and have set our feet upon the Earth, and not even Elf-wisdom may yet say what shall come of it; but the torment and the pain and the tears that we have borne in the way hither shall be sung in song and told in tale by all the folk of the Elfin race hereafter; yea and even among other children of Ior shall some remember it.'

Long time did the Gnome-folk dwell nigh those westward shores in the northern regions of the Earth; and their anguish was lessened. Some were there that fared far afield and gained knowledge of the lands about, and they sought ever to know whither Melko had fled, or where was hidden the gems and treasury of Valinor. [*Struck out*: Then did Gelmir marshal his hosts and three great armies had he, and Golfin his son was captain of the one, and Delin his son of a second, [Oleg >] Lúthien his son of the third, but Gelmir was lord and king.] Thereafter did all the folk move onward to the East and somewhat South, and all the armies of Golfin and of Delin moved ahead unhampered. Now the ice melted, and the snow [?thinned], and the trees grew deep upon the hills, and their hearts knew comfort, till their harps and elfin pipes awoke once more. Then did the rocks ring with the sweet music of the Elves, and countless [?coming] of their many feet; new flowers sprang behind those armies as they trod, for the earth was glad of the coming of the Gnomes, nor had the sun or the white moon yet seen fairer things in those places than their moving field of glinting spears and their goldwrought elfin armoury. But the women and the Gnome-maids and Gnome-children sang as they journeyed after, and no such clear song of hope have the lands heard since, yet was it sad and boding beside that singing that was heard upon [Kôr >] the hill of Tûn while the Two Trees blossomed still.

Of all those scouts and scattered hosts that went far ahead or upon either side of the marching Gnomes none were more eager or burnt with greater fire than Fëanor the gem-smith and his seven sons; but nothing did they discover yet, and came the Gnomes at length unto that magic northern land of which tales often speak, and by reason of its dark woods and grey mountains and its deep

mists the Gnomes named Dor Lómin land of shadows. There lies a lake, Mithrim whose mighty waters reflect a pale image of the encircling hills. Here did the Gnomes rest once more a great while, and Gelmir let build dwellings for the folk about the shores and shoreland woods, but there too he numbered and marshalled all his hosts both of spearmen, and bowmen, and of swordsmen, for no lack of arms did the Gnomes bring out of Valinor and the armouries of Makar to their war with Melko. And three great armies had Gelmir under his lordship, and Golfin his son was captain of one, and Delin his son of another, and Lúthien (not that Lúthien of the Roses who is of another and a later tale) of a third; and Golfin's might was in swordsmen, and Delin had more of those who bore the long . . . . elfin spears, but Lúthien's joy was in the number and . . . . . of his bowmen – and the bow has ever been the weapon wherein the Elf-kin has had the most wondrous skill. Now the colours of the Gnomes were gold and white in those ancient days in memory of the Two Trees, but Gelmir's standard bore upon a silver field a crown of gold, and each captain had a fair banner; and the sign of Golfin in those days was upon gold a silver sword, and of Delin a green beech leaf upon silver diapered with golden flowers, and of Lúthien a golden swallow that winged through an azure field as it were the sky set with silver stars, and the sons of Fëanor wrought that standard and those banners, and they shone by sunlight and by mist and by moonlight and by starless dark by the light of the Gnome-wrought gems that sewed them [sic].

Now it happened on a while that Fëanor got him beyond to the hills that girt Dor Lómin in those parts [northward of >] beyond Artanor where there were open empty lands and treeless hills, and he had no small company and three of his sons were with him. Thus came they on a day nigh evening to a hilltop, and afar off descried a red light leaping in a vale open on that side that looked toward [?them]. Then Fëanor wondered what this fire might be, and he and his folk marched in the still night swiftly thereto, so that ere dawn they looked down into that vale. There saw they an armed company no less than their own, and they sat around a mighty fire of wood. The most were asleep, but some few stirred, and Fëanor stood then up and called in his clear voice so that the dark vale rang: 'Who be ye; men of the Gnomes or other what – say swiftly for 'tis best for [you to] know the children of Fëanor compass you around.'

Then a great clamour broke forth in the vale and the folk of

Fëanor knew full soon that here were no elfin folk, by reason of their harsh voices and unlovely cries, and many arrows came winging in the dark towards that voice, but Fëanor was no longer there. Swiftly had he gone and drawn the most of his folk before the vale's mouth whence a stream issued forth tree-hung

Here the text ends abruptly and near the top of a new page; it is clear that no more was written.

The Noldorin house has still not emerged, but we have a king *Gelmir* of the Gnomes, with his sons *Golfin, Delin, Lúthien* (the last emended from *Oleg*), captains of his three armies. There is no suggestion that Fëanor and his sons were associated with these in any sort of close kinship. In the fragment of the *Lay of the Fall of Gondolin* (see III. 146–7) there appears – for the first time – *Fingolfin*, who steps into Finwë Nólemë's place as the father of Turgon and Isfin, but is not the son of Finwë, rather of *Gelmir*. I have suggested there that this Gelmir, father of Golfin/Fingolfin, is to be identified with Finwë, father of Fingolfin in the alliterative poems and later; and it may be that the name *Gelmir* is formally connected with *Fin-golma*, which in the outlines for *Gilfanon's Tale* is another name for Finwë Nólemë (I. 238–9, and see I. 263, entry *Nólemë*). It is to be remembered that Finwë Nóleme was not in the earliest legend the father of Fëanor and was not slain by Melko in Valinor, but came to the Great Lands. – Of the other sons of Gelmir named in the present text, Delin and Lúthien, there is no trace elsewhere.

It is certainly clear that *Golfin* here is the first appearance of Fingolfin, and by the same token that this text preceded the abandoned beginning of the *Lay of the Fall of Gondolin*. On the other hand, the obscure story of the death of Fëanor in the earliest outlines (I. 238–9) has disappeared, and though the present text breaks off too soon for certainty it seems extremely probable that, had my father continued it a little further, we should have learned of Fëanor's death in battle with the Orcs whom he and his companions had aroused in the valley where they were encamped. It may be, too, that we should have had an explanation of the puzzling lines of the Lay (III. 146):

'Twas the bent blades of the Glamhoth that drank Fingolfin's life as he stood alone by Fëanor.

We are in any case here still a long way from the story of the divided hosts and the treachery of Fëanor.

The encampment of Mithrim (Asgon) is referred to already in the early outlines, but in the later of these there is mention (I. 239) of the first devising of weapons by the Gnomes at this time, whereas in the present text they are said to have brought great store of arms 'out of Valinor and the armouries of Makar'. Here also appears the earliest form of the idea of the flowers springing beneath the marching feet of the Gnomish host.

A characteristic heraldry appears in the armies led by Gelmir's sons, all in gold and silver, in memory of the Two Trees – the banners made (curiously enough) by the sons of Fëanor. In the 'Sketch of the Mythology' the banners of Fingolfin were in blue and silver, as they remained (p. 22).

The name *Ior*, which occurs at the beginning of the text in the expression 'among other children of Ior' (as opposed to 'the Elfin race') and seems therefore to refer to Ilúvatar, occurs elsewhere only in a quite different reference: it is given in the early Gnomish dictionary as the equivalent of Qenya *Ivárë*, 'the famous "piper of the sea"'.

(iii)

Thirdly and lastly, an isolated slip of paper contains a most curious trace of a stage in development between *The Flight of the Noldoli* in the *Lost Tales* and the 'Sketch of the Mythology'.

The Trees stand dark. The Plain is full of trouble. The Gnomes gather by torchlight in Tûn or Côr; Fëanor laments Bruithwir (Felegron) [*emended to* (Feleor)] his father, bids Gnomes depart & seek Melko and their treasures – he longs for the Silmarils – Finweg & Fingolfin speak against him. The Gnomes shout and prepare to depart. The Solosimpi refuse: the wise words of Ethlon (Dimlint). Foamriders [?beaches]. The threats of Fëanor to march to Cú nan Eilch. The arch, the lamplit quays; they seize the boats. One Gilfanon sees his mighty swanwinged swan-feather boat with red oars [?going] & he & his sons run to the arch and threaten the Gnomes. The fight on the arch & Gilfanon's [?curse] ere they throw him into the waves. The Gnomes reach Fangros & repent – burn the boats.

Here Bruithwir (with the additional name Felegron > Feleor) is still the father of Fëanor as in the *Lost Tales*; but Fingolfin and Finweg have emerged, and speak against Fëanor (it is not clear whether Finweg here is Fingolfin's father (Finwë) or Fingolfin's son (later Fingon): see III. 137–8, 146). Narrative features that were never taken up in the later development of 'The Silmarillion' here make their only appearance. What lay behind 'the wise words of Ethlon (Dimlint)' and 'the threats of Fëanor to march to Cú nan Eilch' has now vanished without trace. The name *Fangros* appears once elsewhere, in the alliterative *Children of Húrin*, III. 31 line 631 (earlier *Fangair*), where there is a reference to a song, or songs, being sung

> of the fight at Fangros, and Fëanor's sons'
> oath unbreakable

(the fight and the oath need not be in any way connected). But whatever happened at Fangros is lost beyond recall; and nowhere later is there any suggestion that the burning of the ships arose from repentance. In the *Lost Tales* (I. 168) the Gnomes 'abandoned their stolen ships' when they made the passage of the Ice; Sorontur reported to Manwë (I. 177) that he had seen 'a fleet of white ships that drifted empty in the gales, and some were burning with bright fires'; and Manwë 'knew thereby that the Noldoli were gone for ever and their ships burned or abandoned'.

Lastly, *Gilfanon* appears as an Elf of Alqualondë, one of those hurled by the Gnomes into the sea, though it is not said that he was drowned. Gilfanon of Tavrobel was a Gnome (I. 174–5); and it seems virtually certain that the two Gilfanons were not the same. In that case it is most probable that the Elf of Tavrobel had ceased to be so named; though he had not, as I think, ceased to exist (see p. 274).

II
THE EARLIEST 'SILMARILLION'
(The 'Sketch of the Mythology')

I have earlier (III. 3) given an account of this text, but I repeat the essentials of it here. On the envelope containing the manuscript my father wrote at some later time:

Original 'Silmarillion'. Form orig[inally] composed c. 1926–30 for R. W. Reynolds to explain background of 'alliterative version' of Túrin & the Dragon: then in progress (unfinished) (begun c. 1918).

The 'Sketch' represents a new starting-point in the history of 'The Silmarillion'; for while it is a quite brief synopsis, the further written development of the prose form proceeded from it in a direct line. It is clear from details that need not be repeated here that it was originally written in 1926 (after the *Lay of the Children of Húrin* had been abandoned, III. 3); but it was afterwards revised, in places very heavily, and this makes it a difficult text to present in a way that is both accurate and readily comprehensible. The method I have adopted is to give the text exactly as it was first written (apart from a very few slight alterations of expression in no way affecting the narrative, which are adopted silently into the text), but to break it up into short sections, following each with notes giving the later changes made in that section. I must emphasize that there is no manuscript warrant for the 19 divisions so made: it is purely a matter of convenience of presentation. This method has certain advantages: the later changes can be readily compared with the original text immediately preceding; and since the following version of 'The Silmarillion', the *Quenta*, has been treated in the šame'way and divided into corresponding numbered sections, passages of the one can be easily related to those in the other.

The later changes are referenced by numbers that begin with 1 in each section. The commentary follows at the end of the complete text, and is related to the numbered sections.

Sketch of the mythology with especial reference to the 'Children of Húrin'

1

After the despatch of the Nine Valar for the governance of the world Morgoth (Demon of Dark) rebels against the overlordship of Manwë, overthrows the lamps set up to illumine the world, and floods the isle where the Valar (or Gods) dwelt. He fortifies a palace of dungeons in the North. The Valar remove to the uttermost West, bordered by the Outer Seas and the final Wall, and eastward by the towering Mountains of Valinor which the Gods built. In Valinor they gather all light and beautiful things, and build their mansions, gardens, and city, but Manwë and his wife Bridhil have halls upon the highest mountain (Timbrenting or Tindbrenting in English, Tengwethil in Gnomish, Taníquetil in Elfin) whence they can see across the world to the dark East. Ifan Belaurin[1] plants the Two Trees in the middle of the plain of Valinor outside the gates of the city of Valmar. They grow under her songs, and one has dark green leaves with shining silver beneath, and white blossoms like the cherry from which a dew of silver light falls; the other has golden-edged leaves of young green like the beech and yellow blossom like the hanging blossoms of laburnum which give out heat and blazing light. Each tree waxes for seven[2] hours to full glory and then wanes for seven; twice a day therefore comes a time of softer light when each tree is faint and their light is mingled.

★

1   *Yavanna Palúrien* added in the margin.
2   At both occurrences of *seven* in this sentence my father first wrote *six*, but changed it in the act of writing the manuscript.

2

The Outer Lands are in darkness. The growth of things was checked when Morgoth quenched the lamps. There are forests of darkness, of yew and fir and ivy. There Oromë sometimes hunts, but in the North Morgoth and his demonic broods (Balrogs) and the Orcs (Goblins, also called Glamhoth or people of hate) hold sway. Bridhil looks on the darkness and is moved, and taking all the hoarded light of Silpion (the white tree) she makes and strews the stars.

At the making of the stars the children of Earth awake – the Eldar (or Elves). They are found by Oromë dwelling by the star-lit pool (Cuiviénen, water of awakening) in the East. He rides home to Valinor filled with their beauty and tells the Valar, who are reminded of their duty to the Earth, since they came thither knowing that their office was to govern it for the two races of Earth who should after come each in appointed time. There follows an expedition to the fortress of the North (Angband, Iron-hell), but this is now too strong for them to destroy. Morgoth is nonetheless taken captive, and consigned to the halls of Mandos who dwelt in the North of Valinor.

The Eldalië (people of the Elves) are invited to Valinor for fear of the evil things of Morgoth that still wandered in the dark. A great march is made by the Eldar from the East led by Oromë on his white horse. The Eldar are divided into three hosts, one under Ingwë (Ing) after called the Quendi (or Elves proper, or Light-elves), one under Finwë (Finn) after called the Noldoli (Gnomes or Deep-elves), one under Elwë (Elu) after called the Teleri (Sea-elves, or Solosimpi, the Shoreland Pipers or Foam-riders). Many of them are lost upon the march and wander in the woods of the world, becoming after the various hosts of Ilkorindi (Elves who never dwelt in Côr in Valinor). The chief of these was Thingol, who heard Melian and her nightingales singing and was enchanted and fell asleep for an age. Melian was one of the divine maidens of the Vala Lórien who sometimes wandered into the outer world. Melian and Thingol became Queen and King of woodland Elves in Doriath, living in a hall called the Thousand Caves.

3

The other Elves came to the ultimate shores of the West. In the North these in those days sloped westward in the North until only a narrow sea divided them from the land of the Gods, and this narrow sea was filled with grinding ice. But at the point to which the Elf-hosts came a wide dark sea stretched west.

There were two Valar of the Sea. Ulmo (Ylmir), the mightiest of all Valar next to Manwë, was lord of all waters, but dwelt often in Valinor, or in the 'Outer Seas'. Ossë and the lady Óin,[1] whose tresses lay through all the sea, loved rather the seas of the world that washed the shores beneath the Mountains of Valinor. Ylmir uprooted the half-sunk island where the Valar had first dwelt, and embarking on it the Noldoli and Qendi, who arrived first, bore them to Valinor. The Teleri dwelt some time by the shores of the sea awaiting him, and hence their love of it. While they were being also transported by Ylmir, Ossë in jealousy and out of love for their singing chained the island to the sea-bottom far out in the

Bay of Faërie whence the Mountains of Valinòr could dimly be seen. No other land was near it, and it was called the Lonely Isle. There the Teleri dwelt a long age becoming different in tongue, and learning strange music of Ossë, who made the sea-birds for their delight.

The Gods gave a home in Valinor to the other Eldar. Because they longed even among the Tree-lit gardens of Valinor for a glimpse of the stars, a gap was made in the encircling mountains, and there in a deep valley a green hill, Côr, was built. This was lit from the West by the Trees, to the East it looked out onto the Bay of Faërie and the Lonely Isle, and beyond to the Shadowy Seas. Thus some of the blessed light of Valinor filtered into the Outer Lands, and falling on the Lonely Isle caused its western shores to grow green and fair.

On the top of Côr the city of the Elves was built and called Tûn. The Qendi became most beloved by Manwë and Bridhil, the Noldoli by Aulë (the Smith) and Mandos the wise. The Noldoli invented gems and made them in countless numbers, filling all Tûn with them, and all the halls of the Gods.[2]

The greatest in skill and magic of the Noldoli was Finn's second son Fëanor. (His elder son Fingolfin[3] whose son was Finnweg comes into the tale later.) He contrived three jewels (Silmarils) wherein a living fire combined in the light of the Two Trees was set, they shone of their own light, impure hands were burned by them.

The Teleri seeing afar the light of Valinor were torn between desire to rejoin their kindred and to dwell by the sea. Ylmir taught them craft of boat-building. Ossë yielding gave them swans, and harnessing many swans to their boats they sailed to Valinor, and dwelt there on the shores where they could see the light of the Trees, and go to Valmar if they wished, but could sail and dance in the waters touched to light by the radiance that came out past Côr. The other Eldar gave them many gems, especially opals and diamonds and other pale crystals which were strewn upon the beaches of the Bay of Faërie. They themselves invented pearls. Their chief town was Swanhaven upon the shores northward of the pass of Côr.

★

1   *Uinen* pencilled against *Óin*.
2   The following passage was afterwards added here:

Since the Gnomes or Noldoli afterwards came back into the Great
Lands, and these tales deal mostly with them, it may here be said
that Lord or King of the Noldoli was Finn. His sons were Fëanor,
Fingolfin, and Finrod. Of whom Fëanor was the most skilful, the
deepest in lore, Fingolfin the mightiest and most valiant, Finrod
the fairest, and the most wisehearted and gentle. The seven sons of
Fëanor were Maidros the tall; Maglor a musician and mighty
singer whose voice carried far over hill and sea; Curufin the crafty
who inherited most of his father's skill; Celegorm the fair;
Cranthir the dark; and Damrod and Díriel who after were great
hunters. The sons of Fingolfin were Finweg who was after the king
of the Noldoli in the North of the world, and Turgon of Gondolin;
and his daughter was Isfin the white. The sons of Finrod were
Orodreth, Felagoth, Anrod, and Egnor.

In the last sentence *Felagoth* > *Felagund*, and *Orodreth* moved to
stand after *Felagund*.

3   *Finn's second son Fëanor* and *His elder son Fingolfin* > *Finn's
elder son Fëanor* and *His second son Fingolfin* (an early change,
quite possibly made at the time of the writing of the manuscript).

4

The Gods were now beguiled by Morgoth, who having passed
seven ages in the prisons of Mandos in gradually lightened pain
came before the conclave of the Gods in due course. He looks with
greed and malice upon the Eldar, who also sit there about the
knees of the Gods, and lusts especially after the jewels. He
dissembles his hatred and desire for revenge. He is allowed a
humble dwelling in Valinor, and after a while goes freely about
Valinor, only Ylmir foreboding ill, while Tulcas the strong who
first captured him watches him. Morgoth helps the Eldar in many
deeds, but slowly poisons their peace with lies.

He suggests that the Gods brought them to Valinor out of
jealousy, for fear their marvellous skill, and magic, and beauty,
should grow too strong for them outside in the world. The Qendi
and Teleri are little moved, but the Noldoli, the wisest of the
Elves, become affected. They begin at whiles to murmur against
the Gods and their kindred; they are filled with vanity of their
skill.[1]

Most of all does Morgoth fan the flames of the heart of Fëanor,
but all the while he lusts for the immortal Silmarils, although
Fëanor has cursed for ever anyone, God or Elf or mortal that shall
come hereafter, who touches them. Morgoth lying tells Fëanor

that Fingolfin and his son Finnweg are plotting to usurp the leadership of the Gnomes from Fëanor and his sons, and to gain the Silmarils. A quarrel breaks out between the sons of Finn. Fëanor is summoned before the Gods, and the lies of Morgoth laid bare. Fëanor is banished from Tûn, and with him goes Finn who loves Fëanor best of his sons, and many of the Gnomes. They build a treasury Northward in Valinor in the hills near Mandos' halls. Fingolfin rules the Gnomes that are left in Tûn. Thus Morgoth's words seem justified and the bitterness he sowed goes on after his words are disproved.

Tulcas is sent to put Morgoth in chains once more, but he escapes through the pass of Côr into the dark region beneath the feet of Timbrenting called Arvalin, where the shadow is thickest in all the world. There he finds Ungoliant, Gloomweaver, who dwells in a cleft of the mountains, and sucks up light or shining things to spin them out again in webs of black and choking darkness, fog, and gloom. With her he plots revenge. Only a terrible reward will bring her to dare the dangers of Valinor or the sight of the Gods. She weaves a dense gloom about her to protect her and swings on cords from pinnacle to pinnacle till she has scaled the highest peak of the mountains in the south of Valinor (little guarded because of their height and their distance from the old fortress of Morgoth). She makes a ladder that Morgoth can scale. They creep into Valinor. Morgoth stabs the Trees and Ungoliant sucks up their juices, belching forth clouds of blackness. The Trees succumb slowly to the poisoned sword, and to the venomous lips of Ungoliant.

The Gods are dismayed by a twilight at midday, and vapours of black float in about the ways of the city. They are too late. The Trees die while they wail about them. But Tulcas and Oromë and many others hunt on horseback in the gathering gloom for Morgoth. Wherever Morgoth goes there the confusing darkness is greatest owing to the webs of Ungoliant. Gnomes from the treasury of Finn come in and report that Morgoth is assisted by a spider of darkness. They had seen them making for the North. Morgoth had stayed his flight at the Treasury, slain Finn and many of his men, and carried off the Silmarils and a vast hoard of the most splendid jewels of the Elves.

In the meanwhile Morgoth escapes by Ungoliant's aid northward and crosses the Grinding Ice. When he has regained the northern regions of the world Ungoliant summons him to pay the other half of her reward. The first half was the sap of the Trees of

Light. Now she claims one half of the jewels. Morgoth yields them up and she devours them. She is now become monstrous, but he will not give her any share in the Silmarils. She enmeshes him in a black web, but he is rescued by the Balrogs with whips of flame, and the hosts of the Orcs; and Ungoliant goes away into the uttermost South.

Morgoth returns to Angband, and his power and the numbers of his demons and Orcs becomes countless. He forges an iron crown and sets therein the Silmarils, though his hands are burned black by them, and he is never again free from the pain of the burning. The crown he never leaves off for a moment, and he never leaves the deep dungeons of his fortress, governing his vast armies from his deep throne.

★

1   Added here:

> which Morgoth flatters. The Gods knew also of the coming of mortals or Men that was to be. They had not yet told the Elves, for the time was not near, nor explained what was to be the realm of each race, and their relations. Morgoth tells of Men, and suggests that the Gods are keeping the Elves captive, so that weaker Men shall be controlled more easily by the Gods, and the Elves defrauded of their kingdoms.

> This was an early addition, probably not materially later than the writing of the manuscript.

5

When it became clear that Morgoth had escaped the Gods assemble about the dead Trees and sit in the darkness stricken and dumb for a long while, caring about nothing. The day which Morgoth chose for his attack was a day of festival throughout Valinor. Upon this day it was the custom of the chief Valar and many of the Elves, especially the people of Ing (the Quendi), to climb the long winding paths in endless procession to Manwë's halls upon Timbrenting. All the Quendi and some of the Noldoli (who under Fingolfin dwelt still in Tûn) had gone to Timbrenting, and were singing upon its topmost height when the watchers from afar descried the fading of the Trees. Most of the Noldoli were in the plain, and the Teleri upon the shore. The fogs and darkness drift in now off the seas through the pass of Côr as the Trees die. Fëanor summons the Gnomes to Tûn (rebelling against his banishment).[1]

There is a vast concourse on the square on the summit of Côr about the tower of Ing, lit by torches. Fëanor makes a violent speech, and though his wrath is for Morgoth his words are in part the fruit of Morgoth's lies.[2] He bids the Gnomes fly in the darkness while the Gods are wrapped in mourning, to seek freedom in the world and to seek out Morgoth, now Valinor is no more blissful than the earth outside.[3] Fingolfin and Finweg speak against him.[4] The assembled Gnomes vote for flight, and Fingolfin and Finweg yield; they will not desert their people, but they retain command over a half of the people of the Noldoli.[5]

The flight begins.[6] The Teleri will not join. The Gnomes cannot escape without boats, and do not dare to cross the Grinding Ice. They attempt to seize the swan-ships in Swanhaven, and a fight ensues (the first between the races of the Earth) in which many Teleri are slain, and their ships carried off. A curse is pronounced upon the Gnomes, that they shall after suffer often from treachery and the fear of treachery among their own kindred in punishment for the blood spilled at Swanhaven.[7] They sail North along the coast of Valinor. Mandos sends an emissary, who speaking from a high cliff hails them as they sail by, and warns them to return, and when they will not speaks the 'Prophecy of Mandos' concerning the fate of after days.[8]

The Gnomes come to the narrowing of the seas, and prepare to sail. While they are encamped upon the shore Fëanor and his sons and people sail off taking with them all the boats, and leave Fingolfin on the far shore treacherously, thus beginning the Curse of Swanhaven. They burn the boats as soon as they land in the East of the world, and Fingolfin's people see the light in the sky. The same light also tells the Orcs of the landing.

Fingolfin's people wander miserably. Some under Fingolfin return to Valinor[9] to seek the Gods' pardon. Finweg leads the main host North, and over the Grinding Ice. Many are lost.

★

1   As originally written, this sentence began *Finn and Fëanor summon* &c. This was a mere slip, since Finn's death has already been mentioned in the text as first written (§4), and my father later struck out *Finn and*. He left the plural verb *summon* and *their banishment*; this I have changed to *his banishment*, since it is not said of

the Gnomes who accompanied Fëanor that they left Tûn under banishment (though this is not said of Finn either). The *Quenta* has *his banishment* in this passage (p. 94).

2 Added here hastily in pencil:

He claims the lordship as eldest son now Finn is dead, in spite of the Gods' decree.

[Except for the later pencilled alteration given in note 5, all the changes noted below, mostly concerned to introduce the part of Finrod in the events, were made at the same time, in red ink. Finrod, the third son of Finn/Finwë, appears in the interpolated passage given in §3 note 2.]

3 Added here:

Fëanor and his sons take the unbreakable oath by Timbrenting and the names of Manwë and Briðil to pursue anyone, Elf, Mortal, or Orc, who holds the Silmarils.

4 Added here:

Finrod tries to calm their conflicting anger, but his sons Orodreth, Anrod, and Egnor side with the sons of Fëanor.

5 *a half of the people of the Noldoli* > *a half of the Noldoli of Tûn* (later pencilled change).

6 Added here but then struck out (see note 7):

Finrod does not go, but bids Felagoth (and his other sons) go and cherish the Gnomes of his [?house].

7 Added here:

Finrod is slain at Swanhaven in trying to stay the violence.

This was also struck out (see note 6) and a third version of Finrod's part entered:

Finrod and his sons were not at Swanhaven. They leave Tûn reluctantly, and more than the others carry away memories of it, and even many fair things made there by hands.

8 Added here:

and the curse of war against one another because of Swanhaven.

9 This passage, from *Fingolfin's people wander*, changed to read:

Finrod and his people arrive. The people of Finrod and Fingolfin wander miserably. Some under Finrod return to Valinor, &c.

6

In the meanwhile Manwë summons Ifan Belaurin to the council. Her magic will not avail to cure the Trees. But Silpion under her spells bears one last great silver bloom, and Laurelin one great golden fruit. The Gods fashion the Moon and Sun from these and set them to sail appointed courses from West to East, but afterwards they find it safer to send them in Ylmir's care through the caverns and grottoes beneath the Earth, to rise in the East and come home again high in the air over the mountains of the West, to sink after each journey into the waters of the Outer Seas.

The light of Valinor is henceforth not much greater than that now scattered over the Earth, save that here the ships of Sun and Moon come nearer to Earth, and rest for a while close to Valinor. The Gods and Elves look forward to a future time when the 'magic sun and moon' of the Trees may be rekindled and the old beauty and bliss renewed. Ylmir foretells[1] that it will only be achieved with the aid of the second race of earth. But the Gods, even Manwë, pay little heed to him. They are wroth and bitter because of the slaying at Swanhaven[2] and they fortify all Valinor making the mountains impenetrable, save at Côr which the remaining Elves are commanded to guard, ceaselessly and for ever, and let no bird or beast or Elf or Man land on the shores of Faëry. The magic isles, filled with enchantment, are strung across the confines of the Shadowy Seas, before the Lonely Isle is reached sailing West, to entrap any mariners and wind them in everlasting sleep and enchantment.[3] The Gods sit now behind the mountains and feast, and dismiss the rebel and fugitive Noldoli from their hearts. Ylmir alone remembers them, and gathers news of the outer world through all the lakes and rivers.

At the rising of the first Sun the younger children of earth awoke in the far East. No god came to guide them, but the messages of Ylmir little understood came at whiles to them. They meet Ilkorindi and learn speech and other things of them, and become great friends of the Eldalië. They spread through the earth, wandering West and North.

★

1 *Ylmir foretells* changed at the time of writing from *Bridhil foretells*

2 Added here (hastily in pencil):

   and the flight and ingratitude of the Gnomes

3   Added here:

Thus the many emissaries of the Gnomes in after days never reach Valinor.

7

Now begins the time of the great wars of the powers of the North (Morgoth and his hosts against Men, Ilkorins, and the Gnomes from Valinor). Morgoth's cunning and lies, and the curse of Swanhaven (as well as the oaths of the sons of Fëanor who swore the unbreakable oath by Timbrenting to treat all as foes who had the Silmarils in keeping) in these wars do the greatest injury to Men and Elves.

These stories only tell a part of the deeds of those days, especially such as relate to the Gnomes and the Silmarils, and the mortals who became entangled in their fates. In the early days Eldar and Men were of nearly equal stature and power of body, but the Eldar were blessed with greater wit, skill, and beauty; and those (the Gnomes) who had dwelt in Côr (Koreldar) as much surpassed the Ilkorins as they surpassed mortals. Only in the realm of Doriath, whose queen was of divine race, did the Ilkorins equal the Koreldar. The Elves were immortal, and free from all sickness.[1] But they might be slain with weapons in those days,[2] and then their spirits went back to the halls of Mandos and awaited a thousand years, or the pleasure of the Gods, before they were recalled to free life.[3] Men from the first though slightly bigger were more frail, more easily slain, subject to ills, and grew old and died, if not slain. What happened to their spirits was not known to the Eldalië. They did not go to the halls of Mandos, and many thought their fate was not in the hands of the Valar after death. Though many, associating with Eldar, believed that their spirits went to the western land, this was not true. Men were not born again.[4]

In after days when owing to the triumph of Morgoth Men and Elves became estranged the Eldalië living in the world faded, and Men usurped the sunlight. The Eldar wandered, such as remained in the Outer Lands, took to the moonlight and starlight, the woods and caves.

★

1   *free from all sickness* > *free from death by sickness* (early change, made at the same time as that given in note 4).

2   Added (rough pencilled insertion): *or waste away of sorrow*,
3   Added at the same time as the insertion given in note 2: *and they were reborn in their children, so that the number grows not*.
4   This passage, from *They did not go to the halls of Mandos*, was struck out and replaced by the following:

> They went to the halls of Mandos, but not the same as the halls of awaiting where the Elves were sent. There they too waited, but it was said that only Mandos knew whither they went after the time in his halls – they were never reborn on Earth, and none ever came back from Mandos, save only Beren son of Barahir, who thereafter spoke not to mortal Men. Their fate after death was perchance not in the hands of the Valar.

8

But in these days they were kindred and allies. Before the rising of the Sun and Moon Fëanor and his sons marched into the North and sought for Morgoth. A host of Orcs aroused by the burning ships resisted them and was defeated in the First Battle with such loss that Morgoth pretended to treat with them. Fëanor refused, but he was wounded in the fight by a Balrog chief (Gothmog), and died. Maidros the tall, the elder son, induced the Gnomes to meet Morgoth (with as little intent of faith on his side as on Morgoth's). Morgoth took Maidros captive and tortured him, and hung him from a rock by his right hand. The six remaining sons of Fëanor (Maglor, Celegorm, Curufin, Damrod, Díriel, and Cranthir) are encamped about the lake Mithrim in Hisilómë (Hithlum, or Dorlómin, the land of shadows in the North-west), when they hear of the march of Finweg and his men[1] who have crossed the Grinding Ice. The Sun rises as they march, their blue and silver banners are unfurled, flowers spring beneath the feet of their armies. The Orcs dismayed at the light retreat to Angband. But there is little love between the two hosts of Gnomes encamped now on opposite shores of Mithrim. Vast smokes and vapours are made and sent forth from Angband, and the smoking top of Thangorodrim (the highest of the Iron Mountains around Morgoth's fortress) can be seen from far away. The North shakes with the thunder under the earth. Morgoth is forging armouries. Finweg resolves to heal the feud. Alone he goes in search of Maidros. Aided by the vapours, which are now floating down and filling Hithlum, and by the withdrawal of Orcs and Balrogs to Angband, he finds him, but cannot release him.

Manwë, to whom birds bring news upon Timbrenting of all things which his farsighted eyes do not see upon earth, fashions the race of eagles, and sends them under their king Thorndor to dwell in the crags of the North and watch Morgoth. The eagles dwell out of reach of Orc and Balrog, and are great foes of Morgoth and his people. Finweg meets Thorndor who bears him to Maidros. There is no releasing the enchanted bond upon his wrist. In his agony he begs to be slain, but Finweg cuts off his hand, and they are both borne away by Thorndor, and come to Mithrim. The feud is healed by the deed of Finweg (except for the oath of the Silmarils).

★

1 *the march of Finweg and his men* > *the march of Fingolfin and his sons and his men and Felagoth and the sons of Finrod* (This change belongs with those made in red ink in §5 and concerns the shift from Fingolfin to Finrod as the Gnomish lord who returned to Valinor, see §5 note 9.)

9

The Gnomes march forward and beleaguer Angband. They meet Ilkorins and Men. At that time Men already dwelt in the woods of the North, and Ilkorins also. They long warred with Morgoth.[1] Of Ilkorin race was Barahir and his son Beren. Of mortal race was Húrin son of Gumlin, whose wife was Morwen;[2] they lived in the woods upon the borders of Hithlum. These come after into the tales.

Morgoth sends out his armies and breaks the leaguer of Angband, and from that time the fortunes of his enemies decline.[3] Gnomes and Ilkorins and Men are scattered, and Morgoth's emissaries go among them with lying promises and false suggestions of the greed and treachery of each to each. Because of the curse of Swanhaven these often are believed by the Gnomes.

Celegorm and Curufin found the realm of Nargothrond on the banks of the Narog in the south of the Northern lands.[4] Many Gnomes take service with Thingol and Melian of the Thousand Caves in Doriath. Because of the divine magic of Melian Doriath is the safest from the raids of the Orcs, and it is prophesied that only treachery from within will cause the realm to fall.

★

[This section was substantially interpolated and altered (all in red ink, see §5, except for the change given in note 2).]

1   Added here:

This is the time of Morgoth's retreat, and the growth and prosperity of Men, a time of growth and birth and flowering known as the 'Siege of Angband'.

2   This passage, from *Of Ilkorin race*, was emended to read:

In later times of mortal race was Barahir and his son Beren. Of mortal race also were Húrin and Huor sons of Gumlin. Húrin's wife was Morwen, &c.

3   Here was added *The men of Barahir rescue Celegorm*, but this was struck out and the following insertion made:

In the Leaguer of Angband Fingolfin's host guards the North-west on borders of Hithlum; Felagoth [> Felagund] and the sons of Finrod the South and the [?plains] of Sirion (or Broseliand); the sons of Fëanor the East. Fingolfin is slain when Morgoth breaks the leaguer. Felagoth [> Felagund] is saved by Barahir the Bold a mortal and escapes south to found Nargothrond, swearing a vow of friendship to the race of Barahir. The sons of Fëanor live a wild and nomad life in the East, warring with Dwarves and Orcs and Men. Fingolfin's sons Finweg and Turgon still hold out in the North.

4   This sentence was changed to read:

Felagoth [> Felagund] and his brothers found the realm of Nargothrond on the banks of Narog in the south of the Northern lands. They are aided by Celegorm and Curufin who long while dwelt in Nargothrond.

10

The power of Morgoth begins to spread once more. One by one he overthrows Men and Elves in the North. Of these a famous chieftain of Ilkorindi[1] was Barahir, who had been a friend of Celegorm of Nargothrond. Barahir is driven into hiding, his hiding betrayed, and Barahir slain; his son Beren after a life outlawed flees south, crosses the Shadowy Mountains, and after grievous hardships comes to Doriath. Of this and his other adventures are told in the Lay of Leithian. He gains the love of Tinúviel 'the nightingale' – his own name for Lúthien – the daughter of Thingol. To win her Thingol, in mockery, requires a Silmaril from the crown of Morgoth. Beren sets out to achieve this, is captured, and set in dungeon in Angband, but conceals his real identity and is given as a slave to Thû the hunter.[2] Lúthien is imprisoned by Thingol, but escapes and goes in search of Beren. With the aid of Huan lord of dogs she rescues Beren, and gains entrance to Angband where Morgoth is enchanted and finally wrapped in slumber by her dancing. They get a Silmaril and escape, but are barred at gates of Angband by Carcaras the Wolfward. He bites off Beren's hand which holds the Silmaril, and goes mad with the anguish of its burning within him.

They escape and after many wanderings get back to Doriath. Carcaras ravening through the woods bursts into Doriath. There follows the Wolf-hunt of Doriath, in which Carcaras is slain, and Huan is killed in defence of Beren. Beren is however mortally wounded and dies in Lúthien's arms. Some songs say that Lúthien went even over the Grinding Ice, aided by the power of her divine mother, Melian, to Mandos' halls and won him back; others that Mandos hearing his tale released him. Certain it is that he alone of mortals came back from Mandos and dwelt with Lúthien and never spoke to Men again, living in the woods of Doriath and in the Hunters' Wold, west of Nargothrond.[3]

In the days of his outlawry Beren had been befriended by Húrin of Hithlum, son of Gumlin. In the woods of Hithlum Húrin still remains unbowed to the yoke of Morgoth.

★

1 *a famous chieftain of Ilkorindi* > *a famous chieftain of Men* (cf. §9 note 2).

2 This sentence, following *Beren sets out to achieve this*, was struck through and replaced by the following (in red ink):

> (Beren sets out to achieve this,) and seeks the aid of Felagoth in Nargothrond. Felagoth warns him of the oath of the sons of Fëanor, and that even if he gets the Silmaril they will not, if they can prevent it, allow him to take it to Thingol. But faithful to his own oath he gives him aid. The kingdom is given to Orodreth, and Felagoth and Beren march North. They are overcome in battle. Felagoth and Beren and a small band escape, and creeping back despoil the dead. Disguising themselves as Orcs they get as far as the house of the Lord of Wolves. There they are discovered, and placed in prison – and devoured one by one.
>
> Celegorm discovered what was the secret mission of Felagoth and Beren. He gathers his dogs and hunters and goes a-hunting. He finds the traces of battle. Then he finds Lúthien in the woods.

She flies but is overtaken by Huan the chief of Celegorm's dogs, who is sleepless, and she cannot enchant him. He bears her off. Celegorm offers redress.

From the second sentence *Felagoth warns him of the oath* . . . this entire passage was then struck through and *See tale of Lúthien* written across it; *Felagoth* in the surviving sentence at the beginning was changed to *Felagund*; and *They fall in the power of the Lord of Wolves (Thû)* was added.

3 Here was added, perhaps at the time of the writing of the manuscript:

(But Mandos in payment exacted that Lúthien should become mortal as Beren.)

11

Maidros forms now a league against Morgoth seeing that he will destroy them all, one by one, if they do not unite. The scattered Ilkorins and Men are gathered together. Curufin and Celegorm despatch a host (but not all they could gather, thus breaking their word) from Nargothrond. The Gnomes of Nargothrond refuse to be led by Finweg, and go in search of the hosts of Maidros and Maglor. Men march up from South and East and West and North. Thingol will not send from Doriath.[1] Some say out of selfish policy, others because of the wisdom of Melian and of fate which decreed that Doriath should become the only refuge of the Eldar from Morgoth afterwards. Part was certainly due to the Silmaril, which Thingol now possessed, and which Maidros had demanded with haughty words. The *Gnomes* of Doriath are allowed[2] nonetheless to join the league.

Finweg advances into the Plain of Thirst (Dor-na-Fauglith) before the Iron Mountains and defeats an Orc-army, which falls back. Pursuing he is overwhelmed by countless hordes suddenly loosed on him from the deeps of Angband, and there is fought the field of Unnumbered Tears, of which no elfin songs tell except in lamentation.

The mortal armies, whose leaders had mostly been corrupted or bribed by Morgoth, desert or flee away: all except Húrin's kin. From that day Men and Elves have been estranged, save the descendants of Húrin. Finweg falls, his blue and silver banner is destroyed. The Gnomes attempt to fall back towards the hills and Taur-na-Fuin (forest of night). Húrin holds the rearguard, and all his men are slain, so that not a single man escapes to bring news to

Hithlum. By Morgoth's orders Húrin, whose axe had slain a thousand Orcs, is taken alive. By Húrin alone was Turgon (Finweg's brother) son of Fingolfin enabled to cut his way back into the hills with a part of his people. The remainder of the Gnomes and Ilkorins would have been all slain or taken, but for the arrival of Maidros, Curufin and Celegorm – too late for the main battle.

They are beaten back and driven into the South-east, where they long time dwelt, and did not go back to Nargothrond. There Orodreth ruled over the remnant.[3] Morgoth is utterly triumphant. His armies range all the North, and press upon the borders of Doriath and Nargothrond. The slain of his enemies are piled into a great hill upon Dor-na-Fauglith, but there the grass comes and grows green where all else is desert, and no Orc dare tread upon that hill where the Gnomish swords rust.

Húrin is taken to Angband and defies Morgoth. He is chained in torment. Afterward Morgoth offers him a high captaincy in his forces, a wealth of jewels, and freedom, if he will lead an army against Turgon. None knew whither Turgon had departed save Húrin. Húrin refused and Morgoth devised a torture. He set him upon the highest peak of Thangorodrim and cursed him with never-sleeping sight like the Gods, and he cursed his seed with a fate of ill-hap, and bade Húrin watch the working of it.

★

1   This passage, from *Curufin and Celegorm despatch a host*, was altered by hastily made changes and additions:

> Curufin and Celegorm come from their wandering; but Orodreth because of Felagund his brother will not come: Thingol also sends but few of his folk. The Gnomes of Fëanor's sons refuse to be led by Finweg, and the battle is divided into two hosts, one under Maidros and Maglor, and one under Finweg and Turgon. Men march up from South and East and West and North. Thingol sends but few from Doriath.

2   Added here: *by Thingol*

3   This passage was changed to read:

> They are beaten back and driven into the South-east, where they long time dwelt. In Nargothrond Orodreth ruled still.

12

Morwen wife of Húrin was left alone in the woods. Her son Túrin was a young boy of seven, and she was with child. Only two old men Halog and Mailgond remained faithful to her. The men of Hithlum were slain, and Morgoth breaking his words had driven all men, who had not escaped (as few did) away South, into Hithlum. Now most of these were faithless men who had deserted the Eldar in the battle of Unnumbered Tears. Yet he penned them behind the Shadowy Mountains, nonetheless, and slew such as wandered forth, desiring to keep them from fellowship with Elves. But little love all the same did they show to Húrin's wife. Wherefore it came into her heart to send Túrin to Thingol, because of Beren Húrin's friend who had wedded Lúthien. The 'Children of Húrin' tells of his fate, and how Morgoth's curse pursued him, so that all he did turned out unhappily against his will.

He grew up in Thingol's court, but after a while as Morgoth's power grew no news from Hithlum came and he heard no more of Morwen or of his sister Nienor whom he had not seen. Taunted by Orgof, of the kin of King Thingol, he unwitting of his growing strength killed him at the king's table with a drinking horn. He fled the court thinking himself an outlaw, and took to war against all, Elves, Men, and Orcs, upon the borders of Doriath, gathering a wild band of hunted Men and Elves about him.

One day in his absence his men captured Beleg the bowman, who had befriended Túrin of old. Túrin released him, and is told how Thingol had forgiven his deed long ago. Beleg brings him to abandon his war against Elves, and to assuage his wrath upon the Orcs. The fame of the deeds upon the marches and the prowess of Beleg the Gnome and Túrin son of Húrin against the Orcs is brought to Thingol and to Morgoth. One only of Túrin's band, Blodrin Ban's son, hates the new life with little plunder and harder fighting. He betrays the secret place of Túrin to the Orcs. Their camp is surprised, Túrin is taken and dragged to Angband (for Morgoth has begun to fear he will escape his curse through his valour and the protection of Melian); Beleg is left for dead under a heap of slain. He is found by Thingol's men come to summon them to a feast at the Thousand Caves. Melian heals him, and he sets out to track the Orcs. Beleg is the most skilled in tracking of all who have lived, but the mazes of Taur-na-Fuin bewilder him. There in despair he sees the lamp of Flinding son of Fuilin, a

Gnome of Nargothrond who was captured by Orcs and had long been a thrall in the mines of Morgoth, but escaped.

Of Flinding he learns news of the Orc-band that captured Túrin. They hide and watch the host go by laden with spoil along the Orc-road through the heart of the forest, which the Orcs use when in need of haste. They dread the forest beyond the road as much as Elf or Man. Túrin is seen dragged along and whipped. The Orcs leave the forest and descend the slopes toward Dor-na-Fauglith, and encamp in a dale in sight of Thangorodrim. Beleg shoots the wolf-sentinels and steals with Flinding into the camp. With the greatest difficulty and direst peril they carry the senseless Túrin away and lay him in a dell of thick thorn-trees. In striking off his bonds Beleg pricks Túrin's foot; he is roused, and demented thinks the Orcs are tormenting him, he leaps on Beleg and kills him with his own sword. The covering of Flinding's lamp falls off and seeing Beleg's face he is turned to stone. The Orcs roused by his cries as he leaped upon Beleg discover his escape but are driven far and wide by a dreadful storm of thunder and deluge. In the morning Flinding sees them marching over the steaming waste of Dor-na-Fauglith. Beleg is buried with his bow in the dell.

Flinding leads the dazed unwitting Túrin towards safety. His wits return by Ivrin's lake where are the sources of Narog, and he weeps a great while, and makes a song for Beleg, the 'Bowman's Friendship', which afterwards became a battle-song of the enemies of Morgoth.

13

Flinding leads Túrin to Nargothrond. There Túrin gains the love and loves against his will Finduilas daughter of Orodreth, who had been betrothed before his captivity to Flinding. He fights against his love out of loyalty to Flinding, but Flinding seeing that Finduilas loves Túrin becomes embittered.

Túrin leads the Gnomes of Nargothrond to forsake their secrecy and hidden warfare, and fights the Orcs more openly.[1] He has Beleg's sword forged anew, into a black blade with shining edges, and he is from this given the name of 'Mormakil' or black-sword. The fame of Mormakil reaches even to Thingol. Túrin adopts the name instead of 'Túrin'. For a long while Túrin and the Gnomes of Narog are victorious and their realm reaches to the sources of Narog, and from the western sea to the confines of Doriath. There is a stay in the might of Morgoth.

Morwen and Nienor are able to journey to Thingol leaving their goods in the care of Brodda who had wedded a kinswoman of Morwen. They learn at Thingol's court of the loss of Túrin. News comes to them of the fall of Nargothrond. Morgoth had suddenly loosed a great army on them, and with them one of the first and mightiest[2] of those Dragons that bred in his deep places and for a long while troubled the Northern lands of Men and Elves.[3]

The host of Narog is overwhelmed. Flinding wounded refuses Túrin's succour and dies reproaching him. Túrin hastes back to Nargothrond but the Dragon and Orcs come thither before he can put it in defence, and all the fair halls beneath the earth are plundered, and all the women and maidens of Narog herded as slaves in captivity. Túrin seeks to slay the Dragon, but is held immovable by the spell of his eyes, while the Dragon Glórung[4] taunts him. Glórung then offers him freedom either to follow seeking to rescue his 'stolen love' Finduilas, or to do his duty and go to the rescue of his mother and sister who are living (as he lying says) in great misery in Hithlum. Túrin forsakes Finduilas against his heart (which if he had obeyed his uttermost fate would not have befallen him) and believing the serpent goes to seek Hithlum. Glórung lies in the caves of Narog and gathers beneath him all the gold and silver and gems there hoarded.

Túrin after long wandering goes to Hithlum. But Morwen and Nienor are in Thingol's court, when survivors tell of the fall of Nargothrond, and of Túrin, and some say Túrin escaped alive, and some say he was turned to stone by the eyes of the serpent and lived still in bondage in Nargothrond. Morwen and Nienor at last get Thingol to give them men to go against Glórung, or to spy out his lair at least.

Túrin slays Brodda in his hall, in his anger when he finds Morwen's hall and lands empty and despoiled. Repenting his deed he flies from Hithlum again, and seeks no more after his kin. Desiring to forget his past he takes the name of Turambar (Turmarth) 'Conqueror of Fate', and gathers a new people, 'Men of the Woods', east of Narog, whom he rules, and lives in peace.

The expedition of Thingol, with whom ride Morwen and Nienor, views Narog from a hill-top. The Elves ride down towards the lair,[5] but Glórung coming out lies into the stream and a huge hissing and great vapour goes up, so that their horses turn and fly. Morwen's horse and Nienor's are also panic-stricken and gallop wildly in the mist. When the mist clears Nienor finds herself face to face with the Dragon, whose eye holds her, and a

spell of darkness and utter forgetfulness comes upon her. She
wanders witless in the woods. At last her senses return but she
remembers little.[6] Orcs see her and chase her, but are driven off by
a band of 'Woodmen' under Turambar, who lead her to their
pleasant homes.

As they pass the falls of Silver Bowl a shivering touches her. She
lives amid the woodfolk and is loved by Tamar the Lame, but at
last weds Turambar, who calls her Níniel 'the Tearful' since he
first found her weeping.

Glórung begins to raid across Narog, and Orcs gather to him.
The woodmen slay many of them, and Glórung hearing of their
dwelling comes crawling and filled with fire over Narog and
through the woods against them. He leaves a blasted track behind
him. Turambar ponders how the horror can be warded from his
land. He marches with his men, and Níniel foreboding evil rides
with him,[7] till they can see the burning track of Glórung, and the
smoking place where he lies. Between them runs a stream in a
deep-cloven ravine after falling over the high falls of Silver Bowl.
Turambar asks for volunteers and obtains six only to lie in the
ravine over which the Dragon must pass. The seven depart. They
climb the far side of the ravine at evening and cling near its edge in
the trees. The next morning all have slunk away and Turambar is
alone.

Glórung creeps over. Turambar transfixes him with Gurtholfin[8]
'Wand of Death', his black sword. Glórung coils back in anguish
and lies dying. Turambar comes forth to retrieve his sword, and
places his foot upon Glórung and exults. But the venom of
Glórung gushes out as he tugs out his sword, and he falls in a
swoon. The watchers see that Glórung is slain, but Túrin does not
return. Níniel goes in search of him and finds him lying beside
Glórung. As she is tending him, Glórung opens his eyes and
speaks, and tells her who Turambar is, and lifts his spell from off
her. Then she knows who she is, and knows his tale true from
things Turambar has told her. Filled with horror and anguish she
flies and casts herself over Silver Bowl and none ever found her
body again. Tamar followed her and heard her lament.

Túrin comes back in triumph. He asks for Níniel, but none dare
tell him. Then Tamar comes and tells him. Túrin slays him,
and taking Gurtholfin bids it slay him. The sword answers that his
blood is sweet as any other's, and pierces him to the heart. Túrin is
buried beside Silver Bowl, and his name carved in characters of
Nargothrond upon a rock. Beneath is written Níniel.

Some say Morwen released from spell by Glórung's death came that way and read the stone.

★

1 Added here: *At his advice Narog is bridged* (cf. note 5).
2 *one of the first and mightiest* > *that first and mightiest*
3 Added here: *even Glómund, who was at the Battle of Tears* (see note 4).
4 *Glórung* > *Glómund* here and subsequently, except at the last occurrence.
5 *towards the lair* > *towards the bridge leading to the lair* (cf. note 1).
6 *she remembers little* > *she remembers not even her name.*
7 Added here: *though she is with child,*
8 *Gurtholfin* > *Gurtholfir* at both occurrences.

14

Húrin was released by Morgoth after the end of Túrin and Nienor, for Morgoth thought still to use him. He accused Thingol's faint heart and ungentleness of Túrin's unhappiness, and Húrin wandering bowed with grief pondered his words and was embittered by them.

Húrin and outlaws come to Nargothrond, whom none dare plunder for dread of the spirit of Glórung[1] or even of his memory. They slay Mîm the Dwarf who had taken possession and enchanted all the gold. Húrin casts the gold at Thingol's feet with reproaches. Thingol will not have it, and bears with Húrin, until goaded too far he bids him begone. Húrin wanders away and seeks Morwen, and many for ages after related that they met them together in the woods lamenting their children.

The enchanted gold lays its spell on Thingol. He summons the Dwarves of Nogrod and Belegost to come and fashion it into beautiful things, and to make a necklace of great wonder whereon the Silmaril shall hang. The Dwarves plot treachery, and Thingol bitter with the curse of the gold denies them their reward. After their smithing they are driven away without payment. The Dwarves come back; aided by treachery of some Gnomes who also were bitten by the lust of the gold, they surprise Thingol on a hunt, slay him, and surprise the Thousand Caves and plunder them. Melian they cannot touch. She goes away to seek Beren and Lúthien.

The Dwarves are ambushed at a ford by Beren and the brown and green Elves of the wood, and their king slain, from whose neck Beren takes the 'Nauglafring'[2] or necklace of the Dwarves, with its Silmaril. It is said that Lúthien wearing that jewel is the most beautiful thing that eyes have ever seen outside Valinor. But Melian warned Beren of the curse of the gold and of the Silmaril. The rest of the gold is drowned in the river.

But the 'Nauglafring'[3] remains hoarded secretly in Beren's keeping. When Mandos let Beren return with Lúthien, it was only at the price that Lúthien should become as shortlived as Beren the mortal. Lúthien now fades, even as the Elves in later days faded as Men grew strong and took the goodness of earth (for the Elves needed the light of the Trees). At last she vanished, and Beren was lost, looking in vain for her, and his son Dior ruled after him. Dior re-established Doriath and grew proud, and wore the 'Nauglafring', and the fame of the Silmaril went abroad. After vain bargaining the sons of Fëanor made war on him (the second slaying of Elf by Elf) and destroyed him, and took the 'Nauglafring'. They quarrelled over it, owing to the curse of the gold, until only Maglor was left. But Elwing daughter of Dior was saved and carried away to the mouth of the river Sirion.[4]

★

1 The name *Glórung* is not here emended, as in §13, to *Glómund*, but a *d* is written over the *g*, sc. *Glórund* (the earliest form of the name of the Dragon).

2 At the first occurrence only of *Nauglafring*, *th* is pencilled above, i.e. *Nauglathring* or *Nauglathfring*.

3 Above Nauglafring here my father wrote *Dweorgmene* [Old English, 'Dwarf-necklace']; this was struck out, and *Glingna Nauglir* substituted.

4 The conclusion of this section was changed very soon after it was written, since in §17 already as first written the Nauglafring is with Elwing at the mouth of Sirion:

> After vain bargaining the sons of Fëanor made war on him (the second slaying of Elf by Elf) and destroyed him. But Elwing daughter of Dior, Beren's son, escaped, and was carried away by faithful servants to the mouth of the river Sirion. With her went the Nauglafring.

15

The great river Sirion flowed through the lands South-west; at its mouth was a great delta, and its lower course ran through wide green and fertile lands, little peopled save by birds and beasts because of the Orc-raids; but they were not inhabited by Orcs, who preferred the northern woods, and feared the power of Ylmir – for Sirion's mouth was in the Western Seas.

Turgon Fingolfin's son had a sister Isfin. She was lost in Taur-na-Fuin after the Battle of Unnumbered Tears. There she was trapped by the Dark Elf Eöl. Their son was Meglin. The people of Turgon escaping aided by the prowess of Húrin were lost from the knowledge of Morgoth, and indeed of all in the world save Ylmir. In a secret place in the hills their scouts climbing to the tops discovered a broad valley entirely encircled by the hills in rings ever lower as they came towards the centre. Amid this ring was a wide land without hills, except for one rocky hill that stuck up from the plain, not right at the centre, but nearest to that part of the outer wall which marched close to the edge of Sirion.[1]

Ylmir's messages come up Sirion bidding them take refuge in this valley, and teaching them spells of enchantment to place upon all the hills about, to keep off foes and spies. He foretells that their fortress shall stand longest of all the refuges of the Elves against Morgoth, and like Doriath never be overthrown – save by treachery from within. The spells are strongest near to Sirion, although here the encircling mountains are lowest. Here the Gnomes dig a mighty winding tunnel under the roots of the mountains, that issues at last in the Guarded Plain. Its outer entrance is guarded by the spells of Ylmir; its inner is watched unceasingly by the Gnomes. It is set there in case those within ever need to escape, and as a way of more rapid exit from the valley for scouts, wanderers, and messages, and also as an entrance for fugitives escaping from Morgoth.

Thorndor King of Eagles removes his eyries to the Northern heights of the encircling mountains and guards them against Orc-spies.[2] On the rocky hill, Amon Gwareth, the hill of watching, whose sides they polish to the smoothness of glass, and whose top they level, the great city of Gondolin with gates of steel is built. The plain all about is levelled as flat and smooth as a lawn of clipped grass to the feet of the hills, so that nothing can creep over it unawares. The people of Gondolin grows mighty, and their armouries are filled with weapons. But Turgon does not march to the aid of Nargothrond, or Doriath, and after the slaying of Dior he has no more to do with the son of Fëanor (Maglor).[3] Finally he closes the vale to all fugitives, and forbids the folk of Gondolin to leave the valley. Gondolin is the only stronghold of the Elves left. Morgoth has not forgotten Turgon, but his search is in vain. Nargothrond is destroyed; Doriath desolate; Húrin's children dead; and only scattered and fugitive Elves, Gnomes and Ilkorins, left, except such as work in the smithies and mines in great numbers. His triumph is nearly complete.

★

1   Added here roughly in pencil: *The hill nearest to Angband was guarded by Fingolfin's cairn* (cf. note 2).
2   Added here at the same time as the addition given in note 1: *sitting upon Fingolfin's cairn*.
3   *the son of Fëanor (Maglor)* > *the sons of Fëanor* (this goes with the change at the end of §14, note 4).

16

Meglin son of Eöl and Isfin sister of Turgon was sent by his mother to Gondolin, and there received,[1] although half of Ilkorin blood, and treated as a prince.

Húrin of Hithlum had a brother Huor. The son of Huor was Tuor, younger than Túrin[2] son of Húrin. Rían, Huor's wife, sought her husband's body among the slain on the field of Unnumbered Tears, and died there. Her son remaining in Hithlum fell into the hands of the faithless men whom Morgoth drove into Hithlum after that battle, and he was made a thrall. Growing wild and rough he fled into the woods, and became an outlaw, and a solitary, living alone and communing with none save rarely with wandering and hidden Elves. On a time Ylmir contrived that he should be led to a subterranean river-course leading out of Mithrim into a chasmed river that flowed at last into the Western Sea. In this way his going was unmarked by Man, Orc, or spy, and unknown of Morgoth. After long wanderings down the western shores he came to the mouths of Sirion, and there fell in with the Gnome Bronweg, who had once been in Gondolin. They journey secretly up Sirion together. Tuor lingers long in the sweet land Nan Tathrin 'Valley of Willows'; but there Ylmir himself comes up the river to visit him, and tells him of his mission. He is to bid

Turgon prepare for battle against Morgoth; for Ylmir will turn the hearts of the Valar to forgive the Gnomes and send them succour. If Turgon will do this, the battle will be terrible, but the race of Orcs will perish and will not in after ages trouble Elves and Men. If not, the people of Gondolin are to prepare for flight to Sirion's mouth, where Ylmir will aid them to build a fleet and guide them back to Valinor. If Turgon does Ylmir's will Tuor is to abide a while in Gondolin and then go back to Hithlum with a force of Gnomes and draw Men once more into alliance with the Elves, for 'without Men the Elves shall not prevail against the Orcs and Balrogs'. This Ylmir does because he knows that ere seven[3] full years are passed the doom of Gondolin will come through Meglin.[4]

Tuor and Bronweg reach the secret way,[5] and come out upon the guarded plain. Taken captive by the watch they are led before Turgon. Turgon is grown old[6] and very mighty and proud, and Gondolin so fair and beautiful, and its people so proud of it and confident in its secret and impregnable strength, that the king and most of the people do not wish to trouble about the Gnomes and Elves without, or care for Men, nor do they long any more for Valinor. Meglin approving, the king rejects Tuor's message in spite of the words of Idril the far-sighted (also called Idril Silver-foot, because she loved to walk barefoot) his daughter, and the wiser of his counsellors. Tuor lives on in Gondolin, and becomes a great chieftain. After three years he weds Idril – Tuor and Beren alone of all mortals ever wedded Elves, and since Elwing daughter of Dior Beren's son wedded Eärendel son of Tuor and Idril of them alone has come the strain of Elfinesse into mortal blood.

Not long after this Meglin going far afield over the mountains is taken by Orcs, and purchases his life when taken to Angband by revealing Gondolin and its secrets. Morgoth promises him the lordship of Gondolin, and possession of Idril. Lust for Idril led him the easier to his treachery, and added to his hatred of Tuor.

Morgoth sends him back to Gondolin. Eärendel is born, having the beauty and light and wisdom of Elfinesse, the hardihood and strength of Men, and the longing for the sea which captured Tuor and held him for ever when Ylmir spoke to him in the Land of Willows.

At last Morgoth is ready, and the attack is made on Gondolin with dragons, Balrogs, and Orcs. After a dreadful fight about the walls the city is stormed, and Turgon perishes with many of the most noble in the last fight in the great square. Tuor rescues Idril and Eärendel from Meglin, and hurls him from the battlements. He then leads the remnant of the people of Gondolin down a secret tunnel previously made by Idril's advice which comes out far in the North of the plain. Those who would not come with him but fled to the old way of escape are caught by the dragon sent by Morgoth to watch that exit.

In the fume of the burning Tuor leads his company into the mountains into the cold pass of Cristhorn (Eagles' Cleft). There they are ambushed, but saved by the valour of Glorfindel (chief of the house of the Golden Flower of Gondolin, who dies in a duel with a Balrog upon a pinnacle) and the intervention of Thorndor. The remnant reaches Sirion and journeys to the land at its mouth – the Waters of Sirion. Morgoth's triumph is now complete.

★

[All the changes in this section except that given in note 3 were. late alterations made roughly and hastily.]

1   Added against this sentence: *last of the fugitives from without*
2   *younger than Túrin* > *cousin of Túrin*
3   *seven* early changed to *twelve*
4   Added here: *if they sit still in their halls*.
5   Added here: *which they find by the grace of Ylmir*
6   The word *old* circled for removal.

17

To Sirion's mouth Elwing daughter of Dior comes, and is received by the survivors of Gondolin.[1] These become a seafaring folk, building many boats and living far out on the delta, whither the Orcs dare not come.

Ylmir reproaches the Valar, and bids them rescue the remnants of the Noldoli and the Silmarils in which alone now lives the light of the old days of bliss when the Trees were shining.

The sons of the Valar led by Fionwë Tulcas' son lead forth a host, in which all the Qendi march, but remembering Swanhaven few of the Teleri go with them. Côr is deserted.

Tuor growing old[2] cannot forbear the call of the sea, and builds Eärámë and sails West with Idril and is heard of no more. Eärendel weds Elwing. The call of the sea is born also in him. He builds Wingelot and wishes to sail in search of his father. Ylmir bids him to sail to Valinor.[3] Here follow the marvellous adventures of Wingelot in the seas and isles, and of how Eärendel slew Ungoliant in the South. He returned home and found the Waters of Sirion desolate. The sons of Fëanor learning of the dwelling of Elwing and the Nauglafring had come down on the people of Gondolin. In a battle all the sons of Fëanor save Maidros[4] were slain, but the last folk of Gondolin destroyed or forced to go away and join the people of Maidros.[5] Elwing cast the Nauglafring into the sea and leapt after it,[6] but was changed into a white sea-bird by Ylmir, and flew to seek Eärendel, seeking about all the shores of the world.

Their son (Elrond) who is half-mortal and half-elfin,[7] a child, was saved however by Maidros. When later the Elves return to the West, bound by his mortal half he elects to stay on earth. Through him the blood of Húrin[8] (his great-uncle) and of the Elves is yet among Men, and is seen yet in valour and in beauty and in poetry.

Eärendel learning of these things from Bronweg, who dwelt in a hut, a solitary, at the mouth of Sirion, is overcome with sorrow. With Bronweg he sets sail in Wingelot once more in search of Elwing and of Valinor.

He comes to the magic isles, and to the Lonely Isle, and at last to the Bay of Faërie. He climbs the hill of Côr, and walks in the deserted ways of Tûn, and his raiment becomes encrusted with the dust of diamonds and of jewels. He dares not go further into Valinor. He builds a tower on an isle in the northern seas, to which all the seabirds of the world repair. He sails by the aid of their wings even over the airs in search of Elwing, but is scorched by the Sun, and hunted from the sky by the Moon, and for a long while he wanders the sky as a fugitive star.[9]

★

[In this section again most of the changes (not those in notes 2 and 4) were hastily made in pencil.]

1   This sentence was changed to read:

   At Sirion's mouth Elwing daughter of Dior dwelt, and received the survivors of Gondolin.

2   *growing old* struck out.
3   *Ylmir bids him to sail to Valinor* struck out.
4   *Maidros > Maidros and Maglor*
5   Written in the margin: *Maglor sat and sang by the sea in repentance.*

6 My father first wrote *Elwing cast herself into the sea with the Nauglafring*, but changed it to *Elwing cast the Nauglafring into the sea and leapt after it* in the act of writing.

7 This sentence was changed to read:

Their son (Elrond) who is part mortal and part elfin and part of the race of Valar,

8 *Húrin* struck out, and *Huor and of Beren* written above, together with some illegible words. One might expect *Through him the blood of Huor and of Beren his great-grandfathers*, but the illegible words do not seem to be these. (Húrin was in fact Elrond's great-great-uncle.)

9 The last sentence (*He sails by the aid of their wings . . .*) is an addition, but I think an addition made at the time of writing.

18

The march of Fionwë into the North is then told, and of the Terrible or Last Battle. The Balrogs are all destroyed, and the Orcs destroyed or scattered. Morgoth himself makes a last sally with all his dragons; but they are destroyed, all save two which escape, by the sons of the Valar, and Morgoth is overthrown and bound[1] and his iron crown is made into a collar for his neck. The two Silmarils are rescued. The Northern and Western parts of the world are rent and broken in the struggle.[2]

The Gods and Elves release Men from Hithlum, and march through the lands summoning the remnants of the Gnomes and Ilkorins to join them. All do so except the people of Maidros. Maidros aided by many men[3] prepares to perform his oath, though now at last weighed down by sorrow because of it. He sends to Fionwë reminding him of the oath and begging for the Silmarils. Fionwë replies that he has lost his right to them because of the evil deeds of Fëanor, and of the slaying of Dior, and of the plundering of Sirion. He must submit, and come back to Valinor; in Valinor only and at the judgement of the Gods shall they be handed over.

Maidros and Maglor[4] submit. The Elves set sail from Lúthien (Britain or England) for Valinor.[5] Thence they ever still from time [to time] set sail leaving the world ere they fade.

On the last march Maglor says to Maidros that there are two sons of Fëanor now left, and two Silmarils; one is his. He steals it, and flies, but it burns him so that he knows he no longer has a right to it. He wanders in pain over the earth, and casts himself into a pit.[6] One Silmaril is now in the sea, and one in the earth.[7]

The Gnomes and many of the Ilkorins and Teleri and Qendi repeople the Lonely Isle. Some go back to live upon the shores of Faëry and in Valinor, but Côr and Tûn remain desolate.

★

1   Added here: *by the chain Angainor*
2   Added here: *and the fashion of their lands altered* (late pencilled addition).
3   *aided by many men* struck out.
4   *and Maglor* circled in pencil.
5   This sentence was changed to read:

> The Elves march to the Western shore, and begin to set sail from Leithien (Britain or England) for Valinor.

6   *casts himself into a pit* > *casts it into a fiery pit.*
7   Added here: *Maglor sings now ever in sorrow by the sea.*

19

The judgement of the Gods takes place. The earth is to be for Men, and the Elves who do not set sail for the Lonely Isle or Valinor shall slowly fade and fail. For a while the last dragons and Orcs shall grieve the earth, but in the end all shall perish by the valour of Men.

Morgoth is thrust through the Door of Night into the outer dark beyond the Walls of the World, and a guard set for ever on that Door. The lies that he sowed in the hearts of Men and Elves do not die and cannot all be slain by the Gods, but live on and bring much evil even to this day. Some say also that secretly Morgoth or his black shadow and spirit in spite of the Valar creeps back over the Walls of the World in the North and East and visits the world, others that this is Thû his great chief who escaped the Last Battle and dwells still in dark places, and perverts Men to his dreadful worship. When the world is much older, and the Gods weary, Morgoth will come back through the Door, and the last battle of all will be fought. Fionwë will fight Morgoth on the plain of Valinor, and the spirit of Túrin shall be beside him; it shall be Túrin who with his black sword will slay Morgoth, and thus the children of Húrin shall be avenged.

In those days the Silmarils shall be recovered from sea and earth and air, and Maidros shall break them and Belaurin[1] with their fire rekindle the Two Trees, and the great light shall come forth again, and the Mountains of Valinor shall be levelled so that it goes out over the world, and Gods and Elves and Men[2] shall grow young again, and all their dead awake.[3]

And thus it was that the last Silmaril came into the air. The Gods adjudged the last Silmaril to Eärendel – 'until many things shall come to pass' – because of the deeds of the sons of Fëanor. Maidros is sent to Eärendel and with the aid of the Silmaril Elwing is found and restored. Eärendel's boat is drawn over Valinor to the Outer Seas, and Eärendel launches it into the outer darkness high above Sun and Moon. There he sails with the Silmaril upon his brow and Elwing at his side, the brightest of all stars, keeping watch upon Morgoth.[4] So he shall sail until he sees the last battle gathering upon the plains of Valinor. Then he will descend.

And this is the last end of the tales of the days before the days, in the Northern regions of the Western World. These tales are some of those remembered and sung by the fading Elves, and most by the vanished Elves of the Lonely Isle. They have been told by Elves to Men of the race of Eärendel, and most to Eriol who alone of mortals of later days sailed to the Lonely Isle, and yet came back to Lúthien,[5] and remembered things he had heard in Cortirion, the town of the Elves in Tol Eressëa.

★

1   Against *Belaurin* was written *Palúrien* (cf. §1 note 1).
2   *and Men* struck out.
3   Added here:

   But of Men in that last Day the prophecy speaks not, save of Túrin only.

4   Added here: *and the Door of Night* (late pencilled addition).
5   *Lúthien > Leithien* (cf. §18 note 5).

Commentary on
the *'Sketch of the Mythology'*

While the 'Sketch' is a good and clear manuscript, as it had to be (since it was to be read by R. W. Reynolds), it will be apparent that my father composed it extremely rapidly: I think it quite possible and even probable that he wrote it without consulting the earlier prose tales.

Very great advances have been made towards the form of the story as it appears in the published work; but there is no trace of a prose narrative even in fragmentary or note form that bridges the gap between the *Lost Tales* and this synopsis in the 'Valinórean' part of the mythology (i.e. to the flight of the Noldoli and the making of the Sun and Moon). This is not to say, of course, that none such ever existed, though the fact that my father did undoubtedly preserve a very high proportion of all that he ever wrote leads me to doubt it. I think it far more likely that while working on other things (during his time at Leeds) he had developed his ideas, especially on the 'Valinórean' part, without setting them to paper; and since the prose *Tales* had been set aside a good many years before, it may be that certain narrative shifts found in the 'Sketch' were less fully intended, less conscious, than such shifts in the later development of 'The Silmarillion', where he always worked on the basis of existing writings.

It is in any case often extremely difficult, or impossible, to judge whether features in the *Tales* that are not present in the 'Sketch' were omitted simply for the sake of compression, or whether they had been definitively abandoned. Thus while Eriol – not Ælfwine, see II. 300 – is mentioned at the end, and his coming to Kortirion in Tol Eressëa, there is no trace of the Cottage of Lost Play: the entire narrative framework of the *Lost Tales* has disappeared. But this does not by any means demonstrate that my father had actually rejected it at this time.

The Commentary that follows is divided according to the 19 sections into which I have divided the narrative.

The 'Sketch of the Mythology' is referred to throughout the rest of this book by the abbreviation 'S'.

1

S (the 'Sketch'), which makes no reference to the Creation and the Music of the Ainur, begins with the coming of the Nine Valar 'for the governance of the world': the Nine Valar have been referred to in the alliterative poem *The Flight of the Noldoli* (see III. 133, 137). There now appears the isle (later called Almaren) on which the Gods dwelt after the making of the Lamps, the origin of which is probably to be seen in the tale of *The Coming of the Valar* I. 69–70, where it is said that when the Lamps fell the Valar were gathered on the Twilit Isles, and that 'that island whereon stood the Valar' was dragged westward by Ossë. It might seem that the story of Melko's making the pillars of the Lamps out of ice that melted had been abandoned, but it reappears again later, in the *Ambarkanta* (p. 238).

The use of the word 'plant' of the Two Trees is curious, and might be dismissed simply as a hasty expression if it did not appear in the following version of 'The Silmarillion', the *Quenta* (p. 80). In the old tale, as in the published work, the Trees rose from the ground under the chanted spells of Yavanna. The silver undersides of the leaves of the White Tree now appear, and its flowers are likened to those of a cherry: *Silpion* is translated 'Cherry-moon' in the Name-list to *The Fall of Gondolin* (II.215). The mention of the White Tree first may imply that it had now become the Elder Tree, as it is explicitly in the *Quenta*.

As S was first written the Trees had periods of twelve hours, as in the *Lost Tales* (see I.88 and footnote), but with emendation from 'six' to 'seven' (allowing for the time of 'mingled light') the period becomes fourteen hours. This was a movement towards the formulation in *The Silmarillion* (p. 38), where each Tree 'waxed to full and waned again to naught' in seven hours; but in *The Silmarillion* 'each day of the Valar in Aman contained twelve hours', whereas in S each day was double that length.

The Gnomish name of Varda, *Bridhil*, occurs in the alliterative *Flight of the Noldoli* (changed to *Bredhil*), the *Lay of Leithian*, and the early Gnomish dictionary (I.273, entry *Varda*). On *Timbrenting, Tindbrenting* see III.127, 139; *Tengwethil* (varying with *Taingwethil*) is found in the *Lay of the Children of Húrin*. For *Ifan Belaurin* see I.273, entry *Yavanna*; in the Gnomish dictionary the Gnomish form is *Ifon, Ivon*.

2

The description in S of the 'Outer Lands' (now used of the Great Lands, see III.224), where growth was checked at the downfall of the Lamps, but where there are forests of dark trees in which Oromë goes hunting at times, moves the narrative at this point in one step to its structure in *The Silmarillion*; of the very different account in the *Lost Tales* I noticed in my commentary on *The Chaining of Melko* (I.111): 'In this earliest narrative there is no mention of the beginning of growth during the time when the Lamps shone, and the first trees and low plants appeared under Yavanna's spells in the twilight after their overthrow.'

Whereas in the *Lost Tales* the star-making of Varda took place after the awakening of the Elves (I.113), here they awake 'at the making of the stars'.

In commenting on the *Lost Tales* I noticed (I.111, 131) that the Gods sought out Melko on account of his renewed cosmic violence, before the awakening of the Elves and without respect to them in any way; and that the release of Melko from Mandos took place before the coming of the Eldar to Valinor, so that he played a part in the debate concerning their summons. In S the later story (that the discovery of the Elves led directly to the assault of the Valar on the fortress of Morgoth) is already present, and moreover a motive is ascribed to the intervention of the Valar that is not found in *The Silmarillion*: they are 'reminded of their duty to the Earth, since they came thither knowing that their office was to govern it for the two races of Earth who should after come each in appointed time'. It seems clear also that the old story of the coming of the Elves being known to Manwë independently of their discovery by Oromë (see I. 131) had been abandoned.

In the *Lost Tales* Melko's first fortress was Utumna, and though it was not wholly destroyed to its foundations (I. 104) after his escape back into the Great Lands he was 'busy making himself new dwellings', as Sorontur told Manwë, for 'never more will Utumna open unto him' (I. 176). This second fortress was Angband (Angamandi). In S, on the other hand, the first fortress is Angband, and after his escape Morgoth is able to return to it (§4), for it was too strong for the Gods to destroy (§2). The name Utumna (Utumno) has thus disappeared.

In the passage describing the three hosts of the Elves on the great march from Cuiviénen (which occurs, by emendation, in the *Lay of the Children of Húrin*, III. 18, 23) there appears the later use of *Teleri* for the third kindred (who however still retain the old name *Solosimpi*, the Shoreland Pipers), while the first kindred (the *Teleri* of the *Lost Tales*) now acquire the name *Quendi* (subsequently spelt in S both *Quendi* and *Qendi*). Thus:

Lost Tales	*'Sketch'*	*The Silmarillion*
Teleri	Q(u)endi	Vanyar
Noldoli	Noldoli	Noldor
Solosimpi	Teleri, Solosimpi	Teleri

The formulation at the time of the *Lost Tales* (see I. 235) was that *Qendi* was the original name of all the Elves, and *Eldar* the name given by the Gods and adopted by the Elves of Valinor; those who remained in the Great Lands (Ilkorins) preserved the old name, *Qendi*. There also appear now the terms 'Light-elves', 'Deep-elves', and 'Sea-elves' (as in *The Hobbit*, chapter 8); the meaning of 'the Elves proper', applied to the first kindred, is clear from the *Quenta* (p. 85): 'the Quendi . . . who sometimes are alone called Elves.'

Inwë of the *Lost Tales* now becomes *Ingwë*, with the Gnomish equivalent *Ing* which appears in the alliterative poems, as does Gnomish *Finn* (in *The Flight of the Noldoli*). *Elwë (Elu)* is in the rôle of the later Olwë, leader of the third kindred after the loss of Thingol. In the *Tale of Tinúviel* Tinwelint (Thingol) was indeed originally called *Tinto Ellu* or *Ellu*, but in the tales of *The Coming of the Elves* and *The Theft of Melko*, by later changes, *Ellu* becomes the name of the second lord of the Solosimpi chosen in Tinwelint's place; see II. 50.

Notably absent from the account in S are the initial coming of the three Elvish ambassadors to Valinor, and the Elves who did not leave the Waters of Awakening, referred to in *Gilfanon's Tale* (I. 231): the

Ilkorins are here defined as those who were lost on the great march into the West. On these omissions see the commentary on §2 in the *Quenta*, p. 168.

Other omissions in S are the two starmakings of Varda (see p. 168) and the chain Angainor with which Morgoth was bound (see S §18 note 1).

3

In the tale of *The Coming of the Elves* the island on which the Gods were drawn to the western lands at the time of the fall of the Lamps was the island on which the Elves were afterwards ferried, becoming Tol Eressëa (see I. 118, 134); now, the isle on which the Gods dwelt (see the commentary on §1) is again the isle of the Elves' ferrying. But in *The Silmarillion* there is no connection between the Isle of Almaren and Tol Eressëa.

In the story of the ferrying features of the final narrative emerge in S: the first two kindreds to arrive at the shores of the sea are ferried together on this island, not separately as in the tale; and the love of the sea among the Teleri (Solosimpi) began during their waiting for Ulmo's return. On the other hand the old story of Ossë's rebellious anchoring of Tol Eressëa still survives (see I. 134); but the position of the island after its anchoring has now shifted westwards, to the Bay of Faërie, 'whence the Mountains of Valinor could dimly be seen': contrast the account in the tale, where Ulmo had traversed 'less than half the distance' across the Great Sea when Ossë waylaid it, and where 'no land may be seen for many leagues' sail from its cliffs' (see I. 120–1, and my discussion of this change, I. 134). In the tale, Ossë seized and anchored Tol Eressëa before its journey was done because he 'deemed himself slighted that his aid was not sought in the ferrying of the Elves, but his own island taken unasked' (I. 119); in S his jealousy is indeed mentioned, but also his love of the singing of the Teleri, which was afterwards a prominent motive. Ossë's making of the seabirds for the Teleri (Solosimpi) was retained, though afterwards lost.

In the tale the gap in the Mountains of Valinor was not made by the Valar for the sake of the Elves, nor was the hill of Kôr raised for them: they had existed since distant days, when 'in the trouble of the ancient seas a shadowy arm of water had groped in toward Valinor' (I. 122). In the passage in S can be seen the origin of that in *The Silmarillion* (p. 59). Here in S Côr is the hill and Tûn is the city built upon it (though in §2 there is a reference to Elves dwelling 'in Côr'); see III. 93.

On the 'invention' of gems by the Noldoli see I. 138. The especial love of Mandos 'the wise' for the Noldoli is found neither in the *Lost Tales* nor in *The Silmarillion*, and may seem an improbable attribute of that Vala: cf. *The Coming of the Elves*, I. 117: 'Mandos and Fui were cold to the Eldar as to all else.'

The passage concerning the Noldorin princes, added to the text of S (though probably after no great interval), is the origin of the passage in *The Silmarillion* (p. 60) which begins in the same way: 'The Noldor afterwards came back to Middle-earth, and this tale tells mostly of their deeds . . .' For the details of names and relations in this passage see the Note at the end of this section of the commentary.

The story of the coming of the Teleri (Solosimpi) to Valinor from Tol Eressëa comes in S, in essentials, almost to the form in *The Silmarillion* (p. 61); for the very different account in the tale see I. 124–6. In S, however, it was Ylmir (Ulmo) not Ossë who taught them the craft of shipbuilding, and this of course reflects the difference still underlying: for here Ylmir was still, as in the tale, eager for the coming of the Third Kindred to Valinor, whereas in *The Silmarillion* he had himself bidden Ossë make fast the island to the sea-bottom, and afterwards only 'submitted to the will of the Valar'. – The name *Ylmir* – almost certainly the Gnomish form – appears in the *Lay of the Children of Húrin*, see III. 93; but the form *Óin* for Uinen is not found elsewhere.

Note on the Noldorin princes

Fingolfin as the son of Finwë (Finn) and father of Turgon emerges first in the *Lay of the Fall of Gondolin* (III. 146–7), and is present in the second version of the *Lay of the Children of Húrin* (only by emendation in the first) (III. 137). That Fëanor was Fingolfin's brother is deducible from the alliterative *Flight of the Noldoli (ibid.)*, but from S, as originally written in this section, it is seen that Fëanor was at first the second, not the elder son. Here in S Finwë's third son Finrod first emerges: the mention of him, and his sons, in a note to the *Lay of the Children of Húrin* (III. 80) is certainly later, as is his first appearance in the *Lay of Leithian* (III. 191, 195).

The seven sons of Fëanor with the same name-forms as here in S have appeared in the *Lay of the Children of Húrin* (III. 65, 86); the naming of Damrod and Díriel together in S suggests that they were already twin brothers.

Of the sons of Fingolfin Turgon of course goes back to the *Lost Tales*, where he was the son, not the grandson, of Finwë; the other son Finweg appears in the *Lay of the Children of Húrin*, where the emendation to Fingon (see III. 5, 80) is later than S – and the *Quenta*, where he was still Finweg in the text as first written.

The sons of Finrod first emerge here, and as the inserted passage in S was first written Orodreth was apparently the eldest son; Angrod was Anrod; and Felagund was Felagoth. Felagoth occurs as an intervening stage between Celegorm and Felagund in the A-text of the *Lay of Leithian* (III. 169, 195).

4

In this section again S moves at a step close to the essential structure of the narrative in *The Silmarillion*, though there are important features not yet present. I have discussed previously (I. 156–8) the radical differences between the tale of *The Theft of Melko* and the story in *The Silmarillion*, and it will be seen that it was with S that almost all these differences entered: there is thus no need to repeat the comparison again here. But various more minor matters may be noticed.

The quarrel of the Nóldorin princes has as yet none of the complexity and subtlety that entered into it afterwards with the history of Míriel, the first wife of Finwë and mother of Fëanor; the quarrel is in any case treated with great brevity.

It is said here that 'Fëanor has cursed for ever anyone, God or Elf or mortal that shall come hereafter, who touches [the Silmarils]'. In §5, by a later interpolation, the oath is taken by Fëanor and his sons at the time of the torchlit concourse in Tûn, but the statement in §4 my father allowed to stand, clearly because he overlooked it. In the alliterative fragment *The Flight of the Noldoli*, however, which on general grounds I assume to belong to the earlier part of 1925 (III. 131), the oath is sworn by Fëanor and his sons as in the interpolation in S §5, 'in the mighty square upon the crown of Côr' (see III. 136). I incline to think that the statement here in §4 was a slip of memory.

The events immediately following the council of the Gods in which Morgoth's lies were disclosed and Fëanor banished from Tûn (in S the banishment is not said to be limited to a term of years) are not yet given the form they have in *The Silmarillion*. The entire story of Morgoth's going to Formenos (not yet so named) and his speech with Fëanor before the doors (*The Silmarillion* pp. 71–2) has yet to appear. Morgoth's northward movement up the coast in feint is also absent; rather he comes at once to Arvalin 'where the shadow is thickest in all the world', as is said in *The Silmarillion* (p. 73) of Avathar.

In the story of Morgoth's encounter with Ungoliant and the destruction of the Trees details of the final version appear, as Ungoliant's ascent of the great mountain (later named Hyarmentir) 'from pinnacle to pinnacle', and the ladder made for Morgoth to climb. There is no mention of the great festival, but it appears in §5: it looks as if my father omitted to include it earlier and brought it in a bit further on as an afterthought.

In the tale of *The Theft of Melko* Ungoliant fled south at once after the destruction of the Trees (I. 154), and of Melko's subsequent movements after his crossing of the Ice it is only told (by Sorontur to Manwë, I. 176) that he was busy building himself a new dwelling-place in the region of the Iron Mountains. But in S the story of 'the Thieves' Quarrel' and Morgoth's rescue by the Balrogs emerges suddenly fully-formed.

5

From the account of the great festival (see commentary on §4) is absent both the original occasion for holding it (commemoration of the coming of the Eldar to Valinor, I. 143) and that given in *The Silmarillion* (the autumn feast: pp. 74–5). The later feature that the Teleri were not present appears (see I. 157); but there is no suggestion of the important elements of Fëanor coming alone to the festival from Formenos, the formal reconciliation with Fingolfin, and Fëanor's refusal to surrender the Silmarils before he heard the news of his father's death and the theft of the jewels (*The Silmarillion* pp. 75, 78–9).

In the later emendations to the text of S we see the growth of the story of the divided counsels of the Gnomes, with the introduction of the attempt of Finrod (later Finarfin) to calm the conflicting factions – though this element was present in the tale of *The Flight of the Noldoli*, where Finwë Nólemë plays the part of the appeaser (I. 162). After a good deal of further shifting in this passage in later texts, and the introduction of Galadriel, the alignment, and the motives, of the princes as they appear in *The Silmarillion* are more complex (pp. 83–4); but the element is already present that only one of Finrod's sons sided with him (here Felagund, in *The Silmarillion* Orodreth).

The emendation making Fingolfin and Finweg (Fingon) rule over 'a half of the Noldoli of Tûn' must be incorrect; my father probably intended the revised text to read 'over the Noldoli of Tûn'.

The rapid shifting in the part of Finrod (Finarfin) in these events can be observed in the successive interpolations made in S. It seems that in the original text he did not appear at all (the first mention of him is in the interpolated passage in §3, p. 15). He is said not to have left Tûn; then he is said to have been slain at Swanhaven; and finally it is told that he and his sons were not at Swanhaven, but left Tûn reluctantly, carrying with them many things of their making. Finrod was then introduced as only arriving with his people in the far North after the burning of the ships by the Fëanorians on the other side of the strait. As S was originally written Fingolfin, deserted and shipless, returned to Valinor, and it was his son Finweg (Fingon) who led the main host over the Grinding Ice; but with the introduction of Finrod he becomes the one who returned. (Finweg as the leader of the host was not then changed to Fingolfin, but this was obviously an oversight.)

In the account of the northward journey of the Noldoli after the battle of Swanhaven it seems that all the host was embarked in the ships of the Teleri, since Mandos' emissary hails them from a high cliff 'as they sail by'; but this may be merely due to compression, since in the *Tale* (I. 166) some marched along the shore while 'the fleet coasted beside them not far out to sea', and the same is told in *The Silmarillion* ('some by ship and some by land', p. 87). The storm raised by Uinen is not mentioned.

It is curious that the curse upon the Gnomes, that they should suffer from treachery and the fear of treachery among their own kindred, is separated from the Prophecy of Mandos; but it is not said by whom this curse was pronounced. Nothing is told in S as originally written of the content of the Prophecy of Mandos, save that it concerned 'the fate of after days', but my father subsequently added that it told of 'the curse of war against one another because of Swanhaven', thus bringing the 'curse' into the content of the 'Prophecy', as in *The Silmarillion*. There is no trace of the old prophecies concerning Turgon and Gondolin (I. 167, 172), but nor is there any suggestion of the nature of the doom of the Noldor as it is stated in *The Silmarillion*.

For the original story of the crossing of the Grinding Ice by the Gnomes, where there is no element of treachery (though the blaming of Fëanor was already present), see I. 167-9.

6

The making of the Sun and Moon is here compressed into a couple of phrases. Virtually all of the extremely elaborate account in the old *Tale of the Sun and Moon* has disappeared: the tears of Vána leading to the last fruit of Laurelin, the breaking of the 'Fruit of Noon', the Bath of the Setting Sun where the Sun-maiden and her ship were drawn on coming out of the East, the song of Lórien leading to the last flower of Silpion, the fall of the 'Rose of Silpion' which caused the markings on the Moon, the refusal to allow Silmo to steer the ship of the Moon and the task given instead to Ilinsor, a spirit of the Súruli, Lake Irtinsa where the ship of the Moon was refreshed, and much else. But while it is impossible to say how much of all this my father had 'privately' rejected at this time (see my remarks, I. 200), some elements at least were suppressed for the purposes of this 'Sketch', which is after all only an outline, for they will reappear.

The change in the celestial plan now takes place because the Gods 'find it safer to send [the Sun and Moon] in Ylmir's care through the caverns and grottoes beneath the Earth'. This is wholly different from the old story (I. 215), in which the *original* plan of the Gods was that the Sun and Moon should be drawn beneath the earth; this plan was changed when they found that the Sun-ship 'might not safely come beneath the world' – the very reverse of what is said in S. Though the Moon continued to pass beneath the earth, the Gods now made the Door of Night in the West and the Gates of Morn in the East, through which the Sun passed thenceforward, going into and returning from the Outer Dark (I. 216). The astronomical aspect of the mythology has thus undergone a profound shift, an entire re-making.

The reference to the rekindling of the 'Magic Sun' (here with extension to the Moon, not found in the earliest writings) is a noteworthy survival; and the meaning is explicitly the rebirth of the Trees (see

II. 286). Very remarkable is Ulmo's foretelling to the Valar that the rekindling of the Two Trees and the return of 'the bliss and glory of old' would only come to pass by the aid of Men. It is possible that this is a reference to his own deep designs laid through Turgon, Tuor, and Eärendel; but it is nowhere suggested that these designs issued or were intended to issue in such a way. Perhaps we should see here rather the continued existence in some form of the old prophecy given in II. 285:

> The Elves' prophecy is that one day they will fare forth from Tol Eressëa and on arriving in the world will gather all their fading kindred who still live in the world and march towards Valinor. . . This they will only do with the help of Men. If Men aid them, the fairies will take Men to Valinor – those that wish to go – fight a great battle with Melko in Erumáni and open Valinor. Laurelin and Silpion will be rekindled, and the mountain wall being destroyed then soft radiance will spread over all the world, and the Sun and Moon will be recalled.

In the account of the Hiding of Valinor we move in S from the *Lost Tales* to *The Silmarillion*: I have observed (I. 223) the total absence in the latter of the bitter divisions among the Valar, of Manwë's disgusted withdrawal, of Ulmo's vain pleading for pity on the Noldor – and of my father's explicit view in the tale of *The Hiding of Valinor* that the actions of the Valar at this time, and their failure to make war upon Morgoth, were a profound error arising from indolence and fear. The fear of Morgoth does indeed remain, and is the only motive offered in *The Silmarillion* for the Hiding of Valinor; but the author makes no comment on it. In S however the element of divine anger against the Noldoli is still present (though neither here nor later is there any reference to the peculiar anger of Aulë against them (see I. 176), save that in the *Annals of Valinor* (p. 267) when Finrod and others returned to Valinor after hearing the Doom of Mandos 'Aulë their ancient friend smiled on them no more').

There are differences and omissions in the later versions of the story of the Hiding of Valinor in relation to that in the tale which have been sufficiently discussed already (I. 223–4); but it may be noticed that in S no reason is given for keeping open the pass of Kôr, neither that in the tale nor that in *The Silmarillion*.

It is very clear that with the 'Sketch' the structure of the Valinórean part of the mythology, though not of course the detail, had quite largely reached the stage of development of the published version; and it can be understood why my father wrote on the envelope containing S the words *Original 'Silmarillion'*. It is here that 'The Silmarillion' begins.

7

It will be seen that in this passage S has already the structure and some even of the phrases of the last three paragraphs of chapter 12 ('Of Men') in *The Silmarillion*.

The Fëanorian oath (ascribed here to the sons only) is embodied in the text as written, which probably shows that the interpolated passage, introducing the oath, in §5 (p. 19) was inserted while S was still in process of composition.

The words of S, 'in the early days Eldar and Men were of nearly equal stature and power of body', are echoed in *The Silmarillion*: 'Elves and Men were of like stature and strength of body'; for statements on this matter in earlier writings see II. 326.

The 'higher culture' that my father came to ascribe to the Elves of Doriath (or more widely to the Grey-elves of Beleriand) is now established ('Only in the realm of Doriath . . . did the Ilkorins equal the Koreldar'); contrast the description of the Ilkorins of Tinwelint's following in the old *Tale of Tinúviel* ('eerie they were and strange beings, knowing little of light or loveliness or of musics. . .'), concerning which I noted that Tinwelint's people are there described in terms applicable rather to the wild Avari of *The Silmarillion* (see II. 9, 64). It is however said in this passage of the tale that 'Different indeed did they become when the Sun arose.'

The ideas expressed here concerning the nature of the immortality of the Elves go back largely to the *Lost Tales*; cf. the description of the hall of Mandos in *The Coming of the Valar* (I. 76):

> Thither in after days fared the Elves of all the clans who were by illhap slain with weapons or did die of grief for those that were slain – and only so might the Eldar die, and then it was only for a while. There Mandos spake their doom, and there they waited in the darkness, dreaming of their past deeds, until such time as he appointed when they might again be born into their children, and go forth to laugh and sing again.

Similarly in *The Music of the Ainur* (I. 59) it is said that 'the Eldar dwell till the Great End unless they be slain or waste in grief (for to both of these deaths are they subject)', and 'dying they are reborn in their children, so that their number minishes not, nor grows'. But in the early texts death by sickness is not mentioned, and this appears for the first time in S: where by emendation there is a modification of the idea, from freedom from all sickness to freedom from death by sickness. Moreover in the early texts rebirth in their own children seems to be represented as the universal fate of the Eldar who die; whereas in S they are said to return from Mandos 'to free life'. Rebirth is mentioned in S very briefly and only in a later interpolation.

In S my father's conception of the fate of Men after death is seen evolving (for the extremely puzzling account in the *Lost Tales* see I.77, 90–3). As he first wrote S, there was an explicit assertion that Men did not go to Mandos, did not pass to the western land: this was an idea derived from contact with the Eldar. But he changed this, and wrote instead that Men do indeed go to their own halls in Mandos, for a time; none know whither they go after, save Mandos himself.

On the 'fading' of the Elves who remained 'in the world' see II. 326.

8

Neither the brief outlines for what was to have been Gilfanon's tale of *The Travail of the Noldoli* (I. 237–41) nor the subsequent abandoned narrative given on pp. 6–8 bear much relation to what came after. Enduring features were the camp by Asgon-Mithrim, the death of Fëanor, the first affray with the Orcs, the capture and maiming of Maidros; but these elements had different motivations and concomitants in the earliest writing, already discussed (I. 242–3). With the 'Sketch', however, most of the essentials of the later story appear fully-formed, and the distance travelled from the *Lost Tales* is here even more striking than hitherto.

The first battle of the Gnomes with the forces of Morgoth is not clearly placed in S (cf. *Gilfanon's Tale*, I. 238, 240, where the battle was fought 'in the foothills of the Iron Mountains' or in 'the pass of the Bitter Hills') – but the idea is already present that the Orcs were aroused by the burning of the ships (cf. §5: 'The same light also tells the Orcs of the landing'.)

There now emerge the death of Fëanor at the hand of Gothmog the Balrog, the parley with the enemy and the faithless intentions on both sides, the arrival of the second host, unfurling their blue and silver banners (see p. 9) under the first Sunrise, and the dismay of the Orcs at the new light, the hostile armies of the Gnomes encamped on opposite sides of Lake Mithrim, the 'vast smokes and vapours' rising from Angband. The only important structural element in the narrative that has yet to appear is that of Fingolfin's march to Angband immediately on arrival in Middle-earth and his beating on the doors.

The earlier existence of the story of the rescue of Maidros by Finweg (Fingon) is implied by a reference in the *Lay of the Children of Húrin* (see III. 65, 86) – that in the *Lay of Leithian* is some two years later than S (III. 222). A curious point arises in the account in S: it seems that it was only at this juncture that Manwë brought into being the race of Eagles. In the tale of *The Theft of Melko* Sorontur (the 'Elvish' form of Gnomish Thorndor) had already played a part in the story before the departure of the Noldoli from Valinor: he was the emissary of the Valar to Melko before the destruction of the Trees, and because Melko tried to slay the Eagle between that evil one and Sorontur has there ever since been hate and war, and that was most bitter when Sorontur and his folk fared to the Iron Mountains and there abode, watching all that Melko did (I. 149).

It may be noted that Lake Mithrim is placed in Hisilómë/Hithlum/ Dorlómin; see III. 103.

9

For this section of the narrative the earliest materials are so scanty that we may almost say that the 'Sketch' is the starting-point. In an outline for *Gilfanon's Tale* (I. 238) there is mention of a meeting between Gnomes and Ilkorins, and it was with the guidance of these Ilkorins that Maidros led an army to Angamandi, whence they were driven back with slaughter leaving Maidros a captive; and this was followed by Melko's southward advance and the Battle of Unnumbered Tears. As I have noted (I. 242):

> The entire later history of the long years of the Siege of Angband, ending with the Battle of Sudden Flame (Dagor Bragollach), of the passage of Men over the Mountains into Beleriand and their taking service with the Noldorin Kings, had yet to emerge; indeed these outlines give the effect of only a brief time elapsing between the coming of the Noldoli from Kôr and their great defeat.

In another outline (I. 240) there is a slight suggestion of a longer period, in the reference to the Noldoli 'practising many arts'. In this outline the meeting of Gnomes and Ilkorins takes place at 'the Feast of Reunion' (where Men were also present). But beyond this there is really nothing of the later story to be found in these projections. Nor indeed had S (as originally written) made any very remarkable advances. Men 'already dwelt in the woods of the North', which is sufficiently strange, since according to S Men awoke at the first rising of the Sun (§6), when also Fingolfin marched into Middle-earth (§8), and far too little time had elapsed, one would think, for Men to have journeyed out of 'the far East' (§6) and become established in 'the woods of the North'. Moreover there is no suggestion (even allowing for the brief and concentrated nature of the 'Sketch') that the Leaguer of Angband lasted any great length of time, nor is the breaking of the Leaguer particularly character-ised: Morgoth 'sends out his armies', and 'Gnomes and Ilkorins and Men are scattered'; that is all. But the breaking of the Leaguer was already seen as a turning-point in the history of the Elves of Beleriand. It is perfectly possible that much of the new material that appears at this place in the *Quenta* (see pp. 104 ff.) was already in my father's mind when he wrote S (i.e., S was a précis, but a précis of an unwritten story); for instance, the blasting of the great grassy northern plain in the battle that ended the siege (not even mentioned in S) was already present when the *Lay of the Children of Húrin* was written (III. 55).

With the later interpolations in S enters the idea of the Siege of Angband as an epoch, 'a time of growth and birth and flowering'; and also the disposition of the Gnomish princes, with the essentials of the later history already present – Fingolfin in Hithlum, the Fëanorians in the East (where they afterwards warred with Dwarves, Orcs, and Men), and Felagund guarding the entry into the lands of Sirion. (The reference to *Broseliand* in this passage is noteworthy: the form of the name spelt with -*s*- first appears in the A-text of Canto IV of the *Lay of Leithian* – probably early 1928; III. 195, 197). 'Fingolfin is slain when Morgoth breaks the leaguer' may or may not imply the story of his duel with Morgoth before Angband.

. Gumlin father of Húrin has appeared in the second version of the *Lay of the Children of Húrin* (III. 115, 126); but Huor, named as Húrin's brother in the rewriting of S, here makes his first appearance in the legends.

The complexities of the history of Barahir and Beren and the founding of Nargothrond are best discussed together with what is said in §10; see the commentary on the next section.

10

In §9 as first written Barahir already appears as the father of Beren, replacing Egnor; and they are here Ilkorin Elves, not Men, though this was changed when the passage was revised. In the first version of the *Lay of the Children of Húrin* Beren was still an Elf, while in the second version my father shifted back and forth between Man and Elf (III. 124–5); in the opening cantos of the A-text of the *Lay of Leithian* (in being by the autumn of 1925) Egnor and his son were Men (III. 171); now here in S (early 1926) they are again Elves, though Egnor has become Barahir. Perplexingly, in §10 as first written, while Barahir is 'a famous chieftain of Ilkorindi', on the same page of the manuscript and quite certainly written at the same time Beren 'alone of *mortals* came back from Mandos'. It may well be that the statements in S that Barahir and Beren were Ilkorins were an inadvertent return to the former idea, after the decision that they were Men (seen in the A-text of the *Lay of Leithian*) had been made. (Later in the original text of S, §14, Beren is a mortal.)

The reference in §9 to the founding of Nargothrond by Celegorm and Curufin and in §10 to Barahir having been 'a friend of Celegorm of Nargothrond' belong to the phase of the swiftly-evolving legend represented by alterations to the text of the *Lay of the Children of Húrin* (see III. 83–5), when it was Celegorm and Curufin who founded Nargothrond after the breaking of the Leaguer of Angband and Felagund had not yet emerged; similarly in the A-text of the *Lay of Leithian* (III. 171).

The alterations to S in these sections move the story on to the form

found in the B-text of the *Lay of Leithian*, with Felagund as the one
saved by Barahir and the founder of Nargothrond – though here it is said
specifically that Felagund *and his brothers* founded the realm, with the
aid of Celegorm and Curufin; it seems therefore that the deaths of
Angrod and Egnor in the battle that ended the Leaguer had not yet arisen
(see III. 221, 247).

The very early form of the story of Beren (the first stage of development from the *Tale of Tinúviel*) in S §10 as first written has been
discussed in III. 219–20, 244. There remains an interesting point to
mention in the end of this version: the sentence 'Some songs say that
Lúthien went even over the Grinding Ice, aided by the power of her
divine mother, Melian, to Mandos' halls and won him back.' There is no
suggestion here that Lúthien herself died at the time of Beren's death;
and the same idea seems likely to underlie the lines of the second version
of the *Lay of the Children of Húrin* (III.107):

> ere he winged afar
> to the long awaiting;   thence Lúthien won him,
> the Elf-maiden,   *and the arts of Melian* . . .

In the *Tale of Tinúviel*, on the other hand, it is said (II. 40) that

> Tinúviel crushed with sorrow and finding no comfort or light in all the
> world followed him swiftly down those dark ways that all must tread
> alone

– and this seems quite clear in its meaning.

Beren and Lúthien are here said to have lived, after Beren's return, 'in
the woods of Doriath and in the Hunters' Wold, west of Nargothrond'.
The Land of the Dead that Live was placed in the Hunters' Wold (Hills
of the Hunters) in the *Lay of the Children of Húrin*; see III. 89, where
the previous history of its placing is given.

That Beren and Húrin were friends and fellows-in-arms is stated in the
Lay of the Children of Húrin, and earlier (see III. 25), but it has not
been said before that this relationship arose during the time of Beren's
outlawry.

For the use of 'Shadowy Mountains' to mean the Mountains of Terror
see III. 170–1.

In the rewritten passage (pp. 25–6) the story is seen at an earlier stage
than that in the 'Synopsis II' for Cantos VI and VII of the *Lay of Leithian*
(1928), the text of which is given in III. 221, 233. Celegorm has been
displaced by Felagoth (not yet Felagund); but Celegorm 'discovered
what was the secret mission of Felagoth and Beren' *after* their departure
from Nargothrond, and thus the element of the intervention of Celegorm
and Curufin, turning the Elves of Nargothrond against their king, was
not yet present. Moreover in the northward journey of Beren and his
companions from Nargothrond there is a battle with Orcs, from which
only a small band of the Elves escapes, afterwards returning to the

battlefield to despoil the dead and disguise themselves as Orcs. These two elements are clearly interconnected: Celegorm (and Curufin) do not know why Beren and Felagoth are setting out, and thus there is no reason why the king should not set out with a strong force. When my father wrote 'Synopsis II' he had brought in the element of the intervention of the Fëanorian brothers against Felagund and Beren, and with it the small band that was all they had as companions from their first departure from Nargothrond.

The sequence is thus clearly: S – Synopsis I – interpolation in S – Synopsis II; and in the revision of S here we have an interesting stage in which Felagund (Felagoth) has emerged as the lord of Nargothrond, but the 'Fëanorian intervention' has not, and Celegorm still 'offers redress' to Lúthien, as he did in Synopsis I (III. 244) – for his dog Huan had hurt her.

11

The earliest form of this part of the story (apart from that which relates to Húrin) is extant only in the compressed outlines for *Gilfanon's Tale*. In my comparison of those early outlines with the narrative of *The Silmarillion* I noted (I.242) as essential features of the story that were to survive:

- A mighty battle called the Battle of Unnumbered Tears is fought between Elves and Men and the hosts of Melko;
- Treachery of Men, corrupted by Melko, at that battle;
- But the people of Úrin (Húrin) are faithful, and do not survive it;
- The leader of the Gnomes is isolated and slain;
- Turgon and his host cut their way out, and go to Gondolin;
- Melko is wrathful because he cannot discover where Turgon has gone;
- The Fëanorians come late to the battle;
- A great cairn is piled.

There is no evidence for any narrative of the Battle of Unnumbered Tears in its own right between the outlines for *Gilfanon's Tale* and the 'Sketch'; thus §11 in S shows at a step a very great advance. This is not however to be regarded as a direct evolution from the outlines, for many elements – such as the stories of Beren and Tinúviel, and of Nargothrond – had been developed 'collaterally' in the meantime. As S was originally written in §11, the old 'pre-Felagund' story was present ('Curufin and Celegorm despatch a host from Nargothrond', see commentary on §10), and although the failure of the Union of Maidros to gather together all the Elves of Beleriand into a united force already appears, the alignments were for this reason quite different: the Gnomes of Nargothrond (ruled by Celegorm and Curufin) will not serve under Finweg (Fingon). But with the rewriting of S, made after the emergence of the Felagund-story, an essential element of the later narrative comes into being: Orodreth will not join the league on account of Felagund his brother (cf. *The Silmarillion* p. 188: 'Orodreth would not march forth at the word of any son of Fëanor, because of the deeds of Celegorm and Curufin.') That Thingol sent few (emended from none) out of Doriath is a very old element, appearing already in the *Tale of Turambar* (II. 73), where Tinwelint said to Mavwin, in words echoed in the present passage of S:

> not for love nor for fear of Melko but of the wisdom of my heart and the fate of the Valar did I not go with my folk to the Battle of Unnumbered Tears, who am now become a safety and a refuge . . .

A new factor in Thingol's policy now appears, however, in that he resented the 'haughty words' addressed to him by Maidros, demanding the return of the Silmaril – those 'haughty words' and their effect on the Union of Maidros survived into *The Silmarillion* (p. 189). That Thingol here allows 'the *Gnomes* of Doriath' to join the league is to be related to the statement in S §9: 'Many Gnomes take service with Thingol and Melian' (after the breaking of the Siege of Angband). (In the *Tale of Tinúviel* there were Noldoli in Tinwelint's service: it was they indeed who built the bridge before his doors. II. 9, 43.)

As S was rewritten, the division of the opponents of Morgoth into two hosts was due to the refusal of the Fëanorians to be led by Finweg (Fingon), whereas in *The Silmarillion* account there was good agreement between Himring and Eithel Sirion, and the assault from East and West of the Fëanorians and the Noldor of Hithlum a matter of strategy ('they thought to take the might of Morgoth as between anvil and hammer, and break it to pieces').

The Battle of Unnumbered Tears is still in S in a simple form, but the advance of the Elves of Hithlum into Dor-na-Fauglith in pursuit of a defeated Orc-army, so that they fall prey to much greater hosts loosed from Angband, moves towards the plan of the later narrative; the late arrival of the Fëanorians goes back to an outline for *Gilfanon's Tale* (see above). No detail is given in S concerning the treachery of Men at the battle, nor is any reason suggested for the late coming of the Eastern Noldor.

Finweg (Fingon) had taken the place of Finwë (Nólemë) as the Gnomish king slain in the battle already in the *Lay of the Children of Húrin* (III. 86), and so the story of the Scarlet Heart, emblem of Turgon (I. 241, II. 172), had disappeared; in the second version of the Lay there is mention of his *white banners . . . in blood beaten* (III. 96). In S Turgon is a leader, with his brother Finweg (Fingon), of the Western Noldor from the outset, and was clearly conceived to be dwelling at this time in Hithlum (cf. the interpolation in §9: 'Fingolfin's sons Finweg and Turgon still hold out in the North', i.e. after the ending of the Siege of Angband); and the discovery of the secret valley and the founding of Gondolin follows from the retreat from the disaster of the Battle of Unnumbered Tears. The 'sacrifice of Mablon the Ilkorin' (I.239, 241) has disappeared.

The great mound of the slain on Dor-na-Fauglith, the first trace of which appears in an outline for *Gilfanon's Tale* (I.241, 243), had been described in the *Lay of the Children of Húrin* (III. 58–9), where Flinding said to Túrin as they passed by it in the moonlight:

> A! green that hill   with grass fadeless
> where sleep the swords   of seven kindreds . . .
>
> neath moon nor sun   is it mounted ever
> by Man nor Elf;   not Morgoth's host
> ever dare for dread   to delve therein.

The story of Húrin at the Battle of Unnumbered Tears – his holding of the rearguard with his men while Turgon escaped southwards, his capture, defiance of Morgoth, and torture – had already been told in the *Tale of Turambar* (II.70–1) and in the *Lay of the Children of Húrin* (see III. 23–4, 102). In all these sources Morgoth's concern with Húrin, his attempts to seduce him, and his great rage when defied, arise from his desire to find Turgon; but the element is still of course lacking in S that Húrin had previously visited Gondolin, which at this stage in the development of the legend did not exist as a Noldorin fastness until after the Battle. As the story evolved, this fact, known to Morgoth, gave still more ugency to his wish to take Húrin alive, and to use him against Turgon.

12

It is immediately obvious that S was based on the second version of the *Lay of the Children of Húrin*, so far as it goes – which in relation to the whole narrative is not far: no further than the feast at which Túrin slew Orgof. This is already evident from the preceding portion of S, describing Morgoth's treatment of Húrin in Angband; while in the present section the guardians of Túrin on the journey to Doriath bear the later names Halog and Mailgond (emended in the Lay to Mailrond, III. 119), not Halog and Gumlin.

It is not to be expected that the synopsis of the story in S should show any substantial alteration of that in the first version of the Lay; there is some development nonetheless. It is now explicit that the Men who in the Lay *dwelt in Dorlómin and dealt unkindly* with Húrin's wife, and of whom I noted (III. 24) that 'there is still no indication of who these men were or where they came from', are now explicitly 'faithless men who had deserted the Eldar in the Battle of Unnumbered Tears', penned in Hithlum because Morgoth 'desired to keep them from fellowship with Elves'. The question of whether Nienor was born before Túrin left Hithlum is now resolved: he had never seen her. For the uncertainty on this point in the *Tale of Turambar* see II. 131; in the Lay she was born before Túrin left (III. 9).

Whereas in the Lay Beleg, who was not searching for Túrin when he was captured by the outlaw band, knew nothing of what had happened in the Thousand Caves (see III. 50), in S 'Túrin released Beleg, and is told how Thingol had forgiven his deed long ago'. Blodrin is now again the son of Ban, not of Bor (see III. 52).

There is an interesting note in S that Túrin was taken alive to Angband 'for Morgoth has begun to fear that he will escape his curse through his valour and the protection of Melian'. This idea is seen in the words of the Lay (III. 33) *they haled unhappy   Hurin's offspring/lest he flee his fate*, and goes back to the *Tale of Turambar* (II. 76):

Túrin was overborne and bound, for such was the will of Melko that he be brought to him alive; for behold, dwelling in the halls of Linwë [*i.e.* Tinwelint] about which had that fay Gwedheling the Queen woven much magic and mystery . . . Túrin had been lost out of his sight, and he feared lest he cheat the doom that was devised for him.

There is little else to note in this section beyond the new detail that the Orcs feared Taur-na-Fuin no less than Elves or Men, and only went that way when in haste, and the ancestor of the phrase 'Gwindor saw them marching away over the steaming sands of Anfauglith' (*The Silmarillion* p. 208) in 'Flinding sees them marching over the steaming waste of Dor-na-Fauglith' (cf. the Lay, III. 48: *The dusty dunes   of Dor-na-Fauglith/hissed and spouted*). A very great deal is of course omitted in the synopsis.

13

With the second paragraph of this section, 'Túrin leads the Gnomes of Nargothrond to forsake their secrecy and hidden warfare', S reaches the point where the *Lay of the Children of Húrin* stops, and certain advances made on the *Tale of Turambar* (II. 83 ff.) can be observed. The re-forging of Beleg's sword for Túrin in Nargothrond now appears. In the Lay Flinding put the sword in the hollow of a tree after Beleg's death (III. 56); as I noted (III. 86): 'if the poem had gone further Túrin would have received his black sword in Nargothrond in gift from Orodreth, as happens in the *Tale*'. S thus shows a development from the plot implicit in the Lay. The bridging of Narog by Túrin's counsel enters the story only as a pencilled marginal note. The extent of the victories and reconquest of territory by the Gnomes of Nargothrond at this time is made explicit, and the realm is much as described in *The Silmarillion* (p. 211):

> The servants of Angband were driven out of all the land between Narog and Sirion eastward, and westward to the Nenning and the desolate Falas

(where however its northern border along the southern feet of the Shadowy Mountains is not mentioned; in S 'their realm reaches to the sources of Narog').

The later addition to the text of S, 'even Glómund, who was at the Battle of Tears', is to be related to the absence of any mention of the Dragon in S's account of the battle (§11). As S was first written, the Dragon was named *Glórung*, a change from *Glórund* of the *Lost Tales*; the series was thus *Glórund* > *Glórung* > *Glómund* > *Glaurung*. In the *Lay of Leithian Glómund* replaces *Glórund* (III. 208–9).

The sentence 'Flinding wounded refuses Túrin's succour and dies reproaching him' shows the later form of the story, as in *The Silmarillion* pp. 212–13; for discussion of the substantial change from the *Tale* see II. 124. It is said in S that Túrin forsook Finduilas 'against his heart (which if he had obeyed his uttermost fate would not have befallen him)', and this is no doubt to be related to the passage in the *Tale* (II. 87):

> And truly is it said: 'Forsake not for anything thy friends – nor believe those who counsel thee to do so' – for of his abandoning of Failivrin in danger that he himself could see came the very direst evil upon him and all he loved.

For discussion of this see II. 125.

Of Túrin's return to Hithlum there is little to note, for the synopsis is here very compressed; and I have earlier discussed fully the relationship between the *Tale* and the later story (II. 126–7). The Woodmen with whom Túrin lives after his flight from Hithlum are now given a more definite location 'east of Narog' (see II. 140–1). In S it is made clear that Túrin did not join himself to a people already existing, but 'gathered a new people'. This is in contradiction, strangely enough, both to the *Tale* (II. 91, 102), where they had a leader (Bethos) when Túrin joined them, and to the later story. Túrin now takes the name *Turambar* at this point in the narrative, not as in the *Tale* before the Dragon outside the caves of the Rodothlim (II. 86, 125).

Turning now to the expedition from Doriath to Nargothrond, the only important structural difference from the *Tale* that emerges in the brief account in S is that Morwen (Mavwin) was evidently no longer present at the conversation between Nienor and the Dragon (II. 98–9, 129); on the other hand, it is said at the end of this section that 'Some say Morwen *released from spell by Glórung's death* came that way and read the stone.'

When Nienor-Níniel came to the falls of the Silver Bowl a fit of shivering came on her, as in the later narrative, whereas in the *Tale* it is only said that she was filled with dread (II. 101, 130). Very notably, the statement that Níniel was with child by Turambar was added to S later, just as it was in the *Tale* (see II. 117 note 25, 135).

In the foregoing I have only picked out points that seem to show quite clearly a different conception of the events in S from that in the *Tale*. I have not mentioned the many slight differences (including the very many omissions) that are probably or certainly due to compression.

14

Of this section of the narrative there exists in earlier writing only the conclusion of the *Tale of Turambar* (II. 112–16) and the *Tale of the Nauglafring* (II. 221 ff.) in which the story is continued. The opening passage of S follows the end of the *Tale of Turambar* in Melko's accusation against Thingol of faintheartedness, Húrin's embitterment from the pondering of Melko's words, the gathering to him of a band of outlaws, the fear of the spirit of the dead Dragon that prevented any from plundering Nargothrond, the presence there of Mîm, Húrin's reproaches and the casting of the gold at Thingol's feet, and Húrin's departure. The words of S concerning the fate of Húrin derive from the *Tale*, where however he died in Hithlum and it was his 'shade' that 'fared into the woods seeking Mavwin, and long those twain haunted the woods about the fall of Silver Bowl bewailing their children'.

From this point the source for S (or perhaps more accurately, the previous written form of the narrative) is the *Tale of the Nauglafring*. It is here impossible to say for certain how much of the complex story in the *Tale* had by this time been abandoned.

It is not made clear whether Mîm's presence in Nargothrond goes back to the time of the Dragon (see II. 137), nor whether the outlaws of Húrin's band were Men or Elves (in the *Tale* the text was emended to convert them from Men to Elves); and there is no indication of how the gold was brought to Doriath. The outlaws disappear in S after the slaying of Mîm, and there is no suggestion of the fighting in the Thousand Caves that in the *Tale* led to the mound made over the slain, Cûm an-Idrisaith, the Mound of Avarice.

The next part of the *Tale* (Ufedhin the renegade Gnome and the complex dealings of Thingol with him and with the Dwarves of Nogrod, II. 223–9) is reduced to a few lines in S, which could possibly stand as an extremely abbreviated account of the old story, even though Ufedhin is here not even mentioned. The making of the Necklace was not in the *Tale*, as it is in S, part of the king's request: the idea of it was indeed hatched by

Ufedhin during his captivity as a lure 'for the greater ensnaring of the king' (II. 226); but this also could be set down to compression. I think it is more probable, however, that my father had in fact decided to reduce and simplify the narrative, and that Ufedhin had been abandoned.

The problem of the entry of the Dwarvish army into Doriath, defended by the Girdle of Melian, is still solved by the device – the too simple device, see II. 250 – of 'some treacherous Gnomes' (in the *Tale* there was only one traitor); the slaying of Thingol while hunting remains, and as in the *Tale* Melian, inviolable, left the Thousand Caves seeking Beren and Lúthien. Though it is not so stated, it seems likely that in this version it was Melian who brought the news and the warning to Beren (this is the story in the *Quenta*, p. 134). In the *Tale* it was Huan who brought word to Beren and Lúthien of the assault on Artanor and the death of Tinwelint, and it was Ufedhin, fleeing from the Dwarf-host (after his abortive attempt to slay Naugladur and steal the Nauglafring, and his killing of Bodruith lord of Belegost), who revealed the course that the Dwarves were taking and made possible the ambush at the Stony Ford; but Huan has in S been slain in the Wolf-hunt (§10), and Ufedhin has (as I think) been eliminated.

The ambush at the ford is made by 'Beren and the brown and green Elves of the wood', which goes back to 'the brown Elves and the green', the 'elfin folk all clad in green and brown' ruled by Beren and afterwards by Dior in Hithlum, in the *Tale of the Nauglafring*. But of the vigorous account of the battle at the ford in the *Tale* – the laughter of the Elves at the misshapen Dwarves running with their long white beards torn by the wind, the duel of Beren and Naugladur, whose forge-hammer blows would have overcome Beren had not Naugladur stumbled and Beren swung him off his feet by catching hold of the Nauglafring – there is nothing in S: though equally, nothing to contradict the old story. There is however no mention of the two Dwarf-lords, Naugladur of Nogrod and Bodruith of Belegost, and though both Dwarf-cities are named the Dwarves are treated as an undivided force, with, as it seems, one king (slain at the ford): Thingol summoned those of Belegost as well as those of Nogrod to Doriath for the fashioning of the gold, whereas in the *Tale* (II. 230) the former only enter the story after the humiliating expulsion of the Dwarves of Nogrod, in order to aid them in their revenge. Of the old story of the death of Bodruith and the feud and slaughter among the two kindreds (brought about by Ufedhin) there is no trace.

The drowning of the treasure in the river goes back to the *Tale*; but there however the suggestion is not that the treasure was deliberately sunk: rather it fell into the river with the bodies of the Dwarves who bore it:

> those that waded in the ford cast their golden burdens in the waters and sought affrighted to either bank, but many were stricken with those pitiless darts and fell with their gold into the currents (II. 237).

It is not said in the *Tale* that any of the gold was drowned by the Elves. There, Gwendelin came to Beren and Tinúviel *after* the battle of the Stony Ford, and found Tinúviel already wearing the Nauglafring; there is mention of the greatness of her beauty when she wore it. Gwendelin's warning is only against the Silmaril (the rest of the treasure being drowned), and indeed her horror at seeing the Necklace of the Dwarves on Tinúviel was so great that Tinúviel put it off. This was to Beren's displeasure, and he kept it (II. 239–40). In S the drowning seems to be carried out in response to Melian's warning of the curse upon it, and the story seems to be thus: Melian comes to Beren and Lúthien and warns them of the approach of the Dwarf-host returning out of Doriath; after the battle Lúthien wears the Nauglafring and becomes immeasurably beautiful; but Melian warns them of the curse on the gold and on the Silmaril and they drown the treasure, though Beren keeps the Necklace secretly.

The fading of Lúthien follows immediately on the statement that the Necklace was kept, but no connection is made. In the *Tale* such a connection is explicit: the doom of mortality that Mandos had spoken 'fell swiftly' –

and in this perhaps did the curse of Mîm have [?potency] in that it came more soon upon them (II. 240).

Moreover in a synopsis for a projected revision of the *Lost Tales* it is said that the Nauglafring 'brought sickness to Tinúviel' (II. 246).

The reference to the fading of Lúthien in S retains the words of the *Tale*: Tinúviel slowly faded 'even as the Elves of later days have done'; and, again as in the *Tale*, Lúthien 'vanished'. In the *Tale* Beren was an Elf, and it is said of him that after searching all Hithlum and Artanor for Tinúviel in terrible loneliness 'he too faded from life'. In my discussion of this I said (II. 250):

Since this fading is here quite explicitly the mode in which 'that doom of mortality that Mandos had spoken' came upon them, it is very notable that it is likened to, and even it seems identified with, the fading of 'the Elves of later days throughout the world' – as though in the original idea Elvish fading was a form of mortality.

The passage in S, retaining this idea in respect of Lúthien, but now with the later conception that Beren was a mortal Man, not an Elf, is changed in that Beren is no longer said to have faded: he 'was lost', looking in vain for Lúthien. It is also said here that the price of Beren's return from Mandos was 'that Lúthien should become as shortlived as Beren the mortal'; and in §10, where the story of Beren and Lúthien is briefly told, it is not in fact said that Lúthien died when Beren died in Doriath (see the commentary on that section, p. 55). There is also a sentence added to the MS in §10: 'But Mandos in payment exacted that Lúthien should become mortal as Beren.'

It is possible to conclude from this that, in the conception as it was when S was written, Beren died, as a mortal dies; Lúthien went to Valinor as a living being; and Mandos allowed Beren to return to a second mortal span, but Lúthien now became subject to the same shortness of span as he. In this sense she became 'mortal'; but being an Elf she 'faded' – this was the manner of her death: as it was also the manner of the death of the fading Elves of later ages. Part of the difficulty in all this undoubtedly lies in the ambiguous nature of the words 'mortal' and 'immortal' applied to the Elves: they are 'immortal', both in the sense that they need not die, it is not in their essential nature to die, 'in the world', and also in the sense that, if they did, they did not 'leave the world', did not go to 'a fate beyond the world'; and they are 'mortal' in that they might nonetheless die 'in the world' (by wounds or by grief, but not from sickness or age). Lúthien became 'mortal' in that, although an Elf, she *must* die – she *must* fade.

It may be noted that the words 'as Men grew strong and took the goodness of earth' derive from the *Lay of the Children of Húrin* (III. 44, 54):

> for in days long gone
> ... Men were of mould   less mighty builded
> ere the earth's goodness   from the Elves they drew.

Cf. *The Silmarillion*, p. 105: 'In after days, when because of the triumph of Morgoth Elves and Men became estranged, as he most wished, those of the Elven-race that lived still in Middle-earth waned and faded, and Men usurped the sunlight.'

Lastly, in the story of Dior and the ruin of Doriath as told in S, there are various developments. The son of Dior, Auredhir (II. 240) has disappeared. The 'vain bargaining' between Dior and the Sons of Fëanor perhaps refers to the passage in the *Tale* (II. 241) where Dior asserts that to return the Silmaril the Nauglafring must be broken, and Curufin (the messenger of the Fëanorians) retorts that in that case the Nauglafring must be given to them unbroken. In the *Tale* Maglor, Díriel, Celegorm, and Cranthir (or the earlier equivalents of their names) were killed in the battle (which there took place in Hithlum, where Dior ruled after his father); but in S, as first written, the story takes a very strange turn, in that the Fëanorians did get their hands on the Nauglafring, but then so quarrelled over it that in the end 'only Maglor was left'. How the story would have gone in this case is impossible to discern.

15 and 16

The two sections describing Gondolin and its fall are discussed together in the following commentary.

At the beginning of §15 the brief reference to the story of Isfin and Eöl shows development from what was said in the *Lay of the Fall of Gondolin* (III.146): for in the poem Isfin was seeking, together with her mother, for her father Fingolfin when she was entrapped by Eöl in the dark forest. The larger history has evolved since then, and now Isfin 'was lost in Taur-na-Fuin after the Battle of Unnumbered Tears'. We can only surmise how she came to be there. Either she left Gondolin soon after its settlement bent on some purpose unrecorded, or else she was lost in the retreat from the battle. (It is, incidentally, a curious aspect of the earlier conception of Gondolin's foundation that there were women and children to people it as well as warriors; for one would suppose that Turgon had left the old men, the women, and the children of his people in Hithlum – why should he do otherwise? But in the outlines for *Gilfanon's Tale* there are references to Turgon's having 'rescued a part of the women and children', and having 'gathered women and children from the camps' as he fled south down Sirion (I.239, 241).) Meglin is still, as in the poem, 'sent by his mother to Gondolin', while she remained with her captor.

In the account of Gondolin and its history S is fairly close to the tale of *The Fall of Gondolin*, but there are some developments, if mostly of a minor kind. There is first a notable statement that 'Ylmir's messages come up Sirion bidding them [i.e. the host of Turgon retreating from the battle] take refuge in this valley'; this is unlike the *Tale*, where Tuor speaking the words of Ulmo in Gondolin says: 'There have come to the ears of Ulmo whispers of your dwelling and your hill of vigilance against the evil of Melko, and he is glad' (II.161, 208). Here in S we have the first appearance of the idea that the foundation of Gondolin was a part of Ulmo's design. But Tuor's journey is as in the old story, and the visitation of Ulmo is in Nan·Tathrin, not at Vinyamar. The bidding of Ulmo offers Turgon similar choices, to prepare for war, or, if he will not, then to send people of Gondolin down Sirion to the sea, to seek for Valinor. Here, however, there are differences. In the *Tale*, Ulmo offers scarcely more than a slender hope that such sailors from Gondolin would reach Valinor, and if they did, that they would persuade the Valar to act:

[The Gods] hide their land and weave about it inaccessible magic that no evil come to its shores. Yet still might thy messengers win there and turn their hearts that they rise in wrath and smite Melko . . . (II.161–2).

In S, on the other hand, the people of Gondolin, if they will not go to war against Morgoth, are to desert their city ('the people of Gondolin are to prepare for flight') – cf. *The Silmarillion* p. 240: '[Ulmo] bade him depart, and abandon the fair and mighty city that he had built, and go down Sirion to the sea' – and at the mouths of Sirion Ylmir will not only aid them in the building of a fleet but will himself guide them over the ocean. But if Turgon will accept Ylmir's counsel, and prepare for war, then Tuor is to go to Hithlum with Gnomes from Gondolin and 'draw Men once more into alliance with the Elves, for "without Men the Elves shall not prevail against the Orcs and Balrogs".' Of this strange bidding there is no trace in the *Tale*; nor is it said there that Ulmo knew of Meglin, and knew that this treachery would bring about the end of Gondolin at no distant time. These features are absent also from *The Silmarillion*; Ulmo does indeed foresee the ruin of the city, but his foreseeing is not represented as being so precise: 'Thus it may come to pass that the curse of the Noldor shall find thee too ere the end, and treason awake within thy walls. Then they shall be in peril of fire' (p. 126).

The description of the Vale of Gondolin in S is essentially as in the *Tale*, with a few added details. As in the *Tale*, the rocky height of Amon Gwareth was not in the centre of the plain but nearest to Sirion – that is, nearest to the Way of Escape (II. 158, 177). In S, the level top of the hill is said to have been achieved by the people of Gondolin themselves, who also 'polished its sides to the smoothness of glass'. The Way of Escape is still, as in the *Tale* (II. 163), a tunnel made by the Gnomes – the Dry River and the Orfalch Echor have not yet been conceived; and the meaning of the name 'Way of Escape' is made very clear: both a way of escape from Gondolin, if the need should ever arise, and a way of escape from the outer world and from Morgoth. In the *Tale* (*ibid.*) it is said only that there had been divided counsels concerning its delving, 'yet pity for the enthralled Noldoli had prevailed in the end to its making'. The 'Guarded Plain' into which the Way of Escape issued is the Vale of Gondolin. An additional detail in S is that the hills were lower in the region of the Way of Escape, and the spells of Ylmir there strongest (because nearest to Sirion).

The cairn of Fingolfin, added in pencil in S, is an element that entered the legends in the *Quenta* (p. 107) and the *Lay of Leithian* (III. 286–7); the duel of Fingolfin with Morgoth does not appear in S (p. 54). – Here in S it is said that Thorndor 'removed his eyries to the Northern heights of the encircling mountains'. In the *Tale* the eyries in Cristhorn, the Eagles' Cleft, were in the mountains south of Gondolin, but in S Cristhorn is in the northern heights: this is already the case in the Fragment of an alliterative *Lay of Eärendel* (III. 143). Thorndor had come there from Thangorodrim (stated in the *Quenta*, p. 137); cf. the 'later *Tuor*' in *Unfinished Tales* (p. 43 and note 25): 'the folk of Thorondor, who dwelt once even on Thangorodrim ere Morgoth grew so mighty, and dwell now in the Mountains of Turgon since the fall of Fingolfin.' This goes back to the tale of *The Theft of Melko*, where there is a reference (I. 149) to the time 'when Sorontur and his folk fared to the Iron Mountains and there abode, watching all that Melko did'.

Some other points concerning the story of Gondolin may be noticed. The escort of Noldoli, promised to Tuor by Ulmo in the Land of Willows, of whom Voronwë (in S given the Gnomish form of the name, Bronweg) was the only one who did not desert him (II. 155–6), has disappeared; and 'Bronweg had once been in Gondolin', which is not the case in the *Tale* (II. 156–7). – In the *Tale* Tuor wedded Idril when he 'had dwelt among the Gondothlim many years' (II. 164); in S this took place three years after his coming to the hidden city, in *The Silmarillion* seven years after (p. 241). – In the *Tale* there is no mention of Meglin's support of Turgon's rejection of Ulmo's bidding (cf. *The Silmarillion* p. 240: 'Maeglin spoke ever against Tuor in the councils of the King'), nor of the opposition of Idril to her father (this is not in *The Silmarillion*). – The closing of Gondolin to all fugitives and the forbidding of the people to leave the valley is mentioned in S but not explained.

The sentence 'Meglin . . . purchases his life when taken to Angband *by revealing Gondolin* and its secrets' shows almost certainly, I think, that an important structural change in the story of the fall of the city had now entered. In the *Tale* Melko had discovered Gondolin *before* Meglin was captured, and his treachery lay in his giving an exact account of the structure of the city and the preparations made for its defence (see II. 210–11); but the words 'by revealing Gondolin' strongly suggest the later story, in which Morgoth did not know where it lay.

Lastly, there is a development in the early history of Tuor: that he became a slave of 'the faithless men' in Hithlum after the Battle of Unnumbered Tears. Moreover Tuor's parentage is now finally established. Huor has been mentioned in a rewritten passage of S (§9), but not named as father of Tuor; and this is the first occurrence of his mother Rían, and so of the story that she died seeking Huor's body on the battlefield. It cannot be said whether the story of Tuor's birth in the wild and his fostering by Elves had yet arisen.

17

In commenting on the conclusion of the mythology in S, here comprised in the three sections 17–19, I point to features that derive from or contradict those outlines and notes from an earlier period that are collected in Vol. II chapter V and the earlier part of Chapter VI. S is here an extremely abbreviated outline, composed very rapidly – my father was indeed changing his conceptions as he wrote.

For the narrative of §17 the primary extant early sources are the 'schemes' or plot-outlines which I have called 'B' and 'C', in the passages given in II. 253 and 254–5 respectively.

At the beginning of this section, before emendation, the survivors of Gondolin were already at the Mouths of Sirion when Elwing came there; and this goes back to B and C ('Elwing . . . flees to them [i.e. Tuor and Idril] with the Nauglafring', II. 254). But earlier in S (§ 15) the destruction of Dior took place before the fall of Gondolin; hence the revision here, to make Elwing 'receive the survivors of Gondolin'. (In the *Tale of the Nauglafring*, II. 242, the fall of Gondolin and the attack on Dior took place on the same day.)

Following this, there is a major development in S. In the early outlines there is the story, only glimpsed, of the March of the Elves of Valinor into the Great Lands; and in B (only) there is a reference to 'the sorrow and wrath of the Gods', of which I said in my discussion of these outlines (II. 257): 'the meaning can surely only be that the March of the Elves from Valinor was undertaken in direct opposition to the will of the Valar, that the Valar were bitterly opposed to the intervention of the Elves of Valinor in the affairs of the Great Lands.' On the other hand, the bare hints of what happened when the assault on Melko took place show that greater powers than the Eldar alone were present: Noldorin (the Vala Salmar, who entered the world with Ulmo, and loved the Noldoli), and Tulkas himself, who overthrew Melko in the Battle of the Silent Pools (outline C, II. 278). The only hint in the outlines of Ulmo's intervention is his saving of Eärendel from shipwreck, bidding him sail to Kôr with the words 'for this hast thou been brought out of the Wrack of Gondolin' (B, similarly in C). The March of the Eldar from Valinor was brought about by the coming of the birds from Gondolin.

In S, on the other hand, it is Ulmo (Ylmir) who directly brings about the intervention from the West by his reproaches to the Valar, bidding them rescue the remnants of the Noldoli and the Silmarils; and the host is led by 'the sons of the Valar', commanded by Fionwë – who is here the son of Tulkas! Fionwë is frequently named in the *Lost Tales* as the son of Manwë, while the son of Tulkas was Telimektar (who became the constellation Orion). The naming Fionwë son of Tulkas may have been a simple slip, though the same is said in the *Quenta* as first written (p. 149); subsequently Fionwë again becomes the son of Manwë (p. 154).

'Remembering Swanhaven few of the Teleri go with them': in the outline B the presence of the Solosimpi on the March is referred to without comment, while in C they only agreed to accompany the expedition on condition that they remained by the sea (see II. 258), and this was in some way associated with their remembrance of the Kinslaying.

The desertion of Kôr at this time is referred to in the outlines, but only in connection with Eärendel's coming there and finding it empty; I noted (II. 257) that 'it seems at least strongly implied that Kôr was empty because the Elves of Valinor had departed into the Great Lands', and this is now seen to be certain.

The narrative in S now turns to Tuor. The statement that he grew old at Sirion's mouths – a statement that was struck out – goes back to the old schemes. His ship is now *Eärámë*, untranslated; previously it was *Alqarámë* 'Swanwing', while *Eärámë* was Eärendel's earlier ship, translated 'Eaglepinion', which foundered. In *The Silmarillion* Tuor's ship is *Eärrámë*, as in S, with the meaning 'Sea-Wing'.

In S, Idril departs in company with Tuor. This is different from the original schemes, where Tuor leaves alone, and Idril 'sees him too late', 'laments', and afterwards 'vanishes'. But in the outline C it seems that she found him, for 'Tuor and Idril some say sail now in Swanwing and may be seen going swift down the wind at dawn and dusk'.

In S, the earlier history of Eärendel's ship-building and shipwrecks in the Fiord of the Mermaid and at Falasquil has, apparently, been abandoned entirely, and Wingelot is his first and only ship; but there remains the motive that Eärendel wishes to seek for his father, whereas Ylmir bids him sail to Valinor (this last being afterwards struck out). His adventures in Wingelot are referred to in S but not otherwise indicated, save for the slaying of Ungoliant 'in the South'; there is no mention of the Sleeper in the Tower of Pearl. In C the long voyage of Eärendel, accompanied by Voronwë, that finally took them to Kôr, included an encounter with Ungweliantë, though this was after his southern voyage: 'Driven west. Ungweliantë. Magic Isles. Twilit Isle. Littleheart's gong awakes the Sleeper in the Tower of Pearl.' In another outline Eärendel encounters Wirilómë (Gloomweaver) in the South (II. 260). In the account in S he does not on this great voyage come to Kôr, though from it, as in B and C, he returns to 'the Waters of Sirion' (the delta) and finds the dwellings there desolate. Now however enters the motive of the last desperate attempt of the Fëanorians to regain the Silmaril of Beren and Lúthien, their descent on the Havens of Sirion, and their destruction. Thus the raid on the Havens has remained, but it is no longer the work of Melko (see II. 258) and is brought into the story of the Oath of Fëanor. As S was first written only Maidros survived; but Maglor was added. (In §14, as written, all the Sons of Fëanor save Maglor were slain at the time of the attack on Dior, though this passage was afterwards struck out. In *The Silmarillion* Celegorm, Curufin, and Caranthir were slain at that time, and Amrod and Amras (later names of Damrod and Díriel) were slain in the attack on the Havens of Sirion, so that only Maidros and Maglor were left.)

In the old outlines Elwing was taken captive (as is to be deduced, by Melko); there is no mention of her release from captivity, and she next appears in references to the sinking of her ship (on the way to Tol Eressëa) and the loss of the Nauglafring; after which she becomes a seabird to seek Eärendel. Eärendel returning from his long voyage and finding the dwellings at Sirion's mouth sacked, goes with Voronwë to the ruins of Gondolin, and in an isolated note (II. 264, xv) he 'goes even to the empty Halls of Iron seeking Elwing'.

All this has disappeared in S, with the new story of Elwing casting herself and the Nauglafring into the sea, except that she still becomes a seabird (thus changed by Ulmo) and flies to seek Eärendel about all the shores of the world. The early outlines are then at variance: in C it is said that Eärendel dwelt on the Isle of Seabirds and hoped that Elwing would come to him, 'but she is seeking him wailing along all the shores' – yet 'he will find Elwing at the Faring Forth', while in the short outline E (II. 260) she came to him as a seamew on the Isle of Seabirds. But in S Elwing is further mentioned only as being sought by Eärendel when he sets sail again, until she reappears at the end (§19) and is restored to Eärendel.

The introduction of Elrond in S is of great interest. He has no brother as yet; and he is saved by Maidros (in *The Silmarillion*, p. 247, Elrond and Elros were saved by Maglor). When the Elves return into the West he elects to stay 'on earth', being 'bound by his mortal half'. It is most remarkable that although the idea of a choice of fate for the Half-elven is already present, it takes a curiously different form from that which it was to take afterwards, and which became of great importance in *The Lord of the Rings*; for afterwards, Elrond, unlike his brother Elros Tar-Minyatur, elected to remain an Elf – yet his later choice derives in part from the earlier conception, for he elected also not to go into the West. In S, to choose his 'elfin half' seems to have meant to choose the West; afterwards, it meant to choose Elvish immortality.

Eärendel learnt what had happened at the Mouths of Sirion from Bronweg (earlier it was Littleheart son of Bronweg who survived the sack of the havens, II. 276 note 5), and with Bronweg he sails again in Wingelot and comes to Kôr, which he finds deserted, and his raiment becomes encrusted with the dust of diamonds; not daring to go further into Valinor he builds a tower on an isle in the northern seas, 'to which all the sea-birds of the world repair'. Bronweg is not further mentioned. Almost all of this, other than the statement that Eärendel did not dare venture further into Valinor, goes back to the outline C. The tower on the Isle of Seabirds, which survives in *The Silmarillion* (p. 250), is mentioned in an isolated note on the Eärendel story (II. 264, xvii).

In the early outlines Eärendel now set out on his last voyage. In B, which is here very brief, his sailing to the Isle of Seabirds is followed by 'his voyage to the firmament'. In C he sails with Voronwë to the halls of Mandos seeking for tidings of Tuor, Idril, and Elwing; he 'reaches the bar at the margin of the world and sets sail on the oceans of the firmament in order to gaze over the Earth. The Moon mariner chases him for his brightness and he dives through the Door of Night.' In the outline E (II. 260) 'Elwing as a seamew comes to him. He sets sail over the margent of the world.' In the early note associated with the poem 'The Bidding of the Minstrel' (II. 261) he 'sails west again to the lip of the world, just as the Sun is diving into the sea', and 'sets sail upon the sky'; and in the preface to 'The Shores of Faëry' (II. 262) he

sat long while in his old age upon the Isle of Seabirds in the Northern Waters ere he set forth upon a last voyage. He passed Taniquetil and even Valinor, and drew his bark over the bar at the margin of the world, and launched it on the Oceans of the Firmament. Of his ventures there no man has told, save that hunted by the orbed Moon he fled back to Valinor, and mounting the towers of Kôr upon the rocks of Eglamar he gazed back upon the Oceans of the World.

The passage in S is different from all of these, in that here Eärendel's voyage into the sky is achieved with the aid of the wings of seabirds, and it introduces the idea of his being scorched by the Sun as well as hunted by the Moon. I suggested (II. 259) that Eärendel originally sailed into the sky in continuing search for Elwing, and this is now corroborated.

18 and 19

The story in S now leaves Eärendel, wandering the sky 'as a fugitive star', and comes to the march of Fionwë and the Last Battle (a term that is used in S both of the Last Battle in the mythological record, in which the hosts of Valinor overthrew Morgoth, and of the Last Battle of the world, declared in prophecy, when Morgoth will come back through the Door and Fionwë will fight him on the plains of Valinor). Almost all of this now enters the mythology for the first time; and almost all of what very little survives from the earliest period on the subject of the March of the Elves of Valinor (II. 278–80) has disappeared. There is no mention of Tulkas, of his battle with Melko, of Noldorin, of the hostility of Men; virtually the only point in common is that after the overthrow of Morgoth Elves depart into the West. In the old story the Silmarils play no part at the end (cf. the jotting 'What became of the Silmarils after the capture of Melko?' II. 259); but now in S there appear the lineaments of a story concerning their fate. Now also we have the first mention anywhere of the breaking of the Northwestern world in the struggle to overthrow Morgoth; and (in an addition to the text) the chain Angainor appears from the *Lost Tales*. (Angainor is not named in the earlier passage in S (§2) concerning the binding of Morgoth. It appears (later) in the *Lay of Leithian*, in a puzzling reference to 'the chain Angainor that *ere Doom* / for Morgoth *shall by Gods be wrought*'; see III. 205, 209–10.)

In the story of the fate of the Silmarils, Maglor says to Maidros that there are two sons of Fëanor now left, and two Silmarils. Does this imply that the Silmaril of Beren was lost when Elwing cast herself into the sea with the Nauglafring (unlike the later story)? The answer is certainly yes; the story in S is not comprehensible otherwise. Thus when Maglor casts himself (changed to casts the jewel) into the fiery pit, having stolen one of the Silmarils of the Iron Crown from Fionwë, 'one Silmaril is now in the sea, and one in the earth'. The third was the Silmaril that remained in Fionwë's keeping; and it was that one that was bound to Eärendel's brow. We thus have a remarkable stage of transition, in which the Silmarils have at last achieved primary importance, but where the fate of each has not arrived at the final form; and the conclusion, seen to be inevitable once reached, that it was the Silmaril regained by Beren and Lúthien that became the Evening Star, has not been achieved. In S, Eärendel becomes a star before receiving the Silmaril; but originally, as I have said (II.265), 'there is no suggestion that the Valar hallowed his ship and set him in the sky, nor that his light was that of the Silmaril'. In this respect also S is transitional, for at the end the later story appears.

The Elves of the Outer Lands (Great Lands), after the conquest of Morgoth, set sail from Lúthien (later emended to Leithien), explained as 'Britain or England'. For the forms *Luthany*, *Lúthien*, *Leithian*, *Leithien* and the texts in which they occur see III. 154. It is remarkable that as S was originally written *Lúthien* is both the name of Thingol's daughter and the name of England.

It is further said in S that the Elves 'ever still from time to time set sail [from Lúthien] leaving the world ere they fade'. 'The Gnomes and many of the Ilkorins and Teleri and Qendi repeople the Lonely Isle. Some go back to live upon the shores of Faëry and in Valinor, but Côr and Tûn remain desolate.' Some of this can be brought into relation with the old outlines (see II. 308–9), but how much more was retained in mind, beyond 'The Elves retreated to Luthany' and 'Many of the Elves of Luthany sought back west over the sea and settled in Tol Eressëa', cannot be determined. That even this much was retained is however very instructive. The peculiar relation of the Elves to England keeps a foot-hold, as it were, in the actual articulation of the narrative; as also the idea that if they remained in 'the world' they would fade (see II. 326).

It is not made clear why 'Côr and Tûn' remained desolate, since some of the Elves 'go back to live upon the shores of Faëry and in Valinor'. In the original conception (as I have argued its nature, II. 280) the Eldar of Valinor, when they returned from the Great Lands where they had gone against the will of the Valar, were forbidden to re-enter Valinor and therefore settled in Tol Eressëa, as 'the Exiles of Kôr' (although some did return in the end to Valinor, since Ingil son of Inwë, according to Meril-i-Turinqi (I. 129), 'went back long ago to Valinor and is with Manwë'). But in the story as told in S the idea that the March of the Eldar was against the will of the Valar, and aroused them to wrath, has been abandoned, and 'the sons of the Valar' now lead the hosts out of the West; why then should the Elves of Tûn not return there? And we have the statement in S that Tol Eressëa was repeopled not only by Gnomes (and nothing at all is said of their pardon) and Ilkorins, but also by Qendi (= the later Vanyar) and Teleri, Elves who came from Valinor for the assault on Morgoth. I cannot explain this; and must conclude that my father was only noting down the chief points of his developing conceptions, leaving much unwritten.

There now appears the idea that the Gods thrust Morgoth through the

Door of Night 'into the outer dark beyond the Walls of the World';* and
there is the first reference to the escape of Thû (Sauron) in the Last
Battle. There is also a prophecy concerning the ultimate battle, when the
world is old and the Gods weary, and Morgoth will come back through
the Door of Night; then Fionwë with Túrin beside him shall fight
Morgoth on the plain of Valinor, and Túrin shall slay him with his black
sword. The Silmarils shall be recovered, and their light released, the
Trees rekindled, the Mountains of Valinor levelled so that the light goes
out over all the world, and Gods and Elves shall grow young again. Into
this final resolution of the evil in the world it would prove unprofitable, I
think, to enquire too closely. References to it have appeared in print in
Unfinished Tales, pp. 395–6, in the remarks on Gandalf: 'Manwë will
not descend from the Mountain until the Dagor Dagorath, and the
coming of the End, when Melkor returns', and in the alliterative poem
accompanying this, 'until Dagor Dagorath and the Doom cometh'. The
earliest references are probably in the outline C (II. 282), where (when
the Pine of Belaurin is cut down) 'Melko is thus now out of the world –
but one day he will find a way back, and the last great uproars will begin
before the Great End'. In the *Lost Tales* there are many references to the
Great End, most of which do not concern us here; but at the end of the
tale of *The Hiding of Valinor* is told (I. 219) of 'that great foreboding
that was spoken among the Gods when first the Door of Night was
opened':

For 'tis said that ere the Great End come Melko shall in some wise
contrive a quarrel between Moon and Sun, and Ilinsor shall seek to
follow Urwendi through the Gates, and when they are gone the Gates
of both East and West will be destroyed, and Urwendi and Ilinsor shall
be lost. So shall it be that Fionwë Úrion, son of Manwë, of love for
Urwendi shall in the end be Melko's bane, and shall destroy the world
to destroy his foe, and so shall all things then be rolled away.

(Cf. the outline C, II. 281: 'Fionwë's rage and grief [at the death of
Urwendi]. In the end he will slay Melko.') Whether any of this prophecy
underlies the idea of the ultimate return of Morgoth through the Door of
Night I cannot say. At the end of the *Tale of Turambar*, after the account
of the 'deification' of Túrin and Nienor, there is a prophecy (II. 116) that

Turambar indeed shall stand beside Fionwë in the Great Wrack, and
Melko and his drakes shall curse the sword of Mormakil.

But there is no indication in S of how 'the spirit of Túrin' will survive to
slay Morgoth in the ultimate battle on the plain of Valinor.

*See the commentary on the *Ambarkanta*, p. 252.

That the Mountains of Valinor shall be levelled, so that the light of the rekindled Trees goes out over all the world, is also found in the earliest texts; cf. the isolated passage in C (II. 285) where is told the Elves' prophecy of the (second) Faring Forth:

Laurelin and Silpion will be rekindled, and the mountain wall being destroyed then soft radiance will be spread over all the world, and the Sun and Moon will be recalled.

But this prophecy is associated with other conceptions that had clearly been abandoned.

At the end, with the aid of the Silmaril Elwing is found and restored, but there is no indication of how the Silmaril was used to this purpose. Elwing in this account sails with Eärendel, who bears the third Silmaril, and so he shall sail until he sees 'the last battle gathering upon the plains of Valinor'.

On the reappearance of the name *Eriol* at the very end of S see II. 300.

I do not intend here to relate this version to that in the published work, but will conclude this long discussion of the concluding sections 17–19 with a brief summary. As I have said, S is here extremely condensed, and it is here even harder than elsewhere to know or guess what of the old material my father had suppressed and what was still 'potentially' present. But in any case nothing of the old layer that is not present in S was ever to reappear.

In the present version, Eärendel has still not come to his supreme function as the Messenger who spoke before the Powers on behalf of the Two Kindreds, though the birds of Gondolin have been abandoned as the bringers of tidings to Valinor, and Ulmo becomes the sole agent of the final assault on Morgoth out of the West. The voyages of Eärendel have been simplified: he now has the one great voyage – without Voronwë – in Wingelot, in which he slew Ungoliant, and the second voyage, with Voronwë, which takes him to Kôr – and the desertion of Kôr (Tûn) still depends on the March of the Eldar, which has already taken place when he comes there. His voyage into the sky is now achieved by the wings of birds; and the Silmaril still plays no part in his becoming a star, for the Silmaril of Beren and Lúthien was drowned with the Nauglafring at the Mouths of Sirion. But the Silmarils at last become central to the final acts of the mythological drama, and – unlike the later story – only one of the two Silmarils that remained in the Iron Crown is made away with by a son of Fëanor (Maglor); the second is given to Eärendel by the Gods, and the later story is visible at the end of S, where his boat 'is drawn over Valinor to the Outer Seas' and launched into the Outer Dark, where he sails with the Silmaril on his brow, keeping watch on Morgoth.

The destruction of the people of Sirion's Mouths now becomes the final evil of the Oath of Fëanor. Elrond appears, with a remarkable reference to the choice given to him as half-elven. The coming of the hosts of the West to the overthrow of Morgoth is now an act of the Valar, and the hosts are led by the Sons of the Valar. England, as Lúthien (Leithien), remains as the land from which the Elves of the Great Lands set sail at the end for Tol Eressëa; but I suspect that virtually all the highly complex narrative which I attempted to reconstruct (II.308–9) had gone – Eärendel and Ing(wë) and the hostility of Ossë, the Ingwaiwar, the seven invasions of Luthany.

The original ideas of the conclusion of the Eldar Days (Melko's climbing of the Pine of Belaurin, the cutting down of the Pine, the warding of the sky by Telimektar and Ingil (Orion and Sirius), II.281–2) have disappeared; in S, Morgoth is thrust through the Door of Night, and Eärendel becomes its guardian and guarantee against Morgoth's return, until the End. And lastly, and most pregnant for the future, Thû escapes the Last Battle when Morgoth was overcome, 'and dwells still in dark places'.

III
THE QUENTA

This work is extant in a typescript (made by my father) for which there is no trace of any preliminary notes or drafts. That the *Quenta*, or at any rate the greater part of it, was written in 1930 seems to me to be certainly deducible (see the commentary on §10, pp. 177–8). After a quite different initial section (which is the origin of the *Valaquenta*) this text becomes a reworking and expansion of the 'Sketch of the Mythology'; and it quickly becomes evident that my father had S (the 'Sketch') in front of him when he wrote the *Quenta* (which I shall refer to as 'Q'). The latter moves towards *The Silmarillion* in its published form, both in structure and in language (indeed already in S the first forms of many sentences can be perceived).

Eriol (as in S; not Ælfwine) is mentioned both in the title of Q and at the end of the work, and his coming to Kortirion, but (again as in S) there is no trace of the Cottage of Lost Play. As I have said of its absence from S (p. 42), this does not demonstrate that my father had rejected the conception in its entirety: in S he may have omitted it because his purpose was solely to recount the history of the Elder Days in condensed form, while in the title of Q it is said that the work was 'drawn from the Book of Lost Tales which Eriol of Leithien wrote'. At least then, we may think, some venue in which the *Lost Tales* were told to Eriol in Kortirion still existed.*

The title makes it very plain that while Q was written in a finished manner, my father saw it as a compendium, a 'brief history' that was 'drawn from' a much longer work; and this aspect remained an important element in his conception of 'The Silmarillion' properly so called. I do not know whether this idea did indeed arise from the fact that the starting point of the second phase of the mythological narrative was a condensed synopsis (S); but it seems likely enough, from the step by step continuity that leads from S through Q to the version that was interrupted towards its end in 1937.

It seems very probable that the greater number of the extensions and elaborations found in Q arose in the course of its composition, and that while Q contains features, omitted in S, which go back to the earliest version, these features argue only a recollection of the *Lost Tales* (to be

---

*It is said at the end of the *Quenta* that Eriol 'remembered things that he had heard in fair Cortirion'. But this Book of Lost Tales was composed by Eriol (according to the title) out of a 'Golden Book' which he *read* in Kortirion. (Previously the Golden Book of Tavrobel was written either by Eriol (Ælwine) himself, or by his son Heorrenda, or by some other person unnamed long after; see II. 291.)

assumed in any case! – and doubtless a very clear recollection), not a close derivation from the actual text. If that had been the case, one might expect to find the re-emergence of actual phrasing here and there; but that seems to be markedly lacking.

The history of the typescript becomes rather complex towards the end (from §15), where my father expanded and retyped portions of the text (though the discarded pages were not destroyed). But I see no reason to think that much time elapsed between the two versions; for near the very end (§19) the original typescript gives out, and only the second version continues to the conclusion of the *Quenta*, which strongly suggests that the revisions belong to the same time as the original text.

Subsequently the whole text was revised throughout, the corrections being made carefully in ink; these changes though frequent are mostly small, and very often no more than slight alterations of expression. This 'layer' of emendation was clearly the first;* afterwards further changes were made at different times, often very hastily and not always legibly in pencil. To present the text as first typed with annotation of every small stylistic improvement is obviously quite unnecessary, and would in any case require the introduction into the text of a forest of reference numbers to the notes. The text given here *includes*, therefore, without annotation, all minor changes that in no way affect the course of the narrative or alter its implications. Those emendations that are not taken up into the text but recorded in the notes are marked as 'late changes' if they are clearly distinguishable, as is not always the case, from the first 'layer' described above.

I have divided the text into the same 19 divisions made in S (see p. 11); but since the opening of Q has nothing corresponding in S this section is not given a number.

★

THE QUENTA

herein is

QENTA NOLDORINWA

or

Pennas-na-Ngoelaidh

This is the brief History of the Noldoli
or Gnomes, drawn from the Book of Lost Tales

---

*The occurrence of *Beleriand* in the original typescript, first in §13, note 10, not as previously by emendation in ink from typescript *Broseliand*, shows that some of this 'layer' was carried out while the typescript was still in process of composition.

which Eriol of Leithien wrote, having read
the *Golden Book*, which the Eldar call *Parma
Kuluina*,* in Kortirion in Tol Eressëa, the
Lonely Isle.

After the making of the World by the Allfather, who in Elvish
tongue is named Ilúvatar, many of the mightiest spirits that dwelt
with him came into the world to govern it, because seeing it afar
after it was made they were filled with delight at its beauty. These
spirits the Elves named the Valar, which is the Powers, though
Men have often called them Gods. Many spirits[1] they brought in
their train, both great and small, and some of these Men have
confused with the Eldar or Elves: but wrongly, for they were
before the world, but Elves and Men awoke first in the world after
the coming of the Valar. Yet in the making of Elves and Men and
in the giving to each of their especial gifts Ilúvatar alone had part;
wherefore they are called the Children of the World or of Ilúvatar.

The chieftains of the Valar were nine. These were the names of
the Nine Gods in Elvish tongue as it was spoken in Valinor,
though other or altered names they have in the speech of the
Gnomes, and their names among Men are manifold. Manwë was
the Lord of the Gods and Prince of the airs and winds and the ruler
of the sky. With him dwelt as spouse the immortal lady of the
heights, Varda the maker of the stars. Next in might and closest in
friendship to Manwë was Ulmo Lord of Waters, who dwells alone
in the Outer Seas, but has in government all waves and waters,
rivers, fountains and springs, throughout the earth. Subject to
him, though he is often of rebellious mood, is Ossë the master of
the seas of the lands of Men, whose spouse is Uinen the Lady of
the Sea. Her hair lies spread through all the waters under skies. Of
might nigh equal to Ulmo was Aulë. He was a smith and a master
of crafts, but his spouse was Yavanna, the lover of fruits and all the
growth of the soil. In might was she next among the ladies of the
Valar to Varda. Very fair was she, and often the Elves named her
Palúrien, the Bosom of the Earth.

The Fanturi were called those brothers Mandos and Lórien.
Nefantur the first was also called, the master of the houses of the
dead, and the gatherer of the spirits of the slain. Olofantur was the
other, maker of visions and of dreams; and his gardens in the land

---

*The Elvish name of the Golden Book in the early dictionary of Qenya is *Parma
Kuluinen* (II. 310).

of the Gods were the fairest of all places in the world and filled with many spirits of beauty and power.

Strongest of all the Gods in limbs and greatest in all feats of prowess and valour was Tulkas, for which reason he was surnamed Poldórëa, the Strong One,[2] and he was the enemy and foe of Melko. Oromë was a mighty lord and little less in strength than Tulkas. He was a hunter, and trees he loved (whence he was called Aldaron and by the Gnomes Tavros,[3] Lord of Forests), and delighted in horses and in hounds. He hunted even in the dark earth before the Sun was lit, and loud were his horns, as still they are in the friths and pastures that Oromë possesses in Valinor. Vana was his spouse, the Queen of Flowers, the younger sister of Varda and Palúrien, and the beauty both of heaven and of earth is in her face and in her works. Yet mightier than she is Nienna who dwells with Nefantur Mandos. Pity is in her heart, and mourning and weeping come to her, but shadow is her realm and night her throne.

Last do all name Melko. But the Gnomes, who most have suffered from his evil, will not speak his name (Moeleg) in their own tongue's form, but call him Morgoth Bauglir, the Black God Terrible. Very mighty was he made by Ilúvatar, and some of the powers of all the Valar he possessed, but to evil uses did he turn them. He coveted the world and the lordship of Manwë, and the realms of all the Gods; and pride and jealousy and lust grew ever in his heart, till he became unlike his wise and mighty brethren. Violence he loved and wrath and destruction, and all excess of cold and flame. But darkness most he used for his works and turned it to evil and a name of horror among Elves and Men.

★

1 *Many spirits > Many lesser spirits* (late change).
2 *the Strong One > the Valiant* (late change).
3 *Tavros > Tauros* (late change).

Accents were put in throughout the work in ink (the typewriter did not possess them), and in addition short marks were put in on certain names in this section: *Fantŭri, Ŏlŏfantur, Ŏrŏmë, Aldăron, Vănă.*

1

In the beginning of the overlordship of the Valar they saw that the world was dark, and light was scattered over the airs and lands and seas. Two mighty lamps they made for the lighting of the world and set them on vast pillars in the North and South. They dwelt upon an island in the seas while they were labouring at their first tasks in the ordering of the earth. But Morgoth contested with them and made war. The lamps he overthrew, and in the confusion of darkness he aroused the sea against their island. Then the Gods removed into the West, where ever since their seats have been, but Morgoth escaped, and in the North he built himself a fortress and great caverns underground. And at that time the Valar could not overcome him or take him captive. Therefore they built then in the uttermost West the land of Valinor. It was bordered by the Outer Sea, and the Wall of the World beyond that fences out the Void and the Eldest Dark; but eastward they built the Mountains of Valinor, that are highest upon earth. In Valinor they gathered all light and all things of beauty, and built their many mansions, their gardens, and their towers. Amidmost of the plain was the city of the Gods, Valmar the beautiful of many bells. But Manwë and Varda have halls upon the highest of the Mountains of Valinor, whence they can look across the world even into the East. Taniquetil the Elves named that holy height, and the Gnomes Taingwethil, which in the tongue of this island of old was Tindbrenting.

In Valinor Yavanna planted two trees in the wide plain not far from the gates of Valmar the blessed. Under her songs they grew, and of all the things which the Gods made most renown have they, and about their fate all the stories of the world are woven. Dark-green leaves had one, that beneath were shining silver, and white blossoms like the cherry it bore, from which a dew of silver light was ever falling. Leaves of young green like the new-opened beech the other had. Their edges were of shining gold. Yellow flowers swung upon its boughs like the hanging blossom of the merry trees Men now call Golden Rain. But from those flowers there issued warmth and blazing light. For seven hours each tree waxed to full glory, and for seven hours it waned.[1] Each followed each, and so twice every day in Valinor there came an hour of softer light, when each tree was faint and their gold and silver radiance was mingled; for when white Silpion for six hours had been in bloom, then golden Laurelin awoke. But Silpion was the elder of the Trees, and the first hour that ever it shone the Gods did not count into the tale of hours, and called it the Hour of Opening, and from that hour dated the beginning of their reign in Valinor; and so at the sixth hour of the first of days Silpion ceased its first time of flower, and at the twelfth was the first blossoming of Laurelin at an end. These Trees the Gnomes called in after times Bansil and Glingol; but Men have no names for them, for their light was slain before the coming of the younger children of Ilúvatar upon earth.[2]

★

1   This sentence was emended to read: *In seven hours each tree waxed to full glory and waned*. Before this emendation, the text was confused, since periods of both fourteen and seven hours are attributed to the Trees; but the following sentence, beginning *Each followed each . . .*, was retyped over erasures that cannot be read, and this no doubt explains the confusion, which was rectified later by the emendation.

2   The typescript page beginning with the words *Sea, and the Wall of the World beyond* and continuing to the end of the section was replaced by another. As far as the end of the first paragraph the replacement is almost identical with the first, but with these differences: Manwë and Varda *had* halls, whence they *could* look out; and new names appear for Taniquetil:

Taniquetil the Elves named that holy height, and Ialassë the Everlasting Whiteness, and Tinwenairin crowned with stars, and many names beside; and the Gnomes spake of it in their later tongue as Amon-Uilas; and in the language of this island of old Tindbrenting was its name.

The replacement page then continues:

In Valinor Yavanna hallowed the mould with mighty song, and Nienna watered it with tears. The Gods were gathered in silence upon their thrones of council in the Ring of Doom nigh unto the golden gates of Valmar the Blessed; and Yavanna Palúrien sang before them, and they watched. From the earth came forth two slender shoots; and silence was over all the world save for the slow chanting of Palúrien. Under her songs two fair trees uprose and grew. Of all things which the Gods made most renown have they, and about their fate all the tales of the world are woven. Dark-green leaves had the one, that beneath were as silver shining, and he bore white blossoms like the cherry, from which a dew of silver light was ever falling, and earth was dappled with the dark and dancing shadows of his leaves amid the pools of gleaming radiance. Leaves of young green like the new-opened beech the other bore; their edges were of glittering gold. Yellow flowers swung upon her boughs like the hanging blossoms of the merry trees Men now call Golden-rain; and from those flowers there came forth warmth and a great light.

In seven hours the glory of each tree waxed to full and waned again to nought; and each awoke to life an hour before the other ceased to shine. Thus in Valinor twice each day there came a gentle hour of softer light, when both Trees were faint, and their gold and silver radiances mingled. Silpion was the elder of the Trees, and came first to full stature and to bloom, and that first hour wherein he shone, the white glimmer of a silver dawn, the Gods reckoned not into the tale of hours, but named it the Opening Hour, and counted therefrom the ages of their reign in Valinor. Wherefore at the sixth hour of the First of Days, and all the joyous days thereafter until the Darkening, Silpion ceased his time of flower; and at the twelfth Laurelin her blossoming. These Trees the Gnomes called in after days Bansil and Glingol; but Men have no names for them, for their light was slain before the coming of the younger children of the world.

On the next page, and obviously associated with this replacement text, is a typed table here represented. At the bottom of the replaced page, and clearly associated with the emendation given in note 1 above, is a simpler table of precisely similar significance, with the note:

'Day' ends every second waning to nought of Laurelin or at end of second hour of mingling of light.

2

In all this time, since Morgoth overthrew the lamps, the Outer[1] Lands east of the Mountains of Valinor were without light. While the lamps had shone growth began therein, which now was checked because of the darkness. But the oldest of all things already grew upon the world: the great weeds of the sea, and on the earth the dark shade of yew and fir and ivy, and small things faint and silent at their feet.[2] In such forests did Oromë sometimes hunt, but save Oromë and Yavanna the Valar went not out of Valinor, while in the North Morgoth built his strength, and gathered his demon broods about him, whom the Gnomes knew after as the Balrogs with whips of flame. The hordes of the Orcs he made of stone, but their hearts of hatred. Glamhoth, people of hate, the Gnomes have called them. Goblins may they be called, but in ancient days they were strong and cruel and fell. Thus he held sway. Then Varda looked on the darkness and was moved. The silver light that dripped from the boughs of Silpion she hoarded, and thence she made the stars. Wherefore she is called Tinwetári, Queen of Stars, and by the Gnomes Tim-Bridhil. The

Hour of Opening

1 . .2 .3 .4 .5 .6 Mingling of Light .7

Silpion in bloom

Mingling of Light . .1 .2 .3 .4 .5 .6 .7

Laurelin in bloom

.1 .2 .3 .4 .5 .6 .7 .8 .9 .10 .11 .12

The First of Days

X

Mingling of Light . .1 .2 .3 .4 .5 .6 .7

Silpion in bloom

.1

unlit skies she strewed with these bright globes of silver flame, and high above the North, a challenge unto Morgoth, she set the crown of Seven mighty Stars to swing, the emblem of the Gods, and sign of Morgoth's doom. Many names have these been called; but in the old days of the North both Elves and Men called them the Burning Briar, and some the Sickle of the Gods.

It is said that at the making of the stars the children of the earth awoke: the elder children of Ilúvatar. Themselves they named the Eldar, whom we call the Elves, but in the beginning mightier and more strong were they, yet not more fair. Oromë it was that found them, dwelling by a star-lit mere, Cuiviénen,[3] Water of Awakening, far in the East. Swift he rode home to Valinor filled with the thought of their beauty. When the Valar heard his tidings they pondered long, and they recalled their duty. For they came into the world knowing that their office was to govern it for the children of Ilúvatar who should after come, each in the appointed time.

Thus came it that because of the Elves the Gods made an assault upon the fortress of Morgoth in the North; and this he never forgot. Little do the Elves or Men know of that great riding of the power of the West against the North and of the war and tumult of the battle[4] of the Gods. Tulkas it was who overthrew Morgoth and bound him captive, and the world had peace for a long age. But the fortress which Morgoth had built was hidden with deceit in dungeons and caverns far beneath the earth, and the Gods did not destroy it utterly, and many evil things of Morgoth lingered there still, or dared to roam in the secret pathways of the world.

Morgoth the Gods drew back to Valinor in chains, and he was set in prison in the great halls of Mandos, from which none, God, Elf, nor Man has ever escaped save by the will of the Valar. Vast they are and strong, and built in the North of the land of Valinor. The Eldalië,[5] the people of the Elves, the Gods invited to Valinor, for they were in love with the beauty of that race, and because they feared for them in the starlit dusk, and knew not what deceits and evil wrought by Morgoth still wandered there.

Of their own free will, yet in awe of the power and majesty of the Gods, the Elves obeyed. A great march therefore they prepared from their first homes in the East. When all was ready Oromë rode at their head upon his white horse shod with gold. Into three hosts were the Eldalië arrayed. The first to march forth were led by that most high of all the elfin race, whose name was Ingwë, Lord of Elves. Ing the Gnomes now make his name, but never came he back into the Outer Lands until these tales were near their end.[6] The Quendi[7] were his own folk called, who sometimes are alone called Elves; they are the Light-elves and the beloved of Manwë and his spouse. Next came the Noldoli. The Gnomes we may call them, a name of wisdom; they are the Deep-elves, and on that march their lord was the mighty Finwë, whom his own folk in their tongue later changed call Finn.[8] His kindred are renowned in elfin song, and of them these tales have much to tell, for they warred and laboured long and sore in the Northern lands of old. Third came the Teleri. The Foam-riders may they be called; they are the Sea-elves, and the Solosimpi[9] they were named in Valinor, the pipers of the shores.[10] Elwë (or Elu) was their lord.[11]

Many of the elfin race were lost upon the long dark roads, and they wandered in the woods and mountains of the world, and never came to Valinor, nor saw the light of the Two Trees. Therefore they are called Ilkorindi, the Elves that dwelt never in Côr,[12] the city of the Eldar in the land of the Gods. The Dark-elves are they, and many are their scattered tribes, and many are their tongues.

Of the Dark-elves the chief in renown was Thingol. For this reason he came never to Valinor. Melian was a fay. In the gardens of Lórien she dwelt, and among all his fair folk none were there that surpassed her beauty, nor none more wise, nor none more skilled in magical and enchanting song. It is told that the Gods would leave their business, and the birds of Valinor their mirth, that Valmar's bells were silent, and the fountains ceased to flow, when at the mingling of the light Melian sang in the gardens of the God of Dreams. Nightingales went always with her, and their song she taught them. But she loved deep shadow, and often strayed on long journey into the Outer Lands, and there filled the silence of the dawning world with her voice and the voices of her birds.

The nightingales of Melian Thingol heard and was enchanted, and left his folk. Melian he found beneath the trees and was cast into a dream and a great slumber, so that his people sought him in vain. In after days Melian and Thingol became Queen and King of the woodland Elves of Doriath; and Thingol's halls were called the Thousand Caves.

★

1   At all three occurrences of *Outer Lands* in this section *Hither* is
     written above *Outer* (which is not struck out).

2 After *at their feet* is added: *and in their thickets dark creatures, old and strong.*
3 *Cuiviénen > Kuiviénen*
4 *the battle > the first battle*
5 Written against *Eldalië*: *Quendi* (late change).
6 This sentence, beginning *Ing the Gnomes now make his name*, was changed to read:

> He entered into Valinor and sits at the feet of the Powers, and all Elves revere his name, but he hath come never back into the Outer Lands.

7 *Quendi > Lindar* (late change).
8 *whom his own folk in their tongue later changed call Finn > wisest of all the children of the world.*
9 *Solosimpi > Soloneldi*
10 *the pipers of the shores > for they made music beside the breaking waves.*
11 *Elwë (or Elu) was their lord > Elwë was their lord, and his hair was long and white.*
12 *Côr > Kôr*

Short marks were written in on the names *Eldălië*, *Tĕlĕri*.

3

In time the hosts of the Eldar came to the last shores of the West.[1] In the North these shores in the ancient days sloped ever westward, until in the northernmost parts of the Earth only a narrow sea divided the land of the Gods from the Outer[2] Lands; but this narrow sea was filled with grinding ice, because of the violence of the frosts of Morgoth. At that place where the elfin hosts first looked upon the sea in wonder a wide dark ocean stretched between them and the Mountains of Valinor. Over the waves they gazed waiting; and Ulmo, sent by the Valar, uprooted the half-sunk island upon which the Gods had first had their dwelling, and drew it to the western shores. Thereon he embarked the Quendi[3] and the Noldoli, for they had arrived first, but the Teleri were behind and did not come until he had gone. The Quendi and the Noldoli he bore thus to the long shores beneath the Mountains of Valinor, and they entered the land of the Gods, and were welcomed to its glory and its bliss. The Teleri thus dwelt long by the shores of the sea awaiting Ulmo's return, and they grew to love the sea, and made songs filled with the sound of it. And Ossë loved them and the music of their voices, and sitting upon the rocks he spoke to them. Great therefore was his grief when Ulmo returned at length to take them to Valinor. Some he persuaded to remain on the beaches of the world, but the most embarked upon the isle and were drawn far away. Then Ossë followed them, and in rebellion, it is said, he seized the isle and chained it to the sea-bottom far out in the Bay of Faërie, whence the Mountains of Valinor could but dimly be descried, and the light of the realms beyond that filtered through the passes of the hills. There it stood for many an age. No other land was near to it, and it was called Tol-Eressëa, or the Lonely Isle. There long the Teleri dwelt, and learned strange music of Ossë, who made the seabirds for their delight. Of this long sojourn apart came the sundering of the tongue of the Foamriders and the Elves of Valinor.

To the other Elves the Valar gave a home and dwelling. Because even among the Tree-lit gardens of the Gods they longed at whiles to see the stars, a gap was made in the encircling mountains, and there in a deep valley that ran down to the sea the green hill of Côr⁴ was raised. From the West the Trees shone upon it; to the East it looked out to the Bay of Faërie and the Lonely Isle and the Shadowy Seas. Thus some of the blessed light of Valinor came into the lands without, and fell upon the Lonely Isle, and its western shore grew green and fair. There bloomed the first flowers that ever were east of the mountains of the Gods.

On the top of Côr the city of the Elves was built, the white walls and towers and terraces of Tûn. The highest of those towers was the tower of Ing,⁵ whose silver lamp shone far out into the mists of the sea, but few are the ships of mortals that have ever seen its marvellous beam. There dwelt the Elves and Gnomes. Most did Manwë and Varda love the Quendi, the Light-elves,⁶ and holy and immortal were all their deeds and songs. The Noldoli, the Deep-elves, that Men call Gnomes, were beloved of Aulë, and of Mandos the wise; and great was their craft, their magic and their skill, but ever greater their thirst for knowledge, and their desire to make things wonderful and new. In Valinor of their skill they first made gems, and they made them in countless myriads, and filled all Tûn with them, and all the halls of the Gods were enriched.⁷

Since the Noldoli afterwards came back into the Great⁸ Lands, and these tales tell mostly of them, here may be said, using the names in form of Gnomish tongue as it long was spoken on the earth, that King of the Gnomes was Finn.⁹ His sons were Fëanor,

Fingolfin, and Finrod. Of these Fëanor was the most skilful, the deepest in lore of all his race; Fingolfin the mightiest and most valiant; Finrod the fairest and most wise of heart. The seven sons of Fëanor were Maidros the tall; Maglor, a musician and mighty singer whose voice carried far over hill and sea; Celegorm the fair, Curufin the crafty, the heir of well nigh all his father's skill, and Cranthir the dark; and last Damrod and Díriel, who after were great hunters in the world, though not more than Celegorm the fair, the friend of Oromë. The sons of Fingolfin were Finweg,[10] who was after king of the Gnomes in the North of the world, and Turgon of Gondolin; and his daughter was Isfin the White. The sons of Finrod were Felagund, Orodreth, Angrod, and Egnor.

In those far days Fëanor began on a time a long and marvellous labour, and all his power and all his subtle magic he called upon, for he purposed to make a thing more fair than any of the Eldar yet had made, that should last beyond the end of all. Three jewels he made, and named them Silmarils. A living fire burned within them that was blended of the light of the Two Trees; of their own radiance they shone even in the dark; no mortal flesh impure could touch them, but was withered and was scorched. These jewels the Elves prized beyond all the works of their hands, and Manwë hallowed them, and Varda said: 'The fate of the Elves is locked herein, and the fate of many things beside.' The heart of Fëanor was wound about the things he himself had made.

Now it must be told that the Teleri seeing afar the light of Valinor were torn between desire to see again their kindred and to look upon the splendour of the Gods, and love of the music of the sea. Therefore Ulmo taught them the craft of shipbuilding, and Ossë, yielding to Ulmo at last, brought to them as his last gift the strong-winged swans. Their fleet of white ships they harnessed to the swans of Ossë, and thus were drawn without help of the winds to Valinor. There they dwelt upon the long shores of Fairyland, and could see the light of the Trees, and could visit the golden streets of Valmar, and the crystal stairs of Tûn, if they wished – but most they sailed the waters of the Bay of Faërie and danced in those bright waves whose crests gleamed in the light beyond the hill. Many jewels the other Eldar gave to them, opals and diamonds and pale crystals that they strewed upon the pools and sands. Many pearls they made, and halls of pearl, and of pearls were the mansions of Elwë at the Haven of the Swans. That was their chief town, and their harbour. A marvellous arch of living rock sea-carven was its gate, and it lay upon the confines of Fairyland, north of the pass of Côr.

★

1   *the last shores of the West* > *the last western shores of the Hither Lands*
2   *Hither* written above *Outer* (see §2 note 1).
3   *Quendi* > *Lindar* at all three occurrences (late change; cf. §2 note 7).
4   *Côr* > *Kôr* at both occurrences (as in §2).
5   *Ing* > *Ingwë* (see §2 note 6).
6   *Light-elves* > *High-elves*, and later to *Fair-elves*.
7   On a separate slip is the following passage in manuscript without precise direction for its insertion, but which seems best placed here:

> But the love of the outer earth and stars remained in the hearts of the Noldoli, and they abode there ever and in the hills and valleys about the city. But the Lindar after a while grew to love rather the wide plains and the full light of Valinor, and they forsook Tûn, and came seldom back; and the Noldoli became a separate folk and their king was Finwë. Yet none dwelt in the tower of Ingwë nor . . . . . save such as tended that unfailing lamp, and Ingwë was held ever as high-king of all the Eldalië.

8   *Hither* written above *Great*.
9   *Finn* > *Finwë* (see §2 note 8).
10   *Finweg* > *Fingon*

4

Now it may be told how the Gods were beguiled by Morgoth. This was the high tide of the glory and the bliss of Gods and Elves, the noontide of the Blessed Realm. Seven[1] ages as the Gods decreed had Morgoth dwelt in the halls of Mandos, each age in lightened pain. When seven ages had passed, as they had promised, he was brought before their conclave. He looked upon the glory of the Valar, and greed and malice was in his heart; he looked upon the fair children of the Eldalië that sat at the knees of the Gods, and hatred filled him; he looked upon their wealth of jewels and lusted for them; but his thoughts he hid and his vengeance he postponed.

There Morgoth humbled himself before the feet of Manwë and sought for pardon; but they would not suffer him to depart from their sight and watchfulness. A humble dwelling he was granted in

Valinor within the gates of the city, and so fair-seeming were all
his deeds and words that after a while he was allowed to go freely
about all the land. Only Ulmo's heart misgave him, and Tulkas
clenched his hands whenever he saw Morgoth his foe go by. Never
has Tulkas the strong forgotten or forgiven a wrong done to
himself or his. Most fair of all was Morgoth to the Elves, and he
aided them in many works, if they would let him. The people of
Ing,[2] the Quendi,[3] held him in suspicion, for Ulmo had warned
them and they had heeded his words. But the Gnomes took
delight in the many things of hidden and secret wisdom that he
could tell to them, and some harkened to things which it had been
better that they had never heard. And when he saw his chance he
sowed a seed of lies and suggestions of evil among such as these.
Bitterly did the folk of the Noldoli atone for it in after days. Often
he would whisper that the Gods had brought the Eldar to Valinor
but out of jealousy, for fear their marvellous skill and beauty and
their magic should grow too strong for them, as they waxed and
spread over the wide lands of the world. Visions he would set
before them of the mighty realms they might have ruled in power
and freedom in the East. In those days, moreover, the Valar knew
of the coming of Men that were to be; but the Elves knew nought
of this, for the Gods had not revealed it, and the time was not yet
near. But Morgoth spoke in secret to the Elves of mortals, though
little of the truth he knew or cared. Manwë alone knew aught
clearly of the mind of Ilúvatar concerning Men, and ever has he
been their friend. Yet Morgoth whispered that the Gods kept the
Eldar captive so that Men coming should defraud them of their
kingdoms, for the weaker race of mortals would be more easily
swayed by them. Little truth was there in this, and little have the
Valar ever prevailed to sway the wills or fates of Men, and least of all to
good. Yet many of the Elves believed or half-believed his evil words.
Gnomes were the most of these. Of the Teleri there were none.

   Thus, ere the Gods were aware, the peace of Valinor was
poisoned. The Gnomes began to murmur against the Valar and
their kindred, and they became filled with vanity, and forgot all
that the Gods had given them and taught them. Most of all did
Morgoth fan the flames of the fierce and eager heart of Fëanor,
though all the while he lusted for the Silmarils. These Fëanor at
great feasts wore on brow and breast, but at other times, locked
fast in the hoards of Tûn, they were guarded close, though there
were no thieves in Valinor, as yet. Proud were the sons of Finn,[4]
and the proudest Fëanor. Lying Morgoth said to him that Fingolfin

and his sons were plotting to usurp the leadership of Fëanor and his sons, and supplant them in the favour of their father and of the Gods. Of these words were quarrels born between the children of Finn, and of those quarrels came the end of the high days of Valinor and the evening of its ancient glory.[5]

Fëanor was summoned before the council of the Gods, and there were the lies of Morgoth laid bare for all to see who had the will. By the judgement of the Gods Fëanor was banished from Tûn. But with him went Finn his father who loved him more than his other sons, and many other Gnomes. Northward in Valinor in the hills near the halls of Mandos they built a treasury and a stronghold; but Fingolfin ruled the Noldoli in Tûn. Thus might Morgoth's words seem justified, and the bitterness he sowed went on, though his lies were disproved, and long after it lived still between the sons of Fingolfin and of Fëanor.[6]

Straight from the midst of their council the Gods sent Tulkas to lay hands on Morgoth and bring him before them in chains once more. But he escaped through the pass of Côr,[7] and from the tower of Ing the Elves saw him pass in thunder and in wrath.

Thence he came into that region that is called Arvalin, which lies south of the Bay of Faërie, and beneath the very eastern feet of the mountains of the Gods, and there are the shadows the thickest in all the world. There secret and unknown dwelt Ungoliant, Gloomweaver, in spider's form. It is not told whence she is, from the outer darkness, maybe, that lies beyond the Walls of the World. In a ravine she lived, and spun her webs in a cleft of the mountains, and sucked up light and shining things to spin them forth again in nets of black and choking gloom and clinging fog. Ever she hungered for more food. There Morgoth met her, and with her plotted his revenge. But terrible was the reward that he must promise her, ere she would dare the perils of Valinor or the power of the Gods.

A great darkness she wove about her to protect her, and then from pinnacle to pinnacle she swung on her black ropes, until she had scaled the highest places of the mountains. In the south of Valinor was this, for there lay the wild woods of Oromë, and there was little watch, since, far from the old fortress of Morgoth in the North, the great walls there looked on untrodden lands and empty sea. On a ladder that she made Morgoth climbed, and he looked down upon the shining plain, seeing afar off the domes of Valinor in the mingling of the light; and he laughed as he sped down the long western slopes with ruin in his heart.

So came evil into Valinor. Silpion was waning fast and Laurelin but just begun to glow, when protected by fate Morgoth and Ungoliant crept unawares into the plain. With his black sword Morgoth stabbed each tree to its very core, and as their juices spouted forth Ungoliant sucked them up, and poison from her foul lips went into their tissues and withered them, leaf and branch and root. Slowly they succumbed, and their light grew dim, while Ungoliant belched forth black clouds and vapours as she drank their radiance. To monstrous form she swelled.

Then fell wonder and dismay on all in Valmar, when twilight and mounting gloom came on the land. Black vapours floated about the ways of the city. Varda looked down from Taniquetil and saw the trees and towers all hidden as in a mist. Too late they ran from hill and gate. The Trees died and shone no more, while wailing throngs stood round them and called on Manwë to come down. Out upon the plain the horses of Oromë thundered with a hundred hooves, and fire started in the gloom about their feet. Swifter than they ran Tulkas on before, and the light of the anger of his eyes was as a beacon. But they found not what they sought. Wherever Morgoth went a darkness and confusion was around him that Ungoliant made, so that feet were bewildered and search was blind.

This was the time of the Darkening of Valinor. In that day there stood before the gates of Valmar Gnomes that cried aloud. Bitter were their tidings. They told how Morgoth had fled North and with him was a great black shape, a spider of monstrous form it had seemed in the gathering night. Sudden he had fallen on the treasury of Finn. There he slew the king of the Gnomes before his doors, and spilled the first elfin blood and stained the land of Valinor. Many others too he slew, but Fëanor and his sons were not there. Bitterly they cursed the chance, for Morgoth took the Silmarils and all the wealth of the jewels of the Noldoli that were hoarded there.

Little is known of the paths or journeys of Morgoth after that terrible deed; but this is known to all, that escaping from the hunt he came at last with Ungoliant over the Grinding Ice and so into the northern lands of this world. There Ungoliant summoned him to give her the promised reward. The half of her pay had been the sap of the Trees of Light. The other half was a full share in the plundered jewels. Morgoth yielded these up, and she devoured them, and their light perished from the earth, and still more huge grew Ungoliant's dark and hideous form. But no share in the

Silmarils would Morgoth give. Such was the first thieves' quarrel.

So mighty had Ungoliant become that she enmeshed Morgoth in her choking nets, and his awful cry echoed through the shuddering world. To his aid came the Orcs and Balrogs that lived yet in the lowest places of Angband. With their whips of flame the Balrogs smote the webs asunder, but Ungoliant was driven away into the uttermost South, where she long dwelt.

Thus came Morgoth back to Angband, and there countless became the number of the hosts of his Orcs and demons.[8] He forged for himself a great crown of iron, and he called himself the king of the world. In sign of this he set the three Silmarils in his crown. It is said that his evil hands were burned black with the touch of those holy and enchanted things, and black they have ever been since, nor was he ever afterward free from the pain of the burning, and the anger of the pain. That crown he never took from his head, and it never was his wont to leave the deep dungeons of his fortress, but he governed his vast armies from his northern throne.

★

1 *Nine* written above *Seven* but then struck out.

2 *Ing* > *Ingwë* at both occurrences, as previously.

3 *Quendi* > *Lindar*, as previously (late change).

4 *Finn* > *Finwë* at all occurrences (except once where overlooked), as previously.

5 The following was added here later faintly in pencil:

And Fëanor spoke words of rebellion against the Gods and plotted to depart from Valinor back into the outer world and deliver the Gnomes, as he said, from thraldom.

6 The following was added here in the same way and at the same time as the passage given in note 5:

But Morgoth hid himself and none knew whither he had gone. And while the Gods were in council, for they feared that the shadows should lengthen in Valinor, a messenger came and brought tidings that Morgoth was in the North of the land, journeying towards the house of Finwë.

7 *Côr* > *Kôr*, as previously.

8 Written here later is the direction: *Here mention making of Orcs (p. 4)*. Page 4 of the typescript contains the sentence (p. 82) *The hordes of the Orcs he made of stone, but their hearts of hatred.* See p. 295.

5

When it became at last all too clear that Morgoth had escaped, the Gods assembled about the dead Trees and sat there in darkness for a long while in dumb silence, and mourned in their hearts. Now that day which Morgoth chose for this assault was a day of high festival throughout Valinor. On this day it was the custom of the chief Valar, all save Ossë who seldom came thither, and of many of the Elves, especially the people of Ing,[1] to climb the long winding paths in white-robed procession to Manwë's halls on the summit of Tindbrenting. All the Quendi[2] and many of the Gnomes, who under Fingolfin still lived in Tûn, were therefore on Tindbrenting's height and were singing before the feet of Varda, when the watchers from afar beheld the fading of the Trees. But most of the Gnomes were in the plain, and all the Teleri, as was their wont, were on the shore. The fogs and darkness now drifted in from off the sea through the pass of Côr,[3] as the Trees died. A murmur of dismay ran through all Elfland, and the Foamriders wailed beside the sea.

Then Fëanor rebelling against his banishment summoned all the Gnomes to Tûn. A vast concourse gathered in the great square on the top of the hill of Côr, and it was lit by the light of many torches which each one that came bore in hand.

Fëanor was a great orator with a power of moving words. A very wild and terrible speech he made before the Gnomes that day, and though his anger was most against Morgoth, yet his words were in great part the fruit of Morgoth's lies. But he was distraught with grief for his father and wrath for the rape of the Silmarils. He now claimed the kingship of all the Gnomes, since Finn[4] was dead, in spite of the decree of the Gods. 'Why should we obey the jealous Gods any longer,' he asked, 'who cannot even keep their own realm from their foe?' He bade the Gnomes prepare for flight in the darkness, while the Valar were still wrapped in mourning; to seek freedom in the world and of their own prowess to win there a new realm, since Valinor was no longer more bright and blissful than the lands outside; to seek out Morgoth and war with him for ever until they were avenged. Then he swore a terrible oath. His seven sons leaped to his side and took the selfsame vow together, each with drawn sword. They swore the unbreakable oath, by the name of Manwë and Varda and the holy mountain,[5] to pursue with hate and vengeance to the ends of the world Vala, Demon, Elf, or Man, or Orc who hold or take or keep a Silmaril against their will.

Fingolfin and his son Finweg[6] spake against Fëanor, and wrath and angry words came near to blows; but Finrod spoke and sought to calm them, though of his sons only Felagund was on his side. Orodreth, Angrod, and Egnor took the part of Fëanor. In the end it was put to the vote of the assembly, and moved by the potent words of Fëanor the Gnomes decided to depart. But the Gnomes of Tûn would not renounce the kingship of Fingolfin, and as two divided hosts therefore they set forth: one under Fingolfin who with his sons yielded to the general voice against their wisdom, because they would not desert their people; the other under Fëanor. Some remained behind. Those were the Gnomes who were with the Quendi upon Tindbrenting. It was long ere they came back into this tale of the wars and wanderings of their people.

The Teleri would not join that flight. Never had they listened to Morgoth. They desired no other cliffs nor beaches than the strands of Fairyland. But the Gnomes knew that they could not escape without boats and ships, and that there was no time to build. They must cross the seas far to the North where they were narrower, but further still feared to venture; for they had heard of Helkaraksë, the Strait of the Grinding Ice, where the great frozen hills ever shifted and broke, sundered and clashed together. But their white ships with white sails the Teleri would not give, since they prized them dearly, and dreaded moreover the wrath of the Gods.

Now it is told that the hosts of Fëanor marched forth first along the coast of Valinor; then came the people of Fingolfin less eager, and in the rear of this host were Finrod and Felagund and many of the noblest and fairest of the Noldoli. Reluctantly they forsook the walls of Tûn, and more than others they carried thence memories of its bliss and beauty, and even many fair things made there by hands. Thus the people of Finrod had no part in the dreadful deed that then was done, and not all of Fingolfin's folk shared in it; yet all the Gnomes that departed from Valinor came under the curse that followed. When the Gnomes came to the Haven of the Swans they attempted to seize by force the white fleets that lay anchored there. A bitter affray was fought upon the great arch of the gate and on the lamplit quays and piers, as is sadly told in the song of the Flight of the Gnomes. Many were slain on either side, but fierce and desperate were the hearts of the people of Fëanor, and they won the battle; and with the help beside of many even of the Gnomes of Tûn they drew away the ships of the Teleri, and manned their oars as best they might, and took them north along the coast.

After they had journeyed a great way and were come to the northern confines of the Blessed Realm, they beheld a dark figure standing high upon the cliffs. Some say it was a messenger, others that it was Mandos himself. There he spoke in a loud dread voice the curse and prophecy that is called the Prophecy of Mandos,[7] warning them to return and seek for pardon, or in the end to return only at last after sorrow and endless misery. Much he foretold in dark words, which only the wisest of them understood, of things that after befell; but all heard the curse he uttered upon those that would not stay, because they had at Swanhaven spilled the blood of their kindred, and fought the first battle between the children of earth unrighteously. For that they should suffer in all their wars and councils from treachery and from the fear of treachery among their own kindred. But Fëanor said: 'He saith not that we shall suffer from cowardice, from cravens or the fear of cravens', and that proved true.[8]

All too soon did the evil begin to work. They came at last far to the North and saw the first teeth of the ice that floated in the sea. Anguish they had of the cold. Many of the Gnomes murmured, especially of those that followed less eagerly under the banners of Fingolfin. So it came into the heart of Fëanor and his sons to sail off suddenly with all the ships, of which they had the mastery, and 'leave the grumblers to grumble, or whine their way back to the cages of the Gods'. Thus began the curse of the slaying at Swanhaven. When Fëanor and his folk landed on the shores in the West of the northern world, they set fire in the ships and made a great burning terrible and bright; and Fingolfin and his people saw the light of it in the sky. Thereafter those left behind wandered miserably, and were joined by the companies of Finrod that marched up after.

In the end in woe and weariness Finrod led some back to Valinor and the pardon of the Gods – for they were not at Swanhaven – but the sons of Finrod and Fingolfin[9] would not yield, having come so far. They led their host far into the bitterest North, and dared at last the Grinding Ice. Many were lost there wretchedly, and there was small love for the sons of Fëanor in the hearts of those that came at last by this perilous passage into the Northern lands.

★

1   *Ing* > *Ingwë*, as previously.
2   At neither of the occurrences of *Quendi* is the name changed, as previously, to *Lindar*, clearly through oversight.

3 *Côr* > *Kôr* at both occurrences, as previously.
4 *Finn* not emended to *Finwë* as previously, through oversight.
5 This sentence was rewritten:

> They swore an oath which none shall break, and none should take,
> by the name of the Allfather, calling the Everlasting Dark upon
> them, if they kept it not, and Manwë they named in witness, and
> Varda, and the Holy Mount, vowing

6 *Finweg* > *Fingon*, as in §3, note 10.
7 *Prophecy of Mandos* > *Prophecy of the North*
8 Here is written lightly in pencil: *Finrod returned*.
9 *the sons of Finrod and Fingolfin* > *Fingolfin and the sons of
Finrod*. (This emendation was made, I think, simply for clarity, the
original text having been intended to mean 'the sons of Finrod,
together with Fingolfin': for Fingolfin, not his son Finweg/Fingon,
has become the leader of the hosts across the Grinding Ice, since
Finrod is now the one who returned to Valinor – see the commentary
on S §5, p. 48.)

6

When the Gods heard of the flight of the Gnomes they were
aroused from their grief. Manwë summoned then to his council
Yavanna; and she put forth all her power, but it availed not to heal
the Trees. Yet beneath her spells Silpion bore at last one great and
single silver bloom, and Laurelin a great golden fruit. Of these, as
is said in the song of the Sun and Moon, the Gods fashioned the
great lamps of heaven, and set them to sail appointed courses
above the world. Rána they named the Moon, and Ûr the Sun;
and the maiden who guided the galleon of the sun was Úrien,[1] and
the youth who steered the floating island of the Moon was Tilion.
Úrien was a maiden who had tended the golden flowers in the
gardens of Vana, while still joy was in the Blissful Realm, and
Nessa daughter of Vana[2] danced on the lawns of never-fading
green. Tilion was a hunter from the company of Oromë, and he
had a silver bow. Often he wandered from his course pursuing the
stars upon the heavenly fields.

At first the Gods purposed that the Sun and Moon should sail
from Valinor to the furthest East, and back again, each following
the other to and fro across the sky. But because of the waywardness of Tilion and his rivalry with Úrien, and most because of the
words of Lórien and Nienna, who said that they had banished all
sleep and night and peace from the earth, they changed their
design. The Sun and Moon were drawn by Ulmo or his chosen

spirits through the caverns and grottoes at the roots of the world, and mounted then in the East, and sailed back to Valinor, into which the Sun descended each day at time of Evening. And so is Evening the time of greatest light and joy in the land of the Gods, when the Sun sinks down to rest beyond the rim of earth upon the cool bosom of the Outer Sea. Tilion was bidden not to mount until Úrien was fallen from the sky, or far had journeyed to the West, and so it is that they are now but seldom seen in the heaven together.

Still therefore is the light of Valinor more great and fair than that of other lands, because there the Sun and Moon together rest a while before they go upon their dark journey under the world, but their light is not the light which came from the Trees before ever Ungoliant's poisonous lips touched them. That light lives now only in the Silmarils. Gods and Elves therefore look forward yet to a time when the Magic Sun and Moon, which are the Trees, may be rekindled and the bliss and glory of old return. Ulmo foretold to them that this would only come to pass by the aid, frail though it might seem, of the second race of earth, the younger children of Ilúvatar. Little heed did they pay to him at that time. Still were they wroth and bitter because of the ingratitude of the Gnomes, and the cruel slaying at the Haven of the Swans. Moreover for a while all save Tulkas feared the might and cunning of Morgoth. Now therefore they fortified all Valinor, and set a sleepless watch upon the wall of hills, which they now piled to a sheer and dreadful height – save only at the pass of Côr.[3] There were the remaining Elves set to dwell, and they went now seldom to Valmar or Tindbrenting's height, but were bidden to guard the pass ceaselessly that no bird nor beast nor Elf nor Man, nor anything beside that came from the lands without, should approach the shores of Faërie, or set foot in Valinor. In that day, which songs call the Hiding of Valinor, the Magic Isles were set, filled with enchantment, and strung across the confines of the Shadowy Seas, before the Lonely Isle is reached sailing West, there to entrap mariners and wind them in everlasting sleep. Thus it was that the many emissaries of the Gnomes in after days came never back to Valinor – save one, and he came too late.[4]

The Valar sit now behind the mountains and feast, and dismiss the exiled Noldoli from their hearts, all save Manwë and Ulmo. Most in mind did Ulmo keep them, who gathers news of the outer world through all the lakes and rivers that flow into the sea.

At the first rising of the Sun over the world the younger children of earth awoke in the land of Eruman[5] in the East of East.[6] But of Men little is told in these tales, which concern the oldest days before the waning of the Elves and the waxing of mortals, save of those who in the first days of Sunlight and Moonsheen wandered into the North of the world. To Eruman there came no God to guide Men or to summon them to dwell in Valinor. Ulmo nonetheless took thought for them, and his messages came often to them by stream and flood, and they loved the waters but understood little the messages. The Dark-elves they met and were aided by them, and were taught by them speech and many things beside, and became the friends of the children of the Eldalië who had never found the paths to Valinor, and knew of the Valar but as a rumour and a distant name. Not long was then Morgoth come back into the earth, and his power went not far abroad, so that there was little peril in the lands and hills where new things, fair and fresh, long ages ago devised in the thought of Yavanna, came at last to their budding and their bloom.

West, North, and South they spread and wandered, and their joy was the joy of the morning before the dew is dry, when every leaf is green.

★

1   *Úrien > Árien* at all occurrences.
2   *daughter of Vana* struck out. See p. 275.
3   *Côr > Kôr*, as previously.
4   *and he came too late > the mightiest mariner of song.*
5   At the first occurrence the name *Eruman* was later underlined in pencil, as if for correction, but not at the second.
6   Added here:

> for measured time had come into the world, and the first of days; and thereafter the lives of the Eldar that remained in the Hither Lands were lessened, and their waning was begun.

7

Now began the times of the great wars of the powers of the North, when the Gnomes of Valinor and Ilkorins and Men strove against the hosts of Morgoth Bauglir, and went down in ruin. To this end the cunning lies of Morgoth that he sowed amongst his foes, and the curse that came of the slaying at the Haven of the

Swans, and the oath of the sons of Fëanor, were ever at work; the greatest injury they did to Men and Elves.

Only a part do these tales tell of the deeds of those days, and most they tell concerning the Gnomes and the Silmarils and the mortals that became entangled in their fate. In the early days Eldar and Men were of little different stature and bodily might; but the Eldar were blessed with greater skill, beauty, and wit, and those who had come from Valinor as much surpassed the Ilkorins in these things as they in turn surpassed the people of mortal race. Only in the realm of Doriath, whose queen Melian was of the kindred of the Valar, did the Ilkorins come near to match the Elves of Côr.[1] Immortal were the Elves, and their wisdom waxed and grew from age to age, and no sickness or pestilence brought them death. But they could be slain with weapons in those days, even by mortal Men, and some waned and wasted with sorrow till they faded from the earth. Slain or fading their spirits went back to the halls of Mandos to wait a thousand years, or the pleasure of Mandos[2] according to their deserts, before they were recalled to free life in Valinor, or were reborn,[3] it is said, into their own children.[4] More frail were Men, more easily slain by weapon or mischance, subject to ills, or grew old and died. What befell their spirits the Eldalië knew not. The Eldar said that they went to the halls of Mandos, but that their place of waiting was not that of the Elves, and Mandos under Ilúvatar knew alone whither they went after the time in his wide halls beyond the western sea. They were never reborn on earth, and none ever came back from the mansions of the dead, save only Beren son of Barahir, who after spoke never to mortal Men. Maybe their fate after death was not in the hands of the Valar.

In after days, when because of the triumphs of Morgoth Elves and Men became estranged, as he most wished, those of the Eldalië that lived still in the world faded, and Men usurped the sunlight. Then the Eldar wandered in the lonelier places of the Outer[5] Lands, and took to the moonlight and to the starlight, and to the woods and caves.[6]

★

1   *Côr > Kôr*, as previously.
2   *Mandos > Nefantur*
3   *or were reborn > or sometimes were reborn*
4   Added here:

And of like fate were those fair offspring of Elf and mortal, Eärendel, and Elwing, and Dior her father, and Elrond her child.

5   *Hither* written above *Outer*, but *Outer* not struck out.
6   Added at the end:

and became as shadows, wraiths and memories, such as set not sail unto the West and vanished from the world, as is told ere the tale's ending.

8

But in these days Elves and Men were kindred and allies. Before the rising of the Sun and Moon Fëanor and his sons marched into the North seeking for Morgoth. A host of Orcs aroused by the light of the burning ships came down on them, and there was battle on the plain renowned in song. Yet young and green it stretched[1] to the feet of the tall mountains upreared over Morgoth's halls; but afterward it became burnt and desolate, and is called the Land of Thirst, Dor-na-Fauglith in the Gnomish tongue. There was the First Battle.[2] Great was the slaughter of the Orcs and Balrogs, and no tale can tell the valour of Fëanor or of his sons. Yet woe entered into that first great victory. For Fëanor was wounded to the death by Gothmog Lord of Balrogs, whom Ecthelion after slew in Gondolin. Fëanor died in the hour of victory, looking upon the gigantic peaks of Thangorodrim, the greatest of hills of the world;[3] and he cursed the name of Morgoth, and laid it on his sons never to treat or parley with their foe. Yet even in the hour of his death there came to them an embassy from Morgoth acknowledging his defeat, and offering to treat, and tempting them with a Silmaril. Maidros the tall persuaded the Gnomes to meet Morgoth at the time and place appointed, but with as little thought of faith on his side as there was on the part of Morgoth. Wherefore each embassy came in far greater force than they had sworn, but Morgoth brought the greater, and they were Balrogs. Maidros was ambushed and most of his company was slain; but Maidros was taken alive by the command of Morgoth, and carried to Angband and tortured, and hung from the face of a sheer precipice upon Thangorodrim by his right wrist alone.

Then the six sons of Fëanor dismayed drew off and encamped by the shores of Lake Mithrim, in that northern land which was after called Hisilómë, Hithlum or Dorlómin by the Gnomes, which is the Land of Mist. There they heard of the march of

Fingolfin and Finweg[4] and Felagund, who had crossed the Grinding Ice.

Even as these came the first Sun arose; their blue and silver banners were unfurled, and flowers sprang beneath their marching feet. The Orcs dismayed at the uprising of the great light retreated to Angband, and Morgoth thwarted pondered a long while in wrathful thought.

Little love was there between the two hosts encamped upon the opposing shores of Mithrim, and the delay engendered by their feud did great harm to the cause of both.

Now vast vapours and smokes were made in Angband and sent forth from the smoking tops of the Mountains of Iron, which even afar off in Hithlum could be seen staining the radiance of those earliest mornings. The vapours fell and coiled about the fields and hollows, and lay on Mithrim's bosom dark and foul.

Then Finweg the valiant resolved to heal the feud. Alone he went in search of Maidros. Aided by the very mists of Morgoth, and by the withdrawal of the forces of Angband, he ventured into the fastness of his enemies, and at last he found Maidros hanging in torment. But he could not reach him to release him; and Maidros begged[5] him to shoot him with his bow.

Manwë to whom all birds are dear, and to whom they bring news upon Tindbrenting of all things which his farsighted eyes do not see, sent[6] forth the race of Eagles. Thorndor was their king. At Manwë's command they dwelt in the crags of the North and watched Morgoth and hindered his deeds, and brought news of him to the sad ears of Manwë.

Even as Finweg sorrowing bent his bow, there flew down from the high airs Thorndor king of eagles. He was the mightiest of all birds that ever have been. Thirty feet[7] was the span of his outstretched wings. His beak was of gold. So the hand of Finweg was stayed, and Thorndor bore him to the face of the rock where Maidros hung. But neither could release the enchanted bond upon the wrist, nor sever it nor draw it from the stone. Again in agony Maidros begged them to slay him, but Finweg cut off his hand above the wrist, and Thorndor bore them to Mithrim, and Maidros' wound was healed, and he lived to wield sword with his left hand more deadly to his foes than his right had been.

Thus was the feud healed for a while between the proud sons of Finn[8] and their jealousy forgotten, but still there held the oath of the Silmarils.

★

1 *Yet young and green* > *Yet dark beneath the stars* (and later *it stretched* > *the plain stretched*). (This change was made no doubt because the Sun had not yet risen; but it destroys the force of the antithesis with *but afterward it became burnt and desolate*.)
2 Added here: *the Battle under Stars*.
3 *the world* > *the hither world*
4 *Finweg* > *Fingon*, as previously, at all occurrences.
5 The typescript had present tenses, *finds*, *cannot*, *begs*, early emended to *found*, *could not*, *begged*; an indication that my father was closely following the S manuscript. Present tenses are occasionally found later in Q as originally typed.
6 *sent* > *had sent*
7 *feet* > *fathoms*
8 *Finn* > *Finwë*, as previously.

9

Then the Gnomes marched forward and beleaguered Angband from West, South, and East. In Hithlum and on its borders in the West lay the hosts of Fingolfin. The South was held by Felagund son of Finrod and his brethren. A tower they had on an island in the river Sirion, which guarded the valley between the northward bending mountains on the borders of Hithlum and the slopes where the great pine-forest grew, which Morgoth after filled with such dread and evil that not even the Orcs would go through it, save by a single road and in great need and haste, and the Gnomes came to call it Taur-na-Fuin, which is Deadly Nightshade. But in those days it was wholesome, if thick and dark,[1] and the people of Orodreth, of Angrod and Egnor, ranged therein and watched from its eaves the plain below, that stretched to the Mountains of Iron. Thus they guarded the plain of Sirion, most fair of rivers in elfin song, most loved of Ulmo, and all that wide land of beech and elm and oak and flowering mead that was named Broseliand.[2]

In the east lay the sons of Fëanor. Their watchtower was the high hill of Himling, and their hiding place the Gorge of Aglon, cloven deep between Himling and Taur-na-Fuin, and watered by the river of Esgalduin the dark and strong, which came out of secret wells in Taur-na-Fuin and flowed into Doriath and past the doors of Thingol's halls. But they needed little a hiding place in those days, and ranged far and wide, even to the walls of Angband in the North, and east to the Blue Mountains,[3] which are the borders of the lands of which these tales tell. There they made war upon[4] the Dwarves of Nogrod and Belegost; but they did not discover whence that strange race came, nor have any since. They are not friend of Valar[5] or of Eldar or of Men, nor do they serve Morgoth; though they are in many things more like his people, and little did they love the Gnomes.[6] Skill they had well-nigh to rival that of the Gnomes, but less beauty was in their works, and iron they wrought rather than gold and silver, and mail and weapons were their chief craft. Trade and barter was their delight and the winning of wealth of which they made little use. Long were their beards and short and squat their stature. Nauglir the Gnomes called them, and those who dwelt in Nogrod they called Indrafangs, the Longbeards, because their beards swept the floor before their feet. But as yet little they troubled the people of earth, while the power of the Gnomes was great.

This was the time that songs call the Siege of Angband. The swords of the Gnomes then fenced the earth from the ruin of Morgoth, and his power was shut behind the walls of Angband. The Gnomes boasted that never could he break their leaguer, and that none of his folk could ever pass to work evil in the ways of the world.

A time of solace it was beneath the new Sun and Moon, a time of birth and blossoming. In those days befell the first meeting of the Gnomes with the Dark-elves, and the Feast of Meeting that was held in the Land of Willows was long recalled in after days of little joy. In those days too Men came over the Blue Mountains into Broseliand[7] and Hithlum,[8] the bravest and fairest of their race. Felagund it was that found them, and he ever was their friend. On a time he was the guest of Celegorm in the East, and rode a-hunting with him. But he became separated from the others,[9] and at a time of night he came upon a dale in the western foothills of the Blue Mountains. There were lights in the dale and the sound of rugged song. Then Felagund marvelled, for the tongue of those songs was not the tongue of Eldar or of Dwarves.[10] Nor was it the tongue of Orcs, though this at first he feared. There were camped the people of Bëor, a mighty warrior of Men, whose son was Barahir the bold. They were the first of Men to come into Broseliand. After them came Hador the tall, whose sons were Haleth and Gumlin, and the sons of Gumlin Huor and Húrin,[11] and the son of Huor Tuor, and the son of Húrin Túrin. All these were tangled in the fates of the Gnomes and did mighty deeds which the Elves still remember among the songs of the deeds of their own lords and kings.

But Hador was not yet seen in the camps of the Gnomes. That

night Felagund went among the sleeping men of Bëor's host and sat by their dying fires where none kept watch, and he took a harp which Bëor had laid aside, and he played music on it such as mortal ear had never heard, having learned the strains of music from the Dark-elves alone. Then men woke and listened and marvelled, for great wisdom was in that song, as well as beauty, and the heart grew wiser that listened to it. Thus came it that Men called Felagund, whom they met first of the Noldoli, Wisdom;[12] and after him they called his race the Wise, whom we call the Gnomes.[13]

Bëor lived till death with Felagund, and Barahir his son was the greatest friend of the sons of Finrod.[14] But the sons of Hador were allied to the house of Fingolfin, and of these Húrin and Túrin were the most renowned. The realm of Gumlin was in Hithlum, and there afterward Húrin dwelt and his wife Morwen Elfsheen, who was fair as a daughter of the Eldalië.[15]

Now began the time of the ruin of the Gnomes. It was long before this was achieved, for great was their power grown, and they were very valiant, and their allies were many and bold, Dark-elves and Men.

But the tide of their fortune took a sudden turn. Long had Morgoth prepared his forces in secret. On a time of night at winter he let forth great rivers of flame that poured over all the plain before the Mountains of Iron and burned it to a desolate waste. Many of the Gnomes of Finrod's sons perished in that burning, and the fumes of it wrought darkness and confusion among the foes of Morgoth. In the train of the fire[16] came the black armies of the Orcs in numbers such as the Gnomes had never before seen or imagined. In this way Morgoth broke the leaguer of Angband and slew by the hands of the Orcs a great slaughter of the bravest of the besieging hosts. His enemies were scattered far and wide, Gnomes, Ilkorins, and Men. Men he drove for the most part back over the Blue Mountains, save the children of Bëor and of Hador who took refuge in Hithlum beyond the Shadowy Mountains, where as yet the Orcs came not in force. The Dark-elves fled south to Broseliand[17] and beyond, but many went to Doriath, and the kingdom and power of Thingol grew great in that time, till he became a bulwark and a refuge of the Elves. The magics of Melian that were woven about the borders of Doriath fenced evil from his halls and realm.

The pine-forest Morgoth took and turned it to a place of dread

as has been told, and the watchtower of Sirion he took and made it
into a stronghold of evil and of menace. There dwelt Thû the chief
servant of Morgoth, a sorcerer of dreadful power, the lord of
wolves.[18] Heaviest had the burden of that dreadful battle, the
second battle and the first defeat[19] of the Gnomes, fallen upon the
sons of Finrod. There were Angrod and Egnor slain. There too
would Felagund have been taken or slain, but Barahir came up
with all his men and saved the Gnomish king and made a wall of
spears about him; and though grievous was their loss they fought
their way from the Orcs and fled to the fens of Sirion to the South.
There Felagund swore an oath of undying friendship and aid in
time of need to Barahir and all his kin and seed, and in token of his
vow he gave to Barahir his ring.

Then Felagund went South,[20] and on the banks of Narog established after the manner of Thingol a hidden and cavernous city,
and a realm. Those deep places were called Nargothrond. There
came Orodreth after a time of breathless flight and perilous
wanderings, and with him Celegorm and Curufin, the sons of
Fëanor, his friends. The people of Celegorm swelled the strength
of Felagund, but it would have been better if they had gone rather
to their own kin, who fortified the hill of Himling[21] east of Doriath
and filled the Gorge of Aglon with hidden arms.

Most grievous of the losses of that battle was the death of
Fingolfin mightiest of the Noldoli. But his own death he sought in
rage and anguish seeing the defeat of his people. For he went to the
gates of Angband alone and smote upon them with his sword, and
challenged Morgoth to come out and fight alone. And Morgoth
came. That was the last time in those wars that he left the gates of
his strong places, but he could not deny the challenge before the
faces of his lords and chieftains. Yet it is said that though his
power and strength is the greatest of the Valar and of all things
here below, at heart he is a craven when alone, and that he took not
the challenge willingly. The Orcs sing of that duel at the gates, but
the Elves do not, though Thorndor looked down upon it and has
told the tale.

High Morgoth towered above the head of Fingolfin, but great
was the heart of the Gnome, bitter his despair and terrible his
wrath. Long they fought. Thrice was Fingolfin beaten to his knees
and thrice arose. Ringil was his sword, as cold its blade and as
bright as the blue ice, and on his shield was the star on a blue field
that was his device. But Morgoth's shield was black without a
blazon and its shadow was like a thundercloud. He fought with a

mace like a great hammer of his forges. Grond the Orcs called it, and when it smote the earth as Fingolfin slipped aside, a pit yawned and smoke came forth. Thus was Fingolfin overcome, for the earth was broken about his feet, and he tripped and fell, and Morgoth put his foot, that is heavy as the roots of hills, upon his neck. But this was not done before Ringil had given him seven wounds, and at each he had cried aloud. He goes halt in his left foot for ever, where in his last despair Fingolfin pierced it through and pinned it to the earth.[22] But the scar upon his face Fingolfin did not give. This was the work of Thorndor. For Morgoth took the body of Fingolfin to hew it and give it to his wolves. But Thorndor swept down from on high amid the very throngs of Angband that watched the fight, and smote his claw[23] into the face of Morgoth and rescued the body of Fingolfin, and bore it to a great height. There he set his cairn upon a mountain, and that mountain looks down upon the plain of Gondolin, and over the Mount of Fingolfin no Orc or demon ever dared to pass for a great while, till treachery was born among his kin.

But Finweg[24] took the kingship of the Gnomes, and held yet out, nighest of the scattered Gnomes to the realm of their foe, in Hithlum and the Shadowy Mountains of the North that lie South and East of the Land of Mist, between it and Broseliand and the Thirsty Plain. Yet each of their strongholds Morgoth took one by one, and ever the Orcs growing more bold wandered far and wide, and numbers of the Gnomes and Dark-elves they took captive and carried to Angband and made thralls, and forced them to use their skill and magic in the service of Morgoth, and to labour unceasingly in tears in his mines and forges.[25] And Morgoth's emissaries went ever among the Dark-elves and the thrall-Gnomes and Men (to whom in those days he feigned the greatest friendship while they were out of his power), and lying promises they made and false suggestions of the greed and treachery of each to each; and because of the curse of the slaying at Swanhaven often were the lies believed; and the Gnomes feared greatly the treachery of those of their own kin who had been thralls of Angband, so that even if they escaped and came back to their people little welcome they had, and wandered often in miserable exile and despair.[26]

★

1   Added here: *and it was called Taur Danin* (late change).
2   *Broseliand > Beleriand* (see note 7), and the following added:

in Gnomish tongue; and Noldórien has it been called, [Geleithian>] Geleidhian, the kingdom of the Gnomes, and Ingolondë the fair and sorrowful.

3   *east to the Blue Mountains* > *east unto Erydluin, the Blue Mountains.* Against *Erydluin* was pencilled later *Eredlindon*.
4   *made war upon* > *had converse with* (late change).
5   This sentence was emended to read: *Little friendship was there between Elf and Dwarf, for these are not friend of Valar,* &c. (late change).
6   *and little did they love the Gnomes* bracketed for exclusion (late change).
7   *Broseliand* > *Beleriand* at all occurrences (see note 2).
8   *and Hithlum* struck out.
9   Added here: *and passed into Ossiriand* (late change).
10   Almost illegible words were pencilled above *Eldar or of Dwarves: the* [*?Valar*] *or of* [*?Doriath*] *nor yet of the Green Elves.*
11   This sentence was emended to read: *After them came Hador the Golden-haired, whose sons were Gundor and Gumlin, and the sons of Gumlin Húrin and Huor,* &c. (late change).
     At the bottom of the page, without direction for its insertion, is written: *Haleth the hunter, and little later*
12   *Wisdom* > *Gnome that is Wisdom* > *Gnome or Wisdom*
13   Added here: *Took F*[*elagund*] *to be a god* (late change).
14   Added here: *but he abode in Dorthonion* (late change).
15   Written here, with mark of insertion: *Dagor Aglareb and the Foreboding of the Kings* (late addition).
16   *In the train of the fire* > *In the front of that fire came Glómund the golden, the father of dragons, and in his train*
17   Above *Beleriand* (emended from *Broseliand*, see note 7) is pencilled *Geleidhian* (see note 2).
18   Scribbled against this: *Sauron his servant in Valinor whom he suborned.*
19   *the second battle and the first defeat* > *the Second Battle, the Battle of Sudden Flame, and the first defeat* (and later *Second* > *Third*).
20   Added here: *and West*
21   *Himling* > *Himring* (late change; at the first two occurrences of the name, near the beginning of this section, it was not emended).
22   *and pinned it to the earth* struck through (late change).
23   *claw* > *bill*
24   *Finweg* > *Fingon*, as previously.
25   In this sentence *magic* > *craft* and *in tears in his mines and forges* to an uncertain reading, probably *and tears and torment were their wages* (late changes).

26   A page of the typescript ends here, and at the bottom of the page is
     written *Turgon* (late addition).

10

In these days of doubt and fear, after the Second[1] Battle, many
dreadful things befell of which but few are here told. It is told that
Bëor was slain and Barahir yielded not to Morgoth, but all his land
was won from him and his people scattered, enslaved or slain, and
he himself went in outlawry with his son Beren and ten faithful
men. Long they hid and did secret and valiant deeds of war against
the Orcs. But in the end, as is told in the beginning of the lay of
Lúthien and Beren, the hiding place of Barahir was betrayed, and
he was slain and his comrades, all save Beren who by fortune was
that day hunting afar. Thereafter Beren lived an outlaw alone,
save for the help he had from birds and beasts which he loved; and
seeking for death in desperate deeds found it not, but glory and
renown in the secret songs of fugitives and hidden enemies of
Morgoth, so that the tale of his deeds came even to Broseliand,[2]
and was rumoured in Doriath. At length Beren fled south from the
ever-closing circle of those that hunted him, and crossed the
dreadful Mountains of Shadow,[3] and came at last worn and hag-
gard into Doriath. There in secret he won the love of Lúthien
daughter of Thingol, and he named her Tinúviel, the nightingale,
because of the beauty of her singing in the twilight beneath the
trees; for she was the daughter of Melian.

But Thingol was wroth and he dismissed him in scorn, but did
not slay him because he had sworn an oath to his daughter. But he
desired nonetheless to send him to his death. And he thought in
his heart of a quest that could not be achieved, and he said: If thou
bring me a Silmaril from the crown of Morgoth, I will let Lúthien
wed thee, if she will. And Beren vowed to achieve this, and went
from Doriath to Nargothrond bearing the ring of Barahir. The
quest of the Silmaril there aroused the oath from sleep that
the sons of Fëanor had sworn, and evil began to grow from it.
Felagund, though he knew the quest to be beyond his power, was
willing to lend all his aid to Beren, because of his own oath to
Barahir. But Celegorm and Curufin dissuaded his people and
roused up rebellion against him. And evil thoughts awoke in their
hearts, and they thought to usurp the throne of Nargothrond,
because they were sons of the eldest line. Rather than a Silmaril

should be won and given to Thingol, they would ruin the power of Doriath and Nargothrond.

So Felagund gave his crown to Orodreth and departed from his people with Beren and ten faithful men of his own board. They waylaid an Orc-band and slew them and disguised themselves by the aid of Felagund's magic as Orcs. But they were seen by Thû from his watchtower, which once had been Felagund's own, and were questioned by him, and their magic was overthrown in a contest between Thû and Felagund. Thus they were revealed as Elves, but the spells of Felagund concealed their names and quest. Long they were tortured in the dungeons of Thû, but none betrayed the other.

In the meanwhile Lúthien learning by the far sight of Melian that Beren had fallen into the power of Thû sought in her despair to fly from Doriath. This became known to Thingol, who imprisoned her in a house in the tallest of his mighty beeches far above the ground. How she escaped and came into the woods, and was found there by Celegorm as they hunted on the borders of Doriath, is told in the lay of Lúthien. They took her treacherously to Nargothrond, and Curufin the crafty became enamoured of her beauty. From her tale they learned that Felagund was in the hands of Thû; and they purposed to let him perish there, and keep Lúthien with them, and force Thingol to wed Lúthien to Curufin,[4] and so build up their power and usurp Nargothrond and become the mightiest of the princes of the Gnomes. They did not think to go in search of the Silmarils, or suffer any others to do so, until they had all the power of the Elves beneath themselves and obedient to them. But their designs came to nought save estrangement and bitterness between the kingdoms of the Elves.

Huan was the name of the chief of the hounds of Celegorm. He was of immortal race from the hunting-lands of Oromë. Oromë gave him to Celegorm long before in Valinor, when Celegorm often rode in the train of the God and followed his horn. He came into the Great[5] Lands with his master, and dart nor weapon, spell nor poison, could harm him, so that he went into battle with his lord and saved him many times from death. His fate had been decreed that he should not meet death save at the hands of the mightiest wolf that should ever walk the world.

Huan was true of heart, and he loved Lúthien from the hour that he first found her in the woods and brought her to Celegorm. His heart was grieved by his master's treachery, and he set Lúthien free and went with her to the North.

There Thû slew his captives one by one, till only Felagund and Beren were left. When the hour for Beren's death came Felagund put forth all his power, and burst his bonds, and wrestled with the werewolf that came to slay Beren; and he killed the wolf, but was himself slain in the dark. There Beren mourned in despair, and waited for death. But Lúthien came and sang outside the dungeons. Thus she beguiled Thû to come forth, for the fame of the loveliness of Lúthien had gone through all lands and the wonder of her song. Even Morgoth desired her, and had promised the greatest reward to any who could capture her. Each wolf that Thû sent Huan slew silently, till Draugluin the greatest of his wolves came. Then there was fierce battle, and Thû knew that Lúthien was not alone. But he remembered the fate of Huan, and he made himself the greatest wolf that had yet walked the world, and came forth. But Huan overthrew him, and won from him the keys and the spells that held together his enchanted walls and towers. So the stronghold was broken and the towers thrown down and the dungeons opened. Many captives were released, but Thû flew in bat's form to Taur-na-Fuin. There Lúthien found Beren mourning beside Felagund. She healed his sorrow and the wasting of his imprisonment, but Felagund they buried on the top of his own island hill, and Thû came there no more.

Then Huan returned to his master, and less was the love between them after. Beren and Lúthien wandered careless in happiness, until they came nigh to the borders of Doriath once more. There Beren remembered his vow, and bade Lúthien farewell, but she would not be sundered from him. In Nargothrond there was tumult. For Huan and many of the captives of Thû brought back the tidings of the deeds of Lúthien, and the death of Felagund, and the treachery of Celegorm and Curufin was laid bare. It is said they had sent a secret embassy to Thingol ere Lúthien escaped, but Thingol in wrath had sent their letters back by his own servants to Orodreth.[6] Wherefore now the hearts of the people of Narog turned back to the house of Finrod, and they mourned their king Felagund whom they had forsaken, and they did the bidding of Orodreth. But he would not suffer them to slay the sons of Fëanor as they wished. Instead he banished them from Nargothrond, and swore that little love should there be between Narog and any of the sons of Fëanor thereafter. And so it was.

Celegorm and Curufin were riding in haste and wrath through the woods to find their way to Himling,[7] when they came upon Beren and Lúthien, even as Beren sought to part from his love.

They rode down on them, and recognizing them tried to trample Beren under their hooves. But Curufin swerving lifted Lúthien to his saddle. Then befell the leap of Beren, the greatest leap of mortal Men. For he sprang like a lion right upon the speeding horse of Curufin, and grasped him about the throat, and horse and rider fell in confusion upon the earth, but Lúthien was flung far off and lay dazed upon the ground. There Beren choked Curufin, but his death was very nigh from Celegorm, who rode back with his spear. In that hour Huan forsook the service of Celegorm, and sprang upon him so that his horse swerved aside, and no man for fear of the terror of the great hound dared go nigh. Lúthien forbade the death of Curufin, but Beren despoiled him of his horse and weapons, chief of which was his famous knife, made by the Dwarves. It would cut iron like wood. Then the brothers rode off, but shot back at Huan treacherously and at Lúthien. Huan they did not hurt, but Beren sprang before Lúthien and was wounded, and Men remembered that wound against the sons of Fëanor, when it became known.

Huan stayed with Lúthien, and hearing of their perplexity and the purpose Beren had still to go to Angband, he went and fetched them from the ruined halls of Thû a werewolf's coat and a bat's. Three times only did Huan speak with the tongue of Elves or Men. The first was when he came to Lúthien in Nargothrond. This was the second, when he devised the desperate counsel for their quest. So they rode North, till they could no longer go on horse in safety. Then they put on the garments as of wolf and bat, and Lúthien in guise of evil fay rode upon the werewolf.

In the lay of Lúthien is all told how they came to Angband's gate, and found it newly guarded, for rumour of he knew not what design abroad among the Elves had come to Morgoth. Wherefore he fashioned the mightiest of all wolves, Carcharas[8] Knife-fang, to sit at the gates.[9] But Lúthien set him in spells, and they won their way to the presence of Morgoth, and Beren slunk beneath his chair. Then Lúthien dared the most dreadful and most valiant deed that any of the women of the Elves have ever dared; no less than the challenge of Fingolfin is it accounted, and may be greater, save that she was half-divine. She cast off her disguise and named her own name, and feigned that she was brought captive by the wolves of Thû. And she beguiled Morgoth, even as his heart plotted foul evil within him; and she danced before him, and cast all his court in sleep; and she sang to him, and she flung the magic robe she had woven in Doriath in his face, and she set a binding dream upon him – what song can sing the marvel of that deed, or the wrath and humiliation of Morgoth, for even the Orcs laugh in secret when they remember it, telling how Morgoth fell from his chair and his iron crown rolled upon the floor.

Then forth leaped Beren casting aside the wolvish robe, and drew out the knife of Curufin. With that he cut forth a Silmaril. But daring more he essayed to gain them all. Then the knife of the treacherous Dwarves snapped, and the ringing sound of it stirred the sleeping hosts and Morgoth groaned. Terror seized the hearts of Beren and Lúthien, and they fled down the dark ways of Angband. The doors were barred by Carcharas, now aroused from the spell of Lúthien. Beren set himself before Lúthien, which proved ill; for ere she could touch the wolf with her robe or speak word of magic, he sprang upon Beren, who now had no weapon. With his right he smote at the eyes of Carcharas, but the wolf took the hand into his jaws and bit it off. Now that hand held the Silmaril. Then was the maw of Carcharas burned with a fire of anguish and torment, when the Silmaril touched his evil flesh; and he fled howling from before them, so that all the mountains shuddered, and the madness of the wolf of Angband was of all the horrors that ever came into the North[10] the most dire and terrible. Hardly did Lúthien and Beren escape, ere all Angband was aroused.

Of their wanderings and despair, and of the healing of Beren, who ever since has been called Beren Ermabwed the One-handed, of their rescue by Huan, who had vanished suddenly from them ere they came to Angband, and of their coming to Doriath once more, here there is little to tell.[11] But in Doriath many things had befallen. Ever things had gone ill there since Lúthien fled away. Grief had fallen on all the people and silence on their songs when their hunting found her not. Long was the search, and in searching Dairon the piper of Doriath was lost, who loved Lúthien before Beren came to Doriath. He was the greatest of the musicians of the Elves, save Maglor son of Fëanor, and Tinfang Warble.[12] But he came never back to Doriath and strayed into the East of the world.[13]

Assaults too there were on Doriath's borders, for rumours that Lúthien was astray had reached Angband. Boldog captain of the Orcs was there slain in battle by Thingol, and his great warriors Beleg the Bowman and Mablung Heavyhand were with Thingol in that battle. Thus Thingol learned that Lúthien was yet free of Morgoth, but that he knew of her wandering; and Thingol was

filled with fear. In the midst of his fear came the embassy of
Celegorm in secret, and said that Beren was dead, and Felagund,
and Lúthien was at Nargothrond. Then Thingol found it in his
heart to regret the death of Beren, and his wrath was aroused at the
hinted treachery of Celegorm to the house of Finrod, and because
he kept Lúthien and did not send her home. Wherefore he sent
spies into the land of Nargothrond and prepared for war. But he
learned that Lúthien had fled and that Celegorm and his brother
were gone to Aglon. So now he sent an embassy to Aglon, since his
might was not great enough to fall upon all the seven brethren,
nor was his quarrel with others than Celegorm and Curufin. But
this embassy journeying in the woods met with the onslaught of
Carcharas. That great wolf had run in madness through all the
woods of the North, and death and devastation went with him.
Mablung alone escaped to bear the news of his coming to Thingol.
Of fate, or the magic of the Silmaril that he bore to his torment, he
was not stayed by the spells of Melian, but burst into the inviolate
woods of Doriath, and far and wide terror and destruction was
spread.

Even as the sorrows of Doriath were at their worst came Lúthien
and Beren and Huan back to Doriath. Then the heart of Thingol
was lightened, but he looked not with love upon Beren in whom he
saw the cause of all his woes. When he had learned how Beren had
escaped from Thû he was amazed, but he said: 'Mortal, what of
thy quest and of thy vow?' Then said Beren: 'Even now I have a
Silmaril in my hand.' 'Show it to me,' said Thingol. 'That I
cannot,' said Beren, 'for my hand is not here.' And all the tale he
told, and made clear the cause of the madness of Carcharas, and
Thingol's heart was softened by his brave words, and his for-
bearance, and the great love that he saw between his daughter and
this most valiant Man.

Now therefore did they plan the wolf-hunt of Carcharas. In that
hunt was Huan and Thingol and Mablung and Beleg and Beren
and no more. And here the sad tale of it must be short, for it is
elsewhere told more fully. Lúthien remained behind in foreboding, as they went forth; and well she might, for Carcharas was
slain, but Huan died in the same hour, and he died to save Beren.[14]
Yet Beren was hurt to the death, but lived to place the Silmaril in
the hands of Thingol, when Mablung had cut it from the belly of
the wolf. Then he spoke not again, until they had borne him with
Huan at his side back to the doors of Thingol's halls. There
beneath the beech, wherein before she had been imprisoned,

Lúthien met them, and kissed Beren ere his spirit departed to the halls of awaiting. So ended the long tale of Lúthien and Beren. But not yet was the lay of Leithian, release from bondage, told in full. For it has long been said that Lúthien failed and faded swiftly and vanished from the earth, though some songs say that Melian summoned Thorndor, and he bore her living unto Valinor. And she came to the halls of Mandos, and she sang to him a tale of moving love so fair that he was moved to pity, as never has befallen since. Beren he summoned, and thus, as Lúthien had sworn as she kissed him at the hour of death, they met beyond the western sea. And Mandos suffered them to depart, but he said that Lúthien should become mortal even as her lover, and should leave the earth once more in the manner of mortal women, and her beauty become but a memory of song. So it was, but it is said that in recompense Mandos gave to Beren and to Lúthien thereafter a long span of life and joy, and they wandered knowing thirst nor cold in the fair land of Broseliand, and no mortal Man thereafter spoke to Beren or his spouse.[15] Yet he came back into these tales when one more sad than his was done.

★

1   *Second > Third* (late change); see §9 note 19.
2   *Broseliand > Beleriand*, as previously.
3   *Mountains of Shadow > Mountains of Terror* (see III.170–1).
4   *Curufin* struck through and *Cele[gorm]* written above (late change).
5   *Great > Hither* (cf. §3 note 8).
6   This sentence, from *Thingol in wrath*, emended to: *Thingol was wroth, and would have gone to war with them as is later told.*
7   *Himling > Himring*, as in §9 note 21 (late change).
8   *Carcharas > Carcharoth* at all occurrences.
9   Added here: *Dire and dreadful was that beast; and songs have also named him Borosaith, Everhungry, and Anfauglin, Jaws of Thirst.*
10 Added here: *ere Angband's fall*
11 Late addition in the margin: *Thorndor bore them over Gondolin to Brethil.*
12 *save Maglor son of Fëanor, and Tinfang Warble > and Maglor son of Fëanor and Tinfang Gelion alone are named with him.*
13 Added here: *where long he made secret music in memory of Lúthien.*
14 Added here: *and he bade him farewell, and that was the third and last time Huan spoke.*

15   This sentence emended to: *and they wandered knowing neither thirst nor cold upon the confines of Geleidhian in fair Ossiriand, Land of Seven Streams, Gwerth-i-cuina, the Living Dead; and no mortal Man thereafter*, &c.

11

Now[1] it must be told that Maidros son of Fëanor perceived that Morgoth was not unassailable after the deeds of Huan and Lúthien and the breaking of the towers of Thû,[2] but that he would destroy them all one by one, if they did not form again a league and council. This was the Union of Maidros and wisely planned. The scattered Ilkorins and Men were gathered together, while the forces of Maidros made ever fiercer assaults from Himling,[3] and drove back the Orcs and took their spies. The smithies of Nogrod and Belegost were busy in those days making mail and sword and spear for many armies, and much of the wealth and jewelry of Elves and Men they got into their keeping in that time, though they went not themselves to war. 'For we do not know the rights of this quarrel,' they said, 'and we are friends of neither side – until it hath the mastery.' Thus great and splendid was the army of Maidros, but the oath and the curse did injury to his design.

All the hosts of Hithlum, Gnomes and Men, were ready to his summons, and Finweg[4] and Turgon and Huor and Húrin were their chiefs.[5] Orodreth would not march from Narog at the word of Maidros, because of the death of Felagund, and the deeds of Curufin and Celegorm.[6] Yet he suffered a small company of the bravest, who would not endure to be idle when the great war was afoot, to go North. Their leader was the young Flinding son of Fuilin, most daring of the scouts of Nargothrond; but they took the devices of the house of Finweg and went beneath his banners, and came never back, save one.[7]

From Doriath none came.[8] For Maidros and his brethren had before sent unto Doriath and reminded Thingol with exceedingly haughty words of their oath, and summoned him to yield up the Silmaril. This Melian counselled him to do, and maybe he would have done, but their words were overproud, and he thought how the jewel had been gained by the sorrows of Thingol's people,[9] and despite the crooked deeds of the sons of Fëanor; and greed[10] too, it may be, had some part in the heart of Thingol, as afterwards was shown. Wherefore he sent the messengers of Maidros back in scorn. Maidros said nought, for at that time he was beginning to ponder[11] the reunion of the forces of the Elves. But Celegorm and Curufin vowed aloud to slay Thingol or any of his folk they should ever see, by night or day, in war or peace.[12]

For this reason Thingol went not forth,[13] nor any out of Doriath save Mablung, and Beleg who obeyed no man.

Now came the day when Maidros sent forth his summons and the Dark-elves, save out of Doriath, marched to his banner, and Men from East and South. But Finweg and Turgon and the Men of Hithlum were gathered in the West upon the borders of the Thirsty Plain, waiting for the signal of the advancing standards from the East. It may be that Maidros delayed too long gathering his forces; certain it is that secret emissaries of Morgoth went among the camps, thrall-Gnomes or things in elfin form, and spread foreboding and thoughts of disunion. To Men they went most, and the fruit of their words was later seen.

Long the army waited in the West, and fear of treachery fell upon them, when Maidros came not, and the hot hearts of Finweg and Turgon became impatient.[14] They sent their heralds across the plain and their silver trumpets rang; and they summoned the hosts of Morgoth to come out. Then Morgoth sent forth a force, great and yet not too great. And Finweg was moved to attack from the woods at the feet of the Shadowy Mountains where he lay hid. But Húrin spoke against it.

Then Morgoth led forth one of the heralds of Finweg that he had wrongfully taken prisoner and slew him upon the plain, so that the watchers from afar might see – for far and clear do the eyes of the Gnomes behold things in bright air. Then the wrath of Finweg burst its bonds and his army leaped forth to sudden onslaught. This was as Morgoth designed, but it is said that he reckoned not the true number of their array, nor knew yet the measure of their valour, and well nigh his plan went ill. Ere his army could be succoured they were overwhelmed, and that day there was a greater slaughter of the servants of Morgoth than there yet had been, and the banners of Finweg were raised before the walls of Angband.

Flinding, it is said, and the men of Nargothrond burst even within the gates; and fear came on Morgoth on his throne. But they were slain or taken, for no help came.[15] By other secret gates Morgoth let issue forth the main host that he had kept in waiting, and Finweg and the Men of Hithlum were beaten back from the walls.

Then in the plain began the Battle of Unnumbered Tears,[16] of which no song or tale tells the full, for the voice of the teller is whelmed in lamentation. The host of the Elves was surrounded. Yet in that hour there marched up at last the banners of Maidros and his allies from the East. Even yet the Elves might have won the day, for the Orcs wavered. But as the vanguard of Maidros came upon the Orcs, Morgoth let loose his last forces, and all Angband was empty. There came wolves and serpents, and there came Balrogs like fire, and there came the first of all the dragons, the eldest of all the Worms of Greed. Glómund was his name and long had his terror been noised abroad, though he was not come to his full growth and evil, and seldom had he been seen.[17] Thus Morgoth strove to hinder the joining of the hosts of the Elves, but this the Eldar say he would not even so have achieved, had not the captains of Men in the hosts of Maidros turned and fled, and their number was very great. Treachery or cowardice or both was the cause of that grievous wrong. But worse is to tell, for the swart Men, whom Uldor the Accursed led, went over to the foe and fell upon Maidros' flank. From that day were Elves estranged from Men, unless it be from the children of the children of Hador.[18]

There Finweg fell in flame of swords, and a fire it is said burst from his helm when it was cloven; but he was beaten to the earth and his white banners were trodden under foot. Then the army of the West, sundered from Maidros, fell back as best it could win its way, step by step, towards the Shadowy Mountains or even the dreadful fringes of Taur-na-Fuin. But Húrin did not retreat,[19] and he held the rearguard, and all the Men of Hithlum and his brother Huor were there slain about him in a heap, so that not one came back with tidings to their home. The valiant stand of Húrin is still remembered by the Elves, for by it was Turgon enabled to cleave his way from the field and save part of his battle, and rescue his people from the hills, and escape southward to Sirion. Renowned in song is the axe of Húrin that slew a hundred Orcs, but the magic helm that Gumlin his sire bequeathed him he did not wear that day. Thereon was set in mockery the image of the head of Glómund, and oft it had gone into victory, so that the Men of Hithlum said: We have a dragon of more worth than theirs. It was Telchar's work, the great smith of Belegost, but it would not have availed Húrin on that field, for by the command of Morgoth he was taken alive, grasped by the hideous arms of the uncounted Orcs, till he was buried beneath them.

Maidros and the sons of Fëanor wrought great slaughter on Orc and Balrog and traitor Man that day, but the dragon they did not slay and the fire of his breath was the death of many. And they were driven in the end far away, and the Gorge of Aglon was filled with Orcs and the hill of Himling with the people of Morgoth. But the seven sons of Fëanor, though each was wounded, were not slain.[20]

Great was the triumph of Morgoth. The bodies of his enemies that were slain were piled in a mound like a great hill upon Dor-na-Fauglith, but there the grass came and grew green in that place alone in all the desert, and no Orc thereafter trod upon the earth beneath which the Gnomish swords crumbled into rust. The realm of Finweg was no more, the sons of Fëanor wandered in the East, fugitives in the Blue Mountains.[21] The armies of Angband ranged all the North. To Hithlum Morgoth sent Men who were his servants or afraid of him. South and East his Orcs went in plunder and ruin; well nigh all Broseliand[22] they overran. Doriath yet held where Thingol lived, and Nargothrond. But he heeded these not much as yet, maybe because he knew little of them. But one thing grievously marred his triumph, and great was his wrath when he thought of it. This was the escape of Turgon, and in no way could he learn whither that king had gone.[23]

Húrin was now brought before Morgoth and defied him. He was chained in torment. Afterward Morgoth remembering that treachery or the fear of it, and especially the treachery of Men, alone would work the ruin[24] of the Gnomes, came to Húrin and offered him honour and freedom and a wealth of jewels, if he would lead an army against Turgon, or even tell him whither that king had gone; for he knew that Húrin was close in the counsels of the sons of Fingolfin. But Húrin mocked him. Therefore Morgoth devised a cruel punishment. Upon the highest peak of Thangorodrim he set him chained upon a chair of stone, and he cursed him with a curse of never-sleeping sight like unto the Gods, but his kin and seed he cursed with a fate of sorrow and ill-chance, and bade Húrin sit there and watch the unfolding of it.

★

The first part of this section was heavily but hastily and roughly emended, on top of the careful alterations that belong to an earlier 'layer'. In three of the following notes (7, 14, 15) I give the final text of the passages that were most changed.

1   Scribbled in the margin is *Swarthy Men*, apparently with a mark of insertion to this point in the narrative.

2   *the towers of Thû > Sauron's tower* (late change).

3   This sentence emended to read: *The Dark-elves were summoned again from afar, and Men of the East were gathered together; and the forces of Maidros sallied forth from Himling* (late change). *Himling > Himring* subsequently.

4   *Finweg > Fingon* throughout, as previously.

5   Added here: *Yet less was the aid that Maidros had of Men than should have been, because of the wounding of Beren in the wood; and (Orodreth would not march, &c.)*

6   *Celegorm > Celegorn* at both occurrences (this change has not been made previously).

7   This paragraph, after the changes given in notes 4–6, was rewritten later (introducing the later story of the foundation of Gondolin), thus:

> All the hosts of Hithlum, Gnomes and Men, were ready to his summons; and Fingon and Huor and Húrin were their chiefs. And Turgon himself deeming that haply the hour of deliverance was at hand came forth himself unlooked for, and he brought a great army, and they encamped before the West Pass in sight of the walls of Hithlum, and there was joy among the people of Fingon his brother. [*An addition here was struck out, no doubt at the time of writing, and replaced by a different statement about the folk of Haleth below*: The folk of Haleth made ready in the forest of Brethil.] Yet less was the aid that Maidros had of Men than should have been, because of the wounding of Beren in the wood; for the folk of Haleth abode in the forest, and few came to war. Orodreth, moreover, would not march from Narog at the word of Maidros, because of the death of Felagund, and the deeds of Curufin and Celegorn. Yet he suffered a small company of the bravest, who would not endure to be idle when great war was afoot, to go North. Their leader was Gwindor son of Guilin, a very valiant prince; but they took the devices of the house of Fingon and went beneath his banners, and came never back, save one.

8   *From Doriath none came > From Doriath too came scanty aid.*

9   Added here: *and the anguish of Lúthien*

10 *greed > covetice*

11 *beginning to ponder > already beginning to devise* (late change).

12 This sentence changed to read: *vowed aloud to slay Thingol, and destroy his folk, if they came victorious from war, and the jewel were not yielded of free-will.*

13 *Thingol went not forth* > *Thingol fortified his realm, and went not forth*

14 From the beginning of the preceding paragraph (*Now came the day* . . .) the text was extensively rewritten in the later 'layer' of change:

> At length having gathered at last all the strength that he might Maidros appointed a day, and sent word to Fingon and Turgon. Now for a while the Gnomes had victory, and the Orcs were driven out of Beleriand, and hope was renewed; but Morgoth was aware of all that was done, and he took counsel against their uprising, and he sent forth his spies and emissaries among Elves and Men, but especially did these come unto the Swarthy Men, and to the sons of Ulfang. Upon the East under the banner of Maidros were all the folk of the sons of Fëanor, and they were many; and the Dark-elves coming from the South were with him, and the battalions of the Easterlings, with the sons of Bor and Ulfang. But Fingon and Turgon and the Men of Hithlum and such as came from the Falas and from Nargothrond were gathered ready in the West upon the borders of the Thirsty Plain, waiting under the banner of Fingon for the signal of the advancing standards from the East. But Maidros was delayed upon the road by the machinations of Uldor the Accursed son of Ulfang, and ever the secret emissaries of Morgoth went among the camps, thrall-Gnomes or things in elvish form, and spread foreboding and thoughts of treason.
>
> Long the army waited in the West, and fear of treachery grew in their thought, when Maidros came not. Then the hot hearts of Fingon and Turgon became impatient.

15 This passage, from *Flinding, it is said*, was changed by late emendation to read:

> Gwindor son of Guilin, it is said, and the men of Nargothrond were in the forefront of the battle and burst within the gates; and they slew the Orcs in the very halls of Morgoth, and fear came on Morgoth on his throne. But at the last Gwindor and his men were all slain or taken, for no help came to them.

16 Added here: *Nirnaith Arnediad* (late change).

17 Added here: *since the second battle of the North*.

18 Added here: *and of Bëor* (late change).

19 *But Húrin did not retreat* > *But there Húrin turned to bay*

20 The following passage was added here:

> But their arms were scattered, and their folk minished and dispersed and their league broken; and they took to a wild and woodland life, beneath the feet of Eryd-luin [*later* > Ered-luin],

mingling with the Dark-elves, and forgetting their power and glory of old.

21 *wandered in the East, fugitives in the Blue Mountains* >
    wandered as leaves before the wind.
22 *Broseliand* > *Beleriand*, as previously.
23 The following passage was added here:

> and his anger was the greater, for it is said that of all the Gnomes he feared and hated most the house and people of Fingolfin, who had harkened never to his lies and blandishments, and came into the North, as has been told, only out of loyalty to their kin.

24 *the ruin* > *the final ruin*

12

Morwen[1] the wife of Húrin was left in Hithlum and with her were but two old men too old for war, and maidens and young boys. One of these was Húrin's child, Túrin son of Húrin renowned in song. But Morwen was with child once more, and so she stayed and mourned in Hithlum, and went not like Rían wife of Huor to seek for tidings of her lord. The Men[2] of the faithful race were slain, and Morgoth drove thither in their stead those who had betrayed the Elves, and he penned them behind the Shadowy Mountains, and slew them if they wandered to Broseliand[3] or beyond; and such was all they got of the love and rewards he had promised them. Yet their hearts were turned to evil, and little love they showed to the women and children of the faithful who had been slain, and most of them they enslaved. Great was the courage and majesty of Morwen, and many were afraid of her, and whispered that she had learned black magics of the Gnomes.[4] But she was poor and well nigh alone, and was succoured in secret by her kinswoman Airin whom Brodda, one of the incoming Men, and mighty among them, had taken to wife. Wherefore it came into her heart to send Túrin, who was then seven years of age, to Thingol, that he might not grow up a churl or servant; for Húrin and Beren had been friends of old. The fate of Túrin is told in the 'Children of Húrin', and it need not in full be told here, though it is wound with the fates of the Silmarils and the Elves. It is called the Tale of Grief, for it is very sorrowful, and in it are seen the worst of the deeds of Morgoth Bauglir.

Túrin grew up in Thingol's court, but after a while as Morgoth's power grew news came no more from Hithlum, for it was a long and perilous road, and he heard no more of Nienor his sister who was born after he left his home, nor of Morwen his mother; and his heart was dark and heavy. He was often in battle on the borders of the realm where Beleg the Bowman was his friend, and he came little to the court, and wild and unkempt was his hair and his attire, though sweet his voice and sad his song. On a time at the table of the king he was taunted by a foolish Elf, Orgof by name, with his rough garb and strange looks. And Orgof in jest slighted the maidens and wives of the Men of Hithlum. But Túrin unwitting of his growing strength slew Orgof with a drinking vessel at the king's board.

He fled then the court, and thinking himself an outlaw took to war against all, Elves, Men, or Orcs, that crossed the path of the desperate band he gathered upon the borders of the kingdom, hunted Men and Ilkorins and Gnomes. One day, when he was not among them, his men captured Beleg the Bowman and tied him to a tree, and would have slain him; but Túrin returning was smitten with remorse, and released Beleg and forswore war or plunder against all save the Orcs. From Beleg he learned that Thingol had pardoned his deed the day that it was done. Still he went not back to the Thousand Caves; but the deeds that were done on the marches of Doriath by Beleg and Túrin were noised in Thingol's halls, and in Angband they were known.

Now one of Túrin's band was Blodrin son of Ban, a Gnome,[5] but he had lived long with the Dwarves and was of evil heart and joined Túrin for the love of plunder. He loved little the new life in which wounds were more plentiful than booty. In the end he betrayed the hiding-places of Túrin[6] to the Orcs, and the camp of Túrin was surprised. Blodrin was slain by a chance arrow of his evil allies in the gloom, but Túrin was taken alive, as Húrin had been, by the command of Morgoth. For Morgoth began to fear that in Doriath behind the mazes of Melian, where his deeds were hidden from him, save by report,[7] Túrin would cheat the doom that he had devised. Beleg was left for dead beneath a heap of slain. There he was found by Thingol's messengers who came to summon them to a feast in the Thousand Caves. Taken back thither he was healed by Melian, and set off alone to track Túrin. Beleg was the most marvellous of all woodsmen that have ever been, and his skill was little less than Huan in the following of a trail, though he followed by eye and cunning not by scent. Nonetheless he was bewildered in the mazes of Deadly Nightshade and wandered there in despair, until he saw the lamp of Flinding

Fuilin's son,[8] who had escaped from the mines of Morgoth, a bent and timid shadow of his former shape and mood. From Flinding he learned news of the Orc-band that had captured Túrin; and it had delayed long in the lands plundering East among Men, but was now come in great haste, owing to the angry message of Morgoth, and was passing along the Orc-road through Taur-na-Fuin itself.

Near the issuing of this road, where it reaches the edge of the forest upon the face of the steep[9] slopes that lie to the south of the Thirsty Plain, Flinding and Beleg lay and watched the Orcs go by. When the Orcs left the forest and went far down the slopes to camp in a bare dale in sight of Thangorodrim, Beleg and his companion followed them. At night Beleg shot the wolf-sentinels of the Orc-camp, and stole with Flinding into its midst. With the greatest difficulty and direst peril they lifted Túrin, senseless in a sleep of utter weariness, and brought him out of the camp and laid him in a dell of thick thorn trees high up on the hillside. In striking[10] off the bonds Beleg pricked Túrin's foot; and he, roused in sudden fear and anger, for the Orcs had often tormented him, found himself free. Then in his madness he seized Beleg's sword, and slew his friend thinking him a foe. The covering of Flinding's lamp fell off at that moment, and Túrin saw Beleg's face; and his madness left him and he was turned as to stone.

The Orcs, awakened by his cries as he leaped on Beleg, discovered the escape of Túrin, but were scattered by a terrible storm of thunder and a deluge of rain. In the morning Flinding saw them marching away over the steaming sands of Dor-na-Fauglith. But through all the storm Túrin sat without movement; and scarcely could he be roused to help in the burying of Beleg and his bow in the dell of thorns. Flinding afterwards led him, dazed and unwitting, towards safety; and his mind was healed when he drank of the spring of Narog by Ivrin's lake. For his frozen tears were loosed, and he wept, and after his weeping made a song for Beleg, the Bowman's Friendship, which became a battle song of the foes of Morgoth.

★

1   Written in the margin against the opening of this section is *Take in Helm of Gumlin from page 34*. Page 34 in the typescript contains the passage concerning the Helm in §11, p. 118.

2   *The Men > Most of the Men*

3   *Broseliand > Beleriand*, as previously.
4   *whispered that she had learned black magics from the Gnomes >
    whispered that she was a witch* (late change).
5   *a Gnome > a Gnome of Fëanor's house*
6   *the hiding-places of Túrin > the hiding-places of Túrin beyond the
    eaves of Doriath*
7   *save by report > or upon its borders whence came but uncertain
    report*
8   *Flinding Fuilin's son > Gwindor son of Guilin*, and subse-
    quently *Flinding > Gwindor* (late changes; see §11 note 15).
9   *steep > long*
10 Added after *high up on the hillside*:

> Then Beleg drew his renowned sword, made of iron that fell from
> heaven as a blazing star, and it would cut all earth-dolven iron.
> But fate was that day more strong, for in striking, &c.

13

Flinding[1] led Túrin in the end to Nargothrond. There in days
long gone[2] Flinding had loved Finduilas daughter of Orodreth,
and he called her Failivrin, which is the gleam on the waters of the
fair lake whence Narog comes. But her heart was turned against
her will to Túrin, and his to her. Out of loyalty[3] he fought against
his love and Finduilas grew wan and pale, but Flinding perceiving
their hearts grew bitter.

Túrin grew great and mighty in Nargothrond, but he loved not
their secret manner of fighting and ambush, and began to long for
brave strokes and battle in the open. Then he caused to be forged
anew the sword of Beleg, and the craftsmen of Narog made thereof
a black blade with shining edges of pale fire; from which sword he
became known among them as Mormaglir.[4]

With this sword he thought to avenge the death of Beleg the
Bowman, and with it he did many mighty deeds; so that the fame
of Mormaglir, the Black-sword of Nargothrond, came even unto
Doriath and to the ears of Thingol, but the name of Túrin was not
heard. And long victory dwelt with Mormaglir and the host of the
Gnomes of Nargothrond who followed him; and their realm
reached even to the sources of Narog, and from the western sea to
the marches of Doriath; and there was a stay in the onset of
Morgoth.

In this time of respite and hope Morwen arose, and leaving her
goods in the care of Brodda, who had to wife[5] her kinswoman

Airin, she took with her Nienor her daughter, and adventured the long journey to Thingol's halls. There did new grief await her, for she learnt of the loss and vanishing of Túrin; and even as she dwelt a while as the guest of Thingol, in sorrow and in doubt, there came to Doriath the tidings of the fall of Nargothrond; whereat all folk wept.

Biding his hour Morgoth had loosed upon the folk of Narog at unawares a great army that he had long prepared, and with the host came that father of the dragons, Glómund, who wrought ruin in the Battle of Unnumbered Tears. The might of Narog was overwhelmed upon the Guarded Plain, north of Nargothrond; and there fell Flinding son of Fuilin,[6] mortally wounded, and dying he refused the succour of Túrin, reproaching him, and bidding him, if he would amend the evil he had wrought his friend, to hasten back to Nargothrond to rescue even with his life, if he could, Finduilas whom they loved, or to slay her else.

But the Orc-host and the mighty dragon came upon Nargothrond before Túrin could put it in defence, and they overthrew Orodreth and all his remaining folk, and the great halls beneath the earth were sacked and plundered, and all the women and maidens of the folk of Narog were herded as slaves and taken into Morgoth's thraldom. Túrin only they could not overcome, and the Orcs fell back before him in terror and amaze, and he stood alone. Thus ever did Morgoth achieve the downfall of men by their own deeds; for but little would men have accounted the woe of Túrin had he fallen in brave defence before the mighty doors of Nargothrond.

Fire was in the eyes of Túrin, and the edges of his sword shone as with flame, and he strode to battle even with Glómund, alone and unafraid. But it was not his fate that day to rid the world of that creeping evil; for he fell under the binding spell of the lidless eyes of Glómund, and he was halted moveless; but Glómund[7] taunted him, calling him deserter of his kin, friend-slayer, and love-thief. And the dragon offered him his freedom either to follow seeking to rescue his 'stolen love' Finduilas, or to do his duty and go to the rescue of his mother and sister, who were living in great misery in Hithlum (as he said and lied) and nigh to death. But he must swear to abandon one or the other.

Then Túrin in anguish and in doubt forsook Finduilas against his heart, and against his last word to Flinding[8] (which if he had obeyed, his uttermost fate had not befallen him), and believing the words of the serpent whose spell was upon him, he left the realm of Narog and went to Hithlum. And it is sung that he stopped in vain his ears to keep out the echo of the cries of Finduilas calling on his name as she was borne away; and that sound hunted him through the woods. But Glómund, when Túrin had gone, crept back to Nargothrond and gathered unto himself the greater part of its wealth of gold and gems, and he lay thereon in its deepest hall, and desolation was about him.

It is said that Túrin came at length to Hithlum, and he found not his mother or his kin; for their hall was empty and their land despoiled, and Brodda had added their goods unto his own. In his wooden hall at his own board Túrin slew Brodda; and fought his way from the house, but must needs afterward flee from Hithlum.⁹

There was a dwelling of free Men in the wood, the remnant of the people of Haleth, son of Hador and brother of Gumlin the grandsire of Túrin. They were the last of the Men that were Elf-friends to linger in Beleriand,¹⁰ neither subdued by Morgoth, nor penned in Hithlum beyond the Shadowy Mountains. They were small in numbers, but bold, and their houses were in the green woods about the River Taiglin that enters the land of Doriath ere it joins with the great waters of Sirion, and maybe some magic of Melian had yet protected them. Down from the sources of Taiglin that issues from the Shadowy Mountains Túrin came seeking for the trail of the Orcs that had plundered Nargothrond and must pass that water on their road back to the realm of Morgoth.

Thus he came upon the woodmen and learned tidings of Finduilas; and then he thought that he had tasted his fill of woe, yet it was not so. For the Orcs had marched nigh to the borders of the woodmen, and the woodmen had ambushed them, and come near to rescuing their captives. But few had they won away, for the Orc-guards had slain most of them cruelly; and among them Finduilas had been pierced with spears,¹¹ as those few who had been saved told him amid their tears. So perished the last of the race of Finrod fairest of Elven-kings, and vanished from the world of Men.

Grim was the heart of Túrin and all the deeds and days of his life seemed vile; yet the courage of the race of Hador was as a core of unbent steel. There Túrin vowed to renounce his past, his kin, his name, and all that had been his, save hatred of Morgoth; and he took a new name, Turambar (Turumarth¹² in the forms of Gnomish speech), which is Conqueror of Fate; and the woodmen gathered to him, and he became their lord, and ruled a while in peace.

Tidings came now more clear to Doriath of the fall of Orodreth and the destruction of all the folk of Narog, though fugitives no more than could be counted on the hands came ever into safety there, and uncertain was their report. Yet thus was it known to Thingol and to Morwen that Mormaglir was Túrin; and yet too late; for some said that he had escaped and fled,[13] and some told that he had been turned to stone by the dreadful eyes of Glómund and lived still enthralled in Nargothrond.

At last Thingol yielded so far to the tears and entreaties of Morwen that he sent forth a company of Elves toward Nargothrond to explore the truth. With them rode Morwen, for she might not be restrained; but Nienor was bidden to remain behind. Yet the fearlessness of her house was hers, and in evil hour, for love and care of her mother, she disguised herself as one of the folk of Thingol, and went with that ill-fated riding.

They viewed Narog afar from the summit of the tree-clad Hill of Spies to the east of the Guarded Plain, and thence they rode down greatly daring towards the banks of Narog. Morwen remained upon the hill with scanty guard and watched them from afar. Now in the days of victory when the folk of Narog had gone forth once more to open war, a bridge had been built across the river before the doors of the hidden city (and this had proved their undoing). Towards this bridge the Elves of Doriath now came, but Glómund was aware of their coming, and he issued forth on a sudden and lay into the stream, and a vast and hissing vapour arose and engulfed them. This Morwen saw from the hill-top, and her guards would not stay longer but fled back to Doriath taking her with them.

In that mist the Elves were overwhelmed, and their horses were stricken with panic, and they fled hither and thither and could not find their fellows; and the most part returned never back to Doriath. But when the mist cleared Nienor found that her wandering had taken her only back unto the banks of Narog, and before her lay Glómund, and his eye was upon her. Dreadful was his eye, like to the eye of Morgoth his master who had made him; and as she gazed perforce upon it a spell of darkness and utter forgetfulness fell upon her mind. Thence she wandered witless in the woods, as a wild creature without speech or thought.

When her madness left her, she was far from the borders of Nargothrond, she knew not where; and she remembered not her name or home. Thus was she found by a band of Orcs and pursued as a beast of the woods; but she was saved by fate. For a party of the woodmen of Turambar in whose land they were fell upon the Orcs and slew them; and Turambar himself placed her upon his horse and bore her to the woodmen's pleasant homes. He named her Níniel, Tear-maiden, for he had first seen her weeping. There is a narrow gorge and a high and foaming fall in the river Taiglin, that the woodmen called the Falls of Silver-bowl;[14] and this fair place they passed as they rode home, and would camp there as they were wont; but Níniel would not stay, for a chill and a mortal shivering took her in that place.

Yet afterwards she found some peace in the dwellings of the woodmen, who treated her with kindliness and honour. There she won the love of Brandir, son of Handir, son of Haleth; but he was lame of foot, being wounded by an Orc-arrow as a child, and uncomely and of less might than many, wherefore he had yielded the rule to Túrin at the choice of the woodfolk. He was gentle of heart and wise of thought, and great was his love, and he was ever true to Turambar; yet bitter was his soul when he might not win the love of Níniel. For Níniel would not be parted ever from the side of Turambar, and great love was ever between those twain from the hour of their first meeting. Thus Túrin Turambar thinking to cast off his ancient woes was wed to Nienor Níniel, and fair was the feast in the woods of Taiglin.

Now the power and malice of Glómund waxed apace and well-nigh all the realm of Nargothrond of old he laid waste, both west of Narog and beyond it to the east; and he gathered Orcs to him and ruled as a dragon-king; and there were battles on the marches of the woodmen's land, and the Orcs fled. Wherefore learning of their dwelling, Glómund issued from Nargothrond, and came crawling, filled with fire, over the lands and to the borders of the woods of Taiglin, leaving behind him a trail of burning. But Turambar pondered how the horror could be warded from his people; and he marched forth with his men, and Níniel rode with them, her heart foreboding ill, until they could descry afar the blasted track of the dragon and the smoking place where he now lay, west of the deep-cloven bed of Taiglin. Between them lay the steep ravine of the river, whose waters had in that spot fallen, but a little way before, over the foaming fall of Silver-bowl.

There Turambar thought of a desperate counsel, for he knew but too well the might and malice of Glómund. He resolved to lie in wait in the ravine over which the dragon must pass, if he would reach their land. Six of his boldest men begged to come with him; and at evening they climbed up the further side of the ravine and clung in hiding among the bushes at its brink. In the night the great dragon moved nigh to the river, and the rumour of his approach filled them with fear and loathing. Indeed in the morning all had slunk away leaving Turambar only.

The next evening, when Turambar was now nearly spent, Glómund began the passage of the ravine, and his huge form passed over Turambar's head. There Turambar transfixed Glómund with Gurtholfin, Wand-of-Death, his black sword; and Glómund coiled back in anguish and lay dying nigh to the river's brink and came not into the woodmen's land. But he wrested the sword from Turambar's grasp in his throes, and Turambar came now forth from hiding, and placed his foot upon Glómund and in exultation drew out his sword. Greedy was that blade and very fast in the wound, and as Turambar wrenched it with all his might, the venom of the dragon spouted on his hand and in the anguish of its burning he fell in a swoon.

So it was that the watchers from afar perceived that Glómund had been slain, yet Turambar did not return. By the light of the moon Níniel went forth without a word to seek him, and ere she had long gone Brandir missed her and followed after. But Níniel found Turambar lying as one dead beside the body of Glómund. There as she wept beside Turambar and sought to tend him, Glómund opened his eyes for the last time, and spake, telling her the true name of Turambar; and thereafter he died, and with his death the spell of forgetfulness was lifted from Níniel, and she remembered her kin. Filled with horror and anguish, for she was with child, she fled and cast herself over the heights of Silver-bowl, and none ever found her body. Her last lament ere she cast herself away was heard only by Brandir; and his back was bowed and his head turned grey in that night.

In the morn Túrin awoke and found that one had tended his hand. Though it pained him grievously, he returned in triumph filled with joy for the death of Glómund, his ancient foe; and he asked for Níniel, but none dared tell him, save Brandir. And Brandir distraught with grief reproached him; wherefore Túrin slew him, and taking Gurtholfin red with blood bade it slay its master; and the sword answered that his blood was as sweet as any other, and it pierced him to the heart as he fell upon it.

Túrin they buried nigh to the edge of Silver-bowl, and his name Túrin Turambar was carved there upon a rock. Beneath was written Nienor Níniel. Men changed the name of that place thereafter to Nen-Girith, the Shuddering Water.

So ended the tale of Túrin the unhappy; and it has ever been held the worst of the works of Morgoth in the ancient world. Some have said that Morwen, wandering woefully from Thingol's halls, when she found Nienor not there on her return, came on a time to that stone and read it, and there died.

★

1 *Flinding* > *Gwindor* at all occurrences, as previously (late changes).
2 *in days long gone* > *in days before* (late change).
3 *Out of loyalty* > *Out of loyalty to Gwindor* (late change).
4 Added here: *but the sword he named Gurtholfin, Wand-of-Death.*
5 The words *Brodda, who had to wife* struck through (late change), so the sentence reads *leaving her goods in the care of her kinswoman Airin*
6 *Flinding son of Fuilin* > *Gwindor son of Guilin* (late change).
7 This passage, from *and he was halted moveless*, was extended:

   and long time he stood there as one graven of stone silent before the dragon, until they two alone were left before the doors of Nargothrond. Then Glómund taunted him, &c.

8 *and against his last word to Flinding* struck through.
9 This sentence rewritten to read:

   Then Túrin knew the lie of Glómund, and in his anguish and in his wrath for the evil that had been done to his mother he slew Brodda at his own board and fought his way from the house; and in the night, a hunted man, he fled from Hithlum.

10 *Belèriand* here as originally typed, not emended from *Broseliand*; and subsequently.
11 *and among them Finduilas had been pierced* > *and Finduilas they fastened to a tree and pierced*
12 *Turumarth* > *Turamarth*
13 This passage, from *came ever into safety there*, was altered thus:

   . . . came ever into safety in Doriath. Thus was it known to Thingol and to Morwen that Mormaglir was Túrin himself; and yet too late they learned this; for some said that he was slain, and some told, &c.

14 *Falls of Silver-bowl* > *Falls of Celebros, Foam-silver*; and subsequently *Silver-bowl* > *Celebros*.

14

But after the death of Túrin and Nienor, Húrin was released by Morgoth, for Morgoth thought still to use him; and he accused Thingol of faint heart and ungentleness, saying that only thus had his purpose been brought about; and Húrin distraught, wandering bowed with grief, pondered these words, and was embittered by them, for such is the way of the lies of Morgoth.

Húrin gathered therefore a few outlaws of the woods unto him, and they came to Nargothrond, which as yet none, Orc, Elf, or Man, had dared to plunder, for dread of the spirit of Glómund and his very memory. But one Mîm the Dwarf they found there. This is the first coming of the Dwarves into these tales[1] of the ancient world; and it is said that Dwarves first spread west from Erydluin,[2] the Blue Mountains, into Beleriand after the Battle of Unnumbered Tears. Now Mîm had found the halls and treasure of Nargothrond unguarded; and he took possession of them, and sat there in joy fingering the gold and gems, and letting them run ever through his hands; and he bound them to himself with many spells. But the folk of Mîm were few, and the outlaws filled with the lust of the treasure slew them, though Húrin would have stayed them; and at his death Mîm cursed the gold.

And the curse came upon the possessors in this wise. Each one of Húrin's company died or was slain in quarrels upon the road; but Húrin went unto Thingol and sought his aid, and the folk of Thingol bore the treasure to the Thousand Caves. Then Húrin bade cast it all at the feet of Thingol, and he reproached the Elf-king with wild and bitter words. 'Receive thou,' said he, 'thy fee for thy fair keeping of my wife and kin.'

Yet Thingol would not take the hoard, and long he bore with Húrin; but Húrin scorned him, and wandered forth in quest of Morwen his wife, but it is not said that he found her ever upon the earth; and some have said that he cast himself at last into the western sea, and so ended the mightiest of the warriors of mortal Men.

Then the enchantment of the accursed dragon gold began to fall even upon the king of Doriath, and long he sat and gazed upon it, and the seed of the love of gold that was in his heart was waked to growth. Wherefore he summoned the greatest of all craftsmen that now were in the western world, since Nargothrond was no more (and Gondolin was not known), the Dwarves of Nogrod and Belegost, that they might fashion the gold and silver and the gems (for much was yet unwrought) into countless vessels and fair things; and a marvellous necklace of great beauty they should make, whereon to hang the Silmaril.

But the Dwarves coming were stricken at once with the lust and desire of the treasure, and they plotted treachery. They said one to another: 'Is not this wealth as much the right of the Dwarves as of the elvish king, and was it not wrested evilly from Mîm?' Yet also they lusted for the Silmaril.

And Thingol, falling deeper into the thraldom of the spell, for his part scanted his promised reward for their labour; and bitter words grew between them, and there was battle in Thingol's halls. There many Elves and Dwarves were slain, and the howe wherein they were laid in Doriath was named Cûm-nan-Arasaith, the Mound of Avarice. But the remainder of the Dwarves were driven forth without reward or fee.

Therefore gathering new forces in Nogrod and in Belegost they returned at length, and aided by the treachery of certain Elves on whom the lust of the accursed treasure had fallen they passed into Doriath secretly. There they surprised Thingol upon a hunt with but small company of arms; and Thingol was slain, and the fortress of the Thousand Caves taken at unawares and plundered; and so was brought well nigh to ruin the glory of Doriath, and but one stronghold of the Elves against Morgoth now remained, and their twilight was nigh at hand.

Queen Melian the Dwarves could not seize or harm, and she went forth to seek Beren and Lúthien. Now the Dwarf-road to Nogrod and Belegost in the Blue Mountains passed through East Beleriand and the woods about the River Ascar,[3] where aforetime were the hunting grounds of Damrod and Díriel, sons of Fëanor. To the south of those lands between the river and the mountains lay the land of Assariad, and there[4] lived and wandered still in peace and bliss Beren and Lúthien, in that time of respite which Lúthien had won, ere both should die; and their folk were the Green Elves of the South, who were not of the Elves of Côr,[5] nor of Doriath, though many had fought at the Battle of Unnumbered Tears. But Beren went no more to war, and his land was filled with loveliness and a wealth of flowers; and while Beren was and Lúthien remained Men called it oft Cuilwarthien,[6] the Land of the Dead that Live.

To the north of that region is a ford across the river Ascar, near to its joining with Duilwen[7] that falls in torrents from the mountains; and that ford is named Sarn-athra,[8] the Ford of Stones. This ford the Dwarves must pass ere they reached their homes;[9] and there Beren fought his last fight, warned of their approach by Melian. In that battle the Green Elves took the Dwarves unawares as they were in the midst of their passage, laden with their plunder; and the Dwarvish chiefs were slain, and well nigh all their host. But Beren took the Nauglafring,[10] the Necklace of the Dwarves, whereon was hung the Silmaril; and it is said and sung that Lúthien wearing that necklace and that immortal jewel on her white breast was the vision of greatest beauty and glory that has ever been seen outside the realms of Valinor, and that for a while the Land of the Dead that Live became like a vision of the land of the Gods, and no places have been since so fair, so fruitful, or so filled with light.

Yet Melian warned them ever of the curse that lay upon the treasure and upon the Silmaril. The treasure they had drowned indeed in the river Ascar, and named it anew Rathlorion,[11] Golden-Bed, yet the Silmaril they retained. And in time the brief hour of the loveliness of the land of Rathlorion departed. For Lúthien faded as Mandos had spoken, even as the Elves of later days faded, when Men waxed strong and usurped the goodness of the earth; and she vanished from the world; and Beren died, and none know where their meeting shall be again.[12]

Thereafter was Dior Thingol's heir, child of Beren and Lúthien, king in the woods, most fair of all the children of the world, for his race was threefold: of the fairest and goodliest of Men, and of the Elves, and of the spirits divine of Valinor; yet it shielded him not from the fate of the oath of the sons of Fëanor. For Dior went back to Doriath and for a time a part of its ancient glory was raised anew, though Melian no longer dwelt in that place, and she departed to the land of the Gods beyond the western sea, to muse on her sorrows in the gardens whence she came.

But Dior wore the Silmaril upon his breast and the fame of that jewel went far and wide; and the deathless oath was waked once more from sleep. The sons of Fëanor, when he would not yield the jewel unto them, came[13] upon him with all their host; and so befell the second slaying of Elf by Elf, and the most grievous. There fell Celegorm and Curufin and dark Cranthir, but Dior was slain,[14] and Doriath was destroyed and never rose again.

Yet the sons of Fëanor gained not the Silmaril; for faithful servants fled before them and took with them Elwing the daughter of Dior, and she escaped, and they bore with them the Nauglafring, and came in time to the mouth of the river Sirion by the sea.

★

1   *This is the first coming of the Dwarves into these tales* > *Now for the first time did the Dwarves take part in these tales*

2   *Eryd-luin* > *Ered-luin* (late change).

3   *Ascar* > *Flend* > *Gelion* at the first two occurrences, but left unchanged at the third.

4   This sentence emended to read: *To the south of those lands between the river Flend* [> *Gelion*] *and the mountains lay the land of Ossiriand, watered by seven streams, Flend* [> *Gelion*]*, Ascar, Thalos, Loeglin* [> *Legolin*]*, Brilthor, Duilwen, Adurant. There lived, &c.*

    (The rivers were first written *Flend, Ascar, Thalos, Loeglin, Brilthor, Adurant. Duilwen* was then added between *Thalos* and *Loeglin*; then *Legolin* replaced *Loeglin* and *Duilwen* was moved to stand between *Brilthor* and *Adurant*.)

5   *Côr* > *Kôr*, as previously.

6   *Men called it oft Cuilwarthien* > *Elves called it oft Gwerth-i-cuina* (see §10 note 15).

7   *Duilwen* > *Ascar* (see p. 232, entry *Dwarf-road*).

8   *Sarn-athra* > *Sarn-athrad*.

9   *ere they reached their homes* > *ere they reached the mountain passes that led unto their homes*

10   *Nauglafring* > *Nauglamír* at both occurrences (late changes).

11   *Rathlorion* > *Rathloriel* at both occurrences (late changes).

12   Added here:

    Yet it hath been sung that Lúthien alone of Elves hath been numbered among our race, and goeth whither we go to a fate beyond the world.

    A large pencilled X is made in the margin against the sentence in the typescript beginning *For Lúthien faded* . . .; in my father's manuscripts this always implies that there is some misstatement in the text that requires revision.

13   The words *The sons of Fëanor, when* were struck out, and the sentence enlarged thus:

    For while Lúthien wore that peerless gem no Elf would dare assail her, and not even Maidros dared ponder such a thought. But now hearing of the renewal of Doriath and Dior's pride, the seven gathered again from wandering; and they sent unto Dior to claim their own. But he would not yield the jewel unto them; and they came, &c.

14   Added here: *and his young sons Eldûn and Elrûn* (late change).

15

[For much of this section there exist two typescript texts, the later of the two being longer. Subsequently there is a lot more of such replacement, and I shall call the earlier 'Q I', the later 'Q II'. Q II is given after the notes to Q I.]

Here must be told of Gondolin. The great river Sirion, mightiest in elvish song, flowed through all the land of Beleriand and its course was south-west; and at its mouth was a great delta and its lower course ran through green and fertile lands, little peopled save by birds and beasts. Yet the Orcs came seldom there, for it was far from the northern woods and fells, and the power of Ulmo waxed ever in that water, as it drew nigh to the sea; for the mouths of that river were in the western sea, whose uttermost borders are the shores of Valinor.

Turgon, Fingolfin's son, had a sister, Isfin the white-handed. She was lost in Taur-na-Fuin after the Battle of Unnumbered Tears. There she was captured by the Dark-elf Eöl, and it is said that he was of gloomy mood, and had deserted the hosts ere the battle; yet he had not fought on Morgoth's side. But Isfin he took to wife, and their son was Meglin.

Now the people of Turgon escaping from the battle, aided by the prowess of Húrin, as has been told, escaped from the knowledge of Morgoth and vanished from all men's eyes; and Ulmo alone knew whither they had gone. Their scouts climbing the heights had come upon a secret place in the mountains: a broad valley[1] entirely circled by the hills, ringed about it in a fence unbroken, but falling ever lower as they came towards the middle. In the midmost of this marvellous ring was a wide land and a green plain, wherein was no hill, save for a single rocky height. This stood up dark upon the plain, not right at its centre, but nearest to that part of the outer wall that marched close to the borders of Sirion. Highest were the Encircling Mountains towards the North and the threat of Angband, and on their outer slopes to East and North began the shadow of dread Taur-na-Fuin; but they were crowned with the cairn of Fingolfin, and no evil came that way, as yet.

In this valley the Gnomes took refuge,[2] and spells of hiding and enchantment were set on all the hills about, that foes and spies might never find it. In this Turgon had the aid of the messages of Ulmo, that came now up the river Sirion; for his voice is to be heard in many waters, and some of the Gnomes had yet the lore to harken. In those days Ulmo was filled with pity for the exiled Elves in their need, and in the ruin that had now almost overwhelmed them. He foretold that the fortress of Gondolin should stand longest of all the refuges of the Elves against the might of Morgoth,[3] and like Doriath never be overthrown save by treachery from within. Because of his protecting might the spells of concealment were strongest in those parts nearest to Sirion, though there the Encircling Mountains were at their lowest. There the Gnomes dug a great winding tunnel under the roots of the hills, and its issue was in the steep side, tree-clad and dark, of a gorge through which Sirion ran, at that point still a young stream flowing strongly through the narrow vale between the shoulders of the Encircling Mountains and the Shadowy Mountains, in whose northern heights it took its rise.

The outer entrance of that passage, which they made at first to be a way of secret issue for themselves and for their scouts and spies, and for a way of return to safety for fugitives, was guarded by their magic and the power of Ulmo,[4] and no evil thing found it; yet its inner gate which looked upon the vale of Gondolin was guarded unceasingly by the Gnomes.[5]

Thorndor King of Eagles removed his eyries from Thangorodrim to the northward heights of the Encircling Mountains, and there he kept watch, sitting upon the cairn of King Fingolfin. But on the rocky hill amid the vale, Amon Gwareth, the Hill of Watch, whose sides they polished to the smoothness of glass, and whose top they levelled, the Gnomes built the great city of Gondolin with gates of steel, whose fame and glory is greatest of all dwellings of the Elves in the Outer Lands. The plain all about they levelled, that it was as smooth and flat as a lawn of grass until nigh unto the feet of the hills; and nothing might walk or creep across unseen.

In that city the folk waxed mighty, and their armouries were filled with weapons and with shields, for they purposed yet to come forth to war when the hour was ripe. But as the years drew on they grew to love that place, and desired no better, and few ever issued forth;[6] they shut them behind their impenetrable and enchanted hills, and suffered none to enter, fugitive or foe, and tidings of the outer world came but faint and far, and they heeded them little, and forgot the messages of Ulmo. They succoured not Nargothrond or Doriath, and the wandering Elves knew not how to find them; and when Turgon learned of the slaying of Dior, he vowed never to march with any son of Fëanor, and closed his realm, forbidding any of his folk to go ever forth.[7]

Gondolin now alone remained of all the strongholds of the Elves. Morgoth forgot not Turgon, and knew that without knowledge of that king his triumph could not be achieved; yet his search unceasing was in vain. Nargothrond was void, Doriath desolate, the sons of Fëanor driven away to a wild woodland life in the South and East, Hithlum was filled with evil men, and Taur-na-Fuin was a place of nameless dread; the race of Hador was at an end, and the house of Finrod; Beren came no more to war, and Huan was slain; and all Elves and Men bowed to his will, or laboured as slaves in the mines and smithies of Angband, save only the wild and wandering, and few there were of these save far in the East of once fair Beleriand. His triumph was near complete, and yet was not quite full.[8]

★

1   This sentence was rewritten thus:

Ulmo alone knew whither they had gone; for they returned to the hidden city of Gondolin that Turgon had built. In a secret place in the mountains there was a broad valley, &c.

2   *the Gnomes took refuge* > *Turgon had taken refuge*
3   At this point the replacement text Q II begins.
4   *the power of Ulmo* > *the power of Sirion beloved of Ulmo*
5   The following passage was added in pencil in the margin without direction for insertion. For its place in Q II, where it is embodied in the text, see below.

For Turgon deemed after the Battle of Unnumbered Tears that Morgoth had grown too mighty for Elves and Men, and that it were better to ask the forgiveness and aid of the Valar ere all was lost. Wherefore some of his folk would at whiles go down Sirion, and a small and secret haven they there made, whence ever and anon ships would set forth into the West. Some came back driven by contrary winds, but many never returned; and none reached Valinor.

6   Added here: *and they sent no more messengers into the West*;
7   Here the replacement text Q II ends.
8   Added at the end: *In this wise came the fall of Gondolin*.

§15 in the Q II version
(see note 3 above)

and like Doriath never be overthrown save by treachery from within. Because of his protecting might the spells of concealment were strongest in those parts nearest to Sirion, though there the

Encircling Mountains were at their lowest. In that region the Gnomes dug a great winding tunnel under the roots of the hills, and its issue was in the steep side, tree-clad and dark, of a gorge through which the blissful river ran. There he was still a young stream, but strong, flowing down the narrow vale that lies between the shoulders of the Encircling Mountains and the Mountains of Shadow, Eryd-Lómin,[1] the walls of Hithlum, in whose northern heights he took his rise.[2]

That passage they made at first to be a way of return for fugitives and for such as escaped from the bondage of Morgoth; and most as an issue for their scouts and messengers. For Turgon deemed, when first they came into that vale after the dreadful battle,[3] that Morgoth Bauglir had grown too mighty for Elves and Men, and that it were better to seek the forgiveness and aid of the Valar, if either might be got, ere all was lost. Wherefore some of his folk went down the river Sirion at whiles, ere the shadow of Morgoth yet stretched into the uttermost parts of Beleriand, and a small and secret haven they made at his mouth; thence ever and anon ships would set forth into the West bearing the embassy of the Gnomish king. Some there were that came back driven by contrary winds; but the most never returned again, and none reached Valinor.

The issue of that Way of Escape was guarded and concealed by the mightiest spells they could contrive, and by the power that dwelt in Sirion beloved of Ulmo, and no thing of evil found it; yet its inner gate, which looked upon the vale of Gondolin, was watched unceasingly by the Gnomes.

In those days Thorndor[4] King of Eagles removed his eyries from . Thangorodrim, because of the power of Morgoth, and the stench and fumes, and the evil of the dark clouds that lay now ever upon the mountain-towers above his cavernous halls. But Thorndor dwelt upon the northward heights of the Encircling Mountains, and he kept watch and saw many things, sitting upon the cairn of King Fingolfin. And in the vale below dwelt Turgon Fingolfin's son. Upon Amon Gwareth, the Hill of Defence, the rocky height amidst the plain, was built Gondolin the great, whose fame and glory is mightiest in song of all dwellings of the Elves in these Outer Lands. Of steel were its gates and of marble were its walls. The sides of the hill the Gnomes polished to the smoothness of dark glass, and its top they levelled for the building of their town, save amidmost where stood the tower and palace of the king. Many fountains there were in that city, and white waters fell shimmering down the glistening sides of Amon Gwareth. The plain all about they smoothed till it became as a lawn of shaven grass from the stairways before the gates unto the feet of the mountain wall, and nought might walk or creep across unseen.

In that city the folk waxed mighty, and their armouries were filled with weapons and with shields; for they purposed at first to come forth to war, when the hour was ripe. But as the years drew on, they grew to love that place, the work of their hands, as the Gnomes do, with a great love, and desired no better. Then seldom went any forth from Gondolin on errand of war or peace again. They sent no messengers more into the West, and Sirion's haven was desolate. They shut them behind their impenetrable and enchanted hills, and suffered none to enter, though he fled from Morgoth hate-pursued; tidings of the lands without came to them faint and far, and they heeded them little; and their dwelling became as a rumour, and a secret no man could find. They succoured not Nargothrond nor Doriath, and the wandering Elves sought them in vain; and Ulmo alone knew where the realm of Turgon could be found. Tidings Turgon heard of Thorndor concerning the slaying of Dior, Thingol's heir, and thereafter he shut his ear to word of the woes without; and he vowed to march never at the side of any son of Fëanor; and his folk he forbade ever to pass the leaguer of the hills.

Changes made to this passage

1 *Eryd-Lómin > Eredwethion*
2 *in whose northern heights he took his rise* struck through.
3 This sentence marked with an X in the margin.
4 *Thorndor > Thorondor* throughout.

16

[A substantial part of this section is again extant both in the original typescript (Q I) and in a replacement text (Q II).]

On a time Eöl was lost in Taur-na-Fuin, and Isfin came through great peril and dread unto Gondolin, and after her coming none entered until the last messenger of Ulmo, of whom the tales speak more ere the end. With her came her son Meglin, and he was there received by Turgon his mother's brother,[1] and though he was half of Dark-elfin[2] blood he was treated as a prince of Fingolfin's line.

He was swart but comely, wise and eloquent, and cunning to win men's hearts and minds.

Now Húrin of Hithlum had a brother Huor. The son of Huor was Tuor. Rían Huor's wife sought her husband among the slain upon the field of Unnumbered Tears, and there bewailed him, ere she died. Her son was but a child, and remaining in Hithlum fell into the hands of the faithless Men whom Morgoth drove into that land after the battle; and he became a thrall. Growing of age, and he was fair of face and great of stature, and despite his grievous life valiant and wise, he escaped into the woods, and he became an outlaw and a solitary, living alone and communing with none save rarely wandering and hidden Elves.[3]

On a time Ulmo contrived, as is told in the *Tale of the Fall of Gondolin*, that he should be led to a river-course that flowed underground from Lake Mithrim in the midst of Hithlum into a great chasm, Cris-Ilfing,[4] the Rainbow-cleft, through which a turbulent water ran at last into the western sea. And the name of this chasm was so devised by reason of the rainbow that shimmered ever in the sun in that place, because of the abundance of the spray of the rapids and the waterfalls.

In this way the flight of Tuor was marked by no Man nor Elf; neither was it known to the Orcs or any spy of Morgoth, with whom the land of Hithlum was filled.

Tuor wandered long by the western shores, journeying ever South; and he came at last to the mouths of Sirion, and the sandy deltas peopled by many birds of the sea. There he fell in with a Gnome, Bronweg,[5] who had escaped from Angband, and being of old of the people of Turgon, sought ever to find the path to the hidden places of his lord, of which rumour ran among all captives and fugitives. Now Bronweg had come thither by far and wandering paths to the East, and little though any step back nigher to the thraldom from which he had come was to his liking, he purposed now to go up Sirion and seek for Turgon in Beleriand. Fearful and very wary was he, and he aided Tuor in their secret march, by night and twilight, so that they were not discovered by the Orcs.

They came first into the fair Land of Willows, Nan-Tathrin which is watered by the Narog and by Sirion; and there all things were yet green, and the meads were rich and full of flowers, and there was song of many birds; so that Tuor lingered there as one enchanted, and it seemed sweet to him to dwell there after the grim lands of the North and his weary wandering.

There Ulmo came and appeared before him, as he stood in the long grass at evening; and the might and majesty of that vision is told of in the song of Tuor that he made for his son Eärendel. Thereafter the sound of the sea and the longing for the sea was ever in Tuor's heart and ear; and an unquiet was on him at whiles that took him at last into the depths of the realm of Ulmo.[6] But now Ulmo bade him make all speed to Gondolin, and gave him guidance for the finding of the hidden door; and words were set in his mouth to bear to Turgon, bidding him prepare for battle with Morgoth ere all was lost, and promising that Ulmo would win the hearts of the Valar to send him succour. That would be a mortal and a terrible strife, yet if Turgon would dare it, Morgoth's power should be broken and his servants perish and never after trouble the world. But if Turgon would not go forth to this war, then he must abandon Gondolin and lead his people down Sirion, ere Morgoth could oppose him, and at Sirion's mouth Ulmo would befriend him, and lend his aid to the building of a mighty fleet wherein the Gnomes should sail back at last to Valinor, but then grievous would be the fate of the Outer Lands. Tuor's part if Turgon should accept the counsels of Ulmo, would be to go forth when Turgon marched to war and lead a force into Hithlum and draw its Men once more into alliance with the Elves, for 'without Men the Elves shall not prevail against the Orcs and Balrogs'.

This errand did Ulmo himself perform out of his love of Elves and of the Gnomes, and because he knew that ere twelve years were passed the doom of Gondolin would come, strong though it seemed, if its people sat still behind their walls.

Obedient to Ulmo Tuor and Bronweg journeyed North, and came to the hidden door; and passing down the tunnel neath the hills they came to the inner gate and looked upon the vale of Gondolin, the city of seven names, shining white flushed with the rose of dawn upon the plain. But there they were made captive by the guard of the gate and led before the king. Tuor spoke his embassy to Turgon in the great square of Gondolin before the steps of his palace; but the king was grown proud and Gondolin so fair and beautiful and he was so trustful of its secret and impregnable strength, that he and the most of his folk wished no longer to trouble with the Gnomes and Men without, nor did they long more to return to the lands of the Gods.

Meglin spake against Tuor in the councils of the king, and Turgon rejected the bidding of Ulmo, and neither did he go forth to war nor seek to fly to the mouths of Sirion; but there were some of his wiser counsellors who were filled with disquiet, and the king's daughter spake ever for Tuor. She was named Idril, one of the fairest of the maidens of the Elves of old, and folk called her Celebrindal, Silver-foot, for the whiteness of her slender feet, and she walked and danced ever unshod.

Thereafter Tuor sojourned in Gondolin, and grew a mighty man in form and in wisdom, learning deeply of the lore of the Gnomes; and the heart of Idril was turned to him, and his to her. At which Meglin ground his teeth, for he loved Idril, and despite his close kinship purposed to wed her; indeed already he was planning in his heart to oust Turgon and to seize the throne, but Turgon loved and trusted him. Tuor wedded Idril nonetheless, for he had become beloved by all the Gnomes of Gondolin, even Turgon the proud, save only Meglin and his secret following. Tuor and Beren alone of mortal Men ever wedded Elves of old, and since Elwing daughter of Dior son of Beren after wedded Eärendel son of Tuor and Idril, of them alone has come the elfin blood into mortal Men. But yet Eärendel was an infant; and he was a child surpassing fair: a light was in his face as of heaven, and he had the beauty and the wisdom of Elfinesse[7] and the strength and hardihood of the Men of old; and the sea spoke ever in his ear and heart, even as with Tuor his father.

On a time when Eärendel was yet young, and the days of Gondolin were full of joy and peace (and yet Idril's heart misgave her, and foreboding crept upon her spirit like a cloud), Meglin was lost. Now Meglin loved mining and quarrying after metals above other craft; and he was master and leader of the Gnomes who worked in the mountains distant from the city, seeking for metals for their smithying of things both of peace and war. But often Meglin went with few of his folk beyond the leaguer of the hills, though the king knew not that his bidding was defied; and so it came to pass, as fate willed, that Meglin was taken prisoner by the Orcs and taken before Morgoth. Meglin was no weakling or craven, but the torment wherewith he was threatened cowed his soul, and he purchased his life and freedom by revealing unto Morgoth the place of Gondolin and the ways whereby it might be found and assailed. Great indeed was the joy of Morgoth; and to Meglin he promised the lordship of Gondolin, as his vassal, and the possession of Idril, when that city should be taken. Lust for Idril and hatred of Tuor led Meglin the easier to his foul treachery. But Morgoth sent him back to Gondolin, lest men should suspect the betrayal, and so that Meglin should aid the assault from within when the hour came; and Meglin abode in the halls of the king with a smile on his face and evil in his heart, while the gloom gathered ever deeper upon Idril.

At last, and Eärendel was then seven years of age, Morgoth was ready, and he loosed upon Gondolin his Orcs and his Balrogs and his serpents; and of these, dragons of many and dire shapes were new devised for the taking of the city. The host of Morgoth came over the Northern hills where the height was greatest and the watch less vigilant, and it came at night at a time of festival, when all the folk of Gondolin were upon the walls to wait upon the rising sun and sing their songs at its uplifting; for the morrow was the feast which they named the Gates of Summer. But the red light mounted the hills in the North and not in the East; and there was no stay in the advance of the foe until they were beneath the very walls of Gondolin, and Gondolin was beleaguered without hope.

Of the deeds of desperate valour there done, by the chieftains of the noble houses and their warriors, and not least by Tuor, is much told in *The Fall of Gondolin*; of the death of Rog without the walls; and of the battle of Ecthelion of the Fountain with Gothmog lord of Balrogs in the very square of the king, where each slew the other; and of the defence of the tower of Turgon by the men of his household, until the tower was overthrown; and mighty was its fall and the fall of Turgon in its ruin.

Tuor sought to rescue Idril from the sack of the city, but Meglin had laid hands upon her and Eärendel; and Tuor fought on the walls with him, and cast him down to death. Then Tuor and Idril led such remnants of the folk of Gondolin as they could gather in the confusion of the burning down a secret way that Idril had let prepare in the days of her foreboding. This was not yet complete, but its issue was already far beyond the walls and in the North of the plain where the mountains were long distant from Amon Gwareth. Those who would not come with them, but fled to the old Way of Escape that led into the gorge of Sirion, were caught and destroyed by a dragon that Morgoth had sent to watch that gate, being apprised of it by Meglin. But of the new passage Meglin had not heard, and it was not thought that fugitives would take a path towards the North and the highest parts of the mountains and the nighest to Angband.

The fume of the burning, and the steam of the fair fountains of Gondolin withering in the flame of the dragons of the North, fell upon the vale in mournful mists; and thus was the escape of Tuor and his company aided, for there was still a long and open road to follow from the tunnel's mouth to the foothills of the mountains. They came nonetheless into the mountains, in woe and misery, for the high places were cold and terrible, and they had among them many women and children and many wounded men.

There is a dreadful pass, Cristhorn[8] was it named, the Eagle's Cleft, where beneath the shadow of the highest peaks a narrow path winds its way, walled by a precipice to the right and on the left a dreadful fall leaps into emptiness. Along that narrow way their march was strung, when it was ambushed by an outpost of Morgoth's power; and a Balrog was their leader. Then dreadful was their plight, and hardly would it have been saved by the deathless valour of yellow-haired Glorfindel, chief of the House of the Golden Flower of Gondolin, had not Thorndor[9] come timely to their aid.

Songs have been sung of the duel of Glorfindel with the Balrog upon a pinnacle of rock in that high place; and both fell to ruin in the abyss. But Thorndor bore up Glorfindel's body and he was buried in a mound of stones beside the pass, and there came after a turf of green and small flowers like yellow stars bloomed there amid the barrenness of stone. And the birds of Thorndor stooped upon the Orcs and drove them shrieking back; and all were slain or cast into the deeps, and rumour of the escape from Gondolin came not until long after to Morgoth's ears.

Thus by weary and dangerous marches the remnant of Gondolin came unto Nan-Tathrin and there rested a while, and were healed of their hurts and weariness, but their sorrow could not be cured. There they made feast in memory of Gondolin and those that had perished, fair maidens, wives, and warriors and their king; but for Glorfindel the well-beloved many and sweet were the songs they sang. And there Tuor in song spoke to Eärendel his son of the coming of Ulmo aforetime, the sea-vision in the midst of the land, and the sea-longing awoke in his heart and in his son's. Wherefore they removed with the most part of the people to the mouths of Sirion by the sea, and there they dwelt, and joined their folk to the slender company of Elwing daughter of Dior, that had fled thither little while before.

Then Morgoth thought in his heart that his triumph was fulfilled, recking little of the sons of Fëanor, and of their oath, which had harmed him never and turned always to his mightiest aid. And in his black thought he laughed, regretting not the one Silmaril he had lost, for by it he deemed the last shreds of the elvish race should vanish yet from the earth and trouble it no more. If he knew of the dwelling by the waters of Sirion he made no sign, biding his time, and waiting upon the working of oath and lie.

★

1   *mother's brother* > *sister-son*; no doubt *as his sister-son* was intended.
2   *Dark-elfin* > *Dark-elven*
3   This paragraph was largely struck out, as well as some hasty emendations that had been made to it (introducing the idea of Tuor's being born 'in the wild' and fostered by Dark-elves, and Rían's dying on the Hill of Slain – which is here called *Amon Dengin*). The passage was then rewritten:

> Now Húrin of Hithlum had a brother Huor, and as has been told Rían his wife went forth into the wild and there her son Tuor was born, and he was fostered by the Dark-elves; but Rían laid herself down and died upon the Hill of Slain. But Tuor grew up in the woods of Hithlum, and he was fair of face and great of stature, and valiant and wise; and he walked and hunted alone in the woods, and he became a solitary, living alone and communing with none save rarely wandering and hidden Elves.

4   *Cris-Ilfing* > *Kirith Helvin*
5   *Bronweg* > *Bronwë* at the first two occurrences, but not at the third, which occurs in the part replaced by the Q II text.
6   At this point the replacement text Q II begins.
7   Here the replacement text Q II ends.
8   *Cristhorn* > *Kirith-thoronath*
9   *Thorndor* > *Thorondor*, as previously.

§16 in the Q II version
(see note 6 above)

But now Ulmo bade him make all speed to Gondolin, and gave him guidance for the finding of the hidden door; and a message he gave him to bear from Ulmo, friend of Elves, unto Turgon, bidding him to prepare for war, and battle with Morgoth ere all was lost; and to send again his messengers into the West. Summons too should he send into the East and gather, if he might, Men (who were now multiplying and spreading on the earth) unto his banners; and for that task Tuor was most fit. 'Forget,' counselled Ulmo, 'the treachery of Uldor the accursed, and remember Húrin; for without mortal Men the Elves shall not prevail against the Balrogs and the Orcs.' Nor should the feud with the sons of Fëanor be left unhealed; for this should be the last gathering of the hope of the Gnomes, when every sword should count. A terrible and mortal strife he foretold, but victory if Turgon would dare it, the breaking of Morgoth's power, and the healing of feuds, and friendship between Men and Elves, whereof the greatest good should come into the world, and the servants of Morgoth trouble it no more. But if Turgon would not go forth to this war, then he should abandon Gondolin and lead his people down Sirion, and build there his fleets and seek back to Valinor and the mercy of the Gods. But in this counsel there was danger more dire than in the other, though so it might not seem; and grievous thereafter would be the fate of the Outer¹ Lands.

This errand Ulmo performed out of his love of the Elves, and because he knew that ere many years were passed the doom of Gondolin would come, if its people sat still behind its walls; not thus should anything of joy or beauty in the world be preserved from Morgoth's malice.

Obedient to Ulmo Tuor and Bronweg² journeyed North, and came at last to the hidden door; and passing down the tunnel reached the inner gate, and were taken by the guard as prisoners. There they saw the fair vale Tumladin³ set like a green jewel amid the hills; and amidst Tumladin Gondolin the great, the city of seven names, white, shining from afar, flushed with the rose of dawn upon the plain. Thither they were led and passed the gates of steel, and were brought before the steps of the palace of the king. There Tuor spake the embassy of Ulmo, and something of the power and majesty of the Lord of Waters his voice had caught, so that all folk looked in wonder on him, and doubted that this were a Man of mortal race as he declared. But proud was Turgon become, and Gondolin as beautiful as a memory of Tûn, and he trusted in its secret and impregnable strength; so that he and the most part of his folk wished not to imperil it nor leave it, and they desired not to mingle in the woes of Elves and Men without; nor did they any longer desire to return through dread and danger to the West.

Meglin spoke ever against Tuor in the councils of the king, and his words seemed the more weighty in that they went with Turgon's heart. Wherefore Turgon rejected the bidding of Ulmo; though some there were of his wisest counsellors who were filled with disquiet. Wise-hearted even beyond the measure of the daughters of Elfinesse was the daughter of the king, and she spoke ever for Tuor, though it did not avail, and her heart was heavy. Very fair and tall was she, well nigh of warrior's stature, and her hair was a fountain of gold. Idril was she named, and called Celebrindal, Silver-foot, for the whiteness of her foot; and she walked and danced ever unshod in the white ways and green lawns of Gondolin.

Thereafter Tuor sojourned in Gondolin, and went not to summon the Men of the East, for the blissfulness of Gondolin, the beauty and wisdom of its folk, held him enthralled. And he grew high in the favour of Turgon; for he became a mighty man in stature and in mind, learning deeply of the lore of the Gnomes. The heart of Idril was turned to him, and his to her; at which Meglin ground his teeth, for he desired Idril, and despite his close kinship purposed to possess her; and she was the only heir of the king of Gondolin. Indeed in his heart he was already planning how he might oust Turgon and seize his throne; but Turgon loved and trusted him. Nonetheless Tuor took Idril to wife; and the folk of Gondolin made merry feast, for Tuor had won their hearts, all save Meglin and his secret following. Tuor and Beren alone of mortal Men had Elves to wife, and since Elwing daughter of Dior son of Beren after wedded Eärendel son of Tuor and Idril of Gondolin, of them alone has come the elfin[4] blood into mortal race. But as yet Eärendel was a little child: surpassing fair was he, a light was in his face as the light of heaven, and he had the beauty and the wisdom of Elfinesse

Changes made to this passage

1   *Outer* > *Hither*
2   *Bronweg* > *Bronwë* (see note 5 above).
3   *Tumladin* > *Tumladen*
4   *elfin* > *elven*

17

[The whole of this section is extant in the two typescript versions Q I and Q II.]

Yet by Sirion there grew up an elfin folk, the gleanings of Doriath and Gondolin, and they took to the sea and to the making of fair ships, and they dwelt nigh unto its shores and under the shadow of Ulmo's hand.

But in Valinor Ulmo spake grievous words unto the Valar and unto the Elves the kinsfolk of the exiled and ruined Gnomes, and he called on them to forgive, and to rescue the world from the overmastering might of Morgoth, and win back the Silmarils wherein alone now bloomed the light of the days of ancient bliss when the Two Trees still shone. And the sons of the Valar prepared for battle, and Fionwë son of Tulcas was the captain of the host. With him marched the host of the Quendi, the Light-elves, the folk of Ingwë, and among them such of the race of the Gnomes [as] had not left Valinor; but remembering Swan Haven the Teleri came not forth. Tûn was deserted and the hill of Côr knew no more the feet of the elder children of the world.

In those days Tuor felt old age creep upon him, and he could not forbear the longing that possessed him for the sea; wherefore he built a great ship Eärámë, Eagle's Pinion, and with Idril he set sail into the sunset and the West, and came no more into any tale. But Eärendel the shining became the lord of the folk of Sirion and took to wife fair Elwing; and yet he could not rest. Two thoughts were in his heart blended as one: the longing for the wide sea; and he thought to sail thereon following after Tuor and Idril Celebrindal who returned not, and he thought to find perhaps the last shore and bring ere he died a message to the Gods and Elves of the West, that should move their hearts to pity on the world and the sorrows of Mankind.

Wingelot he built, fairest of the ships of song, the Foam-flower; white were its timbers as the argent moon, golden were its oars, silver were its shrouds, its masts were crowned with jewels like stars. In the Lay of Eärendel is many a thing sung of his adventures in the deep and in lands untrod, and in many seas and many isles; and most of how he fought and slew Ungoliant in the South and her darkness perished, and light came to many places which had yet long been hid. But Elwing sat sorrowing at home.

Eärendel found not Tuor, nor came he ever on that journey to the shores of Valinor; and at last he was driven by the winds back East, and he came at a time of night to the havens of Sirion, unlooked for, unwelcomed, for they were desolate. Bronweg alone sat there in sorrow, the companion of his father of old, and his tidings were filled with new woe.

The dwelling of Elwing at Sirion's mouth, where still she possessed the Nauglafring and the glorious Silmaril, became known to the sons of Fëanor; and they gathered together from their wandering hunting-paths. But the folk of Sirion would not yield that jewel which Beren had won and Lúthien had worn, and for which fair Dior had been slain. And so befell the last and cruellest slaying of Elf by Elf, the third woe achieved by the accursed oath; for the sons of Fëanor came down upon the exiles of Gondolin and the remnant of Doriath, and though some of their folk stood aside and some few rebelled and were slain upon the other part aiding Elwing against their own lords, yet they won the day. Damrod was slain and Díriel, and Maidros and Maglor alone now remained of the Seven; but the last of the folk of Gondolin were destroyed or forced to depart and join them to the people of Maidros. And yet the sons of Fëanor gained not the Silmaril; for Elwing cast the Nauglafring into the sea, whence it shall not return until the End; and she leapt herself into the waves, and took the form of a white sea-bird, and flew away lamenting and seeking for Eärendel about all the shores of the world.

But Maidros took pity upon her child Elrond, and took him with him, and harboured and nurtured him, for his heart was sick and weary with the burden of the dreadful oath.

Learning these things Eärendel was overcome with sorrow; and with Bronweg he set sail once more in search of Elwing and of Valinor. And it is told in the Lay of Eärendel that he came at last unto the Magic Isles, and hardly escaped their enchantment, and found again the Lonely Isle, and the Shadowy Seas, and the Bay of Faërie on the borders of the world. There he landed on the immortal shore alone of living Men, and his feet clomb the marvellous hill of Côr; and he walked in the deserted ways of Tûn, where the dust upon his raiment and his shoes was a dust of diamonds and gems. But he ventured not into Valinor. He came too late to bring messages to the Elves, for the Elves had gone.[1]

He built a tower in the Northern Seas to which all the sea-birds of the world might at times repair, and ever he grieved for fair Elwing looking for her return to him. And Wingelot was lifted on their wings and sailed now even in the airs searching for Elwing; marvellous and magical was that ship, a starlit flower in the sky. But the Sun scorched it and the Moon hunted it in heaven, and long Eärendel wandered over Earth, glimmering as a fugitive star.

★

1   At the foot of the page is written very quickly and faintly in pencil:

Make *Eärendel* move the Gods. And it is said that there were Men
of Hithlum repentant of their evil in that day, and that so were
fulfilled Ulmo's words, for by Eärendel's embassy and the aid of
valiant Men the Orcs and Balrogs were destroyed, yet not as utterly
as might have been.

At the top of the next page is written: *Men turned the* [*tide*] (the last
word is illegible).

§17 in the Q II version

·Yet by Sirion and the sea there grew up an elfin[1] folk, the
gleanings of Gondolin and Doriath, and they took to the waves
and to the making of fair ships, dwelling ever nigh unto the shores
and under the shadow of Ulmo's hand.

In Valinor Ulmo spoke unto the Valar of the need of the Elves,
and he called on them to forgive and send succour unto them and
rescue them from the overmastering might of Morgoth, and win
back the Silmarils wherein alone now bloomed the light of the
days of bliss when the Two Trees still were shining. Or so it is
said, among the Gnomes, who after had tidings of many things
from their kinsfolk the Quendi, the Light-elves beloved of
Manwë, who ever knew something of the mind of the Lord of the
Gods. But as yet Manwë moved not, and the counsels of his heart
what tale shall tell? The Quendi have said that the hour was not yet
come, and that only one speaking in person for the cause of both
Elves and Men, pleading for pardon upon their misdeeds and pity
on their woes, might move the counsels of the Powers; and the
oath of Fëanor perchance even Manwë could not loose, until it
found its end, and the sons of Fëanor relinquished the Silmarils,
upon which they had laid their ruthless claim. For the light which
lit the Silmarils the Gods had made.

In those days Tuor felt old age creep upon him, and ever a
longing for the deeps of the sea grew stronger in his heart.
Wherefore he built a great ship Eärámë, Eagle's Pinion,[2] and with
Idril he set sail into the sunset and the West, and came no more
into any tale or song.[3] Bright Eärendel was then lord of the folk of
Sirion and their many ships; and he took to wife Elwing the fair,
and she bore him Elrond Half-elfin.[4] Yet Eärendel could not rest,
and his voyages about the shores of the Outer[5] Lands eased not his
unquiet. Two purposes grew in his heart, blended as one in
longing for the wide sea: he sought to sail thereon, seeking after
Tuor and Idril Celebrindal who returned not; and he thought to

find perhaps the last shore and bring ere he died the message of Elves and Men unto the Valar of the West, that should move the hearts of Valinor and of the Elves of Tûn to pity on the world and the sorrows of Mankind.

Wingelot[6] he built, fairest of the ships of song, the Foam-flower; white were its timbers as the argent moon, golden were its oars, silver were its shrouds, its masts were crowned with jewels like stars. In the Lay of Eärendel is many a thing sung of his adventures in the deep and in lands untrodden, and in many seas and many isles. Ungoliant[7] in the South he slew, and her darkness was destroyed, and light came to many regions which had yet long been hid. But Elwing sat sorrowing at home.

Eärendel found not Tuor nor Idril, nor came he ever on that journey to the shores of Valinor, defeated by shadows and enchantment, driven by repelling winds, until in longing for Elwing he turned him homeward toward the East. And his heart bade him haste, for a sudden fear was fallen on him out of dreams, and the winds that before he had striven with might not now bear him back as swift as his desire.

Upon the havens of Sirion new woe had fallen. The dwelling of Elwing there, where still she possessed the Nauglafring[8] and the glorious Silmaril, became known unto the remaining sons of Fëanor, Maidros and Maglor and Damrod and Díriel; and they gathered together from their wandering hunting-paths, and messages of friendship and yet stern demand they sent unto Sirion. But Elwing and the folk of Sirion would not yield that jewel which Beren had won and Lúthien had worn, and for which Dior the Fair was slain; and least of all while Eärendel their lord was in the sea, for them seemed that in that jewel lay the gift of bliss and healing that had come upon their houses and their ships.

And so came in the end to pass the last and cruellest of the slayings of Elf by Elf; and that was the third of the great wrongs achieved by the accursed oath. For the sons of Fëanor came down upon the exiles of Gondolin and the remnant of Doriath and destroyed them. Though some of their folk stood aside, and some few rebelled and were slain upon the other part aiding Elwing against their own lords (for such was the sorrow and confusion of the hearts of Elfinesse in those days), yet Maidros and Maglor won the day. Alone they now remained of the sons of Fëanor, for in that battle Damrod and Díriel were slain; but the folk of Sirion perished or fled away, or departed of need to join the people of Maidros, who claimed now the lordship of all the Elves of the

Outer Lands. And yet Maidros gained not the Silmaril, for Elwing seeing that all was lost and her child Elrond[9] taken captive, eluded the host of Maidros, and with the Nauglafring upon her breast she cast herself into the sea, and perished as folk thought.

But Ulmo bore her up and he gave unto her the likeness of a great white bird, and upon her breast there shone as a star the shining Silmaril, as she flew over the water to seek Eärendel her beloved. And on a time of night Eärendel at the helm saw her come towards him, as a white cloud under moon exceeding swift, as a star over the sea moving in strange course, a pale flame on wings of storm. And it is sung that she fell from the air upon the timbers of Wingelot, in a swoon, nigh unto death for the urgency of her speed, and Eärendel took her unto his bosom. And in the morn with marvelling eyes he beheld his wife in her own form beside him with her hair upon his face; and she slept.

But great was the sorrow of Eärendel and Elwing for the ruin of the havens of Sirion, and the captivity of their son, for whom they feared death, and yet it was not so. For Maidros took pity on Elrond, and he cherished him, and love grew after between them, as little might be thought; but Maidros' heart was sick and weary[10] with the burden of the dreadful oath. Yet Eärendel saw now no hope left in the lands of Sirion, and he turned again in despair and came not home, but sought back once more to Valinor with Elwing at his side. He stood now most oft at the prow, and the Silmaril he bound upon his forehead; and ever its light grew greater as they drew unto the West. May be it was due in part to the puissance of that holy jewel that they came in time to the waters that as yet no vessels save those of the Teleri had known; and they came unto the Magic Isles and escaped their magic;[11] and they came into the Shadowy Seas and passed their shadows; and they looked upon the Lonely Isle and they tarried not there; and they cast anchor in the Bay of Faërie[12] upon the borders of the world. And the Teleri saw the coming of that ship and were amazed, gazing from afar upon the light of the Silmaril, and it was very great.

But Eärendel landed on the immortal shores alone of living Men; and neither Elwing nor any of his small company would he suffer to go with him, lest they fell beneath the wrath of the Gods, and he came at a time of festival even as Morgoth and Ungoliant had in ages past, and the watchers upon the hill of Tûn were few, for the Quendi were most in the halls of Manwë on Tinbrenting's[13] height.[14]

The watchers rode therefore in haste to Valmar, or hid them in the passes of the hills; and all the bells of Valmar pealed; but Eärendel clomb the marvellous hill of Côr[15] and found it bare, and he entered into the streets of Tûn and they were empty; and his heart sank. He walked now in the deserted ways of Tûn and the dust upon his raiment and his shoes was a dust of diamonds, yet no one heard his call. Wherefore he went back unto the shores and would climb once more upon Wingelot his ship; but one came unto the strand and cried unto him: 'Hail Eärendel, star most radiant, messenger most fair![16] Hail thou bearer of light before the Sun and Moon, the looked-for that comest unawares, the longed-for that comest beyond hope! Hail thou splendour of the children of the world, thou slayer of the dark! Star of the sunset hail! Hail herald of the morn!'

And that was Fionwë the son of Manwë, and he summoned Eärendel before the Gods; and Eärendel went unto Valinor and to the halls of Valmar, and came never again back into the lands of Men.[17] But Eärendel spake the embassy of the two races[18] before the faces of the Gods, and asked for pardon upon the Gnomes and pity for the exiled Elves and for unhappy Men, and succour in their need.

Then the sons of the Valar prepared for battle, and the captain of their host was Fionwë son of Manwë. Beneath his white banner marched also the host of the Quendi, the Light-elves, the folk of Ingwë, and among them such of the Gnomes of old as had never departed from Valinor;[19] but remembering Swan Haven the Teleri went not forth save very few, and these manned the ships wherewith the most of that army came into the Northern lands; but they themselves would set foot never on those shores.

Eärendel was their guide; but the Gods would not suffer him to return again, and he built him a white tower upon the confines of the outer world in the Northern regions of the Sundering Seas; and there all the sea-birds of the earth at times repaired. And often was Elwing in the form and likeness of a bird; and she devised wings for the ship of Eärendel, and it was lifted even into the oceans of the air. Marvellous and magical was that ship, a starlit flower in the sky, bearing a wavering and holy flame; and the folk of earth beheld it from afar and wondered, and looked up from despair, saying surely a Silmaril is in the sky, a new star is risen in the West. Maidros said unto Maglor:[20] 'If that be the Silmaril that riseth by some power divine out of the sea into which we saw it fall, then let us be glad, that its glory is seen now by many.' Thus hope arose and a promise of betterment; but Morgoth was filled with doubt.

Yet it is said that he looked not for the assault that came upon him from the West. So great was his pride become that he deemed none would ever again come against him in open war; moreover he thought that he had estranged the Gnomes for ever from the Gods and from their kin, and that content in their Blissful Realm the Valar would heed no more his kingdom in the world without. For heart that is pitiless counteth not the power that pity hath, of which stern anger may be forged and a lightning kindled before which mountains fall.

★

1   *elfin > elven*
2   *Eárámë, Eagle's Pinion > Eärrámë, Sea-wing*
3   Added here:

> But Tuor alone of mortal Men was numbered among the elder race, and joined with the Noldoli whom he loved, and in after time dwelt still, or so it hath been said, [*struck out*: in Tol Eressëa] ever upon his ship voyaging the seas of Fairyland [*>* the Elven-lands], or resting a while in the harbours of the Gnomes of Tol Eressëa; and his fate is sundered from the fate of Men.

4   *and she bore him Elrond Half-elfin > and she bore him Elros and Elrond, who are called the Halfelven.*
5   *Outer > Hither* at both occurrences.
6   *Wingelot > Vingelot* at all three occurrences; at the first only, *Vingelot* later *> Wingilot*
7   *Ungoliant > Ungoliantë* at both occurrences.
8   *Nauglafring > Nauglamír* at both occurrences (cf. §14 note 10).
9   *her child Elrond > her children Elros and Elrond*
10 This passage was rewritten thus:

> But great was the sorrow of Eärendel and Elwing for the ruin of the havens of Sirion, and the captivity of their sons; and they feared that they would be slain. But it was not so. For Maglor took pity on Elros and Elrond, and he cherished them, and love grew after between them, as little might be thought; but Maglor's heart was sick and weary, &c.

11 *and they came unto the Magic Isles and escaped their magic > and they came to the Enchanted Isles and escaped their enchantment*
12 *Bay of Faërie > Bay of Elvenhome*
13 *Tinbrenting's > Tindbrenting's*

14   This paragraph was emended at different times, and it is not perfectly clear what was intended. The first change was the addition, after *lest they fell beneath the wrath of the Gods*, of: *And he bade farewell to all whom he loved upon the last shore, and was taken from them for ever.* Subsequently *nor any of his small company* seems to have been removed, with the result: *and he would not suffer Elwing to go with him, lest she fell beneath the wrath of the Gods*: but the previous addition was not struck out.

15   *Côr* > *Kôr*, as previously.

16   This passage was altered to read:

> Wherefore he turned back towards the shores thinking to set sail once more upon Vingelot his ship; but one came unto him and cried: 'Hail Eärendel, radiant star, messenger most fair!

17   *came never again back into the lands of Men* > *never again set foot upon the lands of Men.*

18   *races* > *kindreds*

19   Added here: *and Ingwiel son of Ingwë was their chief;*

20   This passage, from the beginning of the paragraph, was extensively rewritten:

> In those days the ship of Eärendel was drawn by the Gods beyond the edge of the world, and it was lifted even into the oceans of the air. Marvellous and magical was that ship, a starlit flower in the sky, bearing a wavering and holy flame; and the folk of Earth beheld it from afar and wondered, and looked up from despair, saying surely a Silmaril is in the sky, a new star is risen in the West. But Elwing mourned for Eärendel yet found him never again, and they are sundered till the world endeth. Therefore she built a white tower upon the confines of the outer world in the Northern regions of the Sundering Seas; and there all the sea-birds of the earth at times repaired. And Elwing devised wings for herself, and desired to fly to Eärendel's ship. But [?she fell back] . . . . But when the flame of it appeared on high Maglor said unto Maidros:

18

[The whole of this section is again extant in the two typescript versions Q I and Q II.]

Of the march of Fionwë to the North little is said, for in that host there were none of the Elves who had dwelt and suffered in the Outer Lands, and who made these tales; and tidings only long after did they learn of these things from their distant kinsfolk the

Elves of Valinor. The meeting of the hosts of Fionwë and of Morgoth in the North is named the Last Battle, the Battle Terrible, the Battle of Wrath and Thunder. Great was Morgoth's amaze when this host came upon him from the West, and all Hithlum was ablaze with its glory, and the mountains rang; for he had thought that he had estranged the Gnomes for ever from the Gods and from their kin, and that content in their blissful realm the Gods would heed no further his kingdom in the world without. For heart that is pitiless counts not the power that pity hath; nor foresees that of gentle ruth for anguish and for valour overthrown stern anger may be forged, and a lightning kindled before which mountains fall.[1]

There was marshalled the whole power of the Throne of Hate, and well nigh measureless had it become, so that Dor-na-Fauglith might by no means contain it, and all the North was aflame with war. But it availed not. All the Balrogs were destroyed, and the uncounted hosts of the Orcs perished like straw in fire, or were swept away like shrivelled leaves before a burning wind. Few remained to trouble the world thereafter. And Morgoth himself came forth, and all his dragons were about him; and Fionwë for a moment was driven back. But the sons of the Valar in the end overthrew them all, and but two escaped. Morgoth escaped not. Him they threw down, and they bound him with the chain Angainor, wherewith Tulkas had chained him aforetime, and whence in unhappy hour the Gods had released him; but his iron crown they beat into a collar for his neck, and his head was bowed unto his knees. The Silmarils Fionwë took and guarded them.

Thus perished the power and woe of Angband in the North and its multitude of captives came forth into the light again beyond all hope, and looked upon a world all changed. Thangorodrim was riven and cast down, and the pits of Morgoth uncovered, roofless and broken, never to be rebuilt; but so great was the fury of those adversaries that all the Northern and Western parts of the world were rent and gaping, and the sea roared in in many places; the rivers perished or found new paths, the valleys were upheaved and the hills trod down; and Sirion was no more. Then Men fled away, such as perished not in the ruin of those days, and long was it ere they came back over the mountains to where Beleriand once had been, and not till the tale of those days had faded to an echo seldom heard.

But Fionwë marched through the lands summoning the remnants of the Gnomes and the Dark-elves that never yet had looked on Valinor to join with the captives released from Angband, and depart; and with the Elves should those of the race of Hador and Bëor alone be suffered to depart, if they would. But of these only Elrond was now left, the Half-elfin; and [he] elected to remain, being bound by his mortal blood in love to those of the younger race; and of Elrond alone has the blood of the elder race and of the seed divine of Valinor come among mortal Men.

But Maidros would not obey the call, preparing to fulfil even yet the obligation of his oath, though with weary loathing and despair. For he would have given battle for the Silmarils, if they were withheld from him, though he should stand alone in all the world save for Maglor his brother alone. And he sent unto Fionwë and bade him yield up those jewels which of old Morgoth stole from Fëanor. But Fionwë said that the right that Fëanor and his sons had in that which they had made, had perished, because of the many and evil deeds they had wrought blinded by their oath, and most of all the slaying of Dior and the assault upon Elwing. To Valinor must Maidros and Maglor return and abide the judgement of the Gods, by whose decree alone would he yield the jewels to any keeping other than his own.

Maidros was minded to submit, for he was sad at heart, and he said: 'The oath decrees not that we shall not bide our time, and maybe in Valinor all shall be forgiven and forgot, and we shall be vouchsafed our own.' But Maglor said that if once they returned and the favour of the Gods was not granted them, then would their oath still remain, and be fulfilled in despair yet greater; 'and who can tell to what dreadful end we shall come if we disobey the Powers in their own land, or purpose ever to bring war into their Guarded Realm again?' And so came it that Maidros and Maglor crept into the camps of Fionwë, and laid hands on the Silmarils; and they took to their weapons when they were discovered. But the sons of the Valar arose in wrath and prevented them, and took Maidros prisoner; and yet Maglor eluded them and escaped.

Now the Silmaril that Maidros held – for the brothers had agreed each to take one, saying that two brethren alone now remained, and but two jewels – burned the hand of Maidros, and he had but one hand as [has] been before told, and he knew then that his right thereto had become void, and that the oath was vain. But he cast the Silmaril upon the ground, and Fionwë took it; and for the anguish of his pain and the remorse of his heart he took his own life, ere he could be stayed.

It is told too of Maglor that he fled far, but he too could not endure the pain with which the Silmaril tormented him; and in an agony he cast it from him into a yawning gap filled with fire, in the rending of the Western lands, and the jewel vanished into the bosom of the Earth. But Maglor came never back among the folk of Elfinesse, but wandered singing in pain and in regret beside the sea.

In those days there was a mighty building of ships on the shores of the Western Sea, and most upon the great isles, which in the disruption of the Northern world were fashioned of old Beleriand. Thence in many a fleet the survivors of the Gnomes, and of the Western companies of the Dark-elves, set sail into the West and came no more into the lands of weeping and of war; and the Light-elves marched back beneath the banners of their king following in the train of Fionwë's victory. Yet not all returned, and some lingered many an age in the West and North, and especially in the Western Isles. Yet ever as the ages drew on and the Elf-folk faded on the Earth, they would still set sail at eve from our Western shores; as still they do, when now there linger few anywhere of the lonely companies.

But in the West the Gnomes returned rehabited for the most part the Lonely Isle that looks both East and West; and with them were mingled the Dark-elves, especially such as had once belonged to Doriath. And some returned even to Valinor, and were welcomed amid the bright companies of the Quendi, and admitted to the love of Manwë and the pardon of the Gods; and the Teleri forgave their ancient bitterness, and the curse was laid to rest. But Tûn was never again inhabited; and Côr stands still a hill of silent and untrodden green.

★

1　The content of this passage, from *Great was Morgoth's amaze . . .,* has been given at the end of §17 in the Q II version, since it appears there before the words *Of the march of the host of Fionwë* with which I begin §18.

§18 in the Q II version

Of the march of the host of Fionwë to the North little is said, for in his armies came none of those Elves who had dwelt and suffered in the Outer[1] Lands, and who made these tales; and tidings only long after did they learn of these things from their kinsfolk the Light-elves of Valinor. But Fionwë came, and the challenge of his trumpets filled the sky, and he summoned unto him all Men and Elves from Hithlum unto the East; and Beleriand was ablaze with the glory of his arms, and the mountains rang.

The meeting of the hosts of the West and of the North is named the Great Battle, the Battle Terrible, the Battle of Wrath and Thunder. There was marshalled the whole power of the Throne of Hate, and well nigh measureless had it become, so that Dor-na-Fauglith could not contain it, and all the North was aflame with war. But it availed not. All the Balrogs were destroyed, and the uncounted hosts of the Orcs perished like straw in fire, or were swept like shrivelled leaves before a burning wind. Few remained to trouble the world thereafter. And it is said that there many Men of Hithlum repentant of their evil servitude did deeds of valour, and many beside of Men new come out of the East;[2] and so were fulfilled in part the words of Ulmo; for by Eärendel son of Tuor was help brought unto the Elves, and by the swords of Men were they strengthened on the fields of war.[3] But Morgoth quailed and he came not forth; and he loosed his last assault, and that was the winged dragons.[4] So sudden and so swift and ruinous was the onset of that fleet, as a tempest of a hundred thunders winged with steel, that Fionwë was driven back; but Eärendel came and a myriad of birds were about him, and the battle lasted all through the night of doubt. And Eärendel slew Ancalagon the black and the mightiest of all the dragon-horde, and cast him from the sky, and in his fall the towers of Thangorodrim were thrown down. Then the sun rose of the second day and the sons[5] of the Valar prevailed, and all the dragons were destroyed save two alone; and they fled into the East. Then were all the pits of Morgoth broken and unroofed, and the might of Fionwë descended into the deeps of the Earth, and there Morgoth was thrown down. He was bound[6] with the chain Angainor, which long had been prepared, and his iron crown they beat into a collar for his neck, and his head was bowed unto his knees. But Fionwë took the two Silmarils that remained and guarded them.

Thus perished the power and woe of Angband in the North, and its multitude of thralls came forth beyond all hope into the light of day, and they looked upon a world all changed; for so great was the fury of those adversaries that the Northern regions of the Western world were rent and riven, and the sea roared in through many chasms, and there was confusion and great noise; and the rivers perished or found new paths, and the valleys were upheaved and the hills trod down; and Sirion was no more. Then Men fled away, such as perished not in the ruin of those days, and long was it ere they came back over the mountains to where Beleriand once had been, and not until the tale of those wars had faded to an echo seldom heard.

But Fionwë marched through the Western lands summoning the remnants of the Gnomes, and the Dark-elves that had yet not looked on Valinor, to join with the thralls released and to depart. But Maidros would not harken, and he prepared, though with weary loathing and despair, to perform even yet the obligation of his oath. For Maidros and Maglor would have given battle for the Silmarils, were they withheld, even against the victorious host of Valinor, and though they stood alone in all the world. And they sent unto Fionwë and bade him yield now up those jewels which of old Morgoth stole from Fëanor. But Fionwë said that the right to the work of their hands which Fëanor and his sons had formerly possessed now had perished, because of their many and evil deeds blinded by their oath, and most of all the slaying of Dior and the assault upon Elwing; the light of the Silmarils should go now to the Gods whence it came, and to Valinor must Maidros and Maglor return and there abide the judgement of the Gods, by whose decree alone would Fionwë yield the jewels from his charge.

Maglor was minded to submit, for he was sad at heart, and he said: 'The oath says not that we may not bide our time, and maybe in Valinor all shall be forgiven and forgot, and we shall come into our own.' But Maidros said that if once they returned and the favour of the Gods were withheld from them, then would their oath still remain, to be fulfilled in despair yet greater; 'and who can tell to what dreadful doom we shall come, if we disobey the Powers in their own land, or purpose ever to bring war again into their Guarded Realm?' And so it came that Maidros and Maglor crept into the camps of Fionwë, and laid hands on the Silmarils, and slew the guards; and there they prepared to defend themselves to the death. But Fionwë stayed his folk; and the brethren departed and fled far away.

Each took a single Silmaril, saying that one was lost unto them and two remained, and but two brethren. But the jewel burned the hand of Maidros in pain unbearable (and he had but one hand as has before been told); and he perceived that it was as Fionwë had said, and that his right thereto had become void, and that the oath was vain. And being in anguish and despair he cast himself into a gaping chasm filled with fire, and so ended; and his Silmaril was taken into the bosom of the Earth.

And it is told also of Maglor that he could not bear the pain with which the Silmaril tormented him; and he cast it at last into the sea, and thereafter wandered ever upon the shore singing in pain and regret beside the waves; for Maglor was the mightiest of the singers of old, but he came never back among the folk of Elfinesse.

In those days there was a mighty building of ships on the shores of the Western Sea, and especially upon the great isles, which in the disruption of the Northern world were fashioned of ancient Beleriand. Thence in many a fleet the survivors of the Gnomes and of the Western companies of the Dark-elves set sail into the West and came not again into the lands of weeping and of war; but the Light-elves marched back beneath the banners of their king following in the train of Fionwë's victory, and they were borne back in triumph unto Valinor.[7] But in the West the Gnomes and Dark-elves rehabited for the most part the Lonely Isle, that looks both East and West; and very fair did that land become, and so remains. But some returned even unto Valinor, as all were free to do who willed; and the Gnomes were admitted again to the love of Manwë and the pardon of the Valar, and the Teleri forgave their ancient grief, and the curse was laid to rest.

Yet not all would forsake the Outer Lands where they had long suffered and long dwelt; and some lingered many an age in the West and North, and especially in the western isles and the lands of Leithien. And among these were Maglor as has been told; and with him Elrond the Half-elfin,[8] who after went among mortal Men again, and from whom alone the blood of the elder race[9] and the seed divine of Valinor have come among Mankind (for he was son of Elwing, daughter of Dior, son of Lúthien, child of Thingol and Melian; and Eärendel his sire was son of Idril Celebrindal, the fair maid of Gondolin). But ever as the ages drew on and the Elf-folk faded on the Earth, they would still set sail at eve from our Western shores; as still they do, when now there linger few anywhere of their lonely companies.

★

1   *Hither* written above or replacing *Outer* at both occurrences.
2   In this sentence, in the first 'layer' of emendation, *many Men > some few Men* and *many beside of Men > some beside of Men*. Later the sentence was rewritten rapidly in pencil:

> And it is said that all that were left of the three Houses of the Fathers of Men fought for Fionwë, and to them were joined some of the Men of Hithlum who repenting of their evil servitude did deeds of valour against the Orcs; and so were fulfilled, &c.

See note 3.

3   Added here at the same time as the rewriting given in note 2:

> But most Men, and especially those new come out of the East, were on the side of the Enemy.

4   Added here:

> for as yet had none of these creatures of his cruel thought assailed the air.

5   *sons > children* (late change).

6   *and there Morgoth was thrown down* altered and expanded thus:

> and there Morgoth stood at last at bay; and yet not valiant. He fled unto the deepest of his mines and sued for peace and pardon. But his feet were hewn from under him, and he was hurled upon his face. Then was he bound, &c.

7   Added here:

> Yet little joy had they in their return, for they came without the Silmarils, and these could not be again found, unless the world was broken and re-made anew.

8   *Half-elfin > Half-elven* (cf. §17 in the Q II version, note 4).
9   *the elder race > the Firstborn*

19

[Q I comes to an end soon after the beginning of this section.]

Thus did the Gods adjudge when Fionwë and the sons of the Valar returned unto Valmar: the Outer Lands should thereafter be for Men, the younger children of the world; but to the Elves alone should the gateways of the West stand ever open; but if they would not come thither and tarried in the world of Men, then should they slowly fade and fail. And so hath it been; and this is the most grievous of the fruits of the works and lies of Morgoth.

For a while his Orcs and Dragons breeding again in dark places troubled and affrighted the world, as in far places they do yet; but ere the End all shall perish by the valour of mortal Men.

But Morgoth the Gods thrust through the Door of Timeless Night into the Void beyond the Walls of the World; and a guard is set for ever on that door. Yet the lies that

[Here the Q I text gives out, at the foot of a typescript page, but Q II continues to the end.]

This was the judgement of the Gods, when Fionwë and the sons of the Valar had returned unto Valmar: thereafter the Outer Lands should be for Mankind, the younger children of the world; but to the Elves alone should the gateways of the West stand ever open; and if they would not come thither and tarried in the world of Men, then they should slowly fade and fail. This is the most grievous of the fruits of the lies and works that Morgoth wrought, that the Eldalië should be sundered and estranged from Men. For a while his Orcs and his Dragons breeding again in dark places affrighted the world, and in sundry regions do so yet; but ere the End all shall perish by the valour of mortal Men.

But Morgoth the Gods thrust through the Door of Timeless Night into the Void, beyond the Walls of the World; and a guard is set for ever on that door, and Eärendel keeps watch upon the ramparts of the sky. Yet the lies that Melko,[1] Moeleg the mighty and accursed, Morgoth Bauglir the Dark Power Terrible, sowed in the hearts of Elves and Men have not all died, and cannot by the Gods be slain, and they live to work much evil even to this later day. Some say also that Morgoth at whiles secretly as a cloud that cannot be seen or felt, and yet is, and the poison is,[2] creeps back surmounting the Walls and visiteth the world; but others say that this is the black shadow of Thû, whom Morgoth made, and who escaped from the Battle Terrible, and dwells in dark places and perverts Men[3] to his dreadful allegiance and his foul worship.

After the triumph of the Gods Eärendel sailed still in the seas of heaven, but the Sun scorched him and the Moon hunted him in the sky, [and he departed long behind the world voyaging the Outer Dark a glimmering and fugitive star.][4] Then the Valar drew his white ship Wingelot[5] over the land of Valinor, and they filled it with radiance and hallowed it, and launched it through the Door of Night. And long Eärendel set sail into the starless vast, Elwing at his side,[6] the Silmaril upon his brow, voyaging the Dark behind the world, a glimmering and fugitive star. And ever and anon he returns and shines behind the courses of the Sun and Moon above the ramparts of the Gods, brighter than all other stars, the mariner of the sky, keeping watch against Morgoth upon the confines of the world. Thus shall he sail until he sees the Last Battle fought upon the plains of Valinor.

Thus spake the prophecy of Mandos, which he declared in Valmar at the judgement of the Gods, and the rumour of it was whispered among all the Elves of the West: when the world is old and the Powers grow weary, then Morgoth shall come back through the Door out of the Timeless Night; and he shall destroy the Sun and the Moon, but Eärendel shall come upon him as a white flame and drive him from the airs. Then shall the last battle be gathered on the fields of Valinor. In that day Tulkas shall strive with Melko, and on his right shall stand Fionwë and on his left Túrin Turambar, son of Húrin, Conqueror of Fate;[7] and it shall be the black sword of Túrin that deals unto Melko his death and final end; and so shall the children of Húrin and all Men be avenged.

Thereafter shall the Silmarils[8] be recovered out of sea and earth and air; for Eärendel shall descend and yield up that flame that he hath had in keeping. Then Fëanor shall bear the Three and yield them unto Yavanna Palúrien; and she will break them and with their fire rekindle the Two Trees, and a great light shall come forth; and the Mountains of Valinor shall be levelled, so that the light goes out over all the world. In that light the Gods will again grow young, and the Elves awake and all their dead arise, and the purpose of Ilúvatar be fulfilled concerning them. But of Men in that day the prophecy speaks not, save of Túrin only, and him it names among the Gods.[9]

Such is the end of the tales of the days before the days in the Northern regions of the Western world. Some of these things are sung and said yet by the fading Elves; and more still are sung by the vanished Elves that dwell now on the Lonely Isle. To Men of the race of Eärendel have they at times been told, and most to Eriol,[10] who alone of the mortals of later days, and yet now long ago, sailed to the Lonely Isle, and came back to the land of Leithien[11] where he lived, and remembered things that he had heard in fair Cortirion, the city of the Elves in Tol Eressëa.

★

1   *Melko* > *Melkor* (but only at the first occurrence).
2   *and yet is, and the poison is* > *and yet is venomous*
3   This sentence was rewritten:

> but others say that this is the black shadow of Sauron, who served Morgoth and became the greatest and most evil of his underlings; and Sauron escaped from the Great Battle, and dwelt in dark places and perverted Men, &c.

4   This sentence survives from an earlier point in the narrative in Q I (end of §17, p. 150); in Q II the latter part of it, *and he departed long behind the world voyaging the Outer Dark a glimmering and fugitive star*, was struck out, since it recurs immediately below.
5   *Wingelot* not here emended (as in §17 in the Q II version, note 6) to *Vingelot*.
6   *Elwing at his side* struck out.
7   Added here in pencil: *coming from the halls of Mandos*
8   *Thereafter shall the Silmarils* > *Thereafter Earth shall be broken and re-made, and the Silmarils*
9   *among the Gods* emended in pencil to *among the sons of the Gods*
10   Apparently changed, in pencil, to *Ereol*.
11   *Leithien* emended in pencil to *Britain*.

Commentary on the *Quenta*

Opening Section

This passage, to which there is nothing corresponding in S, may be compared with the *Lost Tales* I. 58, 66–7 on the one hand and with the *Valaquenta* (*The Silmarillion* pp. 25 ff.) on the other. This opening section of Q is the origin and precursor of the *Valaquenta*, as may be seen from the fall of its sentences and from many details of wording; while brief as it is it offers no actual contradictions to the text of the *Lost Tales*, save in a few details of names. The Nine Valar, referred to in S§1 and in the alliterative *Flight of the Noldoli* (III. 133), are now for the first time identified. This number was to remain in the Eight *Aratar* (eight, because 'one is removed from their number', *The Silmarillion* p. 29), though there was much shifting in the composition of the number in later writings; in the *Lost Tales* there were 'four great ones' among the Valar, Manwë, Melko, Ulmo, Aulë (I. 58).

The name of Mandos in the *Lost Tales*, Vefántur 'Fantur of Death', who 'called his hall with his own name Vê' (I. 66, 76), now becomes *Nefantur*. Nowhere is there any indication of the meaning of the first element; but the new name bears a curious resemblance to the Old English name of Mandos found in a list of such names of the Valar (p. 208): *Néfréa* (Old English *né(o)* 'corpse', *fréa* 'lord'). The late change of *Tavros* to *Tauros* is made also to the B-text of the *Lay of Leithian* (III. 195, 282).

Vána (here specifically given as *Văna*) is now the younger sister of Varda and Palúrien (in the *Lost Tales* these goddesses are not said to be 'related'); in *The Silmarillion* Vána remains the younger sister of Yavanna. We meet here the Gnomish name of Melko, *Moeleg*, which the Gnomes will not use; cf. the *Valaquenta* (p. 31): 'the Noldor, who among the Elves suffered most from his malice, will not utter it [Melkor], and they name him Morgoth, the Dark Enemy of the World'. The original Gnomish form was *Belcha* (II. 44, 67).

1

In this section of Q, before the replacement page (see note 2) was written, the only important developments from S are the reduction of the periods of the Trees from fourteen hours to seven (and this only came in with an alteration to the typescript, see note 1), and the explicit statement that Silpion was the elder of the Trees, and shone alone for a time (the Opening Hour). It is also said that the Gnomes afterwards called the Trees *Bansil* and *Glingol*. In the tale of *The Fall of Gondolin* these names were expressly those of the Trees of Gondolin (see II. 214–16), but (especially since *Glingol* occurs in a rejected reading in *The Cottage of Lost Play* (I. 22) as a name of the Golden Tree of Valinor) it seems clear that they were the Gnomish names of the original Trees, which were transferred to their scions in Gondolin; in the *Lay of the Children of Húrin* and in the *Lay of Leithian*, as here in Q, Glingol and Bansil (later emended to *Glingal* and *Belthil*) are the Trees of Valinor. But in *The Silmarillion* Glingal and Belthil are the particular names of Turgon's images of the Trees in Gondolin.

With the replacement page in this section (note 2) there are several further developments, and the passage describing the periods of the Trees and the mingling of the lights is effectively the final form, only differing from that in *The Silmarillion* (pp. 38–9) in some slight rhythmical changes in the sentences. Yavanna no longer 'plants' the Trees, and Nienna is present at their birth (replacing Vána of the *Lost Tales*, I. 71–2); the Valar sit upon their 'thrones of council' in the Ring of Doom near the golden gates of Valmar; and the moving shadows of Silpion's leaves, not mentioned in S or in Q as first written, reappear from the *Lost Tales* (see I. 88). Here also appear the names of Taniquetil, *Ialassë* 'Everlasting Whiteness', Gnomish *Amon-Uilas*, and *Tinwenairin* 'crowned with stars'; cf. *The Silmarillion* p. 37:

Taniquetil the Elves name that holy mountain, and Oiolossë Everlasting Whiteness, and Elerrína Crowned with Stars, and many names beside; but the Sindar spoke of it in their later tongue as Amon Uilos.

'Elves' is still used here in contradistinction to 'Gnomes'; on this usage see p. 44.

2

Q remains close to S in this section. I have noticed in commenting on S the absence of certain features that are found both in the *Lost Tales* and in *The Silmarillion*: (1) the coming of the three Elvish ambassadors to Valinor, (2) the Elves who did not leave the Waters of Awakening, (3) the two starmakings of Varda, and (4) the chain Angainor with which Morgoth was bound; and there is still no mention of them. As I have said (p. 76), the *Quenta* though written in a finished manner is still very much an outline, and the absence of these elements may be thought to be due merely to its compressed nature. Against this, however, in respect of (1), is the statement in Q that Thingol 'came never to Valinor', whereas in the old story (I. 115) as in *The Silmarillion* (p. 52) Tinwelint/Thingol was one of the three original ambassadors; and in respect of (3), Varda is said in Q to have strewn 'the unlit skies' with stars. As regards (4), it is said later in Q (§18) that Morgoth was bound after the Last Battle 'with the chain Angainor, wherewith Tulkas had chained him aforetime'.

The constellation of the Great Bear is called the Burning Briar, and the Sickle of the Gods, in the *Lay of Leithian*.

It is said here that the Elves named themselves *Eldar*, in contrast both to the old idea (I. 235) that *Eldar* was the name given to them by the Gods, and to *The Silmarillion* (p. 49), where Oromë 'named them in their own tongue Eldar, the people of the stars'.

The original statement in Q that Ingwë 'never came back into the Outer Lands until these tales were near their end' is a reference to his leadership of the March of the Elves of Valinor in the second assault on Morgoth, in which he perished (I. 129). The revised statement given in note 6, saying that Ingwë never came back from the West, is virtually the same as that in *The Silmarillion* (p. 53); see the Commentary on §17. The Gnomish forms of the names of the three leaders, *Ing*, *Finn*, and *Elu*, are removed by the rewritings given in notes 6, 8, and 11; and the use of *Quendi* for the First Kindred ('who sometimes are alone called Elves', see p. 44) is displaced by *Lindar* in a late emendation (note 7), while *Quendi* reappears (note 5) as the name for all the Elves. These late changes belong to a new nomenclature that came in after the *Quenta* was completed.

3

While Q again follows S very closely here, there is one important narrative development: the first appearance of the story of Ossë's sitting on the rocks of the seashore and instructing the Teleri, and of his persuading some to remain 'on the beaches of the world' (the later Elves of the Havens of Brithombar and Eglarest, ruled by Círdan the Shipwright). And with the late addition given in note 7 there appears the removal of the First Kindred (here called the Lindar) from Tûn, and their sunderance from the Gnomes; here there is a detail not taken up into subsequent texts (probably because it was overlooked), that the Noldoli of Tûn left the tower of Ingwë uninhabited, though they tended the lamp.

As in §2, *Finn* was emended to *Finwë* (and *Ing* to *Ingwë*), although the names of the Noldorin princes are said to be given in Gnomish form, and *Ylmir* found in S is not taken up in Q (similarly *Óin* in S§3, but *Uinen* in the opening section of Q).

In the passage on the Noldorin princes (a later addition to S) Celegorm becomes 'the friend of Oromë' (a development arising from the later story of Huan, see §10); Finrod's third son, *Anrod* in S, becomes *Angrod*. On the change *Finweg > Fingon* see p. 46.

4

Many touches found in the story in *The Silmarillion* now make their appearance in Q (as Fëanor's wearing the Silmarils at great feasts, Morgoth's sight of the domes of Valmar far off in the mingling of the lights, his laugh 'as he sped down the long western slopes', his great cry that echoed through the world as Ungoliant's webs enmeshed him). I have noticed in my commentary on S that 'the entire story of Morgoth's going to Formenos (not yet so named) and his speech with Fëanor before the doors has yet to appear', and it has not done so in Q; but the late interpolation given in note 6, stating that a messenger came to the Gods in council with tidings that Morgoth was in the North of Valinor and journeying to the house of Finwë, is the first hint of this element. In *The Silmarillion* (p. 72) messengers came to the Valar from Finwë at Formenos telling of Morgoth's first coming there, and this is followed by the news from Tirion that he had passed through the Calacirya – a movement that appears at this point in S and Q ('he escaped through the pass of Kôr, and from the tower of Ingwë the Elves saw him pass in thunder and in wrath').

There is no mention in S§4 of the great festival at this point in the narrative, and its appearance in §5 looks like an afterthought (see p. 47); that the same is still true in Q shows the close dependence of the later version on the earlier at this stage in the work.

5

In this section Q as usual contains many details and enduring phrases not found in S, such as the wailing of the Foamriders beside the sea,

Fëanor's contempt for the Valar 'who cannot even keep their own realm from their foe', the drawn swords of the oath-takers, the fighting on 'the great arch of the gate and on the lamplit quays and piers' of Swanhaven, and the suggestion that the speaker of the Prophecy may have been Mandos himself. There was no mention in S of the Gnomes who did not join the Flight (they being those who were on Taniquetil celebrating the festival): this now reappears from the *Lost Tales* (I. 176); nor was it said that not all Fingolfin's people shared in the Kinslaying at Swanhaven.

The reference to 'the song of the Flight of the Gnomes' may be to the alliterative poem *The Flight of the Noldoli* (III. 131 ff.), though that was abandoned at the Fëanorian Oath: perhaps my father still thought to continue it one day, or to write a new poem on the subject.*

The pencilled addition 'Finrod returned' (note 8) indicates the later story, according to which Finarfin (Finrod) left the march of the Noldor after hearing the Prophecy of the North (*The Silmarillion* p. 88); in S as emended (note 9) and in Q Finrod only came up with Fingolfin after the burning of the ships by the Fëanorians, and only after that did Finrod return to Valinor.

Helkaraksë reappears in Q from the *Lost Tales*, but is now rendered 'the Strait of the Grinding Ice', whereas its original meaning was 'Ice-fang', and referred to the narrow neck of land which 'ran out from the western land almost to the eastern shores' and was separated from the Great Lands by the Qerkaringa or Chill Gulf (I. 166–7 and note 5).

6

If there ever was a 'song of the Sun and Moon' (called in *The Silmarillion* p. 99 by an Elvish name, *Narsilion*) it has disappeared. The account in Q scarcely expands the extremely cursory passage in S; but the reason now given for the change in the divine plan is not that the Gods 'find it safer' to send the Sun and Moon beneath the Earth: rather it is changed on account of 'the waywardness of Tilion and his rivalry with Úrien', and still more because of the complaints of Lórien and Nienna against the unceasing light. This element re-emerges from the *Tale of the Sun and Moon* (I. 189–90), where the Valar who protested were Mandos and Fui Nienna, Lórien, and Vána. Likewise the names *Rána* and *Úr* given by the Gods to the Moon and Sun go back to the old story, where however *Úr* is said to be the Elvish name: the Gods named the Sun *Sári* (I. 186–7).

The Sun-maiden is now named *Úrien*, emended to *Árien* (her name in *The Silmarillion*), replacing *Urwendi* (< *Urwen*); she is said to have

---

* Later this becomes a reference to 'that lament which is named *Noldolantë*, the Fall of the Noldor, that Maglor made ere he was lost' (*The Silmarillion* p. 87); but I have found no trace of this.

'tended the golden flowers in the gardens of Vana', which clearly derives from the tending of Laurelin by Urwen(di) in the *Lost Tales* (I. 73). Tilion, the hunter with the silver bow from the company of Oromë, not Ilinsor, is now the steersman of the Moon; but as I noted in I. 88, Tilion, who in *The Silmarillion* 'lay in dreams by the pools of Estë [Lórien's wife], in Telperion's flickering beams', perhaps owes something to the figure of Silmo in the *Lost Tales*, the youth whom Lórien loved and who was given the task of 'watering' Silpion. The words of Q concerning Tilion, 'often he wandered from his course pursuing the stars upon the heavenly fields', and the reference to his rivalry with Úrien (Árien), clearly derive from the passage in the old tale (I. 195) where it is told of Ilinsor that he was 'jealous of the supremacy of the Sun' and that 'often he set sail in chase of [the stars]'.

A trace of the old conception of the Moon survives in the reference to 'the floating island of the Moon', a phrase still found in *The Silmarillion* (see I. 202).

The occurrence of the name *Eruman* of the land where Men awoke (*Murmenalda* in *Gilfanon's Tale*, 'far to the east of Palisor', I. 232–3, *Hildórien* in *The Silmarillion*, 'in the eastward regions of Middle-earth') is strange, and can only be regarded as a passing application of it in a wholly different meaning, for it was in fact retained in a refinement of its original sense – the land between the mountains and the sea south of Taniquetil and Kôr, also in the *Lost Tales* called *Arvalin* (which is the name given to it in S and Q): *Eruman* (> *Araman*) afterwards became the wasteland between the mountains and the sea north of Taniquetil (see I. 82–3).

Though the phrase in Q 'the oldest days before the waning of the Elves and the waxing of mortals' was retained in *The Silmarillion* (p. 103), a later addition to Q (note 6), not retained, is more explicit: 'for measured time had come into the world, and the first of days; and thereafter the lives of the Eldar that remained in the Hither Lands were lessened, and their waning was begun.' The meaning of this is undoubtedly that measured time had come into the Great or Hither Lands, for the phrase 'thus measured time came into the Hither Lands' is found in the earliest *Annals of Beleriand* (p. 295). This seems to relate the waning of the Elves to the coming of 'measured time', and may in turn be associated with the following passage from *The Silmarillion* (p. 103):

From this time forth were reckoned the Years of the Sun. Swifter and briefer are they than the long Years of the Trees in Valinor. In that time the air of Middle-earth became heavy with the breath of growth and mortality, and the changing and ageing of all things was hastened exceedingly.

In the earlier writings the waning or fading of the Elves is always, clearly if mysteriously, a necessary concomitant of the waxing of Men.* Since Men came into the world at the rising of the Sun it may be that the conceptions are not fundamentally at variance: Men, and measured time, arose in the world together, and were the sign for the declining of the Elves. But it must be remembered that the doom of 'waning' was, or became, a part of the Prophecy of the North (*The Silmarillion* p. 88):

> And those that endure in Middle-earth and come not to Mandos shall grow weary of the world as with a great burden, and shall wane, and become as shadows of regret before the younger race that cometh after.

On the phrase used of Eärendel: 'he came too late', see II. 257; and cf. Q§17: 'He came too late to bring messages to the Elves, for the Elves had gone.'

7

In this section Q does scarcely more than polish the text of S and embody the later alterations made to it, and the content has been discussed in the commentary on S. In the sentence added to the end of Q (note 6) there is a clear echo of the old idea of the fading Elves of Luthany, and the Elves of Tol Eressëa who have withdrawn from the world 'and there fade now no more' (see II. 301, 326).

8

Q provides here new details but otherwise follows S closely. The site of the First Battle (by later interpolation called 'The Battle under Stars') is now in the great Northern plain, still unnamed before its desolation, when it became Dor-na-Fauglith; in *The Silmarillion* (p. 106) the Orcs attacked through the passes of the Mountains of Shadow and the battle was fought 'on the grey fields of Mithrim'. Fëanor's sight of Thangorodrim as he died now appears, and his cursing of the name of Morgoth as he gazed on the mountain – transferred from Túrin, who did the same after the death of Beleg in the *Lay of the Children of Húrin* (III. 87).

A very minor structural change is found in the story of the feigned offer of a peace-treaty by Morgoth. In S this was made before the death of Fëanor, and Fëanor indeed refused to treat; after his death Maidros 'induced the Gnomes to meet Morgoth'. In Q 'even in the hour of his death there came to [his sons] an embassy from Morgoth acknowledging

---

*See II. 326. In one place it was said that the Elves 'cannot live in an air breathed by a number of Men equal to their own or greater' (II. 283). In the *Lay of the Children of Húrin* (see III. 54) appears the idea of 'the goodness of the earth' being usurped by Men, and this reappears in §14 in both S and Q (in S with the added statement that 'the Elves needed the light of the Trees').

his defeat, and offering to treat, and tempting them with a Silmaril'. The greater force sent by Morgoth is now referred to; and it is seen that the numbers of the Balrogs were still conceived to be very great: 'but Morgoth brought the greater, *and they were Balrogs*' (contrast *The Silmarillion*: 'but Morgoth sent the more, *and there were Balrogs*').

In the story of the rescue of Maidros by Finweg (Fingon) the explicit and puzzling statement of S that it was only now that Manwë 'fashioned the race of eagles' is changed to a statement that it was now that he sent them forth; by the later change of 'sent' to 'had sent' the final text is reached. In Q are found the details that Finweg (Fingon) climbed to Maidros unaided but could not reach him, and of the thirty fathoms of Thorndor's outstretched wings, the staying of Finweg's hand from his bow, the twice repeated appeal of Maidros that Finweg slay him, and the healing of Maidros so that he lived to wield his sword better with his left hand than he had with his right – cf. the *Lay of the Children of Húrin* (III. 65): *his left wieldeth / his sweeping sword*. But there are of course still many elements in the final story that do not appear: as the former close friendship of Maidros and Fingon, the song of Fingon and Maidros' answer, Fingon's prayer to Manwë, and Maidros' begging of forgiveness for the desertion in Araman and waiving of his claim to kingship over all the Noldor.

9

In this section of the narrative Q shows an extraordinary and unexpected expansion of S, much greater than has been the case hitherto, and many elements of the history in the published *Silmarillion* appear here (notably still absent are the entire story of Thingol's cold welcome to the new-come Noldor, and of course the origin at this time of Nargothrond and Gondolin); but S, as emended and interpolated, was still the basis. A few of the new features had in fact already emerged in the poems: thus the Elvish watchtower on Tol Sirion first appears in Canto VII of the *Lay of Leithian* (early 1928); the deaths of Angrod and Egnor in the battle that ended the Siege of Angband, called the Battle of Sudden Flame in one of the earlier additions in this section (note 19), in Canto VI of the Lay (see p. 55); the Gorge of Aglon in Canto VII and Himling in Canto X (both passages written in 1928); Esgalduin already in the *Lay of the Children of Húrin* (but its source in 'secret wells in Taur-na-Fuin' has not been mentioned before). But much of the content of Q in this section introduces wholly new elements into the legends.

The later pencilled alterations and additions given in the notes were put in a good while afterwards, and the names thus introduced (*Taur Danin, Eredlindon, Ossiriand*—which was *Assariad* in Q§14, *Dorthonion, Sauron*) belong to later phases. But it may be noticed here that the change of *Second Battle* to *Third Battle* (note 19) is explained by the development of the Glorious Battle (*Dagor Aglareb*, a late addition given in note 15), so that the Battle of Sudden Flame became the third of the Battles of Beleriand. With 'the Foreboding of the Kings' in note 15 cf. *The Silmarillion* p. 115: 'A victory it was, and yet a warning'; or the reference may be to the foreboding dreams of Turgon and Felagund (*ibid*. p. 114).

The names of Beleriand given in one of the earlier additions (note 2), *Noldórien*, *Geleidhian*, and *Ingolondë* 'the fair and sorrowful', are interesting. With these may be compared the list of names given in III. 160, which include *Noldórinan* and *Golodhinand*, the latter showing *Golodh*, the Sindarin equivalent of Quenya *Noldo*; *Geleidhian* obviously contains the same element (cf. *Annon-in-Gelydh*, the Gate of the Noldor). *Ingolondë* occurs again in the next version of 'The Silmarillion' (the version nearing completion in 1937, see I. 8):

> And that region was named of old in the language of Doriath *Beleriand*, but after the coming of the Noldor it was called also in the tongue of Valinor *Ingolondë*, the fair and sorrowful, the Kingdom of the Gnomes.

If *Ingolondë* means 'the Kingdom of the Gnomes', this name also should probably be associated with the stem seen in *Noldo*, *Golodh*. In much later writing my father gave the original form of the word as *ngolodō*, whence Quenya *ñoldo*, Sindarin *golodh*, noting that *ñ* = 'the Fëanorian letter for the back nasal, the *ng* of *king*'. He also said that the mother-name of Finrod (= Felagund) was *Ingoldo*: this was 'a form of *ñoldo* with syllabic *n*, and being in full and more dignified form is more or less equivalent to "*the* Noldo", one eminent in the kindred'; and he noted that 'the name was never Sindarized (the form would have been *Angoloð*)'.

How significant is the likeness of *Ingolondë* to *England*? I cannot certainly answer this; but it seems plain from the conclusion of Q that England was one of the great isles that remained after the destruction of Beleriand (see the commentary on §18).

The territory of the other sons of Finrod (Finarfin), Orodreth, Angrod, and Egnor, is now set in the pineclad highlands which afterwards were Taur-na-Fuin.

Quite new in Q is the passage concerning the Dwarves, with the notable statement that the Fëanorians 'made war upon' the Dwarves of Nogrod and Belegost, changed afterwards to 'had converse with' them; this led ultimately to the picture in *The Silmarillion* (p. 113) of Caranthir's contemptuous but highly profitable traffic with the Dwarves in Thargelion. The older view of the Dwarves (see II. 247) was still present when my father wrote the *Quenta*: though 'they do not serve Morgoth', 'they are in many things more like his people' (a hard saying indeed); they were naturally hostile to the Gnomes, who as naturally made war on them. The Dwarf-cities of Nogrod and Belegost go back to the *Tale of the Nauglafring*, where the Dwarves are called *Nauglath* (*Nauglir* in Q, *Naugrim* in *The Silmarillion*); but in the *Tale* the Indrafangs are the Dwarves of Belegost.

The Feast of Reunion, which goes back to *Gilfanon's Tale* (I. 240) but is not mentioned in S (where there is only a reference to the 'meeting' of the Gnomes with Ilkorins and Men), reappears in Q ('The Feast of Meeting'); it is held in the Land of Willows, not as in *The Silmarillion* near the pools of Ivrin. The presence of Men at the feast has been excised, and there now enters the story of the passage of Men over the Blue Mountains (called in an addition *Erydluin*, note 3) and the encounter of Felagund, hunting in the East with Celegorm, and Bëor. This passage in Q is the forerunner of that in *The Silmarillion* (p. 140), with the strangeness of the tongue of Men in Felagund's ears, his taking up Bëor's harp, the wisdom that was in Felagund's song, so that Men called him 'Gnome or Wisdom' (note 12). It is interesting to observe that after my father abandoned the use of the word 'Gnome' (see I. 43–4) he retained Nóm as the word for 'wisdom' in the language of the people of Bëor (*The Silmarillion* p. 141). The abiding of Bëor with Felagund until his death is mentioned (and in a late addition the dwelling of the Bëorians on Dorthonion, note 14).

Hador, called the Tall and by a later change (note 11) the Golden-haired, now first enters, and he is one of the two leaders of Men to cross the Mountains into Beleriand. Later, whereas in the House of Bëor the original leader remained, and new generations were introduced beneath him, in the case of the House of Hador the original leader was moved downwards and replaced by Marach; but the two Houses remained known as the House of Bëor and the House of Hador.

Hador has, beside Gumlin (who appeared in the second version of the *Lay of the Children of Húrin* as Húrin's father, III. 115, 126), another son Haleth; and this occurrence of Haleth is not merely an initial application of the name without particular significance, but implies that originally the 'Hadorian' and 'Halethian' houses of the Elf-friends were one and the same: the affinity of the names *Ha*dor, *Ha*leth (though Haleth ultimately became the Lady Haleth) goes back to their origin as father and son. The pencilled words 'Haleth the hunter, and little later' (note 11) were very probably intended to go after the words 'After them came', i.e.

They were the first of Men to come into Beleriand. After them came Haleth the hunter, and little later Hador, &c.

This shows of course the development of the third house of the Elf-friends, later called the Haladin; and with the removal of Haleth to independent status as the leader of a third people the other son of Hador became Gundor (note 11). Thus:

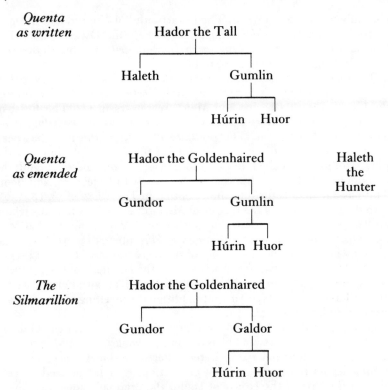

Quenta as written

Hador the Tall

Haleth   Gumlin

Húrin   Huor

Quenta as emended

Hador the Goldenhaired   Haleth the Hunter

Gundor   Gumlin

Húrin Huor

The Silmarillion

Hador the Goldenhaired

Gundor   Galdor

Húrin Huor

Morwen now gains the name 'Elfsheen', and the association of the House of Hador with Fingolfin in Hithlum appears.

The battle that ended the Siege of Angband had already been described in Canto VI (III. 212–13) of the *Lay of Leithian* (March 1928); a second description of it is found in Canto XI of the Lay (III. 275; September 1930). By later additions the name 'The Battle of Sudden Flame' (note 19) and Glómund's presence in it (note 16) are introduced (on the name *Glómund* see p. 60). Here also is the flight of many Dark-elves (not Gnomes as in S) to Doriath, to the increase of Thingol's power.

It is now suggested that Celegorm and Curufin came to Nargothrond after the Battle of Sudden Flame as to a refuge already in being, and with them came Orodreth their friend; this is to be related to the earlier passage in Q (§5): 'Orodreth, Angrod, and Egnor took the part of Fëanor' (in the debate before the Flight of the Noldoli). That Thingol's halls in Doriath were the inspiration for Nargothrond is also suggested.

With the account here of the challenge of Fingolfin and his death compare the *Lay of Leithian* Canto XII. This dates from late September 1930, and is later than this section of Q (see the commentary on §10), as is seen by the reference to Thorndor's 'beak of gold' (line 3616, found already in the A-text of the Lay), in contrast to his 'claw' in Q, emended to 'bill' (note 23).*

10

This version of the legend of Beren and Lúthien is unlike previous sections of the *Quenta*: for whereas hitherto it has been an independent extension of S, here (for a good part of its length) it is a compression of the *Lay of Leithian*. Very slight differences between Q and the Lay are not in my opinion significant, but are merely the result of précis.

At the end of the fight with Celegorm and Curufin, however, Q and the Lay diverge. In the Lay Beren's healing (not mentioned in Q) is followed by debate between him and Lúthien (3148ff.), their return to the borders of Doriath, and Beren's departure alone on Curufin's horse, leaving Huan to guard Lúthien (3219ff.). The narrative in Canto XI begins with Beren's reaching Dor-na-Fauglith and his Song of Parting; then follows (3342ff.) Lúthien's overtaking of Beren, having ridden after him on Huan, Huan's coming to them shortly after with the wolfcoat and batskin from the Wizard's Isle, and his counsel to them. In Q, on the other hand, the story is essentially different, and the difference cannot be explained by compression (admittedly at this point severe): for Huan went off to the Wizard's Isle for the wolfcoat and batskin and *then* Beren and Lúthien rode North together *on horseback*, until they came to a point where they must put on the disguises. This is clearly the form of the story given in Synopsis IV for this part of the Lay (III. 273):

Lúthien heals Beren. They tell Huan of their doubts and debate and he goes off and brings the wolfham and batskin from the Wizard's Isle. Then he speaks for the last time.

They prepare to go to Angband.

But Q is later than Synopsis IV, for the idea had already emerged that Huan spoke thrice, the third time at his death.

It seems at least extremely probable, then, that Q§10 was written when the *Lay of Leithian* extended to about the point where the narrative turns to the events following the routing of Celegorm and Curufin and Huan's desertion of his master. Now against line 3031 is written the date November 1929, probably referring forwards (see the note to this line), and the next date, against line 3220 (the return of Beren and Lúthien to Doriath), is 25 September 1930. In the last week of September of that year my father composed the small amount remaining of Canto X, and Cantos XI and XII, taking the story from Beren's solitary departure on Curufin's horse to the enspelling of Carcharoth at the gates of Angband;

*Cf. also 'thirty feet' as the span of Thorndor's wings emended to 'thirty fathoms' in Q§8 (note 7), 'thirty fathoms' in the Lay (line 3618).

and this part had not, according to the analysis above, been composed when Q§10 was written.* These considerations make 1930 a virtually certain date for the composition of Q or at least the major part of it; and this fits well with my father's statement (see p. 11) that the 'Sketch' was written 'c. 1926–30', for we have seen that the original writing of S dates from 1926 (III. 3), and the interpolations and emendations to it, which were taken up into Q, would belong to the following years. The statement in Q that 'in the lay of Lúthien is all told how they came to Angband's gate' must be an anticipation of further composition of the Lay that my father was at this time premeditating.

From here on there are minor narrative divergences between Q and the Lay. Thus in the prose Morgoth 'fashioned' (rather than bred) Carcharoth (cf. Synopsis III 'fashions', Synopsis V 'fashions' > 'chooses', III. 293–4). The wolf's names Borosaith, Everhungry, and Anfauglin, Jaws of Thirst (an addition given in note 9), are not found in the Synopses or the Lay, but the latter, in the form Anfauglir, reappears in The Silmarillion (p. 180) with the same meaning.

In the prose Lúthien is praised for casting off her disguise and naming her own name, feigning 'that she was brought captive by the wolves of Thû', whereas in the Lay she claims at first to be Thuringwethil, sent to Morgoth by Thû as a messenger, and it seems that her bat-raiment falls from her at Morgoth's command (lines 3959–65), and that he divines who she is without her naming her name. In these features Q agrees rather with Synopsis III, where she does say who she is, and 'lets fall her bat-garb' (III. 305). It is not said in the Lay that 'she flung the magic robe in his face' (but in The Silmarillion p. 181 'she cast her cloak before his eyes'), and there is in the prose the notable detail of the Orcs' secret laughter at Morgoth's fall from his throne. In Q Beren leaps forth, casting aside the wolfcoat, when Morgoth falls, whereas in the Lay Lúthien must rouse him from his swoon. The ascription of the snapping of Curufin's knife to dwarvish 'treachery' agrees however with the verse ('by treacherous smiths of Nogrod made', line 4161) – this feature is not found in The Silmarillion, of course; while the arousing of the sleepers by the sound of its breaking agrees with the A-text of the Lay (lines 4163–6), not with the revised version of B, where the shard struck Morgoth's brow.

From the point where the Lay ends, with the biting off of Beren's hand by the Wolf, the Q account can be compared with the Synopses. The 'wanderings and despair' of Beren and Lúthien and 'their rescue by Huan' clearly associate Q with Synopsis V (III. 312), and the marginal addition (note 11) concerning their rescue by Thorndor, their flight over Gondolin, and their setting down in Brethil, belongs with the brief late outline given in III. 309. The structure of events in Doriath, with

---

*Cf. also the internal evidence given in the commentary on §9 that the Fall of Fingolfin in Canto XII is later than Q's account.

Boldog's raid preceding the embassy from Celegorm to Thingol, agrees with Synopsis IV (III. 310) rather than with Synopsis V (III. 311), where Thingol's host moving against Nargothrond meets Boldog; but Q agrees with Synopsis V in many details, such as the presence of Beleg and Mablung in the battle with Boldog, and Thingol's changed view of Beren.

At the end of this section the Land of the Dead that Live reaches, in the emendation given in note 15, its final placing in Ossiriand, and the name *Gwerth-i-Cuina* appears for the Dead that Live (later in Q as originally written, §14, the names are *Assariad* and *Cuilwarthien*, cf. *i·Cuilwarthon* of the *Lost Tales*). On the name *Geleidhian* for Broseliand/Beleriand, occurring in this emendation, see the commentary on §9.

On the statements at the end of this section concerning Lúthien's fate, and the 'long span of life and joy' granted to Beren and Lúthien by Mandos, see the commentary on §14.

A matter unconcerned with the story of Beren and Lúthien arises at the beginning of this section, where it is said that Bëor was slain in the Battle of Sudden Flame; in §9, on the other hand, 'Bëor lived till death with Felagund'. This can be interpreted to mean that he died in Felagund's service at the time that his son Barahir rescued Felagund, but such an explanation is forced (especially since in the later form of his legend his death was expressly of old age, and was a source of great wonder to the Elves who witnessed it, *The Silmarillion* p. 149). It seems more likely that there is here an inconsistency within Q, admittedly surprising since the two passages are not widely separated.

For the emendation of 'Second Battle' to 'Third Battle' (note 1) see the commentary on §9; and with the change of *Tinfang Warble* to *Tinfang Gelion* (note 12) cf. line 503 in the *Lay of Leithian*, where the same change was made.

11

In this section the *Quenta* becomes, both in structure and in much of its actual wording, the first draft of Chapter 20 ('Of the Fifth Battle') of *The Silmarillion*.

There appears now the unwise and premature demonstration of his gathering strength by Maidros, warning Morgoth of what was afoot among his enemies and allowing him time to send out his emissaries among the Men from the East – though this is less clear and explicit in Q as originally written than it becomes with the rewriting given in note 14, and even then the two phases of the war are not clearly distinguished. Some further development in this had still to come: in *The Silmarillion* the coming of the Easterlings into Beleriand is told at an earlier point (p. 157; cf. note 1 to this section in Q), and it is said that some of them, though not all, 'were already secretly under the dominion of Morgoth, and came at his call'; the entry of his 'spies and workers of treason' was made easier 'for the faithless Men of his secret allegiance were yet deep in the secrets of the sons of Fëanor' (p. 189). Though these agents of Morgoth are said in Q (as rewritten, note 14) to have gone especially to the sons of Ulfang, and though Bor and his sons are mentioned, there is no suggestion here of the good faith of the sons of Bor, who slew Ulfast and Ulwarth in the midst of the battle (*The Silmarillion* p. 193).

The Dwarves now play a part in these events, though only as furnishers of weapons; but in Q they are shown as calculating and indeed cynical ('we are friends of neither side – until it has won'), actuated solely by desire for gain. In *The Silmarillion* the Dwarves actually entered the war on Maedhros' side, and 'won renown': Azaghâl Lord of Belegost wounded Glaurung as the dragon crawled over him (p. 193). But at this time I do not think that my father would have conceived of the Dwarves of the mountains taking any active part in the wars of the Elves.

Whereas in S (as emended, §11 note 1) it is only said that 'Orodreth because of Felagund his brother will not come', there now appears in Q the small company out of Nargothrond who went to the war under the banners of Finweg (Fingon) 'and came never back, save one'; the leader is Flinding son of Fuilin, who comes out of the old *Tale of Turambar* and the *Lay of the Children of Húrin*, and who is thus given a fuller history before he fled from the Mines of Melko to meet Beleg in the Forest of Night. In the tale as in the poem (see III.53) it is only said that he had been of the people of the Rodothlim (of Nargothrond) and that he was captured by Orcs. By later change in Q (note 7) he becomes Gwindor son of Guilin. But it is notable that although the wild onrush of the Gnomes of Nargothrond, that carried them even into Angband and made Morgoth tremble on his throne, was led by Flinding/Gwindor, his heroic fury had as yet no special cause: for the herald of Finweg/Fingon who was murdered on Dor-na-Fauglith in order to provoke the Elves of Hithlum to attack Morgoth's decoy force is not named.* The next and final stage was for the herald to become Gelmir of Nargothrond, Gwindor's brother, who had been captured in the Battle of Sudden Flame: it was indeed grief for the loss of Gelmir that had brought Gwindor out of Nargothrond against the will of Orodreth (*The Silmarillion* p. 188). Thus Flinding/Gwindor, devised long before for a different story, ends by being, in his earlier life, the involuntary cause of the loss of the great battle and the ruin of the kingdoms of the Noldor in Middle-earth.

The account of the behaviour of the people of Haleth in the rewritten passage given in note 7 shows my father in doubt: they made ready for

---

*The statement that 'Morgoth led forth one of the heralds . . . and slew him upon the plain' certainly does not mean, I think, that Morgoth himself came forth and did the deed; rather 'Morgoth' here stands for 'the servants of Morgoth, obeying his command'.

war, then they abode in the forest and few came forth 'because of the wounding of Beren in the wood' (cf. 'Men remembered that wound against the sons of Fëanor', Q§10; 'Men remembered at the Marching Forth', the *Lay of Leithian* line 3103). In the event, the former idea prevailed: 'In the forest of Brethil Halmir, lord of the People of Haleth, gathered his men, and they whetted their axes', and in the battle 'fell most of the Men of Brethil, and came never back to their woods' (*The Silmarillion* pp. 189, 192).

In this same rewritten passage the later story of the foundation of Gondolin *before* the Battle of Unnumbered Tears is present, with Turgon coming forth 'unlooked for' with a great host. It is perhaps strange that in the subsequent passage of rewriting (note 14) Maidros 'appointed a day, and sent word to Fingon *and Turgon*', and 'Fingon *and Turgon* and the Men of Hithlum . . . were gathered ready in the West upon the borders of the Thirsty Plain', which does not at all suggest that Turgon had just arrived, but seems rather to revert to the earlier story (in S, note 1, and in Q as originally written) according to which he was one of the leaders of the Western Elves from the beginning of the preparations for war ('all the hosts of Hithlum . . . were ready to his summons, and Finweg and Turgon and Huor and Húrin were their chiefs'). It seems that the emended narrative in Q represents an intermediate stage: Turgon now emerges from Gondolin already long since in existence, but he does not march up in the nick of time, on the day itself, as in the later story: he comes, certainly unexpected, but in time to take part in the final strategic preparations.

The challenge to Morgoth, summoning by silver trumpets his host to come forth, was afterwards abandoned, but Morgoth's decoying force, 'great and yet not too great', survived, as did Húrin's warning against premature attack. The uncontrollable bursting forth of the Elves of Hithlum and their allies is brought about in the same way as in the later story, even though there is still lacking in Q the fine point that the one slaughtered before their eyes was the brother of Gwindor of Nargothrond; and there is present in the Q narrative the initial success of the hosts of Hithlum, the near-miscarriage of Morgoth's plans, the sweeping of the banners of Finweg (Fingon) over the plain to the very walls of Angband. The final stages of the battle are less fully treated in Q, but all the essential structure is there; several features are indeed still absent, as the death of Fingon at the hands of Gothmog (but the flame from his helm as it was cloven is mentioned, a feature that goes back to the *Lay of the Children of Húrin*, and from which the words *Finweg (Fingon) fell in flame of swords* derive, see III. 103), the fall of the Men of Brethil in the rearguard (see above), the presence of the Dwarves of Belegost (with the death of Azaghâl and the wounding of the dragon), the fateful words between Huor and Turgon that were overheard by Maeglin (*The Silmarillion* p. 194).

Glómund's presence at the Battle of Unnumbered Tears was introduced in a later addition to the text of S (§13, note 3) and is now incorporated in the Q narrative; his earlier appearance at the Battle of Sudden Flame enters with an addition to Q§9 (note 16), and is referred to again here (note 17) – 'the second battle of the North', because the Glorious Battle, Dagor Aglareb, which became the second battle, had not yet been developed. But according to Q the dragon 'was not yet come to his full growth' at the Battle of Unnumbered Tears; later, he was already full grown at the Battle of Sudden Flame (*The Silmarillion* p. 151), and his first, immature emergence from Angband was placed still further back (*ibid.* pp. 116–17).

The Dragon-helm of Dor-lómin here reappears from the *Lay of the Children of Húrin* (see III. 26, 126), where in the second version it is said that it was the work of Telchar, and

> Would that he [Húrin] had worn it   to ward his head
> on that direst day   from death's handstroke!   (665–6)

But only now does the dragon-crest become the image of Glómund. Afterwards the history of the helm was much enlarged: in the *Narn i Hîn Húrin* (*Unfinished Tales* p. 75) it is told that Telchar (of Nogrod, not as in Q of Belegost) made it for Azaghâl of Belegost, and that it was given by him to Maedhros, by Maedhros to Fingon, and by Fingon to Hador, whence it descended to Hador's grandson Húrin. In the *Narn* it is said that Húrin never in fact wore it; and also that the people of Hithlum said 'Of more worth is the Dragon of Dorlómin than the gold-worm of Angband!' – which originated in this passage of Q, 'We have a dragon of more worth than theirs'. A pencilled direction against the beginning of §12 in Q (note 1) postpones the introduction of the Helm to the point where Morwen sends it to Thingol, as it is placed in *The Silmarillion* (p. 199).

Some other minor features now enter, as Melian's counsel to restore the Silmaril to the sons of Fëanor (*The Silmarillion* p. 189), and in additions to the text the presence of Elves of the Falas among the Western hosts at the great battle (note 14), and the especial hatred and fear felt by Morgoth of the House of Fingolfin (note 23; *The Silmarillion* p. 196, where however the reasons for it are their friendship with Ulmo and the wounds that Fingolfin had given him – and Turgon, Fingolfin's son). In emendations to Q (note 6) the name *Celegorm* begins a long uncertainty between that form and *Celegorn*.

The mention of 'Dark-elves, *save out of Doriath*' marching to Maidros' banners shows that my father still naturally used this term of Thingol's people; cf. the Index to *The Silmarillion*, entry *Dark Elves*.

12

It is immediately apparent, from many actual repetitions of wording, that when my father composed the Q version of the tale of Túrin

Turambar he had the 'Sketch' in front of him; while many of the phrases that occur in *The Silmarillion* version are first found here. There are also features in Q's narrative that derive from the *Lay of the Children of Húrin* but which were omitted in S. The statement in Q, repeated from S, that 'the fate of Túrin is told in the "Children of Húrin"' no doubt shows that my father had not yet given up all thought of completing that poem some day.

In this first of the two sections into which the tale of Túrin is here divided there are only minor points to be noticed. Q, though much fuller than S, is still expressly a synopsis, and the entire element of the Dragonhelm is omitted (see note 1 and the commentary on §11), together with the guiding of Túrin by the two old men and the return of one of them to Morwen: the guides (Halog and Mailgond in S) are here not named. Rían Huor's wife has already appeared in S at a later point (§16).

Airin, wife of Brodda and kinswoman of Morwen, re-enters from the old *Tale* (she is mentioned in S§13 but not named),* and the aid she gives to Morwen is secret, which perhaps suggests a movement towards the worsening of Brodda's character as tyrant and oppressor (see II. 127), though later in Q it is still told that Morwen entrusted her goods to him when she left her home (the text was subsequently altered here, §13 note 5). We meet here the expression 'the incoming Men', surviving in the term 'Incomers' used in the *Narn*, and also the element that the Easterlings were afraid of Morwen, whispering that she was a witch skilled in Elvish magic.

There has been virtually no further development in the story of Túrin in Doriath, the slaying of Orgof, and the outlaw band. Blodrin the traitor is now described as a Gnome, and by a later addition (note 5) a member of the House of Fëanor; in the Lay (as in S) it is not made clear who he was, beyond the fact that he was an Elf who had been turned to evil during his upbringing among the Dwarves (III. 52).

In the passage concerned with Taur-na-Fuin there is the new detail that the Orc-band that captured Túrin 'had delayed long in the lands plundering East among Men', which is found in *The Silmarillion* (p. 206): the Orcs 'had tarried on their road, hunting in the lands and fearing no pursuit as they came northward'. This feature clearly arose from a feeling that Beleg would never have caught up with the Orcs if they had returned swiftly to Angband, but in both S and Q they were moving in haste through Taur-na-Fuin, and in Q this is explained by 'the angry message of Morgoth'.

The addition concerning Beleg's sword (note 10) is the first indication that it was of a strange nature; the phrase 'made of iron that fell from heaven as a blazing star, and it would cut all earth-dolven iron' is found in

*In the *Tale* Airin was Morwen's friend (II. 93); in S and Q she was Morwen's kinswoman; in *The Silmarillion* (p. 198) and the *Narn* (p. 69) she was Húrin's kinswoman.

The Silmarillion at a different point (p. 201), where the origin of the sword is more fully told.

13

There are several substantial developments in the latter part of the story of Túrin in Q.

Finduilas' name *Failivrin* is now ascribed to Flinding (Gwindor); in the Lay occur the lines

> the frail Finduilas   that Failivrin,
> the glimmering sheen   on the glassy pools
> of Ivrin's lake   the Elves in love
> had named anew.   (III. 76, lines 2175–8)

In Nargothrond Túrin, as the Black Sword, is *Mormaglir*, not as in S *Mormakil* (cf. the *Tale of Turambar*, II. 84: 'Hence comes that name of Túrin's among the Gnomes, calling him Mormagli or Mormakil according to their speech'). The final form was *Mormegil*. It is now expressly stated that though rumour of the Black Sword of Nargothrond reached Thingol 'the name of Túrin was not heard'; but there is still no suggestion that Túrin deliberately concealed his identity.

The place where the Gnomes of Nargothrond were defeated is not said to be between the rivers Ginglith and Narog (*The Silmarillion* p. 212), but 'upon the Guarded Plain, north of Nargothrond', and as will be seen later the battlefield at this time was east of Narog, not in the triangle of land between it and Ginglith. The impression is given that the reproaches of Flinding (Gwindor) as he died were on account of Finduilas. There is indeed no suggestion here that Túrin's policy of open war was opposed in Nargothrond, nor that it was this policy that revealed Nargothrond to Morgoth; but since these elements were fully present in the *Tale of Turambar* (II. 83–4) their absence from Q must be set down to compression. There is also no mention at this point in Q of the bridge over the Narog (see S§13 notes 1 and 5), but it is referred to later in this section as having proved the undoing of the Elves of Nargothrond. Orodreth was slain at Nargothrond, and not as in *The Silmarillion* on the battlefield.

In an alteration to Q (note 9) a shift is implied in the motive of Túrin's slaying of Brodda. In the *Tale* Túrin struck Brodda's head off in explicit vengeance on 'the rich man who addeth the widow's little to his much' (II. 90); in the revised passage in Q (as afterwards in *The Silmarillion*, p. 215, and most clearly in the *Narn*, pp. 107–8) Túrin's action sprang in part from the fury and agony of his realisation that the dragon had cheated him.*

Whereas in S the Woodmen are placed 'east of Narog', in Q they are

---

*In the *Narn* it is not made clear that Túrin actually intended to kill Brodda when he hurled him across the table.

said to dwell 'in the green woods about the River Taiglin that enters the land of Doriath ere it joins with the great waters of Sirion' – these being the first occurrences of Taiglin and 'Doriath beyond Sirion' in the texts (though both are marked on the earliest 'Silmarillion' map, see pp. 222, 224). I noted in connection with the passage in S that it is strange that whereas in the *Tale* the Woodmen had a leader (Bethos) when Túrin joined them, as also in the later story, in S Túrin 'gathered a new people'. Now in Q the Woodmen have an identity, 'the remnant of the people of Haleth', Haleth being at this time the son of Hador and uncle of Húrin, and the 'Hadorian' and 'Halethian' houses one and the same, as already in §9; but still as in S Túrin at once becomes their ruler. Brandir the Lame, son of Handir son of Haleth, does indeed emerge here, replacing Tamar (son of Bethos the ruler) of the *Tale of Turambar*, who is still present in S, and it is said that Brandir had 'yielded the rule to Túrin at the choice of the woodfolk'; but in the later story it is an important element that Brandir remained the titular ruler until his death, though disregarded by Túrin.

Here is the first mention of Túrin's vain seeking for Finduilas when he came down from Hithlum, and the first account of Finduilas' fate; in the *Tale* and in S there is no suggestion of what became of her. Finduilas is 'the last of the race of Finrod' (later Finarfin) because Galadriel had not yet emerged.

The narrative of Q also advances to the later form in making Nienor accompany the expedition from Doriath in disguise (see II. 128); and the 'high place . . . covered with trees' of the *Tale* and the 'hill-top' of S now becomes 'the tree-clad Hill of Spies'. But in Q it was only Morwen who was set for safety on the Hill of Spies: there is no mention of what Nienor did until she was confronted by Glómund on the banks of Narog (not, as later, on the Hill). This is a movement away both from the *Tale* and from the later story, where Morwen and Nienor remained together until the dragon-fog arose; but towards the later story in that Nienor met the dragon alone (on the treatment of this in S see the commentary). We must suppose that at this stage in the development of the legend Nienor's presence was never revealed, either to her mother or to anyone else save the dragon; in the later story she was discovered at the passage of the Twilit Meres (*The Silmarillion* p. 217, *Narn* pp. 114–15). The 'Mablung-element' is still wholly absent; and it is to be noted that Morwen was taken back in safety to the Thousand Caves, whence she afterwards wandered away when she found that Nienor was gone. – The bridge over Narog seems to have been still standing after the sack (in *The Silmarillion* Glaurung broke it down, p. 214).

By emendation in Q (note 14) appears for the first time the name *Celebros*, translated 'Foam-silver', for Silver-bowl; but in Q (as in S) the falls are still in the Taiglin itself (see II. 132). Later, *Celebros* became the name of the tributary stream in which were the falls; and the falls were named *Dimrost*, the Rainy Stair.

In the story of the slaying of the dragon, the six (not as afterwards two) companions of Turambar still survive through S from the *Tale* (II. 106); though in Q they were not so much the only companions that Turambar could find but rather 'begged to come with him'. In the *Tale* the band of seven clambered up the far side of the ravine in the evening and stayed there all night; at dawn of the second day, when the dragon moved to cross, Turambar saw that he had now only three companions, and when they had to climb back down to the stream-bed to come up under Glórund's belly these three had not the courage to go up again. Turambar slew the dragon by daylight; Níniel went down to the ravine on the *second* evening, and threw herself over the falls at sunrise of the *third* day; and Turambar slew himself in the afternoon of that day. In S the only indication of time is that all six of Turambar's companions deserted him during the night spent clinging to the further lip of the ravine. In Q the six all deserted Turambar during the first night, as in S, but he spent the whole of the following day clinging to the cliff; Glómund moved to pass over the ravine on the *second* night (my father clearly wished to make the dragon-slaying take place in darkness, but achieved this at first by extending the time Turambar spent in the gorge). But Níniel went down and found him, and threw herself over the falls, on that same night. Thus in Q the story has moved closer to that of *The Silmarillion* and the *Narn*, and needed only the contraction of the time before the dragon crossed the ravine, so that all took place in a single night and the following morning. – It seems to be suggested in Q that Glómund in his death-throes hurled himself back on to the bank from which he was coming: he '*coiled back in anguish* . . . and came not into the woodmen's land'. If this is so Níniel must have crossed the ravine to reach Turambar. In the *Tale* (II. 107) it is explicit that 'almost had [the dragon] crossed the chasm when Gurtholfin pierced him, and now he cast himself upon its farther bank', as also in the later versions.

That Níniel was with child by Turambar is now stated in the text as written (in the *Tale* and in S this appears only in later additions).

In the *Tale* (II. 111) Turambar slew himself in the glade of Silver Bowl; it is not said in S or in Q where he died, though in both he was buried beside Silver Bowl. – At the very end appears in Q the name *Nen-Girith*, its first occurrence: 'Men changed the name of that place thereafter to Nen-Girith, the Shuddering Water.' In *The Silmarillion* (p. 220) it is said, in the passage describing the great fit of shuddering that came on Nienor at Dimrost, the falls of Celebros, that – on account of this – 'afterwards that place was called Nen Girith'; and in the *Narn* (p. 123) that 'after that day' it was called Nen Girith. These passages can be taken to mean that the falls of Celebros were renamed Nen Girith simply on account of Nienor's shivering when she first came there. But this is surely absurd; the event was, in itself and without aftermath, far too slight for a renaming – too slight, indeed for narrative mention or legendary recollection, if it had no aftermath: places are not renamed in legend because a person, however important, caught a chill there. Obviously the prophetic element is the whole point, and it goes back to the *Tale*, where before ever the name Nen Girith was devised Nienor 'not knowing why was filled with a dread and could not look upon the loveliness of that foaming water' (II. 101), and in the original story both Nienor and Turambar died in that very place (see II. 134–5). I think that the phrase in the *Narn*, 'after that day', must be interpreted to mean 'after that time', 'after the events which are now to be described had come to pass'. I noted in *Unfinished Tales* (p. 149, note 24):

> One might suppose that it was only when all was over, and Túrin and Nienor dead, that her shuddering fit was recalled and its meaning seen, and Dimrost renamed Nen Girith; but in the legend Nen Girith is used as the name throughout.

Almost certainly, the use of the name 'Nen Girith' in the later narratives *before* the account of the events that must have given rise to the name is to be explained in the same way as that proposed by my father for *Mablung*: concerning which he observed in a very late essay that when Mablung took the Silmaril from the belly of Carcharoth

> the hand [of Beren] and jewel seemed to have so great a weight that Mablung's own hand was dragged earthward and forced open, letting the other fall to the ground. It was said that Mablung's name ('with weighted hand') was prophetic; but it may have been a title derived from the episode *that afterwards became the one that the hero was chiefly remembered by in legend.*

I have no doubt that the story in Q shows the original idea: Nienor shivered with prophetic but unconscious fear when she came to the falls of Celebros; there both she and her brother died horrifyingly; and after their deaths the falls were renamed Nen Girith, the Shuddering Water, because the meaning was understood. 'Afterwards', 'After that day', this became the name of the falls; but in the legendary history, when all was well-known both to the historian and to his audience, the later name became generalised, like that of Mablung.

14

At the beginning of this section it is made clear that Mîm's presence in Nargothrond did not go back to the time of the dragon, since he 'had found the halls and treasure of Nargothrond unguarded'. In the *Lost Tales* my father doubtless saw no particular need to 'explain' Mîm; he was simply there, a feature of the narrative situation, like Andvari the Dwarf in the Norse Völsung legend. But in Q the first step is taken to relate him to the developing conception of the Dwarves of Middle-earth: they spread into Beleriand from the Blue Mountains after the Battle of

Unnumbered Tears. (Ultimately the need to 'explain' Mîm led to the conception of the Petty-dwarves.) But Q's statement that the Dwarves only now enter the tales of the ancient world seems at variance with earlier passages: with §9, where it is said that the Fëanorians made war on the Dwarves of Nogrod and Belegost, and with §11, concerning the furnishing of weapons by the Dwarves to the armies of the Union of Maidros.

Here Mîm has some companions, slain with him by the outlaws of Húrin's band, whom Húrin 'would have stayed'; in the *Tale of Turambar* (II.113) Mîm was alone, and it was Úrin himself who gave him his death-blow. Whereas in the *Tale* Úrin's band – large enough to be called a host – brought the treasure of Nargothrond to the caves of Tinwelint in a mass of sacks and rough boxes (while in S there is no indication whatsoever of how the treasure came to Doriath, and the outlaws are not further mentioned after the slaying of Mîm), in Q Húrin's outlaws are as conveniently got rid of as they were conveniently come by – 'each one died or was slain in quarrels upon the road', deaths ascribed to Mîm's curse; and since Húrin now goes alone to Doriath and gets Thingol's help in the transportation of the treasure the outlaw-band seems to serve very little narrative purpose. The fight in the halls of Tinwelint between the woodland Elves and the outlaws, not mentioned in S, has now therefore been expunged (the emergence in Q of a new fight in the halls, between the Elves and the Dwarves, would demand its removal in any case, if Menegroth were not to appear a permanent shambles).

But the problem remained: how did the gold come to Doriath? It was an essential idea that Húrin, destroyed by what he had seen (or by what Morgoth allowed him to see) and tormented by bitterness and grief, should cast the treasure of Nargothrond at Thingol's feet in a gesture of supreme scorn of the craven and greedy king, as he conceived him to be; but the new story in Q is obviously unsatisfactory – it ruins the gesture, if Húrin must get the king himself to send for the gold with which he is *then* to be humiliated, and it is difficult to imagine the conversation between Húrin and Thingol when Húrin first appeared in Doriath, announcing that the treasure had become available.

However this may be, the gold comes to Doriath, and in all versions Húrin departs: but now in Q, to drown himself in the western sea, without ever finding Morwen again.

I have said in commenting on the corresponding section in S that I think it probable that my father had already decided to simplify the involved story in the *Tale of the Nauglafring* concerning the gold of Nargothrond. In Q, which is a fully articulated narrative, if brief, the absence of Ufedhin can be taken as a clear indication that he had been abandoned, and with him, necessarily, many of the complexities of the king's dealings with the Dwarves. The story has become, then, quite simple. Thingol desires the unwrought gold brought by Húrin to be worked; he sends for the greatest craftsmen on earth, the Dwarves of

Nogrod and Belegost; and they coming desire the treasure for themselves, the Silmaril also, and plot to gain it. The argument that they use –
that the treasure belonged in right to the Dwarves, since it was taken
from Mîm – reappears from the *Tale of the Nauglafring*, where it occurs
in a different context (II. 230: an argument used by Naugladur lord of
Nogrod to support his intention to attack Tinwelint).

The relative wealth or otherwise of Thingol has not been touched on in
Q, but his riches are recounted in the *Lay of the Children of Húrin* (see
III. 26) and in the *Lay of Leithian* (III. 160–1); and this is no doubt the
force of the word 'even' in 'Then the enchantment of the accursed dragon
gold began to fall *even* upon the king of Doriath.'

In S the king drives the Dwarves away without any payment; there is
no mention of any strife at this point, and one would think that even the
most severe compression could hardly have avoided mentioning it. But
in Q the narrative now takes a quite different turn. Thingol 'scanted his
promised reward', and this led to fighting in the Thousand Caves, with
many slain on both sides; and 'the Mound of Avarice', which in the *Tale
of the Nauglafring* covered the bodies of the slain Elves of Artanor after
the battle with the outlaws of Húrin's band, now covers those of the
Dwarves and Elves; the form of the Elvish name is changed from *Cûm
an-Idrisaith* (II. 223) to *Cûm-nan-Arasaith*.

As in S, the sack of Menegroth by the Dwarves is still treated in Q with
the utmost brevity, and central features of the story in the *Tale of the
Nauglafring* do not recur, nor ever would. But (in addition to the loss of
Ufedhin) it seems likely that the 'great host' of Orcs, paid and armed by
Naugladur of Nogrod (II. 230), would by now have been abandoned. Of
course the whole story arose in terms of, and continues to depend on, the
hostile view of the Dwarves which is so prominent in the early writings.

The much emended geographical passage that follows now in Q is best
understood in relation to the first 'Silmarillion' map, and I postpone
discussion of the rivers of Ossiriand and the Dwarf-road to Chapter IV,
pp. 230ff. It is sufficient to notice here that the courses of the six
tributary rivers of Gelion (here called *Ascar*,* before emendation to
Flend and then to *Gelion*, note 3) are drawn on that map in precisely
the same form as they have on that published in *The Silmarillion*, and the
first map names them in order of the original emendation to Q (note 4)
before that was itself changed: i.e., Ascar, Thalos, Duilwen, Loeglin,
Brilthor, Adurant.

It is now made explicit that it was Melian who warned Beren of the
approach of the Dwarves (see p. 62); and the removal of the Land of
the Dead that Live from 'the woods of Doriath and the Hunters' Wold,
west of Nargothrond', where it is still placed in S (§10), to Assariad

---

*It seems probable that the first two occurrences of *Ascar* in this section were mere slips,
for *Flend* (> *Gelion*). At the third occurrence the name is used, as it is on the map, for the
northernmost of the rivers coming down out of the Blue Mountains, afterwards renamed
Rahlorion (> *Rathloriel*).

(Ossiriand) in the East makes the interception of the Dwarves far simpler and more natural: the Stony Ford (which goes back to the *Tale of the Nauglafring* and is there called *Sarnathrod*) now lies on the river that bounds that very land. The geographical shift and development has made the whole organisation of the story here much easier.

Beren's people now at last become 'the Green Elves' (see p. 62); but the story of the ambush at the ford is passed over in Q as sketchily as it was in S: there is now no mention even of the taking of the Nauglafring (> Nauglamír) from the slain king. The story of the drowning of the treasure remains much the same as in S, but there are suggestions of wider implications in the wearing of the Nauglafring: that the Land of the Dead that Live became itself so fruitful and so fair because of the presence of Lúthien wearing the Silmaril. This passage is retained almost word for word in *The Silmarillion* (p. 235). It is clearly to be associated with a later passage, found both in Q (p. 152) and in *The Silmarillion* (p. 247), where the people dwelling at the Havens of Sirion after the fall of Gondolin would not surrender the Silmaril to the Fëanorians 'for it seemed to them that in the Silmaril lay the healing and the blessing that had come upon their houses and their ships'. But the Silmaril was cursed (and this may seem a sufficiently strange conception), and Melian warned Beren and Lúthien against it. In Q it is not said, as it is in S, that the Silmaril was kept secretly by Beren, merely that he and Lúthien 'retained' it. In both texts the fading of Lúthien follows immediately; but while Q again makes no actual connection (see p. 63) the very ordering of its sentences suggests that such a connection was there: 'the Land of the Dead that Live became like a vision of the land of the Gods . . . Yet Melian warned them ever of the curse . . . yet the Silmaril they retained. And in time the brief hour of the loveliness of the land of Rathlorion departed. For Lúthien faded as Mandos had spoken . . .'

The statements made in S§§10 and 14 on the fates of Beren and Lúthien have been discussed at some length (pp. 63–4). When we turn to Q, we find that in the earlier passage (§10, where the first death of Beren and Lúthien's pleading with Mandos is recounted), while there is mention of songs that say that Lúthien was borne living to Valinor by Thorndor, these are discounted, and 'it has long been said that Lúthien failed and faded swiftly and vanished from the earth', and thus came to Mandos: she had died, as Elves might die, of grief (cf. the old *Tale of Tinúviel*, II. 40). And the dispensation of Mandos exacted that 'Lúthien should become mortal even as her lover, *and should leave the earth once more in the manner of mortal women*'. This seems precise: it can surely only mean that Lúthien had become, not an Elf with a peculiar destiny, but a mortal woman. Her nature had changed.*

*The further judgement of Mandos in §10, that 'in recompense' he 'gave to Beren and Lúthien thereafter a long span of life and joy', seems at variance with what is implied here in Q. See III. 125.

Yet Q retains the conception in the present passage of Lúthien's fading – her second fading. I think it can now be seen why my father wrote an X against this sentence (note 12); and note also the marginal addition at this point: 'Yet it hath been sung that Lúthien *alone of Elves hath been numbered among our race,** and goeth whither we go to a fate beyond the world*' (cf. *The Silmarillion* p. 236: 'Beren Erchamion and Lúthien Tinúviel had died indeed, and gone where go the race of Men to a fate beyond the world').

Coming lastly to the story of Dior and the end of Doriath, it is now Celegorm, Curufin, and Cranthir who were slain, as in *The Silmarillion* (p. 236); and by a late addition to the text (note 14) Dior has sons, Eldûn and Elrûn, who were killed with their father. In *The Silmarillion* they were Eluréd and Elurín, who were left by the servants of Celegorm to starve in the forest.

15

In this version of the story of Eöl and Isfin it is told that Eöl 'was of gloomy mood, and had deserted the hosts ere the battle [of Unnumbered Tears]'. Nothing has been said before of how Eöl came to be dwelling in the terrible forest (and later his earlier history was to be wholly changed again: *The Silmarillion* p. 132).

The general description of the plain and city of Gondolin in Q is obviously closely based on S, and shows little more than stylistic development. But Thorndor is here said to have dwelt on Thangorodrim before he moved his eyries to the Encircling Mountains (see p. 66); and there is an interesting reference to the original intention of the people of Gondolin to go to war again when the time was ripe. The most important alteration here is the pencilled addition (note 5), taken up into the Q II text, telling that Turgon after the Battle of Unnumbered Tears sent at times Elves down Sirion to the sea, where they built a small haven and set sail, in vain, for Valinor. This is the forerunner of the passage in *The Silmarillion* (p. 159), where however the building of ships by the Gondolindrim and the setting sail for Valinor 'to ask for pardon and aid of the Valar' is placed after the Dagor Bragollach and the breaking of the Leaguer of Angband (for the foundation of Gondolin took place centuries before the Battle of Unnumbered Tears). But in *The Silmarillion* (p. 196) there was also a further attempt by Turgon to reach Valinor in the time after the great battle, when Círdan of the Falas built for him seven ships, of which the only survivor was Voronwë. The origin of this idea of the fruitless voyages of the Gondolindrim is to be found in the tale of *The Fall of Gondolin* (II. 162), where Ulmo by the mouth of Tuor counselled Turgon to make such voyages, and Turgon replied that he had done so 'for years untold', and would do so now no more.

**'our race': the *Quenta*, according to its title (pp. 77–8), was 'drawn from the Book of Lost Tales which Eriol of Leithien wrote'.

In the replacement text Q II (pp. 138–40), where the old story of the foundation of Gondolin is still present, there is very little to record in narrative development, except that the sending of Elves to Sirion's mouth and the sailing of ships from a secret haven is now incorporated in the text; and it is said that as the years drew on these sailings ceased and the haven was abandoned. It is now explained why it was that Thorndor (> Thorondor) moved his eyries from Thangorodrim.

The passage of time is left entirely vague in these narratives. There is no indication of how many years elapsed between the Battle of Unnumbered Tears or its immediate aftermath – when in the first years of Gondolin Turgon was trying to get his messages to Valinor – and the coming of Tuor, by which time the haven at Sirion's mouth was desolate, none could enter Gondolin from the outside world, and neither the king nor the most part of his people wished any more for return to Valinor (p. 142). But the change in feeling in Gondolin – and all the mighty works of levelling and tunnelling – must imply a long lapse of time ('as the years drew on', pp. 137, 140). This conception goes back to the original *Fall of Gondolin* (see my remarks, II. 208); but at that time Tuor had no associations that would tie him into a chronological framework. Already in S (§16), however, Huor, brother of Húrin, had become Tuor's father, and Huor was slain in the Battle of Unnumbered Tears. Clearly there was a major narrative-chronological difficulty lurking here, and it was not long before my father moved the founding of Gondolin (and with it that of Nargothrond) to a far earlier point in the history. Unhappily, as I have mentioned before (II. 208, footnote), the *Quenta* account was the last that my father ever wrote of the story of Gondolin from Tuor's coming to its destruction; and therefore, though the revised chronological structure is perfectly clear, the latest actual formed narrative retains the old story of the founding of Gondolin after the Battle of Unnumbered Tears. Against the words in the Q II replacement 'For Turgon deemed, *when first they came into that vale after the dreadful battle*' my father wrote an X (note 3); but in all the years that followed he never turned to it again.*

The name *Eryd-Lómin* occurs for the first time† in the Q II replacement text, but its reference is to the Mountains of Shadow fencing Hithlum, and it was later emended (note 1) to *Eredwethion* (*Ered Wethrin* in *The Silmarillion*). The name *Eryd-Lómin* did at this time mean 'Shadowy Mountains', just as *Dor-lómin* meant 'Land of Shadows' (see I. 112, and I. 255 entry *Hisilómë*). Subsequently *Eryd-Lómin*, *Ered*

---

*The passage in *The Silmarillion* (p. 240) is an editorial attempt to use the old narrative within the later structure.

†For the first time in the narrative texts. The actual first occurrence is probably in the caption to my father's painting of Tol Sirion (*Pictures by J. R. R. Tolkien* no. 36) of July 1928, which though it cannot be made out in the reproduction reads: 'The Vale of Sirion, looking upon Dor-na-Fauglith, with Eryd Lómin (the Shadowy Mountains) on the left and the eaves of Taur-na-Fuin on the right.'

Lómin was changed both in meaning ('Shadowy Mountains' to 'Echoing Mountains', with *lóm* 'echo', as also in *Dor-lómin* 'Land of Echoes') and in application, becoming the name of the coastal range to the west of Hithlum.

16

At the beginning of this section we find the first beginnings of the later story of the coming of Isfin and Meglin (Aredhel and Maeglin) to Gondolin, rather than (as still in S) the sending of Meglin by his mother; Eöl was lost in Taur-na-Fuin, and his wife and son came to Gondolin in his absence. There was much further development to come (the story of Maeglin in *The Silmarillion* is one of the latest elements in the book).

In the rewritten passage given in note 3 the birth of Tuor 'in the wild' appears (see p. 67); the implication is no doubt that as in *The Silmarillion* (p. 198) and with more detail in the 'later *Tuor*' (*Unfinished Tales* p. 17) he was born in the wilds of Hithlum, and that it was after his birth that Rían went east to the Hill of Slain (in the rough rewriting of the passage in Q I now first given an Elvish name, *Amon Dengin*). But it is odd that in the rewriting Tuor's servitude among 'the faithless Men', found in S and in Q as first written, is excluded.

In the account of Tuor's flight from Hithlum the name of the Rainbow Cleft as originally written was *Cris-Ilfing* (in the tale of *The Fall of Gondolin* it was *Cris Ilbranteloth* or *Glorfalc*), emended to *Kirith Helvin* (*Cirith Ninniach* in *The Silmarillion*).

Tuor's journey remains unchanged. It was already said in S that Bronweg 'had once been in Gondolin'; now it is added that he had escaped from Angband, and had reached Sirion after long wanderings in the East. That he had been in Angband appears in fact already in the *Lay of the Fall of Gondolin* (III. 148), and is implied in the *Tale* (II. 156–7). The story of his lone survival from the last of the ships sent out on Turgon's orders had not yet arisen; and his escape from Angband makes him a rather obvious parallel to Flinding (Gwindor), or at least points a general likeness between the stories of Túrin and Tuor at this point. In each case a Man is guided by an Elf escaped from Angband to the hidden city of which the Elf was a citizen in the past. – The visitation of Ulmo to Tuor 'as he stood in the long grass at evening' in the Land of Willows goes back to the *Tale*, where he stood 'knee-deep in the grass' (II. 155). This was an essential element never abandoned; see II. 205. The song of Tuor that he made for his son Eärendel is extant, and is given in Appendix 2 to this chapter (p. 213).

Ulmo's instructions to Tuor in Q remain the same as in S; but in the Q II replacement there are important differences. Here, the great war between Gondolin and Angband foreseen by Ulmo is given a larger scope, and its succesful outcome made to seem more plausible: Tuor's errand to Hithlum, where he was to draw the ('evil' and 'faithless') Men of Hithlum (a land full of Morgoth's spies) into alliance with the Elves, a task it would seem of the utmost hopelessness, is now abandoned, and Tuor is to journey into the East and rouse the new nations of Men; the feud with the Fëanorians is to be healed. But in the contrary case, Ulmo no longer makes any promise to aid the people of Gondolin in the building of a fleet. His foreknowledge of the approaching doom of Gondolin is made progressively less precise: in S he knows that it will come through Meglin in seven (> twelve) years, in Q I that it will come in twelve years, but without mention of Meglin, in Q II only that it will come before many years are passed, if nothing is done.

In the story of Meglin's treachery in Q it is expressly stated (as it is not in S, though it is almost certainly implied) that he revealed the actual situation of Gondolin, of which Morgoth was until then ignorant.

There are strong suggestions in this compressed account that Gondolin's rich heraldry of houses and emblems was only in abeyance, not abandoned. The seven names of Gondolin are referred to, though not given, and Ecthelion of the Fountain and Glorfindel of the House of the Golden Flower are named. Indeed so many old features reappear – the Gates of Summer, the 'death of Rog without the walls'* – that it does not need the reference in the text to *The Fall of Gondolin* to show that my father had the *Tale* very fully in mind. In the reference to the 'devising' (rather than 'breeding') of new dragons by Morgoth for the assault on the city there is even a suggestion of the (apparently) inanimate constructions of the *Tale* (see II.213).

The relation between the present short version of the escape of the fugitives and the ambush in Cristhorn (> Kirith-thoronath), which is effectively that in *The Silmarillion* (p. 243), and that in the *Tale* has been discussed in II.213–14. The absence from *The Silmarillion* of the fugitives who went to the Way of Escape and were there destroyed by the dragon lying in wait, an element present in S and Q, is due to editorial excision, based on evidence in a much later text that the old entrance to Gondolin had been blocked up. That text is the basis for the passage in *The Silmarillion* (p. 228) where Húrin after his release from Thangorodrim came to the feet of the Encircling Mountains:

> he looked about him with little hope, standing at the foot of a great fall of stones beneath a sheer rock-wall; and he knew not that this was all that was now left to see of the old Way of Escape: the Dry River was blocked, and the arched gate was buried.

The sentence in *The Silmarillion* p. 240 'Therefore in that time the very entrance to the hidden door in the Encircling Mountains was caused to be blocked up' was an editorial addition.

In Q reappears from the *Tale* the sojourn of the survivors of Gondolin

---

*For the absence of Rog from the passage in *The Silmarillion* (p. 242) see II.211, second footnote.

in the Land of Willows, and the return of the 'sea-longing' to Tuor, leading to the departure from Nan-Tathrin down Sirion to the Sea.

Lastly may be noticed the description of Idril Celebrindal in Q II (p. 148) – tall, 'well nigh of warrior's stature', with golden hair: the prototype of Galadriel (see especially the description of her in *Unfinished Tales* pp. 229–30).

17

In the original Q text in this section the structure of S is closely followed, and in many respects the story is still unchanged where change was very soon to take place.

All trace of Ulmo's urging Eärendel to undertake the voyage to Valinor has disappeared (see S §17 note 3); but it is still Ulmo's 'grievous words' to the Valar that lead to the coming forth of the Sons of the Valar against Morgoth, and still Eärendel 'came too late to bring messages to the Elves, for the Elves had gone' (cf. Q§6: 'he came too late'). There now appears, on the other hand, Eärendel's *wish* to bring 'a message to the Gods and Elves of the West, that should move their hearts to pity on the world', even though, when he came, there were none in Kôr to whom to deliver it. But the ultimate story is noted on the text in pencil (note 1).

In the account of the host that came from Valinor Fionwë is still the son of Tulkas (see p. 68); but now none of the Teleri leave Valinor, while on the other hand there is mention of the Gnomes who had not left Valinor at the time of the Rebellion – cf. the earlier passage in Q (§5): 'Some remained behind . . . It was long ere they came back into this tale of the wars and wanderings of their people.'

Bronweg is still present as in S living alone at Sirion's mouth after the attack by the Fëanorians, and he still sails with Eärendel on the second voyage of Wingelot that brought them to Kôr. Eärendel still at this point in the story builds the Tower of Seabirds; his ship is raised, as in S, on the wings of birds, as he searches for Elwing from the sky, whence he is hunted by the Moon and wanders over the earth as a fugitive star. Elwing still casts the Silmaril into the sea and leaps after it, taking the form of a seabird to seek Eärendel 'about all the shores of the world'. Minor developments are the dissension among the Fëanorians, so that some stood aside and others aided Elwing; the deaths of Damrod and Díriel (see p. 69); the explanation of Maidros' pity for the child Elrond ('for his heart was sick and weary with the burden of the dreadful oath'); and the description of Wingelot. The name of Tuor's ship *Eärámë* is translated 'Eagle's Pinion' (the old explanation of the name, when it was Eärendel's ship), not 'Sea-wing' (see p. 69). The passage in S concerning the choice of Elrond Halfelven is here omitted, but the matter reappears in §18.

With this section the rewriting of Q (as 'Q II') becomes continuous to the end of the work, and the original text ('Q I') in fact gives out before the end. Since substantial stretches of Q I remain unchanged in Q II, I do not suppose that much time elapsed between them; but certain major new strokes are introduced into the legend in the rewriting.

These major developments in the present section are, first, that Ulmo's words to the Valar did *not* achieve the war against Morgoth ('Manwë moved not'); second, that Elwing, borne up as a seabird, *bore the Silmaril on her breast*, and came to Eärendel, returning from his first voyage in Wingelot: so that the Silmaril of Beren was not lost, but became the Evening Star; and third, that Eärendel, voyaging to Valinor *with Elwing*, came before the Valar, and it was his 'embassy of the two kindreds' that led to the assault on Morgoth.*

But there are also many changes of a less structural character in Q II, as: Eärendel's earlier voyages about the shores of the Outer Lands before he built Wingelot; his warning dreams to return in haste to the Mouths of Sirion, which in the event he never came back to, being intercepted by the coming of Elwing as a seabird and her tidings of what had happened there in his absence— hence the disappearance of Bronweg from the story; the healing power of the Silmaril on the people of Sirion (see p. 190); the great light of the Silmaril as Wingelot approached Valinor, and the suggestion that it was the power of the jewel that brought the ship through the enchantments and the shadows; Eärendel's refusal to allow any of those that travelled with him to come with him into Valinor; the new explanation of the desertion of Tûn upon Kôr (for the story still endured that the city of the Elves was empty of its inhabitants when Eärendel came there); the greeting of Eärendel by Fionwë (now again the son of Manwë) as the Morning and Evening Star; the manning by the Teleri of the ships that bore the hosts of the West; and the sighting of the Silmaril in the sky by Maidros and Maglor and the people of the Outer Lands.

By subsequent emendation to Q II some further elements enter. To Tuor is ascribed a fate (note 3) hardly less astonishing than that of his cousin Túrin Turambar. Elrond's brother Elros appears (notes 4 and 9); and Maglor takes over Maidros' rôle as their saviour, and as the less ruthless and single-minded of the two brothers (note 10; see the commentary on §18). The addition in note 19 stating that the leader of the Gnomes who had never departed from Valinor was Ingwiel son of Ingwë is at first sight surprising: one would expect Finrod (> Finarfin), as in *The Silmarillion* (p. 251). I think however that this addition was imperfectly accommodated to the text: the meaning intended was that Ingwiel was the chief of the Quendi (the Light-elves, the Vanyar) among whom the Gnomes of Valinor marched.† In a revision to Q§2 (note 6) the

---

*The first appearance of this central idea is in a hasty pencilled note to Q I (note 1): 'Make *Eärendel* move the Gods.'

†In the final version of this passage my father noticed the (apparent) error, and changed *Ingwiel son of Ingwë* to *Finarfin son of Finwë* (hence the reading in *The Silmarillion*). The result is that whereas in Q II only the leader of the First Kindred is named, Ingwiel, in the final version only the leader of the Noldor of Valinor is named, Finarfin; but the one should not, I think, have replaced the other – rather both should have been named.

original text, saying that Ingwë never came back into the Outer Lands 'until these tales were near their end', was changed to a statement that he never returned. Ingwiel replaces Ingil son of Inwë of the *Lost Tales*, who built Ingil's Tower in Tol Eressëa (I. 16) after his return from the Great Lands.

As Q II was first written

Eärendel was their guide [i.e. of the fleet of the hosts of Valinor]; but the Gods would not suffer him to return again,* and he built him a white tower upon the confines of the outer world in the Northern regions of the Sundering Seas, and there all the sea-birds of the earth at times repaired.

The Tower of Seabirds thus survives in the same place in the narrative as in S and Q, where Eärendel builds the tower after his fruitless visit to Kôr. At the end of this section in S Eärendel

sails by the aid of [the seabirds'] wings even over the airs in search of Elwing, but is scorched by the Sun, and hunted from the sky by the Moon, and for a long while he wanders the sky as a fugitive star.

Virtually the same is said at the end of the section in Q I. In Q II, however, as first written, Elwing was with Eärendel at this time,† in the form of a bird, and it was she who devised wings for his ship, so that 'it was lifted even into the oceans of the air'.

In S and Q I Eärendel does not yet bear a Silmaril when he wanders the sky 'as a fugitive star' (for the Silmaril of Beren is drowned with the Nauglafring, and the others are still in the Iron Crown of Morgoth); whereas in Q II it is at this time that the Silmaril appears in the sky and gives hope to the people of the Outer Lands.

With the revision to Q II given in note 20 enters the idea that it was the Gods themselves who set Eärendel and his ship in the sky. It is now Elwing who builds the Tower of Seabirds, devising wings for herself in order to try to reach him, in vain; *and they are sundered till the end of the world*. This no doubt goes with the revision to Q II given in note 14: 'And he bade farewell to all whom he loved upon the last shore, and was taken from them for ever.'

In *The Silmarillion* the element of a small ship's company remains: the three mariners Falathar, Erellont, and Aerandir (p. 248). These, and Elwing, Eärendil refused to allow to set foot on the shore of Aman; but Elwing leapt into the sea and ran to him, saying: 'Then would our paths be sundered for ever.' There Eärendil and Elwing 'bade farewell to the companions of their voyage, and were taken from them for ever'; but

---

*Cf. the letter of 1967 cited in II. 265: '*Eärendil*, being in part descended from Men, was not allowed to set foot on Earth again.'

†It is not actually said in Q II that Elwing returned to Eärendel after being bidden by him to remain behind when he landed on 'the immortal shores' and went to Kôr; but it is evident that she did, from her having devised wings for his ship.

Elwing did not even so accompany Eärendil to Tirion. She sojourned among the Teleri of Alqualondë, and Eärendil came to her there after he had 'delivered the errand of the Two Kindreds' before the Valar; and they went then together to Valmar and heard Manwë's decree, and the choice of fate that was given to them and to their children,

A curious point arises in the account in Q II of the voyage of Eärendel and Elwing that brought them to the coaast of Valinor. Whereas in Q I it is said that Eärendel 'found again the Lonely Isle, and the Shadowy Seas', in Q II 'they came into the Shadowy Seas *and passed their shadows*; and they looked upon the Lonely Isle . . .' This suggests that the Shadowy Seas had become a region of the Great Sea lying to the east of Tol Eressëa; and the same idea seems to be present in §6 both in S and in Q, for it is said there that at the Hiding of Valinor 'the Magic Isles were . . . strung across the confines of the Shadowy Seas, *before the Lonely Isle is reached* sailing West'. Quite different is the account in the *Lost Tales*, where *'beyond Tol Eressëa* [lying west of the Magic Isles] is the misty wall and those great sea glooms beneath which lie the Shadowy Seas' (I. 125); and the Shadowy Seas extend to the coasts of the western land (I. 68). Conceivably, this development is related to the changed position of Tol Eressëa – anchored in the Bay of Faërie within far sight of the Mountains of Valinor, and not as in the *Lost Tales* in mid-Ocean: a change that entered the geography in S§3.

In emendations to Q II the Magic Isles become the Enchanted Isles (note 11; see II. 324–5) and the Bay of Faërie becomes the Bay of Elvenhome (note 12); also the name *Eärámë* of Tuor's ship becomes *Eärrámë*, with the later interpretation 'Sea-wing' (note 2).

18

There are several interesting developments in the story of the Last Battle and its aftermath as told in the original Q I text of this section. The very brief account in S is here greatly expanded, and much of the final version appears, if still with many differences (notably the absence of Eärendel). That Morgoth had been bound long before by Tulkas in the chain Angainor now re-emerges from the *Lost Tales* (this feature is absent in Q§2; see pp. 71, 168).

The passage describing the rending of Beleriand survives almost unchanged in *The Silmarillion* (p. 252), which in fact adds nothing else. There is a notable statement (retained in Q II) that

> Men fled away, such as perished not in the ruin of those days, and long was it ere they came back over the mountains to where Beleriand once had been, and not till the tale of those days had faded to an echo seldom heard.

I do not know certainly what this refers to (see below, p. 200). Unhappily the evidence for the development of the conception of the drowning of Beleriand is extremely scanty. Later, it was only a small region (Lindon) that remained above the sea west of the Blue Mountains; but this need not by any means yet have been the case. It is also said in Q (again retained in Q II) that

> there was a mighty building of ships on the shores of the Western Sea, and most upon the great isles, which in the disruption of the Northern world were fashioned of old Beleriand.

Of the size and number of these 'great isles' we are not told. On one of my father's sketchmaps made for *The Lord of the Rings* there is the island of Himling, i.e. the summit of the Hill of Himring, and also Tol Fuin, i.e. the highest part of Taur-na-Fuin (see *Unfinished Tales* pp. 13–14); and in *The Silmarillion* (p. 230) it is said that the stone of the Children of Húrin and the grave of Morwen above Cabed Naeramarth stands on Tol Morwen 'alone in the water beyond the new coasts that were made in the days of the wrath of the Valar'. But it seems obvious that my father was at this time imagining far larger islands than these, since it was on them that the great fleets were built at the end of the War of Wrath. Lúthien (> Leithien) as the land from which the Elves set sail, named in S §18 and explained as 'Britain or England', is not named in Q; but the words that follow in S: 'Thence they ever still from time to time set sail leaving the world ere they fade', are clearly reflected in Q:

> Yet not all returned, and some lingered many an age in the West and North, and especially in the Western Isles. Yet ever as the ages drew on and the Elf-folk faded on the Earth, they would still set sail at eve from our Western shores; as still they do, when now there linger few anywhere of the lonely companies.

The relation between these passages strongly suggests that the 'Western Isles' were the British Isles,* and that England still had a place in the actual mythological geography, as is explicitly so in S. In this connection the opening of *Ælfwine of England*, in the final text *Ælfwine II* (II. 312–13), is interesting:

> There was a land called England, and it was an island of the West, and before it was broken in the warfare of the Gods it was westernmost of all the Northern lands, and looked upon the Great Sea that Men of old called Garsecg; but that part that was broken was called Ireland and many names besides, and its dwellers come not into these tales.
>
> All that land the Elves named Lúthien and do so yet. In Lúthien alone dwelt still the most part of the Fading Companies, the Holy Fairies that have not yet sailed away from the world, beyond the

---

*This may seem to be rendered less likely by the form of the passage in Q II, where the first sentence is expanded: 'and especially in the western isles *and the lands of Leithien*'. But I do not think that this phrase need be taken too precisely, and believe that the equation holds.

horizon of Men's knowledge, to the Lonely Island, or even to the Hill of Tûn upon the Bay of Faëry that washes the western shores of the kingdom of the Gods.

It is possible, as I suggested (II. 323–4), that this passage refers to the cataclysm, and its aftermath, that is otherwise first mentioned in S §18. *Ælfwine II* cannot be dated, but *Ælfwine I* on which it was based was probably written in 1920 or not much later. It is also conceivable, if no more, that the meaning of the words in Q, that it was long before Men came back over the mountains to where Beleriand once had been, refers to the bloody invasions of England in later days described in *Ælfwine II*; for there is very little in that text that cannot be readily accommodated to the present passage in S and Q, with the picture of the fading Elves of Lúthien 'leaving our Western shores'.* But a serious difficulty with this idea lies in the coming of Men 'over the mountains' to where Beleriand once had been.

Certainly the most remarkable, even startling, feature of the aftermath of the Last Battle in Q (I) is the statement that when Fionwë marched through the lands summoning the Gnomes and the Dark-elves to leave the Outer Lands, the Men of the Houses of Hador and Bëor were 'suffered to depart, if they would'. But only Elrond was left; and of his choice, as Half-elven, the same is told as in S §17. The implications of this passage are puzzling. It is obvious that 'the race of Hador and Bëor' means those directly descended from Hador and Bëor; afterwards the conception of these Houses became much enlarged – they became clans. But since of the direct descendants only Elrond was left, what does this permission mean? Is it a (very curious) way of offering the choice of departure to the Half-elven, if he (they) wished? – because the Half-elven had only come into existence in the Houses of Hador and Bëor. But this seems too legalistic and contorted to be at all probable. Then does it imply that, if there had in fact been other descendants – if, for example, Gundor son of Hador had had children – they would have been permitted to depart? And what then? Would they have ended their days as mortal Men on Tol Eressëa? The permission seems very obscure on either interpretation; and it was removed from Q II. Nonetheless it represents, as I think, the first germ of the story of the departure of the survivors of the Elf-friends to Númenor.

---

*Two small likenesses may be noticed: in *Ælfwine II* the ships of the Elves weigh anchor from the western haven 'at eve' (II. 315), as in Q; and with 'the lonely companies' of Q cf. 'the Fading Companies' of *Ælfwine II* in the passage cited above.

A further attractive deduction, that this was the origin of the haven of *Belerion* in *Ælfwine of England*, the western harbour 'whence the Elves at times set sail' (a survival of the old name *Beleriand* among the Men of later days when its original reference was forgotten, and 'the tale of those days had faded to an echo seldom heard'), cannot be sustained: for *Ælfwine II* was certainly written long before the earliest occurrences of *Beleriand* (rather than *Broseliand*).

The story of the fate of the Silmarils in Q I advances on S, and here reaches an interesting transitional stage between S and Q II, where the final resolution is achieved. Maidros remains as in S the less fiercely resolute of the two surviving sons of Fëanor in the fulfilment of the oath: in S it is Maglor alone who steals a Silmaril from Fionwë's keeping, and in Q I it is Maidros who is 'minded to submit', but is argued down by Maglor. In Q II the arguments remain, but the parts of Maidros and Maglor are reversed, just as in §17 (by later emendation to Q II, note 10) Maglor becomes the one who saved Elrond and Elros. In Q I both brothers go to steal the Silmarils from Fionwë, as in the final version of the legend; but, as in S, only Maglor carries his away – for in the new story Maidros is captured. Yet, whereas as in S only one of the two remaining Silmarils is consigned to the deep places by the act of one of the brothers (Maglor), and the other is retained by Fionwë and ultimately becomes Eärendel's star – Maidros playing, so far as can be seen, no further part in its fate, in Q I the burning of the unrighteous hand, and the realisation that the right of the sons of Fëanor to the Silmarils is now void, becomes that of Maidros; and, a prisoner of Fionwë, he slays himself, casting the Silmaril on the ground (and though the text of Q I does not go so far as this, the logic of the narrative must lead to the giving of this Silmaril to Eärendel, as in S). The emended version in S (notes 6 and 7), that Maglor casts his Silmaril into a fiery pit and thereafter wanders singing in sorrow by the sea (rather than that he casts himself also into the pit), is taken up into Q I.

In Q II the story has shifted again, to the final harmonious and symmetrical structure: the Silmaril of Beren is not lost, and becomes the star of Eärendel: both Maglor and Maidros take a Silmaril from the camp of Fionwë, and both cast them down into inaccessible places. Maidros still takes his own life, but does so by casting himself into the fiery pit – and this is a return to the original story of Maglor told in S. Maglor now casts his Silmaril into the sea – and thus the Silmarils of earth, sea, and sky are retained, but they are different Silmarils; for in the earlier versions it was one of those from the Iron Crown of Morgoth that became the Evening Star.

This extraordinarily complex but highly characteristic narrative evolution can perhaps be shown more clearly in a table:

S	Q I	Q II
The Silmaril of Beren is cast into the sea by Elwing and lost	As in S	The Silmaril of Beren is brought by Elwing to Eärendel on Wingelot; with it he goes to Valinor
—	*Maidros* is minded to submit, but *Maglor* argues against him	*Maglor* is minded to submit, but *Maidros* argues against him

S	Q I	Q II
Maglor alone steals a Silmaril from Fionwë, and escapes	*Maidros* and *Maglor* together steal both Silmarils from Fionwë, but *Maidros* is captured	As in Q I, but both *Maidros* and *Maglor* are permitted to depart bearing the Silmarils
Maglor knows from the pain of the Silmaril that he no longer has a right to it	*Maidros* knows from the pain of the Silmaril that he no longer has a right to it	As in Q I
Maglor casts himself and the Silmaril into a fiery pit > He casts the Silmaril into a pit and wanders by the shores	*Maidros* casts his Silmaril on the ground and takes his life	*Maidros* casts himself and his Silmaril into a fiery pit
	Maglor casts his Silmaril into a fiery pit and wanders by the shores	*Maglor* casts his Silmaril into the sea and wanders by the shores
Maidros' Silmaril is adjudged by the Gods to Eärendel	[As in S, though this point not reached in Q I]	The Silmaril of Beren, never lost, is retained by Eärendel

We find still in both versions of Q, as in S, the statement that some of the returning Elves went beyond Tol Eressëa and dwelt in Valinor ('as all were free to do who willed', Q II) – and it is made clear in the Q texts that these included some of the exiled Noldoli, 'admitted to the love of Manwë and the pardon of the Gods'. Also retained in Q I (but not in Q II) is the statement that Tûn remained deserted, again without explanation given (see p. 72). But whereas in S Tol Eressëa was repeopled by 'the Gnomes and many of the Ilkorins and Teleri and Qendi', in the Q-texts Teleri and Quendi are not mentioned here, only Gnomes and Dark-elves ('especially such as had once belonged to Doriath', Q I).

In a hasty pencilled note to Q I (§17 note 1) there is a reference to some Men of Hithlum being repentant, and to the fulfilment of Ulmo's foretelling (i.e. 'without Men the Elves shall not prevail against the Orcs and Balrogs', §16): both by the valour of the Men of Hithlum, and by the embassy of Eärendel to the Valar. This is taken up into Q II in the present section, with the addition that many Men new come out of the East fought against Morgoth; but further revision (notes 2 and 3) altered this to say that most Men and especially these newcomers from the East fought on the side of the Enemy, and also that in addition to the repentant Men of Hithlum 'all that were left of the three Houses of the Fathers of Men fought for Fionwë'. This latter phrase indicates both that the house of Hador had now been divided (see the commentary on §9), and also that the houses of the Elf-friends are now enlarged, so that they are not restricted to those descendants of the Fathers who have been mentioned in the narrative. The strange permission of Fionwë to the Men of the houses of Hador and Bëor to depart into the West has disappeared in Q II.

Other developments in Q II are the failure of Morgoth to come forth at the end; the coming of the winged dragons, of which the greatest was Ancalagon the black; the slaying of Ancalagon by Eärendel descending out of the skies with countless birds about him; and the destruction of Thangorodrim by the fall of Ancalagon.

19

In this concluding section the narrative, almost entirely now in the Q II text only, returns again to Eärendel; and, very curiously, the scorching of him by the Sun and the hunting of him by the Moon, and his voyaging as 'a fugitive star', reappears *after* the Last Battle and overthrow of Morgoth; in S and Q this is said of his first uprising into the heavens, at the end of §17. It is only now that

the Valar drew his white ship Wingelot over the land of Valinor, and they filled it with radiance and hallowed it, and launched it through the Door of Night.

It seems plain that in this account this act of the Valar was to protect Eärendel, by setting him to sail in the Void, above the courses of the Sun and Moon and stars (see the diagram in the *Ambarkanta*, p. 243), where also he could guard the Door against Morgoth's return. And in Q II Elwing was beside him in his journeys 'into the starless vast' (this being later struck out, note 6).

We have in fact already encountered, in the rewritten passage given in note 20 to §17 in Q II, the final story, that Wingelot was hallowed by the Gods and set in the heavens *before* the departure of the hosts of the West; but this postdates the writing of the conclusion of Q II. In this passage Elwing herself builds the Tower of Seabirds, devising wings in order to try to reach Eärendel, but they never meet again; and thus the element of the seabirds is removed from any direct association with Eärendel. In the account of the Last Battle in Q II §18 Eärendel descends out of the sky accompanied by 'a myriad of birds', but this of course belongs with the story in Q II §17 that it was Eärendel who built the Tower, and Elwing who devised wings for his ship. One might have expected that the birds that descended with Eärendel on Ancalagon the black would disappear in the later story, where it is the Valar who raise Wingelot, and the bird-wings by which it was formerly lifted up are rejected; but in the final version of the story of 'the last things' they are still present, and so in *The Silmarillion* (p. 252).

I give (p. 204) a table that may serve to show the development of the story of Eärendel and Elwing in these texts more clearly.

The final version of the story is further changed in that Elwing remained with Eärendel in Valinor; the Tower of Seabirds was built for her, and from it she would fly to meet Eärendel as his ship returned to Valinor (*The Silmarillion* p. 250).

S and Q	Q II	Revisions to Q II
Eärendel (with Bronweg) visits Kôr fruitlessly, for the Elves have already gone (§17)	Eärendel (with Elwing, and bearing the Silmaril) goes to Valinor, and forbidding Elwing to accompany him further declares 'the embassy of the Two Kindreds' (§17)	Eärendel bids farewell to Elwing for ever on the shore of Valinor (§17 note 14)
He builds the Tower where all seabirds come (Q: and grieves for the loss of Elwing) (§17)	He guides the fleet out of the West; he builds the Tower of Seabirds, and Elwing is with him (§17)	Eärendel's ship is hallowed by the Valar and set in the sky (§17 note 20)
By birds' wings Wingelot is lifted into the sky (§17)	Elwing devises wings for Wingelot (§17)	Elwing builds the Tower and devises bird-wings for herself, but cannot reach Eärendel, and they are sundered for ever (§17 note 20)
He is scorched by the Sun and hunted by the Moon, and wanders as a fugitive star. He has no Silmaril. (§17)	He sails the sky bearing the Silmaril (?with Elwing), and the star is seen by the people of the Outer Lands (§17)	(Elwing is not with him)
	He descends from the sky to the Last Battle with countless birds about him, and slays Ancalagon (§18)	
After the Last Battle the Silmaril of Maidros is given to Eärendel and Elwing is restored to him; he sails into the Outer Dark with Elwing, bearing the Silmaril (§19) [The Q I text ends before this point is reached]	He is scorched by the Sun and hunted by the Moon, and sails as a fugitive star (§19)	(Elwing is not with him; §19 note 6)
	His ship is hallowed by the Valar and launched through the Door of Night. Elwing is with him (§19)	

Apart from the passage concerning Eärendel, Q II follows S (presumably now the immediate precursor) fairly closely, in its account of the belief that Morgoth comes back in secret from time to time, whereas others declare that it is Thû (> Sauron), who survived the Last Battle; and in the content of the prophecy of the Last Things – which is now given formal existence as 'the Prophecy of Mandos', which Mandos declared in Valmar at the judgement of the Gods. There are however certain changes and developments in the Prophecy: Morgoth when he returns will destroy the Sun and Moon (which must surely contain at least a reminiscence of the passage from the tale of *The Hiding of Valinor* cited on p. 73); Tulkas is now named as the chief antagonist of Melko in the final battle on the plains of Valinor, together with Fionwë and Túrin Turambar; Eärendel will yield up his Silmaril, and Fëanor will bear the Three to Yavanna to break them (in S they are to be broken by Maidros); and with the awakening of the Elves and the rising of their dead the purpose of Ilúvatar will be fulfilled concerning them. The appearance of Túrin at the end remains profoundly mysterious; and here it is said that the Prophecy names him among the Gods, which is clearly to be related to the passage in the old *Tale of Turambar* (II. 116), where it is said that Túrin and Nienor 'dwelt as shining Valar among the blessed ones', after they had passed through Fôs'Almir, the bath of flame. In changes to the text of Q II it is said that Túrin is named among 'the sons of the Gods', rather than among the Gods, and also that he comes 'from the halls of Mandos' to the final battle; about which I can say no more than that Túrin Turambar, though a mortal Man, did not go, as do the race of Men, to a fate beyond the world.

★

APPENDIX 1

Fragment of a translation of the Quenta Noldorinwa into Old English, made by Ælfwine or Eriol; together with Old English equivalents of Elvish names

There are extant fragments of Old English (Anglo-Saxon) versions of the *Annals of Valinor* (three), the *Annals of Beleriand*, and *Quenta Noldorinwa*. All begin at the beginning of the respective works and only one, a version of the *Annals of Valinor*, constitutes a substantial text. The Old English version of the *Quenta* which is given here had no title, but my father later inserted in pencil the title *Pennas*; cf. *Qenta Noldorinwa* or *Pennas-na-Ngoelaidh*, p. 77. In a brief detached list of Elvish names and words that belongs to this period occurs this entry:

Quenta story, tale (*quete-* 'say'). N[oldorin] *pent.*
pennas history (*quentassë*).

At this time *Eriol* and *Ælfwine* reappear together as the Elvish and English names of the mariner who came to Tol Eressëa and there translated various Elvish works into his own language: in the preamble to the *Annals of Valinor* (p. 263) he is 'Eriol of Leithien, that is Ælfwine of the Angelcynn', and in one of the Old English versions of these *Annals* the work is said (p. 281) to have been translated by 'Ælfwine, whom the Elves named Eriol'. (On the earlier relations of the two names see II. 300–1.)

The Old English version of the *Quenta* is a very close equivalent of the Modern English text from its opening 'After the making of the World by the Allfather' to 'shadow is her realm and night her throne' (pp. 78–9), where the Old English ends. It is a manuscript in ink, obviously a first draft, with pencilled emendations (mostly small alterations of word-order and suchlike) which I take up into the text; the last paragraph is written in pencil, very rapidly. Acute accents on long vowels were put in rather sporadically and I have made the usage consistent, as with the Old English texts throughout.

Pennas

Æfter þám þe Ealfæder, se þe on elfisc Ilúuatar hátte, þás worolde geworhte, þá cómon manige þá mihtegostan gǽstas þe mid him wunodon hire to stíeranne; for þon þe hí híe feorran ofsáwon fægre geworhte and hí lustfollodon on hire wlitignesse. þás gǽstas nemdon þá Elfe *Valar*, þæt is þá 5
Mægen, þe men oft siððan swápéah nemdon Godu. Ópre gǽstas manige hæfdon hí on hira folgoðe, ge máran ge lǽssan, 7 þára sume tealdon men siþþan gedwollice mid þǽm Elfum; ac híe lugon, for þám þe ǽr séo worold geworht wǽre hí wǽron, 7 Elfe and Fíras (þæt sindon men) onwócon ǽrest 10
on worolde æfter þára Valena cyme. Ealfæder ána geworhte Elfe and Fíras ond ǽgþerum gedǽlde hira ágene gifa; þý hátað hí woroldbearn oþþe Ealfæderes bearn.

þara Valena ealdoras nigon wǽron. þus hátað þá nigon godu on elfiscum gereorde swá swá þa elfe hit on Valinóre 15
sprǽcon, þéah þe hira naman sind ópre 7 onhwerfede on nold-elfisc, and missenlice sind hira naman mid mannum.

Manwe wæs goda hláford, and winda and wedera wealdend and heofones stýrend. Mid him wunede to his geféran séo undéadlice héanessa hlǽfdige, úprodera cwén, *Varda* 20

tunglawyrhte. Him se nyxta on mægene, and on fréondscipe
se cúðesta, wæs *Ulmo* ágendfréa ealra wætera, se þe ána
wunað on Útgársecge, 7 stýreð swáþéah eallum wǽgum 7
wæterum, éam 7 stréamum, wyllum ond ǽwelmum geond
eorðan ymbhwyrfte. Him underþýded, þéah he him oft   25
unhold bið, is *Osse*, se þe manna landa sǽm stýreð, 7 his
geféra is *Uinen* merehlǽfdige. Hire feax líþ gesprǽdd geond
ealle sǽ under heofenum.

On mægene wæs *Aule* Ulmo swíðost gelíc. He wæs smiþ
and cræftiga, 7 *Yavanna* wæs his geféra, séo þe ofet and   30
hærfest and ealle eorðan wæstmas lufode. Nyxt wæs héo on
mægene þára Valacwéna Vardan. Swíþe wlítig wæs héo, and
híe þá Elfe nemdon oft *Palúrien* þæt is 'eorþan scéat'.

þá gebróþru *Mandos* 7 *Lórien* hátton *Fanturi*. *Nefantur*
háteð se ǽresta, neoærna hláford, and wælcyriga, se þe   35
samnode ofslægenra manna gǽstas. *Olofantur* háteð se óðer,
swefna wyrhta 7 gedwimora; 7 his túnas on goda landum
wǽron ealra stówa fægroste on worolde 7 wǽron gefylde mid
manigum gǽstum wlitigum and mihtigum.

Ealra goda strengest 7 leoþucræftigost and foremǽrost   40
ellendǽdum wæs *Tulkas*; þý háteð he éac þon *Poldórea* se
ellenrófa (se dyhtiga); and he wæs Melkoes unwine and his
wiþerbroca.

Orome wæs mihtig hláford and lýtle lǽssa maegenes þonne
Tulkas sylf. Orome wæs hunta 7 tréowcynn lufode – þý hátte   45
he *Aldaron*, 7 þá noldielfe hine *Tauros* nemdon, þæt is
Wealdafréa – 7 him wǽron léofe hors and hundas. Húru he
éode on huntoð þurh þá deorce land ǽr þám þe séo sunne
wurde gýt atend /onǽled; swíþe hlúde wǽron his hornas, 7
swá béoð gíet on friðum and feldum þe Orome áh on   50
Valinóre. *Vana* hátte his geféra, séo wæs gingra sweostor
hira Vardan 7 Palúrienne, 7 séo fægernes ge heofenes ge
eorðan bið on hire wlite and hire weorcum. Hire mihtigre
swáþéah bið *Nienna*, séo þe mid Nefantur Mandos eardað.
Mildheort bið héo, hire bið geómor sefa, murnende mód;   55
sceadwa bið hire scír 7 hire þrymsetl þéostru.

NOTES

6 *Mægen* ('Powers') was emended to *Reg*. . (*?Regen ?Regin*). Old
   English *regn-* in compounds 'great, mighty', related to Old Norse
   regin 'Gods' (occurring in *Ragnarök*).

10 *Fíras* is an emendation of *Elde* (both are old poetic words for 'men').
    At line 12 *Fíras* is written beside *Elde*, which was emended to *Ælde*
    (and *Elfe* apparently to *Ælfe*).
11 *Valena* genitive plural is an emendation from *Vala*; also in line 14.
23 *on Útgársecge*: *Út-gársecg* 'the Outer Seas'. *Gársecg*, one of many
    Old English names of the sea, is used frequently in *Ælfwine of
    England* of the Great Sea of the West (in one of the texts spelt
    Garsedge to represent the pronunciation).
35 *wælcyriga*: 'chooser of the slain (*wæl*)', the Old English equivalent
    of Old Norse *valkyrja* (Valkyrie).
49 *atend, oncæled*: these words are alternatives, but neither is marked
    for rejection.
55 Cf. *Beowulf* lines 49–50: *him wæs geómor sefa, murnende mód* ('sad
    was their heart and mourning in their soul').

★

Associated with the Old English texts are several lists of Elvish names
with Old English equivalents, some of which are of much interest for the
light they cast on the meaning of Elvish names; though many are not in
fact translations, as will be seen.
    There is firstly a list of the Valar:

The chief gods are Fréan. ós (ése)

[O.E. *fréa* 'ruler, lord'; *ós* 'god' (in proper names as *Oswald*), with
mutated vowel in the plural.]

Manwë is Wolcenfréa [O.E. *wolcen* 'sky'; cf. Modern English *welkin*.]

Ulmo is Gársecges fréa, & ealwæter-fréa [For *Gársecg* see note to
line 23 of the O.E. *Quenta*. In that text Ulmo is called *ágendfréa ealra
wœtera* 'Lord of Waters' (literally 'owning lord of all waters').]

Aulë is Cræftfréa

Tulkas is Afoðfréa [O.E. *afoð, eafoð* 'might, strength'.]

Oromë is Wáðfréa and Huntena fréa [O.E. *wáð* 'hunting'; 'Hunting
Lord and Lord of Hunters'. In the O.E. *Quenta* he is *Wealdafréa*
'Lord of Forests', translating *Tauros*.]

Mandos is Néfréa [O.E. *né(o)* 'corpse'; cf. *néocerna hláford* 'master of
the houses of the dead' in the O.E. *Quenta*. On the Elvish name
Nefantur see p. 166.]

Lórien is Swefnfréa [O.E. *swefn* 'dream'.]

Melko is Mánfréa, Bolgen, Malscor [O.E. *mán* 'evil, wickedness'; *bolgen* 'wrathful'. An O.E. verbal noun *malscrung* is recorded, with the meaning 'bewildering, bewitching'; see the Oxford English Dictionary s.v. *Masker* (verb), 'bewilder'.]

Ossë is Sæfréa

There are also several lists of Old English equivalents of Elvish names of persons and places, and since they all obviously belong to the same period I combine them and give them in alphabetical order:

Aldaron: Béaming [O.E. *béam* 'tree'.]

Amon Uilas: Sinsnáw, Sinsnǽwen [O.E. *sin-* 'perpetual'; *snáw* 'snow', *snǽwen* (not recorded) 'snowy'. *Amon Uilas* appears in the *Quenta*, p. 81 note 2.]

Ancalagon: Anddraca [O.E. *and-* as the first element in compounds denotes opposition, negation (*anda* 'enmity, hatred, envy'); *draca* 'dragon' (see II. 350).]

Angband: Engbend, Irenhell [*Engbend* contains O.E. *enge* 'narrow, strait, oppressive, cruel' and *bend* 'bond, fetter'; it is thus not a translation but a word-play between the two languages.]

Asgar: Bǽning [This river, *Ascar* in Q as in *The Silmarillion*, is also *Asgar* in the *Annals of Beleriand* (p. 307). I cannot interpret *Bǽning*. If a derivative of O.E. *bán* 'bone' (cf. *bǽnen* 'of bone') it might have some meaning like 'the place (i.e. the river) filled with bones', with reference to the Dwarves who were drowned in the river at the battle of the Stony Ford; but this does not seem at all probable.]

Balrog: Bealuwearg, Bealubróga [O.E. *bealu* 'evil', cf. Modern English *bale(ful)*; *wearg* 'felon, outlaw, accursed being' (Old Norse *vargr* 'wolf, outlaw', whence the *Wargs*); *bróga* 'terror'. These O.E. names are thus like *Engbend* ingenious sound-correspondences contrived from O.E. words.]

Bansil: Béansíl, Béansigel [The second element is O.E. *sigel* 'sun, jewel' (cf. J. R. R. Tolkien, *Sigelwara land*, in *Medium Ævum III*, June 1934, p. 106); the first is presumably *béam* 'tree'. This is another case where Ælfwine used Old English words to give a likeness of sound (with of course a suitable meaning), rather than a translation. – In the Name-list to *The Fall of Gondolin Bansil* is translated 'Fair-gleam', II. 214.]

Baragund, Barahir: Beadohun, Beadomær [O.E. *beadu* 'battle'.]

Bauglir: Bróga [O.E. *bróga* 'terror'.]

Beleg: Finboga [O.E. *boga* 'bow'.]

Belegar: Ingársecg, Westsǽ, Wídsǽ [The Gnomish name of the Great Sea, has not yet appeared in the texts. *Ingársecg* = *Gársecg*; *Útgársecg* is the Outer Sea (see note to line 23 of the O.E. *Quenta*).]

Belegost: Micelburg ['Great fortress', the original meaning (see II.336).]

Blodrin Ban's son: Blodwine Banan sunu [*Blodwine* presumably contains O.E. *blód* 'blood'; while *bana* is 'slayer'.]

Doriath: Éaland, Folgen(fold), Infolde, Wudumǽraland [O.E. *éaland*, land by water or by a river – doubtless with reference to the rivers Sirion and Esgalduin. *Folgen(fold)*: O.E. *folgen* is the past participle of *féolan* 'penetrate, make one's way, get to', but the cognate verbs in Gothic and Old Norse have the meaning 'hide', and it may be that *folgen* is here given the sense of Old Norse *fólginn* 'hidden', i.e. 'the hidden (land)'. Gondolin is called *Folgenburg*. *Infolde*, a word not recorded, perhaps has some meaning like 'the inner land', 'the land within'. *Wudumǽraland* no doubt contains *mǽre* 'boundary, border'.]

Dor-lómen: Wómanland [See *Ered-lómen*.]

Drengist: Nearufléot [*Drengist* has not yet appeared in the texts. O.E. *nearu* 'narrow', *fléot* 'arm of the sea, estuary, firth'.]

Ered-lómen: Wómanbeorgas [O.E. *wóma* 'sound, noise', *beorg* 'mountain'; sc. the Echoing Mountains, and similarly *Wómanland* for Dor-lómen, Land of Echoes. This is the later etymology of these names; see pp. 192–3.]

Gelion: Glæden [*Gelion* appears by emendation of *Flend* in the *Quenta* §14. O.E. *glædene* 'iris, gladdon', as in the Gladden Fields and Gladden River in *The Lord of the Rings*.]

Gondolin: Stángaldor(burg), Folgenburg, Galdorfæsten [O.E. *stán* 'stone'; *galdor* 'spell, enchantment'; *fæsten* 'fastness, fortress'. For *Folgenburg* (? 'the hidden city') see *Doriath*.]

Hithlum: Hasuglóm, Hasuland (Hasulendingas) [O.E. *hasu* 'grey'; *glóm* 'gloaming, twilight'. *Hasulendingas* 'the people of Hasuland'.]

Laurelin: Gleng(g)old [O.E. *gleng* 'ornament, splendour'; *Glengold* is not a translation but a sound-imitation of *Glingol* ('Singing-gold', II.216.]

Mithrim: Mistrand, Mistóra [O.E. *óra* 'bank, shore', and *rand* of the same meaning.]

Nargothrond: Hlýdingaburg, Stángaldor(burg) [*Hlýdingaburg* is the city of the *Hlýdingas*, the people of Narog (*Hlýda*). *Stángaldor (burg)* is also given as an O.E. name for Gondolin.]

Narog: Hlýda [*Hlýda* 'the loud one' (O.E. *hlúd* 'loud'; see III. 87–8).]

Silmaril: Sigel, Sigelmǽrels [For *sigel* see *Bansil* above. O.E. *mǽrels* 'rope'; *Sigelmǽrels* is another case of imitation – but it refers to the Necklace of the Dwarves.]

Sirion: Fléot (Fléwet), Scírwendel [*Fléot* must here have the meaning 'river', which is scarcely evidenced in Old English, though it is the general meaning of the word in cognate language (cf. *Drengist* above). *Scírwendel*: O.E. *scír* 'bright'; *wendel* does not occur, but certainly refers to the windings of a river's course – cf. *Withywindle*, the river in the Old Forest, concerning which my father noted: '*-windle* does not actually occur (*Withywindle* was modelled on *withywind*, a name of the convolvulus or bindweed)' (*Guide to the Names in The Lord of the Rings*, in *A Tolkien Compass*, p. 196).]

Taur-na-Danion: Furhweald [In an addition to the *Quenta* §9 (note 1) *Taur Danin* is given as the former name of Taur-na-Fuin, when it was still 'wholesome, if thick and dark'; *Taur-na-Danion* here was changed to *Taur-na-Donion*, precursor of *Dorthonion* 'Land of Pines'. O.E. *furh* 'fir, pine', *weald* 'forest'.]

Taur-na-Fuin: Nihtsceadu, Nihtsceadwesweald, Atol Nihtegesa, Nihthelm unfǽle [O.E. *sceadu* 'shadow'; *weald* 'forest'; *atol* 'dire, terrible'; *egesa* 'terror'; *niht-helm* 'cover of night', a poetic compound found in *Beowulf* and other poems; *unfǽle* 'evil'. Cf. the Modern English translation, found in the long Lays and in the *Quenta*, 'Forest of Deadly Nightshade'.]

Tindbrenting þe þa Brega Taniquetil nemnað ['Tindbrenting which the Valar name Taniquetil': see III. 127, and for *Brega* see *Vala*.]

Vala: Bregu [O.E. *bregu* 'ruler, lord', plural (unrecorded) *brega*. Two other words were added to the list: *Mægen* 'Powers', which is used in the O.E. *Quenta* line 6, and *Ése* (see p. 208).]

Valinor: Breguland, Godéðel [O.E. *éðel* 'country, native land'.]

Valmar: Godaburg, Bregubold [O.E. *bold* 'dwelling'.]

Another page gives Old English equivalents of the names of the Kindreds of the Elves, and of the princes of the Noldoli arranged in a genealogical table. This page is headed:

Fíras. Includes both Men and Elves.

This contradicts the use of *Fíras* in the O.E. *Quenta*, where it appears as an emendation of *Elde* (lines 10 and 12), used in distinction to *Elfe*.

Then follows:

Fíra bearn

§1. þæt eldre cyn: *Elfe* oþþe *Wine*

1. *Ingwine*: *lyftelfe, héahelfe, hwítelfe, Líxend.   Godwine*
2. *Éadwine*: *goldelfe, eorðelfe, déopelfe, Rǽdend.   Finningas*
3. *Sǽwine*: *sǽelfe, mereþyssan, flotwine, Nówend.   Elwingas*

Wine can only be O.E. *wine* (old plural *wine*) 'friend' (a word used of equals, of superiors, and of inferiors); but its use here as a general term equivalent to *Elfe* is curious.

Of the names given to the First Kindred, *lyftelfe* contains O.E. *lyft* 'sky, air'; *Líxend* 'Shining Ones'. The Second Kindred: *Éad-* in the context of the Noldoli is in no doubt to be interpreted 'riches'. I am not sure of the meaning of *Rǽdend*, though it clearly refers to the knowledge and desire for knowledge of the Noldoli in some aspect. *Finningas* 'the people of Finn' (*Ing* and *Finn* as the Gnomish forms of Ingwë and Finwë were still found in Q §2, though removed by later changes to the text). The Third Kindred: O.E. *mereþyssa* 'sea-rusher' (used in recorded O.E. poetry of ships); *flotwine* contains O.E. *flot* 'sea'; *Nówend* 'mariners, shipmasters'.

In the genealogical table that follows Fëanor is given the Old English name *Finbrós Gimwyrhta* ('Jewel-wright'); since his sons are here called *Brósingas* (from *Brósinga mene* 'the necklace of the Brósings' in *Beowulf*, line 1199) *-brós* is presumably a back-formation from *Brósingas*. They are also called *Yrfeloran*: an unrecorded compound, 'those bereft of their inheritance', the Dispossessed. The *Brósingas* or sons of Fëanor are given thus:

1. *Dægred Winsterhand* [O.E. *dægred* 'daybreak, dawn'; *winsterhand* 'left-handed' (for the right hand of Maidros was cut off in his rescue from Thangorodrim, Q §8). I can cast no light on the O.E. equivalent *Dægred* for Maidros, unless an extremely late note on Maidros (Maedhros) is relevant (for ideas long buried so far as written record goes might emerge again many years later): according to this he inherited 'the rare red-brown hair of Nerdanel's kin' (Nerdanel was the wife of Fëanor, *The Silmarillion* p. 64), and was called 'by his brothers and other kin' *Russandol* 'copper-top'.]

2. *Dægmund Swinsere* [I cannot explain *Dægmund* for Maglor. O.E. *mund* is 'hand', also 'protection'; *swinsere* (not recorded) 'musician, singer' (cf. *swinsian* 'make music').]

3. *Cynegrim Fægerfeax* [Celegorm 'Fairfax', i.e. fair-haired. *Cynegrim* is probably the substitution of an O.E. name with some similarity of sound.]

4. *Cyrefinn Fácensearo* [Curufin the Crafty. O.E. *cyre* 'choice'; *fácen* 'deceit, guile, wickedness' (a word of wholly bad meaning); *searu* 'skill, cunning' (also with bad meaning, 'plot, snare, treachery'); *fácensearu* 'treachery'.]

5. *Colþegn Nihthelm* [Cranthir the Dark. O.E. *col* 'coal'; for *nihthelm* see under *Taur-na-Fuin* above.]

6. *Déormód* }
7. *Tirgeld* } *huntan* [Damrod and Díriel the hunters. O.E. *déormód* 'brave-hearted'; *tír* 'glory'; *-geld* (*-gild*) in names, 'of worth'.]

Fingolfin appears as *Fingold Fengel* (O.E. *fengel* 'king, prince'; cf. III. 145), and his sons are *Finbrand* (i.e. Finweg/Fingon) and *Finstán* (i.e. Turgon); the element *stán* 'stone' presumably showing that *-gon* in *Turgon* is *gond* (*gonn*) 'stone', see I. 254. Fingolfin's daughter is *Finhwít* (i.e. Isfin), and Eöl is *Eor*; Meglin is *Mánfrið* (an unrecorded compound of *mán* 'evil deed, wickedness' and *frið* 'peace').

Finbrand (i.e. Finweg/Fingon) here has a son, *Fingár*; and the daughter of *Finstán* (i.e. Turgon) is *Ideshild Silfrenfót* (i.e. Idril Celebrindal).

Finrod (i.e. the later Finarfin) is called *Finred Felanóþ* (*felanóþ* 'very bold'), and his sons are *Ingláf Felahrór* (i.e. Felagund; *felahrór* has the same meaning as *felanóþ*), *Ordred* (i.e. Orodreth), *Angel* (i.e. Angrod), and *Eangrim* (i.e. Egnor).

Ordred (i.e. Orodreth) has two sons, *Ordhelm* and *Ordláf*; his daughter is *Friþuswíþ Fealuléome* (i.e. Finduilas Failivrin; *fealuléome* perhaps 'golden light').

Lastly, there is a fourth child of Finwë given in this table: *Finrún Felageómor* (*felageómor* 'very sorrowful').

The name given to Felagund, *Ingláf Felahrór*, is notable; for *Felagund* was to become his 'nickname', and his true name *Inglor* (as it remained until replaced long afterwards by Finrod, when the original Finrod became Finarfin); see p. 341.

★

APPENDIX 2

The Horns of Ylmir

This poem is unquestionably that referred to in the *Quenta*, p. 142: 'the might and majesty of that vision is told of in the song of Tuor that he made for his son Eärendel.' It is extant in three versions and five texts.

The first version, found only in one manuscript, consists of 40 lines, beginning:

I sat on the ruined margin of the deep-voiced echoing sea

and ending:

and I wake to silent caverns, and empty sands, and peace

(lines 15 and 66 in the text given below). To the manuscript in ink my father added in pencil the title *The Tides*, together with the notes *Dec. 4 1914* and *On the Cornish Coast*. For his visit to the Lizard Peninsula in Cornwall in the summer of 1914 see Humphrey Carpenter, *Biography*, pp. 70–1. But although I have found nothing earlier than this text it is clear from my father's notes to subsequent versions that he remembered the origin of the poem to be earlier than that time.

The second version bears the title *Sea Chant of an Elder Day* (and Old English *Fyrndaga Sǽléoþ*), and is extant in two manuscripts which differ only in small details. The second has some minor emendations, and the date: *Mar. 1915 < Dec. 1914 < 1912*, also *Essay Club* [of Exeter College, Oxford] *March 1915*. This version begins:

In a dim and perilous region, down whose great tempestuous ways
I heard no sound of men's voices; in those eldest of the days,
I sat on the ruined margin of the deep-voiced echoing sea . . .

(i.e. it begins at line 13 in the text, p. 216) and contains two further lines after 'and empty sands, and peace' (where *The Tides* ends):

In a lovely sunlit region down whose old chaotic ways
Yet no sound of men's voices echoed in those eldest of all days.

It is from this version, not that of 1914, that Humphrey Carpenter cites the first six lines (*ibid*. pp. 73–4). The *Sea Chant* differs from *The Tides* both by extension (it has 50 lines as against 40) and in the reconstruction of many verses.

Against the second text of the *Sea Chant* my father wrote in pencil:

This is the song that Tuor told to Eärendel his son what time the Exiles of Gondolin dwelt awhile in Dor Tathrin the Land of Willows after the burning of their city. Now Tuor was the first of Men to see the Great Sea, but guided by Ulmo towards Gondolin he had left the shores of the Ocean and passing through the Land of Willows became enamoured of its loveliness, forgetting both his quest and his former love of the sea. Now Ulmo lord of Vai coming in his deep-sea car sat at twilight in the reeds of Sirion and played to him on his magic flute of hollow shells. Thereafter did Tuor hunger ever after the sea and had no peace in his heart did he dwell in pleasant inland places.*

This very evidently belongs with the tale of *The Fall of Gondolin* (see especially II. 153–6), and was no doubt added at the time of the composition of the tale (and of the third version of the poem), since the *Sea Chant* has no point of contact with the Tuor legend, nor indeed with any feature of the mythology.

The third version, entitled *The Horns of Ulmo*, is extant in a manuscript and in a typescript taken directly from it, and it is only now that the references to Ulmo and Ossë (and to the rending of the Earth by the Gods in the primeval darkness) appear in the poem. A note on the MS, written at the same time as the poem, reads:

1910–11–12 rewr[itten] & recast often. Present shape due to rewriting and adding introd[uction] & ending in a lonely house near Roos, Holderness (Thistle Bridge Camp) Spring 1917

(For Roos see Humphrey Carpenter, *Biography*, p. 97.) A further pencilled note adds: 'poem to "The Fall of Gondolin".'

Thus the absorption of the poem into the legend of Tuor and Eärendel took place at much the same time as the writing of the tale of *The Fall of Gondolin* (see I. 203, II. 146); it should have been given in *The Book of Lost Tales Part II*.

A few small emendations were made to the MS of *The Horns of Ulmo*, notably *Ulmo > Ylmir* (the latter being the Gnomish form, found in the *Lay of the Children of Húrin* and in the 'Sketch'), and the second reference to Ossë (lines 41–2, replacing two earlier verses). The typescript is essentially the same as the manuscript (with the words 'from "The Fall of Gondolin"' added beneath the title), but it has some small alterations made in red ball-point pen, which therefore belong to a much later time. These late changes are not incorporated in the text given here, but are given in notes following the poem.

The Horns of Ylmir
from
'The Fall of Gondolin'

'Tuor recalleth in a song sung to his son Eärendel
the visions that Ylmir's conches once called before
him in the twilight in the Land of Willows.'

Dor Tathrin occurs in the Name-list to *The Fall of Gondolin*, II. 346, and Ulmo's 'deep-sea car' in the tale of *The Chaining of Melko*, I. 101.

'Twas in the Land of Willows where the grass is long and green –
I was fingering my harp-strings, for a wind had crept unseen
And was speaking in the tree-tops, while the voices of the reeds
Were whispering reedy whispers as the sunset touched the meads,
5   Inland musics subtly magic that those reeds alone could weave –
'Twas in the Land of Willows that once Ylmir came at eve.

In the twilight by the river on a hollow thing of shell
He made immortal music, till my heart beneath his spell
Was broken in the twilight, and the meadows faded dim
10   To great grey waters heaving round the rocks where sea-birds swim.

I heard them wailing round me where the black cliffs towered high
And the old primeval starlight flickered palely in the sky.
In that dim and perilous region in whose great tempestuous ways
I heard no sound of men's voices, in those eldest of the days,
15   I sat on the ruined margin of the deep-voiced echoing sea
Whose roaring foaming music crashed in endless cadency
On the land besieged for ever in an aeon of assaults
And torn in towers and pinnacles and caverned in great vaults;
And its arches shook with thunder and its feet were piled with shapes
20   Riven in old sea-warfare from those crags and sable capes.

Lo! I heard the embattled tempest roaring up behind the tide
When the trumpet of the first winds sounded, and the grey sea sang
        and cried
As a new white wrath woke in him, and his armies rose to war
And swept in billowed cavalry toward the walled and moveless shore.
25   There the windy-bannered fortress of those high and virgin coasts
Flung back the first thin feelers of the elder tidal hosts;
Flung back the restless streamers that like arms of a tentacled thing
Coiling and creeping onward did rustle and suck and cling.
Then a sigh arose and a murmuring in that stealthy-whispering van,
30   While, behind, the torrents gathered and the leaping billows ran,
Till the foam-haired water-horses in green rolling volumes came –
A mad tide trampling landward – and their war-song burst to flame.

Huge heads were tossed in anger and their crests were towers of froth
And the song the great seas were singing was a song of unplumbed
        wrath,
35   For through that giant welter Ossë's trumpets fiercely blew,
That the voices of the flood yet deeper and the High Wind louder
        grew;
Deep hollows hummed and fluted as they sucked the sea-winds in;
Spumes and great white spoutings yelled shrilly o'er the din;
Gales blew the bitter tresses of the sea in the land's dark face
40   And wild airs thick with spindrift fled on a whirling race
From battle unto battle, till the power of all the seas

Gathered like one mountain about Ossë's awful knees,
And a dome of shouting water smote those dripping black facades
And its catastrophic fountains smashed in deafening cascades.

*　　*　　*

45 Then the immeasurable hymn of Ocean I heard as it rose and fell
To its organ whose stops were the piping of gulls and the
   thunderous swell;
Heard the burden of the waters and the singing of the waves
Whose voices came on for ever and went rolling to the caves,
Where an endless fugue of echoes splashed against wet stone
50 And arose and mingled in unison into a murmuring drone –
'Twas a music of uttermost deepness that stirred in the profound,
And all the voices of all oceans were gathered to that sound;
'Twas Ylmir, Lord of Waters, with all-stilling hand that made
Unconquerable harmonies, that the roaring sea obeyed,
55 That its waters poured off and Earth heaved her glistening
   shoulders again
Naked up into the airs and the cloudrifts and sea-going rain,
Till the suck and suck of green eddies and the slap of ripples was all
That reached to mine isléd stone, save the old unearthly call
Of sea-birds long-forgotten and the grating of ancient wings.

60 Thus murmurous slumber took me mid those far-off eldest things
(In a lonely twilit region down whose old chaotic ways
I heard no sound of men's voices, in those eldest of the days
When the world reeled in the tumult as the Great Gods tore the
   Earth
In the darkness, in the tempest of the cycles ere our birth),
65 Till the tides went out, and the Wind died, and did all sea musics
   cease
And I woke to silent caverns and empty sands and peace.

Then the magic drifted from me and that music loosed its bands –
Far, far-off, conches calling – lo! I stood in the sweet lands,
And the meadows were about me where the weeping willows grew,
70 Where the long grass stirred beside me, and my feet were drenched
   with dew.
Only the reeds were rustling, but a mist lay on the streams
Like a sea-roke drawn far inland, like a shred of salt sea-dreams.
'Twas in the Land of Willows that I heard th'unfathomed breath
Of the Horns of Ylmir calling – and shall hear them till my death.

NOTES

The following are the late changes made to the typescript, referred to on p. 215:

1 and 6 'Twas to It was
16   The line changed to: Whose endless roaring music crashed in foaming harmony, and marked with an X
21   roaring to rolling
28   The line marked with an X, probably primarily on account of the use of did (cf. III. 153)
65   The line changed to: Till the tides went out, and the Wind ceased, and all sea musics died (but this destroys the rhyme).

---

72   'sea-roke': roke is a medieval English word surviving until recent times in dialect meaning 'mist, fog, drizzling rain'.

IV

THE FIRST 'SILMARILLION' MAP

This map was made on a sheet of examination paper from the University of Leeds (as was most of the A-text of the *Lay of the Children of Hurin*, III.4), which suggests that it originated in association with the Lay, or perhaps rather with the 'Sketch of the Mythology' which was written to accompany it (p. 11). On the other hand, some names which seem to belong with the first making of the map do not appear in the texts before the *Quenta*. Though it was not drawn initially in a way that would suggest that my father intended it to endure, it was his working map for several years, and it was much handled and much altered. Names were emended and places re-sited; the writing is in red ink, black ink, green ink, pencil, and blue crayon, often overlaying each other. Lines representing contours and others representing streams tangle with lines for redirection and lines cancelling other lines. But it is striking that the river-courses as drawn on this first map were scarcely changed at all afterwards.

Associated with the map are two supplementary sheets, giving an Eastern and a Western extension to the main or central map; these are reproduced and annotated subsequently (pp. 227ff.). The main map is on a single sheet but is here reproduced in two halves, Northern and Southern. Names that were written in red ink all seem to belong to the original 'layer' of names, as do some (e.g. *Huan, Mavwin, Turgon*) of those in black ink; but *Taiglin, Geleidhian*, in red, do not otherwise occur before the *Quenta*. Those in green ink are few: *Broseliand*; *Gnomes* on the Northern half beside Gondolin, and on the Southern half beside Nargothrond; and *Wandering Gnomes* in the South-east.

In the following alphabetically-ordered list I take each half in turn* and comment on almost every item, noticing especially where the name in question first appears in the narrative texts.

The Northern Half of the Map

Aglon, Gorge of   The name itself is a hasty later addition. The Gorge of Aglon first occurs in the *Lay of Leithian* (lines 2062, 2995, passages composed in 1928). In the Lay and in Q (§§9, 10) the Gorge is the

---

*The list of names for the northern half includes names as far south as the fold in the original map, which can be seen in the reproductions; thus *Ginglith, Esgalduin, Thousand Caves* appear in the first list, but *Doriath beyond Sirion, Aros* in the second.

dwelling of the Sons of Fëanor, who are placed on the map to the North of it (and circled with an arrow directing to the East).

Angband   The placing of Angband in relation to Thangorodrim shows how my father saw them at the time of the long Lays and the 'Sketch'. In the *Lay of the Children of Húrin* (lines 712–14) the 'hopeless halls of Hell' are

> wrought at the roots   of the roaring cliffs
> of Thangorodrim's   thunderous mountain.

In the *Lay of Leithian* (lines 3526ff.) Angband's gate seems clearly to lie beneath Thangorodrim; and in S (§8) Thangorodrim is 'the highest of the Iron Mountains around Morgoth's fortress'. See further the commentary on the *Ambarkanta*, p. 260.

Angeryd   The Iron Mountains. Cf. *Angorodin* in the *Tale of Turambar* (II. 77).

Angrin Aiglir   *Aiglir Angrin* occurs twice in the *Lay of the Children of Húrin* (lines 711, 1055), emended later to *Eiglir Engrin* (in *The Silmarillion Ered Engrin*).

Aryador   This name reappears, rather surprisingly, from the *Lost Tales*, as a third name of Hithlum. In the tale of *The Coming of the Elves* (I. 119) Aryador is said to be the name among Men for Hisilómë; see also I. 249.

Battle of Unnumbered Tears   The Mound of Slain is placed in the *Lay of the Children of Húrin* (lines 1439 ff.) 'at the furthest end of Dor-na-Fauglith's dusty spaces' (Flinding and Túrin were wandering westward, line 1436); cf. also Q§11 'Finweg and Turgon and the Men of Hithlum were gathered in the West upon the borders of the Thirsty Plain.'

Beleg and Túrin   These names mark the north march of Doriath, where Beleg and Túrin fought together against the Orcs, an element that first entered the story in the *Lay of the Children of Húrin* (see III. 27).

Cristhorn   Placed in the mountains north (not as originally south) of Gondolin, as already in the fragment of the alliterative *Lay of Eärendel* (III. 143).

Deadly Nightshade, Forest of   See *Taur-na-Fuin*.

Dorlómin   See *Hithlum*.

Dor-na-Fauglith   This name arose during the composition of the *Lay of the Children of Húrin* (see III. 55), where also *the Thirsty Plain* is found. On the map this is an emendation of *The Black Plain*.

Dwarf-road to Belegost and Nogrod in the South   It is interesting that the Dwarf-road is shown as leading all the way from Nogrod and

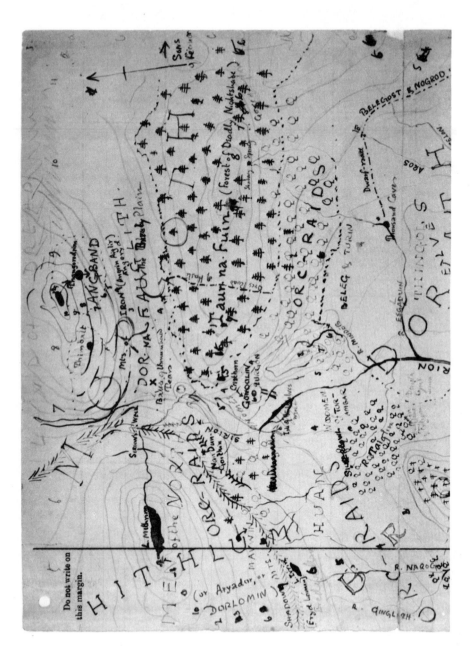

The Northern Half
of the First 'Silmarillion' Map

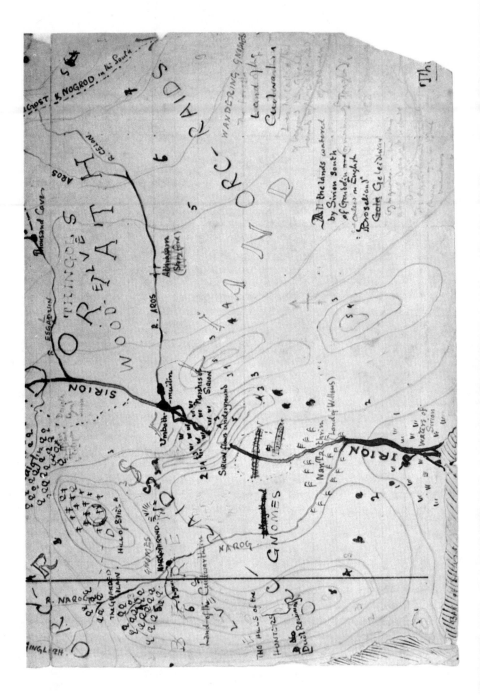

The Southern Half
of the First 'Silmarillion' Map

Belegost in the far South to the very doors of the Thousand Caves. It is possible, if not very likely, that the 'Dwarf-road' on the map merely indicates the path that the Dwarves did in fact take when summoned to Doriath, rather than a beaten track.

Eredwethion   A later replacement of *Eryd Lómin*, as also in Q II §15 (note 1).

Eryd Lómin   This name occurs in the caption to the painting of Tol Sirion of July 1928, where, as on the map and in Q II §15, it refers to the Shadowy Mountains; see pp. 192–3.

Esgalduin   First found in the *Lay of the Children of Húrin* (III.93). It is said in Q (§9) that it 'came out of secret wells in Taur-na-Fuin'; see *Shadowy Spring*. The course of Esgalduin was not afterwards changed.

Ginglith   First occurs in the *Lay of the Children of Húrin* (III.88). Its course was never changed.

Gondolin   Placed as it was to remain. The lines running south and west from the Encircling Mountains perhaps represent the hidden 'Way of Escape'.

Hithlum   Obviously Hithlum was not intended to extend south of the Shadowy Mountains, despite the placing of the M. The contour lines show that the Mountains of Mithrim did not yet exist. *Dorlómin* is given as an alternative name, as it is in S and Q (§8), where Lake Mithrim is placed in Hisilómë/Hithlum/Dorlómin; on the map *Mithrim* is simply and solely the name of the lake (cf. III. 103).

Huan   That a territory, south and east of Ivrin, is assigned to Huan shows a very early stage in the legend of Beren and Lúthien, when Huan was independent of any master (see III. 244).

Isle of the Werewolves   The Isle first appears in the *Lay of Leithian* in a passage written in March 1928 (see III. 234). Originally marked on the map S.W. of Gondolin, and with the river Sirion dividing quite broadly and enclosing a large island, this site was struck out, and an arrow directs from here to a more northerly position, not far south of the battlefield of Unnumbered Tears. The later map brought it somewhat southward again.

Ivrin, Lake   First occurs in the *Lay of the Children of Húrin* (line 1526); it is placed on the map in the position that I think is indicated in the Lay (see III. 87), and where it remained.

Land of Dread   Occurs twice in the *Lay of Leithian* (lines 49, 383) of the realm of Morgoth.

Mavwin   It is curious that the map retains the old name, which goes back to the *Tale of Turambar*, for *Morwen* is found already in the second version of the *Lay of the Children of Húrin* (III.94) and in S. In S (§9) Húrin and Morwen 'lived in the woods on the borders of Hithlum'.

Mindeb   First occurs in the *Lay of Leithian*, line 2924 (April 1928).

Mithrim, Lake   See *Hithlum*.

Mountains of Iron   See *Angeryd, Angrin Aiglir*.

Nan Dun-Gorthin   As the map was originally drawn this was placed west of Sirion, S.W. of Gondolin and very close to the Isle of the Werewolves (as that was originally placed). This cannot be the same placing as in the *Lay of the Fall of Gondolin* (III.148), where the hidden door of Gondolin was actually 'in dark Dungorthin'.

Subsequently *Nan-Dungorthin* was struck out and the name written again further north, still west of Sirion, but close beneath the Shadowy Mountains. This position is clearly that of the *Lay of the Children of Húrin*, where Túrin and Flinding passed the site of the Battle of Unnumbered Tears, crossed Sirion not far from his source, and came to 'the roots . . . of the Shadowy Mountains', where they entered the valley of Nan Dungorthin (see III. 59, 87).

Later again, an arrow was drawn moving Nan Dungorthin to a position east of Sirion and north of Doriath, and so more or less into the position of Nan Dungorthin (Nan Dungortheb) on the later map.

Orcs' Road of Haste   Cf. S §12: 'the Orc-road . . . which the Orcs use when in need of haste.'

Shadowy Mountains   First occurs in the *Lay of the Children of Húrin* (see III. 29). See *Eryd Lómin*.

Shadowy Spring   It is notable that the rivers Aros and Esgalduin arise at the same place, in the *Shadowy Spring* (not previously named in the texts; see *Esgalduin*). In the later map, on which mine in the published *Silmarillion* was based, this is still the case, and my map, showing the two sources as separate, is regrettably in error.

Silver Bowl   Shown in the Taiglin itself (not as later in the tributary stream Celebros), as in the *Tale of Turambar* and still in S and Q (§13).

Sirion   The course of the river was never changed; in the later map my father followed the earlier precisely.

Sirion's Well   This is referred to in the *Lay of the Children of Húrin* (line 1460). Its site remained unchanged.

Sons of Fëanor   See *Aglon*.

Taiglin   This looks like an original element on the map, although the name does not otherwise occur until the *Quenta*, §13 (see p. 185).

Taur-na-Fuin   This name (for *Taur Fuin* of the *Lost Tales*) and its translation *Deadly Nightshade* first occur in the *Lay of the Children of Húrin* (III. 55).

Thangorodrim   See *Angband*.

Thimbalt   This name occurs nowhere else. It is not clear from the map what it represents, but since an area marked out by dots surrounds Angband, and a similar area surrounds Thimbalt, it seems likely that this was another fortress. Thimbalt was struck out in pencil.

Thirsty Plain   See *Dor-na-Fauglith*. *Thirsty* is an emendation in black ink of *Black* in red ink.

Thousand Caves   First occurs in the *Lay of the Children of Húrin*. It is here placed as it was to remain, where Esgalduin bends westward towards Sirion.

Woodmen of Turambar   This is the second and later placing of the Woodmen on the map; see notes on the southern half.

The Southern Half of the Map

Aros, River   Aros has only been named hitherto in the *Tale of the Nauglafring*, where after the sack of Artanor (Doriath) the Dwarves journeying thence to their homes in the South (II. 225) had to pass the 'fierce stream' Aros at Sarnathrod, the Stony Ford (II. 236). It is also said in the same place that Aros, nearer to its spring, ran past the doors of the Caves of the Rodothlim, though against this my father later noted (II. 244 note 15) 'No [?that] is Narog'; while in the *Tale of Turambar* it is said (II. 81) that the Caves were above a stream that 'ran down to feed the river Sirion'. I am not sure how to interpret this. If it is assumed that the Stony Ford in the *Tale of the Nauglafring* was on the (later) Aros, then the Caves of the Rodothlim were on that river also, which is most improbable. On the other hand, if Aros was simply the earlier name of Narog, the question arises why the Dwarves fleeing out of Artanor should have been going in this direction. On the whole I am inclined to think that the phrase in the *Tale of the Nauglafring* saying that Aros ran past the Caves of the Rodothlim was a momentary confusion in a text written at very great speed (II. 221), and that the Stony Ford (but *not* the Caves) was always on the Aros, this river having always borne this name. If this is so, this is still the geography on the map (as originally marked in this detail), where *Athrasarn* (*Stony Ford*) was placed on the Aros halfway between Umboth-muilin and the inflowing of Celon. At this time the Land of the Cuilwarthin was in the North of the Hills of the Hunters; and therefore in the story implied by the map Beren and his Elves crossed Sirion from his land and ambushed the Dwarves on the southern confines of Doriath. It is not clear why the Dwarves were not taking the Dwarf-road from the Thousand Caves, which crossed the Aros much higher up; on this point see the note on the Dwarf-road in the northern half of the map.

Before the first map was laid aside the idea had changed, and when the Land of the Cuilwarthin was moved eastward (see note on *Beren*) the Stony Ford was moved eastward also; for the later history see under the Eastward Extension of this map.

Athrasarn (Stony Ford) See *Aros*.

Beren The first placing of *Beren* and *Land of the Cuilwarthin* (Land of the Dead that Live), in the North of the Hills of the Hunters and in the proximity of Nargothrond, agrees with the *Lay of the Children of Húrin* lines 1545–6 (see III.89), and so still in S (§10). In the *Lost Tales* the Dead that Live Again were *(i·)Guilwarthon*, changed in the *Tale of Tinúviel* (II.41) to *i·Cuilwarthon*; in Q (§14) the land is called *Cuilwarthien*, changed to *Gwerth-i-Cuina*.

Subsequently *Beren* and *Land of the Cuilwarthin* were struck out in this position, and *Land of the Cuilwarthin* re-entered much further to the East, in the empty lands between Sirion and Gelion. This was again struck out, in pencil, with the note 'Lies to the east of this and beyond the Great Lands of the East and of wild men' (on which see *Beren and Lúthien* and *Great Lands* under the Eastward Extension of the map). In Q (§14) the Land of the Dead that Live is in Assariad (>Ossiriand), 'between the river [Gelion] and the [Blue] mountains'.

Broseliand This name occurs first in the *Lay of Leithian*, with the spelling *Broceliand* (III.158–9, 169); *Beleriand* first appears (i.e. as originally typed, not as an emendation of *Broseliand*) in Q §13, and in the *Lay of Leithian* at line 3957. *Broseliand* occurs also in the note in red ink in the south-east corner of the map; this is given together with the later alterations to it at the end of these notes on the southern half.

Celon, River This has not occurred in any text. The course of Celon is the same as on the later map, the river rising (in the Eastward Extension of the present map) in Himling.

Cuilwarthin, Land of the See *Beren*.

Doriath The bounds of Doriath are represented, I think, by Mindeb, by the dotted line (above 'Beleg and Túrin') between Mindeb and Aros, then by Aros and Sirion to the dotted line encircling 'Doriath beyond Sirion', and so back to Mindeb.

Doriath beyond Sirion It is said in Q (§13) that the Taiglin 'enters the land of Doriath *ere it joins with* the great waters of Sirion'. As a name,

'Doriath beyond Sirion' has only occurred in a note on the MS of the *Tale of the Nauglafring* (II. 249).

Duil Rewinion This name of the Hills of the Hunters (also on the Westward Extension of the map) is not found elsewhere.

Dwarf-road See *Aros*.

Geleidhian This occurs in the note in the corner of the map, as the Gnomish name of Broseliand. It is found in additions to Q, §9 (note 2) and §10 (note 15); see p. 174.

Guarded Plain, The First occurs in the *Lay of the Children of Húrin* (III.88). On the later map the name is written over a much larger area further to the North-east, and outside the boundaries of the realm of Nargothrond as shown on that map (see *Realm of Narog beyond Narog*).

Hill of Spies This first appears in Q §13 (see p. 185). If, as would seem natural, the Hill of Spies is the eminence marked by radiating lines a little north of east from Nargothrond, the name itself is placed oddly distant from it, and seems rather to refer to the highland rising N.E. of Nargothrond, between Narog and Taiglin.

Hills of the Hunters, The First named in the *Lay of the Children of Húrin*, though they had been described without being named in the *Tale of Turambar*; see my discussion, III.88. On the map the Hills of the Hunters are shown as extending far southwards towards the coast of the Sea, with the Narog bending south-eastwards along the line of the Hills; and there is an outlying eminence above the unnamed cape in the S.W. corner of the map (later Cape Balar).

Ingwil First occurs in the *Lay of the Children of Húrin* (III. 88–9).

Lúthien caught by Celegorm In the *Lay of Leithian* (lines 2342–7) Celegorm and Curufin hunting out of Nargothrond with Huan on the occasion when Lúthien was captured rode for 'three days',

> till nigh to the borders in the West
> of Doriath a while they rest.

Marshes of Sirion On the later map called 'Fens of Sirion'.

Nan Tathrin (Land of Willows) For the name *Nan Tathrin* see III.89. It was already placed essentially thus in the tale of *The Fall of Gondolin* (see II. 153, 217), and in Q §16 Nan-Tathrin 'is watered by the Narog and by Sirion'.

Nargothrond Nargothrond was placed first further to the South and nearer to the confluence with Sirion; the second site is where it remained – but it is curious that in both sites it is marked as lying on the east side of the river: in the *Lay of the Children of Húrin* it was on the western side (cf. line 1762), and, I would think, always had been. (On the Westward Extension map this is corrected.)

In Q §9, after the Battle of Sudden Flame Barahır and Felagund 'fled to the fens of Sirion to the South'; and after swearing his oath to Barahir Felagund 'went South' (emended to 'South and West') and founded Nargothrond. This would in fact point to the first site of Nargothrond on the map; since the later site is due West from the fens.

Narog   First occurs in the *Lay of the Children of Húrin*. The course of the river was scarcely changed subsequently.

Realm of Narog beyond Narog   This was hastily added to the map in blue crayon, together with the broken line indicating its boundaries. On the later map the 'Realm of Nargothrond beyond the river' covers a much larger territory to the North-east (see *Guarded Plain*).

Sirion   See notes on the northern half.

Sirion flows underground   See *Umboth-muilin*. Sirion's fall is also referred to in the *Lay of the Children of Húrin*, lines 1467–8.

Umboth-muilin   The name goes back to the *Tale of the Nauglafring* (II.225). It emerges from the *Lay of Leithian* (lines 1722 ff.) that the Twilight Meres were north of Sirion's fall and passage underground, whereas in the tale of *The Fall of Gondolin* the reverse was the case (see II.217, III.222–3).

Waters of Sirion   Cf. S §16 'The remnant reaches Sirion and journeys to the land at its mouth – the Waters of Sirion', and §17 'He returned home and found the Waters of Sirion desolate.'

Woodmen of Turambar   The Woodmen were first placed a long way away from their later location – south of Sirion's passage underground and north of Nan Tathrin, with their land (shown by a dotted line) extending on both sides of the river. This position is quite at variance with what was said in the *Tale of Turambar* (II.91): 'that people had houses . . . in lands that *were not utterly far from Sirion* or the grassy hills of that river's *middle course*', which as I said (II.141) 'may be taken to agree tolerably with the situation of the Forest of Brethil'. The first placing of the name was struck out, and the second agrees with Q (§13): 'their houses were in the green woods about the River Taiglin that enters the land of Doriath ere it joins with the great waters of Sirion.'

Note on the south-east corner of the map, in red ink with later pencilled additions:

All the lands watered by Sirion south of Gondolin [*added*: or more usually R. Taiglin] are called in English 'Broseliand', *Geleidhian* by the gnomes. [*Added*: – but this usually does *not* include Doriath. Its east boundary is not shown. It is the Blue Mountains.]

It is interesting that *Broseliand* is said to be the English name; and that Doriath is not usually included in Broseliand.

·   Lastly, it may be mentioned that of the highlands rising on the eastern side of the lower course of Sirion there is no trace on the later map.

THE WESTWARD AND EASTWARD EXTENSIONS TO THE MAP

These supplementary maps were drawn in relation to the main or central map and substantially overlapping it: they are in close accord with it in all features where they overlap. These sheets were carefully laid out, but the actual markings were done extremely rapidly in soft pencil, and are now very faint; the paper is thin and the maps are battered. Some alterations and additions were made in ink (some of the rivers of Ossiriand are written in ink and some in pencil).

The notes on these supplementary maps include almost all names that do not occur on the main map, and a few that occur on both which have features of interest on the extensions.

The Westward Extension

Bridge of Ice   The words in the N.W. corner 'Far north lies the bridge of Ice' refer to the Helkaraksë, but the meaning of the word 'bridge' is only explained in the *Ambarkanta* (see p. 238).

Brithombar (and *Eldorest*)   This is the first occurrence of the Havens of the Falas. That Ossë persuaded some of the Teleri to remain 'on the beaches of the world' is mentioned in Q §3; and in a later rewriting of a passage in Q §11 (note 14) the presence of Elves 'from the Falas' before the Battle of Unnumbered Tears is referred to.

Brithon, River   The first occurrence of the name, as of *Brithombar* the haven at its mouth. The later imposition on the coast-line as originally drawn of the river-mouth and the long cape giving protection to the haven can be seen.

Celegorm and Curufin   They are shown as being lords of a 'fief' N.W. of the Hills of the Hunters, with *Felagund* ruling in Nargothrond.

Eldor, River   The first occurrence of the name. This river was later named *Eglor*, *Eglahir*, and finally *Nenning*, its course remaining unchanged.

Eldorest, Haven of Eldorest   The first occurrence of the name (see *Brithombar*). The haven at the mouth of the Eldor became *Eglorest*

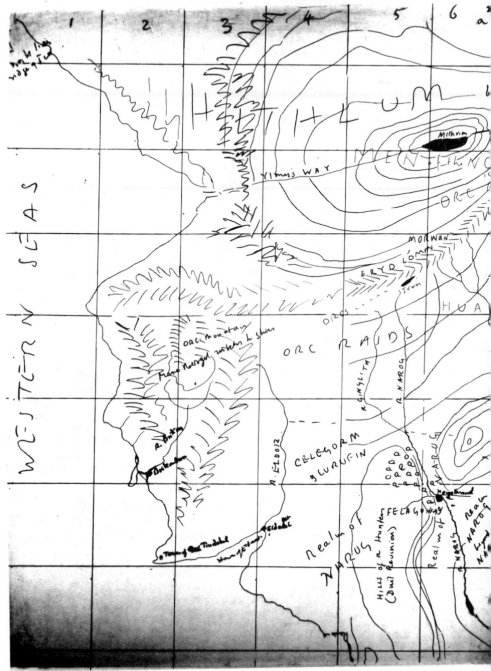

The Westward Extension

when the river became the *Eglor*, and so remained (*Eglarest* in *The Silmarillion*) when the river was again renamed *Nenning*.

Felagund   See *Celegorm* and *Curufin*.

Hithlum   The mountain-range fencing Hithlum on the West (later *Ered Lómin* when that name was transferred from the Shadowy Mountains, see pp. 192–3) is shown.

Morwen   This is written over *Mavwin* (see this entry under the main map).

Nargothrond   is now placed on the west bank of Narog.

Orc-Mountains   Extensive highlands cover the entire region between Brithombar and the range forming the southern fence of what was later called Nevrast. On the later map these highlands are retained in the region between the sources of the Brithon and the Eldor (Nenning), and are too little represented on my map in the published *Silmarillion*.
   Here Morgoth reaches the shores is probably a reference to the story that has not yet emerged in the texts, that in the year after the Battle of Unnumbered Tears 'Morgoth sent great strength over Hithlum and Nevrast, and they came down the rivers Brithon and Nenning and ravaged all the Falas' (*The Silmarillion* p. 196).

Realm of Narog   Of the three occurrences, that in the centre between the Hills of the Hunters and the river was put in at the time of the making of the map; the other two (*Realm of Narog* in the West, and *Realm of Narog beyond Narog* to the East of the river) were entered in blue crayon at the same time as *Realm of Narog beyond Narog* on the main map, as also was the continuation of the broken line, marking the northern boundary, as far as the river Eldor.

Tower of Tindobel   This stands where on the later map is Barad Nimras (the tower raised by Felagund 'to watch the western sea', *The Silmarillion* pp. 120, 196). *Tindobel* is first mentioned in the *Annals of Beleriand* (later than the *Quenta*), p. 331.

Ylmir's Way   *Ylmir*, almost certainly the Gnomish form of *Ulmo*, is found in the *Lay of the Children of Húrin* (III.93) and regularly in S. With 'Ylmir's Way' cf. the tale of *The Fall of Gondolin* (II.149–50):

> Thereafter 'tis said that magic and destiny led [Tuor] on a day to a cavernous opening down which a hidden river flowed from Mithrim. And Tuor entered that cavern seeking to learn its secret, but the waters of Mithrim drove him forward into the heart of the rock and he might not win back into the light. And this, 'tis said, was the will of Ulmo Lord of Waters at whose prompting the Noldoli had made that hidden way.

It is not clear from this passage at what point the river out of Lake Mithrim went underground. In the story of Tuor written long afterwards and given in *Unfinished Tales* Tuor followed 'a sudden spring of water in the hills' (p. 21), and

> he came down from the tall hills of Mithrim and passed out into the northward plain of Dor-lómin; and ever the stream grew as he followed it westward, until after three days he could descry in the west the long grey ridges of Ered Lómin . . . (p. 20).

The Gate of the Noldor, where the stream went underground, was in the eastern foothills of Ered Lómin.

Ylmir's Way issues in a firth that is unnamed on the map (*Drengist* has hitherto only occurred in the list of Old English names, p. 210).

It will be seen that the western coastline is closely similar to that on the later map.

The Eastward Extension

Adurant, River   The most southerly of the tributaries of Gelion, named in an addition to Q §14 (note 4). Its course and relation to the mountains and the other rivers was not changed.

Ascar, River   The name of the northernmost of the tributaries of Gelion occurs in Q §14 (see entry *Flend* below). Its course and relation to the mountains and the other rivers was not changed.

Beren and Lúthien   *Here dwelt Beren and Lúthien before destruction of Doriath in Land of Cuilwarthin.*   On the main map the second placing of this land, between Sirion and Gelion, was rejected with the note: 'Lies to the east of this and beyond the Great Lands of the East and of wild men.' This must mean that my father was moving the Land of the Dead that Live far away into unknown regions (see the entry *Great Lands*); but the Eastward Extension map places it in the final position, in the region of the Seven Rivers: see *Gweirth-i-cuina*.

Blue Mountains   These were first named in Q §9.

Brilthor, River   This, the fifth of the tributaries of Gelion, is named in an addition to Q §14 (note 4); later emendation to Q moved Duilwen further south and brought Brilthor into the fourth place.

Broseliand   *Here is end of Broseliand*, written between the rivers Ascar and Thalos, and against the western feet of the Blue Mountains. Cf. the addition to the note in the corner of the main map (p. 227): 'Its east boundary is not shown. It is the Blue Mountains.'

Cuilwarthin   See *Beren and Lúthien*, *Gweirth-i-cuina*.

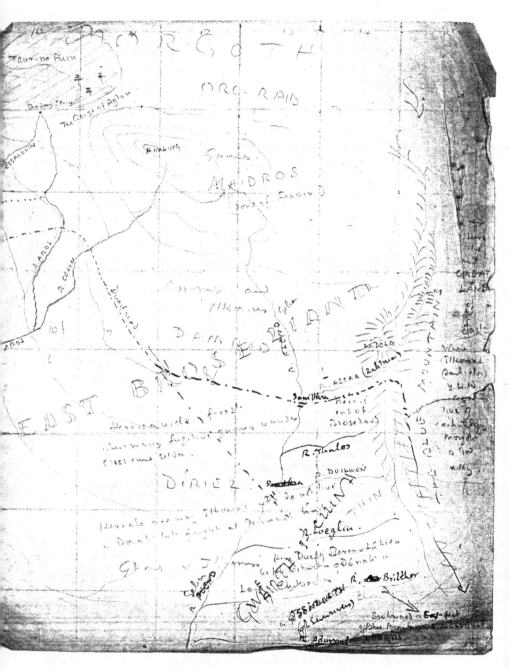

The Eastward Extension

Damrod and Díriel   The note above the name *Díriel* reads: 'Here is a wide forest where many fugitive gnomes wander. Orcs come seldom.' Cf. Q §14: 'the woods about the River [Flend/Gelion], where aforetime were the hunting grounds of Damrod and Díriel.'

The note below the name *Díriel* reads: 'Here also are many Ilkorins who do not live in Doriath but fought at Nirnaith Únoth.' *Nirnaith Únoth* occurs in the *Lay of the Children of Húrin*, replaced by *Nirnaith Ornoth* (III.79, 102, 123). On Dark-elves at the Battle of Un-numbered Tears see S and Q §11.

Dolm, Mt.   This is the first appearance of the mountain afterwards named *Dolmed*, placed as on the later map.

Duilwen   This, the third of the tributaries of Gelion, is named in an addition to Q §14 (note 4), where it is placed as on the map between Thalos and Loeglin. Later emendation to Q gave the final order, with Duilwen moved south to become the fifth tributary.

Dwarf-road and *Sarn Athra*   As the Dwarf-road was first marked on this map, after crossing Aros it bent south-east and ran in that direction in a straight line across East Broseliand, crossing (Flend) Gelion at Sarn Athra, which (having been moved from its position on the main map, where it was on the Aros) was now placed at the confluence of the third tributary river (here Duilwen). The line of the road goes off the map in the south-east corner, with the direction: 'Southward in East feet of Blue Mountains are Belegost and Nogrod.' This site for Sarn Athra agrees with Q §14, where the ford is near the confluence of (Flend) Gelion and Duilwen.

A later route for the Dwarf-road is also marked on this map. Here the road bears more nearly east in the land of Damrod and Díriel and so crosses (Flend) Gelion further north: Sarn Athra is now placed just below the confluence of Ascar with Gelion (this is the reason for the emendation of Duilwen to Ascar in Q §14, note 7). It then follows the course of Ascar on the southern side, crosses the mountains by a pass below Mount Dolm, and then turns sharply south and goes away on the eastern side of the mountains.

On the later map Sarn Athra is placed just *above* the confluence of Ascar and Gelion, and the road therefore goes along the northern bank of Ascar, but still crosses the mountains south of Mount Dolmed; the Dwarf-cities are now placed in the eastern side of the mountains not far from Mount Dolmed.

East Broseliand   The term *East Beleriand* occurs in Q §14.

Flend   In Q §14 the great river of East Beleriand was first named *Ascar*, but since *Ascar* was already in Q the name of the northernmost of the tributaries from the Blue Mountains I think that this was a mere slip (see p. 189 and footnote) for *Flend*, to which it was emended. *Flend* then > *Gelion*, as on the map. The course of Gelion was not changed afterwards, but the map does not show the later eastern tributary arm ('Greater Gelion').

Gelion   See *Flend*.

Great Lands   The note down the right hand side of the map reads: 'Here lie the Great Lands of the East where Ilkorins (dark-elves) and Wild Men live, acknowledging Morgoth as God and King.' This use of *Great Lands* for the lands of Middle-earth *east of the Blue Mountains* is notable; it is used also on the main map, where the third site of the Land of the Dead that Live is said to lie 'beyond the Great Lands of the East and of wild men' (see *Beren and Lúthien*). In the *Lost Tales* the term *Great Lands* always means the lands between the Seas (i.e. the whole of the later *Middle-earth*); in S and Q *Outer Lands* (which in the *Lost Tales* meant the Western Lands) is used of Middle-earth, with later emendation to *Hither Lands* in Q.

The statement here that in the Great Lands of the East both Wild Men and Dark-elves acknowledged Morgoth as God and King is significant for the future. Cf. the emendation to Q II §18, note 3: 'But most Men, and especially those new come out of the East, were on the side of the Enemy.' The corruption of certain Men in the beginning of their days appears in very early synopses (for *Gilfanon's Tale*); see I. 236.

Gweirth-i-cuina   This name, in which *Gweirth-* is apparently emended from *Gwairth-*, is written over *Cuilwarthin*. *Gwerth-i-cuina* (not *Gweirth-* as on the map) has appeared in two emended passages in Q: §10 (note 15) 'they wandered . . . upon the confines of Geleidhian in fair Ossiriand, Land of Seven Streams, Gwerth-i-cuina, the Living Dead' (where the name seems to be used of Beren and Lúthien themselves); and §14 (note 6) 'Elves called it oft Gwerth-i-cuina', where it is used of the land, as on the map.

Himling   The first occurrence is in the *Lay of Leithian* lines 2994–5 (April 1928):

> where Himling's watchful hill
> o'er Aglon's gorge hung tall and still.

Loeglin   As the fourth of the tributaries of Gelion this is named in an addition to Q §14 (note 4). Later emendation moved Duilwen further south and brought Loeglin (> *Legolin*) into the third place.

Nirnaith Únoth   See *Damrod and Díriel*.

Ossiriath (of the Seven rivers)   This form is not found elsewhere. It is written over *Assariad*, which occurs in Q §14, later emended to *Ossiriand* (note 4). *Ossiriand(e)* is found as a rejected alternative to *Broseliand* in Canto I of the *Lay of Leithian* (III. 158–60). The placing of the name, between the sixth and seventh rivers, is odd, but in view of 'of the Seven rivers' probably not significant.

Rathlorion   This is the form of the new name of Ascar found in Q (§14), later emended to *Rathloriel*.

Sarn Athra   See *Dwarf-road*. In Q §14 *Sarn-athra*, emended to *Sarn-athrad* (note 8).

Sons of Fëanor   See entry *Aglon* to the northern half of the main map.

Thalos   This, the second of the tributaries of Gelion, is named in an addition to Q §14 (note 4). Its course and relation to the mountains and the other rivers was not changed.

V

THE AMBARKANTA

This very short work, of cardinal interest (and not least in the associated maps), is entitled at the beginning of the text 'Of the Fashion of the World'; on a title-page loose from but obviously belonging with the work is written:

> *Ambarkanta*
>
> The Shape of the World
>
> Rúmil

together with the word *Ambarkanta* in tengwar. This is the first appearance of Rúmil since the *Lost Tales*; but he is not mentioned in the text itself.

That the *Ambarkanta* is later than the *Quenta* (perhaps by several years) cannot be doubted. The reappearance of the name *Utumna* is an advance on Q, where also the term 'Middle-earth' does not appear; *Eruman* is (aberrantly) the name in Q of the land where Men awoke (pp. 99, 171), whereas in the *Ambarkanta* its name is for the first time *Hildórien*; and there are several cases where the *Ambarkanta* has names and details that are only found in Q by emendation (for example, *Elvenhome* p. 236, but *Bay of Faërie* > *Bay of Elvenhome* in Q (II), p. 155 note 12).

The text consists of six pages of fine manuscript in ink, with very little emendation; I give the final forms throughout, with all rejected readings in the notes that follow the text. Closely associated with the work and here reproduced from the originals are three diagrams of the World, here numbered I, II, and III, and two maps, numbered IV and V. On the pages facing these reproductions I note changes made to names. The text begins with a list of cosmographical words, with explanations; this I give on pp. 240–1.

OF THE FASHION OF THE WORLD

About all the World are the Ilurambar, or Walls of the World. They are as ice and glass and steel, being above all imagination of the Children of Earth cold, transparent, and hard. They cannot be seen, nor can they be passed, save by the Door of Night.

Within these walls the Earth is globed: above, below, and upon all sides is Vaiya, the Enfolding Ocean. But this is more like to sea below the Earth and more like to air above the Earth. In Vaiya below the Earth dwells Ulmo. Above the Earth lies the Air, which is called Vista,[1] and sustains birds and clouds. Therefore it is called above Fanyamar, or Cloudhome; and below Aiwenórë[2] or Bird-land. But this air lies only upon Middle-earth and the Inner Seas, and its proper bounds are the Mountains of Valinor in the West and the Walls of the Sun in the East. Therefore clouds come seldom in Valinor, and the mortal birds pass not beyond the peaks of its mountains. But in the North and South, where there is most cold and darkness and Middle-earth extends nigh to the Walls of the World, Vaiya and Vista and Ilmen[3] flow together and are confounded.

Ilmen is that air that is clear and pure being pervaded by light though it gives no light. Ilmen lies above Vista, and is not great in depth, but is deepest in the West and East, and least in the North and South. In Valinor the air is Ilmen, but Vista flows in at times especially in Elvenhome, part of which is at the eastern feet of the Mountains; and if Valinor is darkened and this air is not cleansed by the light of the Blessed Realm, it takes the form of shadows and grey mists. But Ilmen and Vista will mingle being of like nature, but Ilmen is breathed by the Gods, and purified by the passage of the luminaries; for in Ilmen Varda ordained the courses of the stars, and later of the Moon and Sun.

From Vista there is no outlet nor escape save for the servants of Manwë, or for such as he gives powers like to those of his people, that can sustain themselves in Ilmen or even in the upper Vaiya, which is very thin and cold. From Vista one may descend upon the Earth. From Ilmen one may descend into Valinor. Now the land of Valinor extends almost to Vaiya, which is most narrow in the West and East of the World, but deepest in the North and South. The Western shores of Valinor are therefore not far from the Walls of the World. Yet there is a chasm which sunders Valinor from Vaiya, and it is filled with Ilmen, and by this way one may come from Ilmen above the earth to the lower regions, and to the Earthroots, and the caves and grottoes that are at the foundations of the lands and seas. There is Ulmo's abiding-place. Thence are derived the waters of Middle-earth. For these waters are compounded of Ilmen and Vaiya and Ambar[4] (which is Earth), since Ulmo blends Ilmen and Vaiya and sends them up through the veins of the World to cleanse and refresh the seas and rivers, the lakes and the fountains of Earth. And running water thus possesses the memory of the deeps and the heights, and holds somewhat of the wisdom and music of Ulmo, and of the light of the luminaries of heaven.

In the regions of Ulmo the stars are sometimes hidden, and there the Moon often wanders and is not seen from Middle-earth. But the Sun does not tarry there. She passes under the earth in haste, lest night be prolonged and evil strengthened; and she is drawn through the nether Vaiya by the servants of Ulmo, and it is warmed and filled with life. Thus days are measured by the courses of the Sun, which sails from East to West through the lower Ilmen, blotting out the stars; and she passes over the midst of Middle-earth and halts not, and she bends her course northward or southward, not waywardly but in due procession and season. And when she rises above the Walls of the Sun it is Dawn, and when she sinks behind the Mountains of Valinor it is evening.

But days are otherwise in Valinor than in Middle-earth. For there the time of greatest light is Evening. Then the Sun comes down and rests for a while in the Blessed Land, lying upon the bosom of Vaiya. And when she sinks into Vaiya it is made hot and glows with rosecoloured fire, and this for a long while illumines that land. But as she passes toward the East the glow fades, and Valinor is robbed of light, and is lit only with stars; and the Gods mourn then most for the death of Laurelin. At dawn the dark is deep in Valinor, and the shadows of their mountains lie heavy on the mansions of the Gods. But the Moon does not tarry in Valinor, and passeth swiftly o'er it to plunge in the chasm of Ilmen,[5] for he pursues ever after the Sun, and overtakes her seldom, and then is consumed and darkened in her flame. But it happens at times that he comes above Valinor ere the Sun has left it, and then he descends and meets his beloved, and Valinor is filled with mingled light as of silver and gold; and the Gods smile remembering the mingling of Laurelin and Silpion long ago.

The Land of Valinor slopes downward from the feet of the Mountains, and its western shore is at the level of the bottoms of the inner seas. And not far thence, as has been said, are the Walls of the World; and over against the westernmost shore in the midst of Valinor is Ando Lómen[6] the Door of Timeless Night that pierceth the Walls and opens upon the Void. For the World is set amid Kúma, the Void, the Night without form or time. But none can pass the chasm and the belt of Vaiya and come to that Door, save the great Valar only. And they made that Door when Melko was overcome and put forth into the Outer Dark; and it is guarded by Eärendel.

The Middle-earth lies amidst the World, and is made of land and water; and its surface is the centre of the world from the confines of the upper Vaiya to the confines of the nether. Of old its fashion was thus. It was highest in the middle, and fell away on either side into vast valleys, but rose again in the East and West and again fell away to the chasm at its edges. And the two valleys were filled with the primeval water, and the shores of these ancient seas were in the West the western highlands and the edge of the great land, and in the East the eastern highlands and the edge of the great land upon the other side. But at the North and South it did not fall away, and one could go by land from the uttermost South and the chasm of Ilmen to the uttermost North and the chasm of Ilmen. The ancient seas lay therefore in troughs, and their waters spilled not to the East or to the West; but they had no shores either at the North or at the South, and they spilled into the chasm, and their waterfalls became ice and bridges of ice because of the cold; so that the chasm of Ilmen was here closed and bridged, and the ice reached out into Vaiya, and even unto the Walls of the World.

Now it is said that the Valar coming into the World descended first upon Middle-earth at its centre, save Melko who descended in the furthest North. But the Valar took a portion of land and made an island and hallowed it, and set it in the Western Sea and abode upon it, while they were busied in the exploration and first ordering of the World. As is told they desired to make lamps, and Melko offered to devise a new substance of great strength and beauty to be their pillars. And he set up these great pillars north and south of the Earth's middle yet nearer to it than the chasm; and the Gods placed lamps upon them and the Earth had light for a while.

But the pillars were made with deceit, being wrought of ice; and they melted, and the lamps fell in ruin, and their light was spilled. But the melting of the ice made two small inland seas, north and south of the middle of Earth, and there was a northern land and a middle land and a southern land. Then the Valar removed into the West and forsook the island; and upon the highland at the western side of the West Sea they piled great mountains, and behind them made the land of Valinor. But the mountains of Valinor curve backward, and Valinor is broadest in the middle of Earth, where the mountains march beside the sea; and at the north and south the mountains come even to the chasm. There are those two regions of the Western Land which are not of Middle-earth and are yet outside the mountains: they are dark and empty. That to the North is Eruman, and that to the South is Arvalin; and there is only a narrow strait between them and the corners of Middle-earth, but these straits are filled with ice.

For their further protection the Valar thrust away Middle-earth at the centre and crowded it eastward, so that it was bended, and the great sea of the West is very wide in the middle, the widest of all waters of the Earth. The shape of the Earth in the East was much like that in the West, save for the narrowing of the Eastern Sea, and the thrusting of the land thither. And beyond the Eastern Sea lies the Eastern Land, of which we know little, and call it the Land of the Sun; and it has mountains, less great than those of Valinor, yet very great, which are the Walls of the Sun. By reason of the falling of the land these mountains cannot be descried, save by highflying birds, across the seas which divide them from the shores of Middle-earth.

And the thrusting aside of the land caused also mountains to appear in four ranges, two in the Northland, and two in the Southland; and those in the North were the Blue Mountains in the West side, and the Red Mountains in the East side; and in the South were the Grey Mountains and the Yellow. But Melko fortified the North and built there the Northern Towers, which are also called the Iron Mountains, and they look southward. And in the middle land there were the Mountains of the Wind, for a wind blew strongly there coming from the East before the Sun; and Hildórien the land where Men first awoke lay between these mountains and the Eastern Sea. But Kuiviénen where Oromë found the Elves is to the North beside the waters of Helkar.[7]

But the symmetry of the ancient Earth was changed and broken in the first Battle of the Gods, when Valinor went out against Utumno,[8] which was Melko's stronghold, and Melko was chained. Then the sea of Helkar (which was the northern lamp) became an inland sea or great lake, but the sea of Ringil (which was the southern lamp) became a great sea flowing north-eastward and joining by straits both the Western and Eastern Seas.

And the Earth was again broken in the second battle, when

Melko was again overthrown, and it has changed ever in the wearing and passing of many ages.[9] But the greatest change took place, when the First Design was destroyed, and the Earth was rounded, and severed from Valinor. This befell in the days of the assault of the Númenóreans upon the land of the Gods, as is told in the Histories. And since that time the world has forgotten the things that were before, and the names and the memory of the lands and waters of old has perished.

NOTES

1   *Vista*: at all seven occurrences the original name *Wilwa* was changed, first in pencil then in ink, to *Vista*; so also on the world-diagrams I and II, and on the diagram III (the World Made Round).

2   Original reading *Aiwenor*; so also on diagram I.

3   *Ilmen*: at all the many occurrences the original name *Silma* was carefully erased and changed to *Ilma* (the same change on the map IV); *Ilma* was then itself altered to *Ilmen* (the same succession of changes on diagrams I and II).

4   *Ambar* is an emendation but the underlying word is wholly erased (so also on diagram II; written in later on I).

5   In the margin is written *Ilmen-assa*, changed from *Ilman-assa*.

6   *Ando Lómen* is interpolated into the text, but in all probability not significantly later than the original writing of the MS.

7   The last two sentences of this paragraph (from 'And in the middle land . . .') were added, but to all appearance belong in time with the original writing of the MS.

8   *Utumno* is emended from *Utumna*.

9   The original MS ends here; what follows, concerning the Earth Made Round at the time of the assault of the Númenóreans, was added later (see p. 261).

I give now the list of cosmological words accompanying the *Ambarkanta*. My father made several changes to this list, but since the alterations were mostly made over erasures and the additions belong to the same period it is impossible to know the original form of the list in all points. The changes in the list are however much the same as those made in the text of the *Ambarkanta* and on the world-diagrams; thus *Silma* > *Ilma* > *Ilmen*, *Wilwa* > *Vista*, *Aiwenor* > *Aiwenórë*; *ava*, *ambar*, *Endor* over erasures; *Avakúma*, & *Elenarda Stellar Kingdom* additions. The translation of *Ilmen* as 'Place of light' is an emendation from 'sheen'.

Ilu   The World   World
Ilurambar   The Walls of the World;
ramba   wall

Kúma   darkness, void   Dark
ava   outer, exterior; *Avakúma*

Vaiya   fold, envelope. In nature like   Outer Sea, or Encircling
to water, but less buoyant than air,   Ocean, or Enfolding Ocean
and surrounding   The Outer Sea.*

Ilmen   Place of light. The region above   Sky. Heaven
the air, than which it is thinner and
more clear. Here only the stars and
Moon and Sun can fly. It is called
also *Tinwë-mallë* the Star-street, &
Elenarda Stellar Kingdom.

Vista   air. Wherein birds may fly and   Air
clouds sail. Its upper region is
Fanyamar or Cloudhome, and its
lower *Aiwenórë* or Birdland.

ambar   Earth. *ambar-endya* or   Earth
Middle Earth of which *Endor* is
the midmost point.

ëar   water; sea.   Sea
The roots of the Earth are
Mar-talmar, or *Talmar Ambaren*.

ando   door, gate.

lómë   Night. *Ando Lómen* the Door of
Night, through which Melko was
thrust after the Second War of the
Gods.

All that land that lies above water, between the Seas of the West and East
and the Mountains of North and South is *Pelmar*, the Enclosed
Dwelling.

Commentary on the *Ambarkanta*

This elegant universe, while certainly in many respects an evolution
from the old cosmology of the *Lost Tales*, shows also radical shifts and
advances in essential structure.

*This is very confusing, since Vaiya is apparently said to *surround* the Outer Sea
(though in the right-hand column it is itself defined as 'Outer Sea'). But the word 'The' in
'The Outer Sea' has a capital T; and I think that my father left the preceding sentence
unfinished, ending with 'surrounding', and that he added 'The Outer Sea' afterwards as a
definition of Vaiya, without noticing that the preceding phrase was incomplete.

Diagram I

Some of the names on this diagram were written in over erasures, and in most of the cases only the fact of correction can be seen:

Ilmen (replacing *Ilma* and *Silma*, see note 3 to the text of the *Ambarkanta*); *Vista* (replacing *Wilwa*, see note 1); *Ava-* (in *Ava-kúma*); *Ambarendya*; *Endor*; *Martalmar*. The letter A in the centre, of obscure significance, is also written over an erasure.

Additions are: *Elenarda or*; *-e* added to *Aiwenor* (see note 2); *Ambar* (see note 4).

Much later pencilled changes and additions are: *Ilurambar* to *Earambar* at one only of the occurrences; *Hidden Half* added above the lower occurrence of *Vaiya*; *Ilu* to *Arda* in the title. The note at the right-hand bottom corner is too faint to make out after the words 'Alter story of Sun'; that on the left reads: 'Make world *always a globe* but larger than now. Mountains of East and West prevent anyone from going to Hidden Half.'

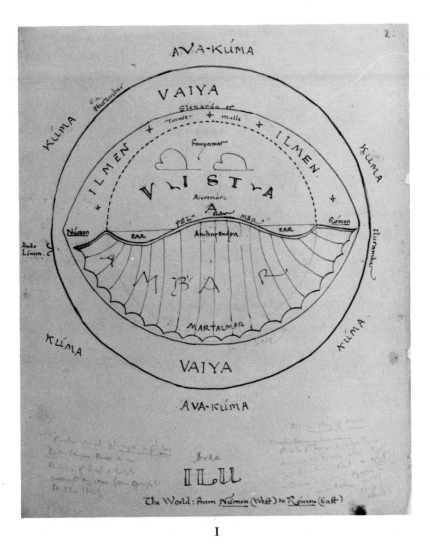

The World: Ilu Númen (West) to Rómen (East)

I

Diagram II

As in diagram I some names were written in over erasures:

Ilmen (from *Ilma* and *Silma*); *Vista* (from *Wilwa*); *Ambar*; *Endor*; *Martalmar*; *Formen* (from *Tormen*) in the title.

Late pencilled changes are: *Ilurambar* to *Earambar* at one of the occurrences, as on diagram I; *Harmen* to *Hyarmen* both on the diagram and in the title; *Tormen* > *Formen* on the diagram.

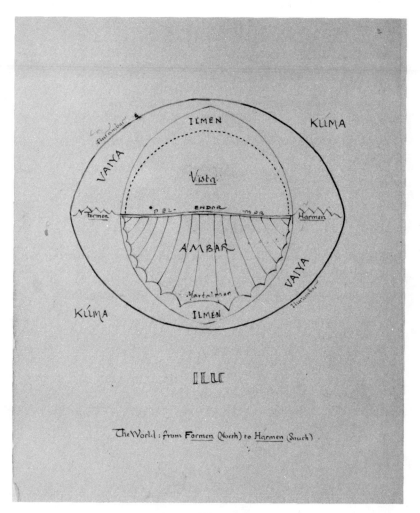

ILU

The World : from Formen (North) to Harmen (South).

II

Diagram III

On this diagram the name *Wilwa* was struck out and replaced by *Vista* (see note 1 to the text of the *Ambarkanta*). Names other than those in capitals are: *The Straight Path* (twice), *Valinor, Eressëa, Old Lands, New Lands*. The title reads: 'The World after the Cataclysm and the ruin of the Númenoreans'.

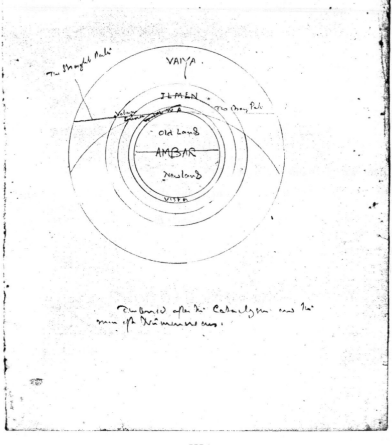

III

Map IV

Changes made to this map were:

Silma to *Ilma* at all three occurrences, and at one only *Ilma* later in pencil to *Ilmen* (see note 3 to the text of the *Ambarkanta*); *Endor* to *Endon* (but *Endor* written again above in pencil); and *Tormen* > *Formen*, *Harmen* > *Hyarmen*, as on diagram II.

V.Y. 500 = Valian Year 500; see p. 263.

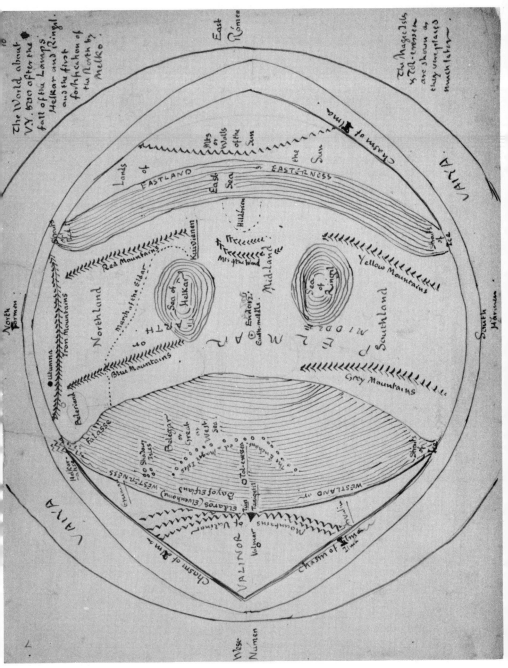

IV

Map V

Some of the names on this map are not easy to read, and I list here all that appear on it:

The West: *Outer Seas, Utgarsecg*
  Eruman (written above this later: *Araman*); *Outer Lands* (*Valinor*); *Alflon*;
  Two Trees; *Tún*; *Valmar*; *Taniquetil*; *Bay of Faery*; *Arvalin* (changed from
  Eruman).
  Lightly pencilled later across the Western Land: *Aman*

The Western Sea: in the extreme North: *Helkaraksë.*
  Great Seas; *The G[rea]t Gulf*; *Beleglo[rn?]*; *(Belegar)*; *Ingarsecg*

The North-west of Middle-earth: *Hithlum*; *Angband*; *Thangorodrim*; *Daidelos*;
  Beleriand

Central regions: *Hither Lands*; *Inland Sea*; *Straits of the World; East Sea*; *Dark
  Land (South Land)*

The East: *Walls of the Sun*; *Burnt Land of the Sun*; *Outer Seas*

Note in the upper right-hand corner: *After the War of the Gods
  (Arvalin was cast up by the Great Sea at the foot of the Mts.* See pp. 260–1.

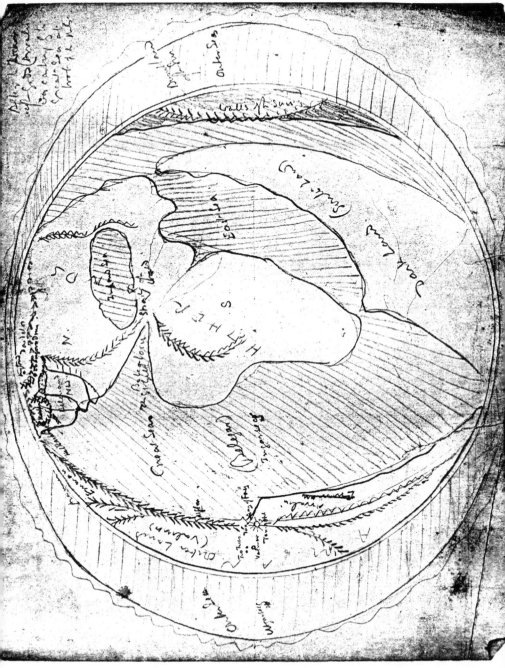

To begin from the Outside: beyond the Walls of the World lies 'the Void, the Night without form or time', *Kúma* (*Ava-kúma*); and this is of course an aboriginal conception, 'the outer dark', 'the limitless dark', 'the starless vast' of the tale of *The Hiding of Valinor* (I.216). The Walls of the World, *Ilurambar*,* are the unbroken, uninterrupted shell of a vast globe; they are cold, invisible, and impassable save by *Ando Lómen*, the Door of Night. This Door was made by the Valar 'when Melko was overcome and put forth into the Outer Dark'; and Eärendel guards it. Already in S (§19) it was said that 'Morgoth is thrust through the Door of Night into the outer dark beyond the Walls of the World, and a guard set for ever on that Door'; this is repeated in the corresponding passage in Q, where the same expressions are used as in the *Ambarkanta*, 'the Door of Timeless Night', 'the Void', and where Eärendel, sailing in the Void, is named as the guardian (see pp. 164–5, 203). It is not however said in these texts that the Door of Night was made *when Melko was overcome*, at the end of the Great Battle.

I have remarked earlier (p. 49) on the great shift in the astronomical myth introduced in S by the passage of the Sun beneath the Earth, rather than departure through the Door of Night followed by the journey through the Outer Dark and return through the Gates of Morn, as described in *The Hiding of Valinor*; in that account the Gods made the Door of Night in order that the Sunship should not have to pass beneath the Earth. Thus the Door of Night has remained, but its purpose and the time of its making have been totally changed.

The conception of a great Wall surrounding the 'World' and fencing it against an outer Emptiness and Darkness goes back to the beginning; in *The Hiding of Valinor* it is called 'the Wall of Things', and Ulmo instructs the Valar that 'Vai runneth from the Wall of Things unto the Wall of Things whithersoever you may fare' (I.214). I have discussed earlier (I.86) the possibility that already in the early cosmology Vaitya (the outermost of the three 'airs') and Vai (the Outer Ocean) constituted 'a continuous enfolding substance', and that the *Ambarkanta* 'only makes explicit what was present but unexpressed in the *Lost Tales*'; and pointed to the difficulties in this idea. In the first draft of *The Hiding of Valinor* (see I.221 note 16) the Wall of Things was evidently imagined, as I have said (I.227), 'like the walls of terrestrial cities, or gardens – walls with a top: a "ring-fence"'; the Walls were lower in the East, so that there was no Door there corresponding to the Door of Night in the West, and the Sun *rode over* the Eastern Wall. In the second draft (I.216) the idea of the Gates of Morn was introduced; but the nature and extent of the Walls was still left obscure, and indeed nothing else is said of them in the *Lost Tales* beyond the statement that they are 'deep-blue' (I.215). A

Ilu is 'the World' in diagrams I and II, and is so defined in the list of words (p. 241); for its early meaning see I.255, entry *Ilwë*. – The changes to *Earambar* in diagrams I and II, like the pencilled note at the bottom of I, were made very much later and do not concern us here.

remarkable sentence in the original tale of *The Music of the Ainur* (I. 56) declares that 'the Ainur marvelled to see how *the world was globed amid the void* and yet separated from it'. How this is to be interpreted in the context of the *Lost Tales* I do not know; but the sentence was retained through all the rewritings of the *Ainulindalë* (cf. *The Silmarillion* p. 17), and so became a precise description of the world of the *Ambarkanta*, whatever my father's original meaning may have been.

In view of the close similarity of wording between Q and the *Ambarkanta* on the subject of the expulsion of Melko through the Door of Night, mentioned above, it is very puzzling that in the same passage of Q (p. 164) it is said that some think that he 'creeps back *surmounting the Walls* and visiteth the world'. The fact that this is only a surmise ('Some say . . .'), and that the Prophecy of Mandos which immediately follows declares that when Morgoth does return it will be through the Door of Night, hardly explains how the idea of his 'surmounting the Walls' (in inescapable contradiction to the *Ambarkanta*, and negating the purpose of Eärendel's guard) could arise.*

It is not indeed explained in the *Ambarkanta* how the Valar entered the world at its beginning, passing through the impassable Walls, and perhaps we should not expect it to be. But the central idea at this time is clear: from the Beginning to the Great Battle in which Melko was overthrown, the world with all its inhabitants was inescapably bounded; but at the very end, in order to extrude Melko into the Void, the Valar were able to pierce the Walls by a Door.

Wholly new is the conception of Ilmen as the pure air that is breathed in Valinor, and whose bounds are the Mountains of Valinor and the mountains called the Walls of the Sun, beyond the Eastern Sea, though 'Vista flows in at times especially in Elvenhome'. In Ilmen journey the Sun, Moon, and Stars, so that this region is called also *Tinwë-mallë*† and *Elenarda* (translated 'Star-street' and 'Stellar Kingdom' in the list of words, p. 241). This partly corresponds to the cosmology of the *Lost Tales*, where the Moon-ship 'saileth in the lower folds of Ilwë threading a white swathe among the stars', and the stars 'could not soar into the dark and tenuous realm of Vaitya that is outside all', but where the Sun 'voyageth even above Ilwë and beyond the stars' (I. 181, 193).

The lowest air, Vista, in which are *Fanyamar* 'Cloudhome' and *Aiwenórë* 'Bird-land', retains the characteristic nature of the earlier Vilna; cf. I.65 'Vilna that is grey and therein may the birds fly safely'. But there is an important corollary to the frontier between Ilmen and

---

*This conception of the Walls reappears much later, and is found in *The Silmarillion* (p. 36): Melkor, returning to Arda after his expulsion by Tulkas into the outer darkness, '*passed over the Walls of the Night* with his host, and came to Middle-earth far in the north'. But this is an aspect of intractable problems arising in the later cosmology that cannot be entered into here.

†See I. 269 (entry *Tinwë Linto*) and 263 (entry *Olórë Mallë*).

Vista in the West: 'clouds come seldom in Valinor, and the mortal birds pass not beyond the peaks of its mountains'.

An aspect of the cosmology that seems puzzling at first sight arises from the statements in the *Ambarkanta* (1) that 'in the North and South . . . Middle-earth extends nigh to the Walls of the World' (p. 236), and (2) that Vaiya is 'most narrow in the West and East of the World, but deepest in the North and South' (*ibid.*). This apparent contradiction is to be explained by the passage (p. 238) describing how the Inner Seas have no shores at North and South, but spilling into the Chasm of Ilmen form ice bridges * that close the chasm, and the ice extends out into Vaiya and even to the Walls of the World. This ice is represented by the mountain-like peaks above the words *Tormen* and *Harmen* in diagram II. Of all this there is no trace in the *Lost Tales*; but it will be found that the *Ambarkanta* here greatly illumines the passage in *The Silmarillion* (p. 89) describing the Helcaraxë:

> For between the land of Aman that in the north curved eastward, and the east-shores of Endor (which is Middle-earth) that bore westward, there was a narrow strait, through which the chill waters of the Encircling Sea and the waves of Belegaer flowed together, and there were vast fogs and mists of deathly cold, and the sea-streams were filled with clashing hills of ice and the grinding of ice deep-sunken.

The passage of the Sun beneath the Earth seems to be differently conceived in the *Ambarkanta* from that of the Moon; for while both pass from East to West through Ilmen, the Sun 'sinks into Vaiya' and is 'drawn through the nether Vaiya by the servants of Ulmo', whereas the Moon plunges into the Chasm of Ilmen.†

Turning now to the surface of the Earth, we meet for the first time the name *Endor*, which does not occur in the text of the *Ambarkanta* itself, but which is defined in the word-list as 'the midmost point' of *Ambarendya* or Middle-earth. *Endor* is marked in also on the 'World-diagrams' I and II, and also on the map IV, where it is shown as a point, the 'Earth-middle', and subsequently changed to *Endon*. The name *Endor* occurs once in *The Silmarillion* (in the passage just cited), but there it is a name of Middle-earth, not of the midmost point of Middle-earth; so also in *The*

---

* Cf. 'Far north lies the bridge of Ice' in the N.W. corner of the Westward Extension of the first 'Silmarillion' map, pp. 227–8.

† The statement in *The Silmarillion* (p. 101) that Tilion (steersman of the Moon) 'would pass swiftly over the western land . . . and plunge in *the Chasm beyond the Outer Sea*' cannot in any way be brought into harmony with the *Ambarkanta*, where the Chasm of Ilmen is reached before Vaiya, and must be so by virtue of the fundamental ideas of the cosmology.

The passage in the 'Silmarillion' version that followed Q and was interrupted at the end of 1937 has: 'But Tilion . . . passes swiftly over the western land . . . and plunges into the chasm between the shores of the Earth and the Outer Sea.' The passage in the published *Silmarillion* derives from a later version written in all probability in 1951–2; but though I retained it I am at loss to explain it.

Lord of the Rings (Appendix E): Quenya *Endórë*, Sindarin *Ennor* 'Middle-earth'. *Ambar-endya* seems to be synonymous with *Pelmar*, since in the word-list the former is defined as 'Middle-earth', while on map IV the region between the two seas of East and West is called 'Pelmar or Middle-earth'; but in diagram I they are marked as if different in reference. Possibly, *Pelmar* (translated in the list of words as 'the Enclosed Dwelling') means strictly the habitable surface, *Ambar-endya* the central raised part of *Ambar*, the Earth.*

The lines drawn downwards from the surface of the Earth to *Martalmar* 'the roots of the Earth' in diagrams I and II are 'the veins of the World' (p. 236); and this passage is important in understanding Ulmo's power and benign influence exerted through the waters of the world (cf. *The Silmarillion* pp. 27, 40, in both of which passages the expression 'the veins of the world' is used).

In the East of the world are the Walls of the Sun, which is a great mountain range symmetrically answering the Mountains of Valinor in the West, as shown on map IV. Of this range there is no mention in the *Lost Tales*, where almost all that is said of the East is contained in Oromë's words to the Valar: 'In the East beyond the tumbled lands there is a silent beach and a dark and empty sea' (I.214); in the East also was the great mountain Kalormë (I.212), and there Aulë and Ulmo 'builded great havens [of the Sun and Moon] beside the soundless sea' (I.215). In the *Ambarkanta* the Gates of Morn, through which the Sun returns from the Outer Dark in the *Lost Tales*, have disappeared.

In the description of evening and dawn in Valinor in the *Ambarkanta* there is an echo of the *Lost Tales*: 'Valinor is filled with mingled light as of silver and gold; and the Gods smile remembering the mingling of Laurelin and Silpion long ago'; cf. I.216 'Then smile the Gods wistfully and say: "It is the mingling of the lights once more."'

The extremely close symmetry of the Eastern and Western lands as displayed on map IV is striking; the chief departure from symmetry being the difference in shape of the great Seas, and this was due to the eastward thrusting or 'crowding' of Middle-earth – 'so that it was bended' – at the time of the making of Valinor and the raising of its protective mountain-chain. This more than Titanic crushing of the new-made world was the origin of the great mountain ranges of Middle-earth, the Blue, the Red, the Yellow, and the Grey. Cf. *The Silmarillion* p. 37:

And the shape of Arda and the symmetry of its waters and its lands was marred in that time, so that the first designs of the Valar were never after restored.

*For the first element in *Pelmar* see the Appendix to *The Silmarillion*, entry *pel-*. Neither this name nor *Ambar*, *Ambar-endya* occur in *The Silmarillion*, but *Ambar-metta* 'world-ending' is found in *The Return of the King* (VI.5). – *Middle-earth* is first found in the *Ambarkanta* and in the *Annals of Valinor*, which belong to the same period but cannot be dated relative to one another. – *Rómen* 'East' appears for the first time in diagram I, and *Hyarmen* 'South' and *Formen* 'North' (< *Harmen*, *Tormen*) in diagram II.

But in *The Silmarillion* this loss of symmetry is not attributed to the deliberate act of the Valar themselves, who in the *Ambarkanta* are ready to contort the very structure of *Ambar* for the sake of their own security. There are some interesting points in the *Ambarkanta* account of the first days of the Valar in the world. Here it is said for the first time that Melko 'descended in the furthest North', whereas the Valar, coming to Middle-earth at its centre, made their island from 'a portion of land' and set it in the Western Sea. The old story of Melko's treacherous assistance of the Valar in their works by devising the pillars of the Lamps out of ice is still present, despite the wording of S, and still more of Q (§1): 'Morgoth contested with them and made war. The lamps he over-threw . . .', which seems to suggest that it had been abandoned. In the tale of *The Coming of the Valar* the name *Ringil* was given (by Melko!) to the northern pillar, and *Helkar* to the southern (I.69); in the *Ambarkanta* the names are applied to the Lamps rather than the pillars, and *Ringil* becomes that of the southern, *Helkar* that of the northern. In the tale there is no mention of the formation of Inland Seas at the time of the fall of the Lamps; rather 'great floods of water poured from [the Lamps] into the Shadowy Seas', and 'so great was their thaw that whereas those seas were at first of no great size but clear and warm, now were they black and wide and vapours lay upon them and deep shades, for the great cold rivers that poured into them' (I.70). Later the names of the Lamps were changed more than once, but *Helcar* remained the name of the Inland Sea 'where aforetime the roots of the mountain of Illuin [the northern Lamp] had been' (*The Silmarillion* p. 49), and it is seen from the *Ambarkanta* that the idea of the sea being formed where the Lamp once stood owed its origin to the melting pillar of ice, although the actual story of Melko's devising of the pillars was abandoned when it became impossible to represent Melko as co-operative, even in seeming, with the Valar. There is no mention in *The Silmarillion* of a southern sea where the other Lamp had stood.

Kuiviénen is said in the *Ambarkanta* to be 'to the North beside the waters of Helkar', as shown on map IV. In the *Lost Tales* (I.115, 117) Koivië-néni was a lake (with 'bare margin', set in a vale 'surrounded by pine-clad slopes') in Palisor, the midmost region; in *The Silmarillion* it is 'a bay in the Inland Sea of Helcar' (p. 49). In the same passage Oromë, on that ride that led him to the finding of the Elves, 'turned north by the shores of Helcar and passed under the shadows of the Orocarni, the Mountains of the East', and this agrees perfectly with map IV (*Orocarni* 'Red Mountains', see the Appendix to *The Silmarillion* entry *caran*). The Blue Mountains oppose them symmetrically in the West; and in the South are the Grey Mountains and the Yellow, again symmetrically opposed both to each other and to the northern ranges. The track of the March of the Elves as marked on map IV is again in complete agreement with *The Silmarillion* (p. 53): 'passing northwards about the Sea of Helcar they turned towards the west'; but of the Misty Mountains

(*Hithaeglir*) and the Great River (*Anduin*) where many Elves of the Third Host turned away South (*ibid*. p. 54) there is no sign. In *The Hobbit* and *The Lord of the Rings* the Grey Mountains (*Ered Mithrin*) are a range beyond Mirkwood in the North of Middle-earth.

It seems that Beleriand, to judge by the placing and size of the lettering of the name on map IV, was relatively a very small region; and the Elves reached the Sea to the south of it, at the *Falassë* (later the *Falas* of Beleriand). But my father circled 'Beleriand' in pencil and from the circle drew an arrow to the point where the track of the March reached the Sea, which probably implies that he wished to show that this was in fact within the confines of Beleriand.

The name *Hildórien* of the land where Men awoke (implying *Hildor*, the Aftercomers) now first appears; for the curious use of the name *Eruman* for this land in Q see pp. 99, 171. Hildórien is a land lying between the Mountains of the Wind and the Eastern Sea; in *The Silmarillion* (p. 103) it is placed, more vaguely, 'in the eastward regions of Middle-earth'.

The placing of *Utumna* (in the *Ambarkanta* emended to *Utumno*, note 8) on map IV is notable, as is also the occurrence of the name itself. Whereas in the *Lost Tales* Melko's first fortress was *Utumna*, and his second *Angband* (see I. 198), in S and Q the original fortress is *Angband*, to which Melko returned after the destruction of the Trees (see p. 44), and *Utumna* is not mentioned in those texts. My father had now reverted to *Utumna* (*Utumno*) as the name of Melko's ancient and original dwelling in Middle-earth (see further below, pp. 259–60).

The archipelagoes in the Western Sea have undergone the great change and simplification that distinguishes the account in *The Silmarillion* from that in the *Lost Tales* (see II. 324–5); there is no sign on the map of the Harbourless Isles or the Twilit Isles, and instead we have 'The Enchanted or Magic Isles' – in Q II §17 *Magic Isles* is emended to *Enchanted Isles* (note 11). The 'Shadowy Isles' lying to the northward of the Enchanted Isles on the map seem to be a new conception.

The name *Eldaros* (not *Eldamar*, see I. 251) appears on map IV with the meaning 'Elvenhome'. *Eldaros* has occurred once previously, in one of the 'Ælfwine' outlines (II. 301): 'Eldaros or Ælfhâm', where the reference is unclear, but seems to be to Tol Eressëa. The words 'Bay of Elfland' are written on the map but no bay is indicated.

In the West the symmetrically formed lands of Eruman and Arvalin between the Mountains and the Sea now appear; for the earlier history see I. 83. *Tún* lies a little to the north of Taniquetil; and the position of *Valmar* is as it was on the little ancient map given in I. 81.

In the *Ambarkanta* something is said of the vast further changes in the shape of the lands and seas that took place in 'the first Battle of the Gods', when Melko was taken captive, concerning which there is nothing in Q (§2) beyond a reference to the 'tumult'. In *The Silmarillion* (p. 51) this is called 'the Battle of the Powers'; and

> In that time the shape of Middle-earth was changed, and the Great Sea that sundered it from Aman grew wide and deep; and it broke in upon the coasts and made a deep gulf to the southward. Many lesser bays were made between the Great Gulf and Helcaraxë far in the north, where Middle-earth and Aman came nigh together. Of these the Bay of Balar was the chief; and into it the mighty river Sirion flowed down from the new-raised highlands northwards: Dorthonion, and the mountains about Hithlum.

The text of the *Ambarkanta* does not mention the Great Gulf or the Bay of Balar, but speaks rather of the vast extension of the sea of Ringil and its joining to the Eastern and Western Seas (it is not clear why it is said that the sea of Helkar 'became an inland sea or great lake', since it was so already). But on the back of the map IV is another map (V) that illustrates all the features of both accounts. This map is however a very rapid pencil sketch, and is in places difficult to interpret, from uncertainty as to the meaning of lines, more especially in the Western Lands (Outer Lands). It is very hard to say how precisely this map should be interpreted in relation to map IV. For example, in map IV the Grey Mountains are very widely separated from the Blue, whereas in map V there is only a narrow space at the head of the Great Gulf between them; the Inland Sea (Helkar) is further to the North; and so on. Again, many features are absent (such as the Straits of Ice), and in such cases one cannot be sure whether their absence is casual or intentional; though the failure to mark in Tol Eressëa or the Enchanted Isles suggests the former. I am inclined to think that map V is a very rough sketch not to be interpreted too strictly.

The narrow ring between the Earth and the Outer Seas clearly represents the Chasm of Ilmen.

In relation to Beleriand in the North-west, and bearing in mind the whole underlying history of Eriol-Ælfwine and Leithien (England), the southern part of the Hither Lands, below the Great Gulf, bears an obvious resemblance to the continent of Africa; and in a vaguer way the Inland Sea could be interpreted as the Mediterranean and the Black Sea. But I can offer nothing on this matter that would not be the purest speculation.

The sea marked 'East Sea' on map V is the former sea of Ringil; cf. the *Ambarkanta*: 'the sea of Ringil . . . became a great sea flowing north-eastward and joining by straits both the Western and Eastern Seas.'

In the North-west the ranges of Eredlómin and Eredwethrin (not named; see pp. 192–3) enclosing Hithlum (which is named) are shown, and the western extension of Eredwethrin that was the southern fence of later Nevrast.* In the version of 'The Silmarillion' that followed Q it is said that in the War of the Gods the Iron Mountains 'were broken and distorted at their western end, and of their fragments were made Eredwethrin and Eredlómin', and that the Iron Mountains 'bent back northward'; and map V, in relation to map IV, agrees well with this. The first 'Silmarillion' map (after p. 220), on the other hand, shows the Iron Mountains curving back strongly to the North-east (it is conceivable that the hasty zigzag lines to the east of Thangorodrim were intended to rectify this).

In the version of 'The Silmarillion' just referred to it is also said that 'beyond the River Gelion the land narrowed suddenly, for the Great Sea ran into a mighty gulf reaching almost to the feet of Eredlindon, and there was a strait of mountainous land between the gulf and the inland sea of Helcar, by which one might come into the vast regions of the south of Middle-earth'. Again, these features are clearly seen on map V, where the 'strait of mountainous land' is called the 'Straits of the World'. The enclosed areas to the east of Eredwethrin and south-east of Thango-rodrim clearly represent the Encircling Mountains about Gondolin and the highlands of Taur-na-Fuin; we see what was later called the Gap of Maglor between those highlands and the Blue Mountains, and the rivers Gelion (with its tributaries, the rivers of Ossiriand), Sirion, and Narog.† With this part of map V compare the first 'Silmarillion' map and its Eastward extension.

Particularly notable is the closeness of Hithlum on map V to the edge of the world (the Chasm of Ilmen).

Angband is placed in very much the same position on map V as is Utumna on map IV: very near to the Chasm of Ilmen and well behind the mountain-wall, in the land that on map V is called *Daidelos* (later *Dor Daedeloth*).‡ As noted above, Utumna had now been resurrected from the *Lost Tales* as Melko's original fortress; and it emerges clearly from later texts that the story now was that when Melko returned to Middle-earth after the destruction of the Trees *he returned to the ruins of Utumna and built there his new fortress, Angband*. This, I think, is why the fortress is called Angband, not Utumna, on map V.

The history was therefore as follows:

Lost Tales	{ *Utumna*	Melko's original fortress
	{ *Angband*	His dwelling when he returned

---

*This range is seen also on the Westward Extension of the first 'Silmarillion' map, p. 228.

†All these north-western features are drawn in ink, whereas the rest of map V is in pencil; but the mountain-ranges (though not the rivers) are inked in over pencil.

‡Similar forms but with different application have occurred earlier: in the *Epilogue* to the *Lost Tales* the High Heath in Tol Eressëa where the battle was fought is *Ladwen-na-Dhaideloth*, *Dor-na-Dhaideloth* ('Sky-roof'), II.287; and in line 946 of the *Lay of the Children of Húrin* Dor-na-Fauglith was first called *Daideloth* ('High plain'), III.49.

S, Q   *Angband*   Melko's original fortress to which he
                                     returned

Ambarkanta   { *Utumna*   Melko's original fortress
maps   { *Angband*   His second fortress built on the site of
                             Utumna when he returned

Much later, Utumno and Angband were both ancient fortresses of
Morgoth, and Angband was that to which he returned (*The Silmarillion*
pp. 47, 81).

Thangorodrim is shown on map V as a point, set slightly out from the
Iron Mountains. This represents a change in the conception of
Thangorodrim from that on the first 'Silmarillion' map, which illustrates
the words of S (§8) that Thangorodrim is 'the highest of the Iron
Mountains around Morgoth's fortress'. The marking of Thangorodrim
on *Ambarkanta* map V shows the later conception, seen in *The Silmarillion* p. 118, where it is said expressly that Melkor made a tunnel
under the mountains which issued south of them, that Thangorodrim
was piled above the gate of issue, and that Angband was behind the
mountain-wall: thus Thangorodrim stood out somewhat from the main
range.

There are extremely puzzling features in the Western Land on map V.
There is now a mountain chain (for so the herring-bone markings must
be interpreted, since that is their meaning elsewhere on the map)
extending up the western coast northwards from Taniquetil to the
Helkaraksë and (as it seems) rising out of the sea, as well as the old
westward curve of the Mountains of Valinor (bending back to the Chasm
of Ilmen) seen on map IV; thus Eruman (with the first occurrence of the
name *Araman* pencilled above it afterwards) is not represented as a
coastal wasteland between the mountains and the sea but is walled in by
mountains both on the East and on the West. I do not understand this;
in any case *The Silmarillion* has the geography shown on map IV.

Equally puzzling is the representation of the lands south of Tûn and
Taniquetil. Here there are herring-bone lines continuing the main line of
mountains southwards from Taniquetil, with again the old westward
curve back to the Chasm; but the area symmetrically corresponding to
Eruman in the North is here left unnamed, and *Arvalin* (emended
from *Eruman*) is shown as a substantial land extending east even of the
'new' mountains, from the southern shore of the Bay of Faëry to the
extreme South of the world. The Bay of Faëry, which is clearly shown on
this map (in contrast to map IV), is in fact partly formed by this 'new'
Arvalin. In a corner of the map is written:

After the War of the Gods (Arvalin was cast up by the Great Sea at the
foot of the Mts.

Though the brackets are not closed after 'Mts.', I think that the first words may have been intended as a title, indicating the period represented by the map. But the following words, coupled with the absence of Arvalin from its expected place on the map, seem to imply that it was only now that Arvalin came into being.

The Old English names *Ingarsecg*, *Utgarsecg* are found in the Old English texts (pp. 207, 210). *Alflon* on the coast north of Tûn is Alqualondë (later Sindarin *alph*, *lond* (*lonn*): see the Appendix to *The Silmarillion*, entries *alqua*, *londë*). The names *Aman*, *Araman* were added to map V many years later (as also *Arda*, *Earambar* on the diagrams).

If this map shows the vastness of the cataclysm that my father conceived as having taken place at the time of the breaking of Utumno and the chaining of Melko, at the end of the *Ambarkanta* he added (see note 9) a passage concerning the far greater cataclysm that took place 'in the days of the assault of the Númenóreans upon the land of the Gods'. This may have been added much later; but the passage is written carefully in ink, not scribbled in pencil, and is far more likely to be contemporary, since the story of Númenor arose about this time. In support of this is the diagram III, 'the World after the Cataclysm and the ruin of the Númenóreans'; for on this diagram the inner air was originally marked *Wilwa* and only later changed to *Vista*. In the *Ambarkanta* and the accompanying list of words, as in diagrams I and II, *Vista* is likewise an emendation from *Wilwa*; it seems therefore that diagram III belongs to the same period.

VI

THE EARLIEST ANNALS
OF VALINOR

I refer to this work as the 'earliest' *Annals of Valinor* because it was followed later in the 1930s by a second version, and then, after the completion of *The Lord of the Rings* and very probably in 1951–2, by a third, entitled *The Annals of Aman*, which though still a part of the continuous evolution of these *Annals* is a major new work, and which contains some of the finest prose in all the Matter of the Elder Days.

These earliest *Annals of Valinor* are comprised in a short manuscript of nine pages written in ink. There is a good deal of emendation and interpolation, some changes being made in ink and probably not much if any later than the first writing of the text, while a second layer of change consists of alterations in faint and rapid pencil that are not always legible. These latter include two quite substantial passages (given in notes 14 and 18) which introduce wholly new material concerning events in Middle-earth.

The text that follows is that of the *Annals* as originally written, apart from one or two insignificant alterations of wording that are taken up silently, and all later changes are given in the numbered notes, other than those made to dates. These are many and complex and are dealt with all together, separately, at the end of the notes.

It is certain that these *Annals* belong to the same period as the *Quenta*, but also that they are later than the *Quenta*. This is seen from the fact that whereas in Q Finrod (= the later Finarfin) returned to Valinor out of the far North after the burning of the ships, and the later story of his return earlier, after the Prophecy of the North, is only introduced in a marginal note (§5 note 8 and commentary p. 170), in the *Annals* the later story is already embodied in the text (Valian Year 2993). The Annals have *Beleriand*, whereas Q, as far as §12, had *Broseliand* emended to *Beleriand*; they have several names that do not occur in Q, e.g. *Bladorion*, *Dagor-os-Giliath*, *Drengist*, *Eredwethion* (this only by later emendation in Q); and *Eredlómin* has its later sense of the Echoing Mountains, not as in Q and on the first map of the Shadowy Mountains (see pp. 192–3). I see no way of showing that the *Annals* are later, or earlier, than the *Ambarkanta*, but the matter seems of no importance; the two texts certainly belong to very much the same time.

Following my commentary on the *Annals*, which I shall refer to as 'AV', I give the Old English versions in an appendix.

ANNALS OF VALINOR

(These and the *Annals of Beleriand* were written by
Pengolod the Wise of Gondolin, before its fall, and after
at Sirion's Haven, and at Tavrobel in Toleressëa after
his return unto the West, and there seen and translated
by Eriol of Leithien, that is Ælfwine of the Angelcynn.)

Here begin the Annals of Valinor

0 At the beginning Ilúvatar, that is 'Allfather', made all
things, and the Valar, that is the 'Powers', came into the
World. These are nine, Manwë, Ulmo, Aulë, Oromë,
Tulkas, Ossë, Mandos, Lórien, and Melko. Of these
Manwë and Melko were most puissant and were brethren, and Manwë was lord of the Valar and holy; but
Melko turned to lust and pride and violence and evil,
and his name is accursed, and is not uttered, but he is
called Morgoth. The spouses of the Valar were Varda,
and Yavanna, who were sisters; and Vana; and the sister
of Oromë, Nessa the wife of Tulkas;[1] and Uinen lady of
the Seas; and Nienna sister of Manwë and Melko; and
Estë. No spouse hath Ulmo or Melko.[2] With them came
many lesser spirits, their children, or beings of their own
kind but of less might; these are the Valarindi.

Time was counted in the world before the Sun and
Moon by the Valar according to ages, and a Valian age
hath 100 of the years of the Valar, which are each as ten
years are now.

In the Valian Year **500**: Morgoth destroyed by deceit
the Lamps[3] which Aulë made for the lighting of the
World, and the Valar, save Morgoth, retired to the West
and built there Valinor between the Outer Seas that
surround the Earth and the Great Seas of the West, and
on the shores of these they piled great mountains. But
the symmetry of land and sea was first broken in those
days.[4]

In the Valian Year **1000**, after the building of Valinor,
and Valmar the city of the Gods, the Valar brought into
being the Two Trees of Silver and of Gold, whose
bloom gave light unto Valinor.

But all this while Morgoth had dwelt in the Middle-earth and made him a great fortress in the North of the World; and he broke and twisted the Earth much in that time.[5]

A thousand Valian Years of bliss and glory followed in Valinor, but growth that began on Middle-earth at the lighting of the Lamps was checked. To Middle-earth came only Oromë to hunt in the dark woods of the ancient Earth, and sometimes Yavanna walked there.

The Valian Year **2000** is accounted the Noontide of the Blessed Realm, and the full season of the mirth of the Gods. Then did Varda make the stars[6] and set them aloft, and thereafter some of the Valarindi strayed into the Middle-earth, and among them was Melian, whose voice was renowned in Valmar. But she returned not thither for many ages, and the nightingales sang about her in the dark woods of the Western Lands.

At the first shining of the Sickle of the Gods which Varda set[7] above the North as a threat to Morgoth and an omen of his fall, the elder children of Ilúvatar awoke in the midmost of the World: they are the Elves.[8] Oromë found them and befriended them; and the most part under his guidance marched West and North to the shores of Beleriand, being bidden by the Gods to Valinor.

But first Morgoth in a great war was bound and made captive and imprisoned in Mandos. There he was confined in punishment for nine ages (900 Valian Years)[9] until he sought for pardon. In that war the lands were rent and sundered anew.[10]

The Quendi[11] and the Noldoli were the first to reach Valinor, and upon the hill of Kôr nigh to the strand they built the city of Tûn. But the Teleri who came after abode an age (100 Valian Years) upon the shores of Beleriand, and some never departed thence. Of these most renowned was Thingol (Sindingul)[12] brother of Elwë, lord of the Teleri, whom Melian enchanted. Her he after wedded and dwelt as a king in Beleriand, but this was after the departure of most of the Teleri, drawn by Ulmo upon Toleressëa.[13] This is the Valian Years **2000** to **2100**.

From **2100** to **2200** the Teleri dwelt on Toleressëa in the Great Sea within sight of Valinor; in **2200** they came in their ships to Valinor, and dwelt upon its eastern strands, and there they made the town and haven of Alqalondë or 'Swan-haven', so called because there were moored their swan-shaped boats.

About **2500** the Noldoli invented and began the fashioning of gems; and after a while Fëanor the smith, eldest son of Finwë chief of the Noldoli, devised the thrice-renowned Silmarils, concerning the fates of which these tales tell. They shone of their own light, being filled with the radiance of the Two Trees, the holy light of Valinor, blended to a marvellous fire.[14]

In **2900** Morgoth sued for pardon, and at the prayers of Nienna his sister, and by the clemency of Manwë his brother, but against the wish of Tulkas and Aulë, he was released, and feigned humility and repentance, obeisance to the Valar, and love and friendship for the Elves, and dwelt in Valinor in ever-increasing freedom. But he lied and dissembled, and most he cozened the Noldoli, for he had much to teach, and they had an over-mastering desire to learn; but he coveted their gems and lusted for the Silmarils.

2900   During two more ages[15] Valinor abode yet in bliss, yet a shadow of foreboding began to gather in many hearts; for Morgoth was at work with secret whisperings and cunning lies; and most he worked, alas, upon the Noldoli, and sowed the seeds of dissension between the sons of Finwë, Fëanor, Fingolfin, and Finrod, and of distrust between Noldoli and Valar. **2950** By the doom of the Gods Fëanor, eldest son of Finwë, and his household and following was deposed from the leadership of the Noldoli – wherefore the house of Fëanor was after called the Dispossessed, for this and because Morgoth after robbed them of their treasure – and the Gods sent also to apprehend Morgoth. But he fled into hiding in Arvalin, and plotted evil.[16]

2990–1   Morgoth now completed his designs and with the aid of Ungoliantë out of Arvalin stole back into Valinor, and destroyed the Trees, escaping in the gathering dark northward, where he sacked the dwellings of Fëanor, and carried off a host of jewels, among them the Silmarils; and he slew Finwë and many Elves and thus defiled Valinor and began slaughter in the World.[17] Though hunted by the Valar he escaped into the North of the Hither Lands and re-established there his stronghold, and bred and gathered once more his evil servants, Orcs and Balrogs.[18]

2991   Valinor lay now in great gloom, and darkness, save only for the stars, fell on all the World. But Fëanor against the will of the Valar returned to Tûn and claimed the kingship of the Noldoli after Finwë, and he summoned to Tûn all the people of that kindred. And Fëanor spoke to them, and his words were filled with the lies of Morgoth, and distrust of the Valar, even though his heart was hot with hate for Morgoth, slayer of his father and robber of his gems.

The most of the Noldoli[19] he persuaded to follow him out of Valinor and recover their realms on earth, lest they be filched by the younger children of Ilúvatar, Men (herein he echoed Morgoth unwitting); and war for ever on Morgoth seeking to recover their treasure. At that meeting Fëanor and his sons swore their dreadful oath to slay or pursue any soever that held a Silmaril against their will.

2992   The march began, though the Gods forbade (and yet hindered not), but under divided leadership, for Fingolfin's house held him for king. Long was the people preparing. Then it came into Fëanor's heart that never should that great host, both warriors and other, and store of goods make the vast leagues unto the North (for Tûn beneath Taniquetil is upon the Girdle of the Earth, where the Great Seas are measurelessly wide) save with the help of ships. But the Teleri alone had ships, and they would not yield or lend them against the will of the Valar.

Thus about **2992** of Valian Years befell the dreadful battle about Alqalondë, and the Kin-slaying evilly renowned in song, where the Noldoli distraught furthered Morgoth's work. But the Noldoli overcame the Teleri and took their ships, and fared slowly north along the rocky coasts in great peril and hardship and amid dissensions.

In **2993** it is said they came to a place where a high rock stands above the shores, and there stood either Mandos or his messenger and spoke the Doom of Mandos. For the kin-slaying he cursed the house of Fëanor, and to a less degree all who followed them or shared in their emprise, unless they would return to abide the doom and pardon of the Valar. But if they would not, then should evil fortune and disaster befall them, and ever from treachery of kin towards kin; and their oath should turn against them; and a measure of mortality should visit them, that they should be lightly slain with weapons, or torments, or sorrow, and in the end fade and wane before the younger race. And much else he foretold darkly that after befell, warning them that the Valar would fence Valinor against their return.[20]

But Fëanor hardened his heart and held on, and so also but reluctantly did Fingolfin's folk, feeling the constraint of their kindred and fearing for the doom of the Gods (for not all of Fingolfin's house had been guiltless of the kin-slaying). Felagund and the other sons of Finrod went forward also, for they had aforetime great fellowship, Felagund with the sons of Fingolfin, and Orodreth, Angrod, and Egnor with Celegorm and Curufin sons of Fëanor. Yet the lords of this third house were less haughty and more fair than the others, and had had no part in the kin-slaying, and many with Finrod himself returned unto Valinor and the pardon of the Gods. But Aulë their ancient friend smiled on them no more, and the Teleri were estranged.

2994 The Noldoli came to the bitter North, and further they would not dare, for there is a strait between the Western Land (whereon Valinor is built) that curveth east, and the Hither Lands which bear west, and through this the chill waters of the Outer Seas and the waves of the Great Sea flow together, and there are vast mists of deathly cold, and the streams are filled with clashing hills of ice and with the grinding of ice submerged. This strait was named Helkaraksë.

But the ships that remained, many having been lost,

were too few to carry all across, and dissensions awoke between Fëanor and Fingolfin. But Fëanor seized the ships and sailed east;[21] and he said: 'Let the murmurers whine their way back to the shadows of Valinor.' And he burned the ships upon the eastern shore, and so great was its fire that the Noldoli left behind saw its redness afar off.

Thus about **2995** Fëanor came unto Beleriand and the shores beneath Eredlómin the Echoing Mountains, and their landing was at the narrow inlet Drengist that runs into Dorlómen. And they came thence into Dorlómen and about the north of the mountains of Mithrim, and camped in the land of Hithlum in that part that is named Mithrim and north of the great lake that hath the same name.

2996   And in the land of Mithrim they fought an army of Morgoth aroused by the burning and the rumour of their advance; and they were victorious and drove away the Orcs with slaughter, and pursued them beyond Eredwethion (the Shadowy Mountains) into Bladorion. And that battle is the First Battle of Beleriand, and is called Dagor-os-Giliath, the Battle under Stars; for all was as yet dark. But the victory was marred by the death of Fëanor, who was wounded mortally by Gothmog, lord of Balrogs, when he advanced unwarily too far upon Bladorion;[22] and Fëanor was borne back to Mithrim and died there, reminding his sons of their oath. To this they now added an oath of vengeance for their father.

2997   But Maidros eldest son of Fëanor was caught in the snares of Morgoth. For Morgoth feigned to treat with him, and Maidros feigned to be willing, and either purposed evil to the other, and came with force to the parley; but Morgoth with the more, and Maidros was made captive.

Then Morgoth held him as hostage, and swore only to release him if the Noldoli would march away either to Valinor, if they could, or from Beleriand and away to the far South; and if they would not he would torment Maidros.

But the Noldoli trusted not that he would release

Maidros if they departed, nor were they willing to do so whatever he might do. Wherefore in **2998** Morgoth hung Maidros by the right wrist in a band of hellwrought steel above a precipice upon Thangorodrim, where none could reach him.

Now it is told that Fingolfin and the sons of Finrod[23] won their way at last with grievous losses and with minished might into the North of the World. And they came perforce over Helkaraksë, being unwilling to retrace their way to Valinor, and having no ships; but their agony in that crossing was very great and their hearts were filled with bitterness against Fëanor.

And even as they came the First Ages of the World were ended;[24] and these are reckoned as 30000 years or **3000** years of the Valar; whereof the first Thousand was before the Trees, and Two Thousand save nine were Years of the Trees or of the Holy Light, which lived after and lives yet only in the Silmarils. And the Nine are the Years of Darkness or the Darkening of Valinor.

But towards the end of this time as is elsewhere told the Gods made the Sun and Moon and sent them forth over the World, and light came unto the Hither Lands.[25] And Men awoke in the East of the World even at the first Dawn.[26]

But with the first Moonrise Fingolfin set foot upon the North; for the Moonrise came ere the Dawn, even as Silpion of old bloomed ere Laurelin and was the elder of the Trees. But the first Dawn shone upon Fingolfin's march, and his banners blue and silver were unfurled, and flowers sprang beneath his marching feet, for a time of opening and growth was come into the Earth, and good of evil as ever happens.

But Fingolfin marched through the very fastness of Morgoth's land, Dor-Daideloth[27] the Land of Dread, and the Orcs fled before the new light amazed, and hid beneath the earth; and the Elves smote upon the gates of Angband and their trumpets echoed in Thangorodrim's towers.

They came thus south unto Mithrim, and little love[28] was there between them and the house of Fëanor; and the folk of Fëanor removed and camped upon the southern shores, and the lake lay between the peoples. And from this time are reckoned the Years of the Sun, and these things happened in the first year. And after came measured time into the World, and the growth and change and ageing of all things was thereafter more swift even in Valinor, but most in the Hither Lands,[29] the mortal regions between the Seas of East and West. And what else happened is recorded in the *Annals of Beleriand*, and in the *Pennas* or *Qenta*, and in many songs and tales.

NOTES

1 Added here in pencil: *daughter of Yavanna.*
2 This passage, from *and Nienna* . . ., was emended in pencil to read: *and Vairë; and Estë. No spouse hath Ulmo or Melko or Nienna, Manwë's sister and Melko's.*
3 Cf. the title to the *Ambarkanta* map IV (p. 249): *The World about V.Y. 500 after the fall of the Lamps.*
4 *But the symmetry of land and sea was first broken in those days* is an addition, but was probably made at the time of writing of the text. Cf. pp. 255–6 and the citation from *The Silmarillion* given there.
5 *and he broke and twisted the Earth much in that time* is another addition probably made at the time of writing.
6 The paragraph to this point was emended in ink to read: *But on a time (1900) Varda began the making of the stars* . . . The sentence *The Valian Year 2000 is accounted the Noontide of the Blessed Realm, and the full season of the mirth of the Gods* was removed to a later point: see note 10.
7 Added here in ink: *last and* (i.e. *the Sickle of the Gods which Varda set last and above the North*)
8 Added here in ink: *Hence are they called the children of the stars.*
9 *nine ages (900 Valian Years)* emended in ink to *seven ages (700 Valian Years).*
10 At this point the sentence *The Valian Year 2000* . . . was reintroduced (see note 6).
11 *Quendi > Lindar* in pencil.
12 *Sindingul > Tindingol* in pencil.
13 Added here in pencil: *His folk looked for him in vain, and his sleep lasted till they had gone.*
14 Added here in pencil:

2700 Here the Green-elves or Laiqi or Laiqeldar came to Ossiriand at length after many wanderings and long sojourns in diverse places. It is told that a company of the Noldoli under Dan forsook the host of Finwë early in the march and turned south, but again finding the lands barren and dark turned north, and they came about 2700 over Eredlindon under Denithor son of Dan, and dwelt in Ossiriand, and they were allies of Thingol.

The name *Denithor* is an emendation, probably of *Denilos* (see note 18).

15 This second entry for 2900 was written after the first was changed to 2700 (see note 9, and the note on dates below).

16 This passage was emended and extended thus in pencil:

> ... robbed them of their treasure. But Morgoth hid himself in the North of the land, as was known only to Finwë and Fëanor, who dwelt now apart.
> 2950 The Gods sent to apprehend Morgoth, but he fled over the mountains into Arvalin, and plotted evil for a long while, gathering the strength of darkness into him.

The date 2950 earlier in the paragraph was struck out at the same time.

17 Added here in pencil: *This reward got Finwë for his friendship*.
18 Added here in ink:

> Then fear came into Beleriand, and Thingol made his mansions in Menegroth, and Melian wove magics of the Valar about the land of Doriath, and the most of the Elves of Beleriand withdrew within its protection, save some that lingered in the western havens, Brithombar and Eglorest, beside the Great Seas.

To this was added, in faint and hasty pencil:

> and the remnant of the Green-elves of Ossiriand behind the rivers and the might of Ulmo. But Thingol with his ally Denilos of the Green-elves kept the Orcs for a while from the South. But at length Denilos son of Dan was slain, and Thingol

Here the pencilled note ends abruptly. Above *-los* of *Denilos* at the first occurrence is an alternative reading, illegible, but in view of *Denithor* probably < *Denilos* in note 14, no doubt *-thor*.

19 *Noldoli* emended from *Gnomes* at the time of writing.
20 Added here in pencil: *Here endeth that which Rúmil wrote*. See pp. 292–3.
21 Added here in ink: *with all his folk and no others save Orodreth, Angrod, and Egnor, whom Celegorm and Curufin loved*;
22 Added here in pencil: *but he . . . . duel and Fëanor fell wrapped in fire.*
23 *Fingolfin and the sons of Finrod* emended in ink to *Fingolfin and Felagund* (cf. note 21).
24 Added here in pencil: *for they had tarried long in despair upon the shores of the West*. The next sentence begins: *And these . . .*

25   Added here in pencil: *But the Moon was the first to set sail.*
26   *Sun-rise* written in pencil above *Dawn*.
27   *Dor-Daideloth* is an emendation in ink of (almost certainly) *Dor-Daidelos*; cf. the *Ambarkanta* map V, and p. 259.
28   This sentence emended in pencil to read: *Then being wary of the wiles of Morgoth they turned unto Mithrim, that the Shadowy Mountains should be their guard. But little love . . .*
29   Added in pencil: *of Middle-earth*.

Note on changes made to the dates

(i)   *Dates in the period up to the Valian Year 2200*

The mention of the Noontide of the Blessed Realm was displaced (notes 6 and 10) in order to date the starmaking and other events earlier than 2000. The beginning of the starmaking was then dated 1900 (note 6), and against *At the first shining of the Sickle of the Gods* was written in the date 1950. Against the march of the Elves led by Oromë was written in 1980–1990; and against the arrival of the Quendi (Lindar) and Noldoli in Valinor 2000.

In the sentence *But the Teleri who came after abode an age (100 Valian Years) upon the shores of Beleriand* the words *an age* were struck out, *100* changed to *10*, and the dates 2000–2010 written in. In the sentence *This is the Valian Years 2000 to 2100* the second date was likewise changed to 2010.

In the concluding part of the period, by pencilled changes perhaps later than the foregoing, the dates of the dwelling of the Teleri on Tol Eressëa, originally 2100 to 2200, were changed to 2010 to 2110; and the coming of the Teleri to Valinor in 2200 was changed to 2111. The result of these changes may be shown in a table:

Original Annals	After changes	
2000	1900	Making of the stars by Varda begun
	1950	Making of the Sickle of the Gods (end of the starmaking)
	1980–1990	March of the Elves
2000	2000	Noontide of the Blessed Realm
	2000	Coming of the first two kindreds of the Elves to Valinor
2000–2100	2000–2010	Teleri on the shores of Beleriand
2100–2200	2010–2110	Teleri dwelling in Tol Eressëa
2200	2111	Coming of the Teleri to Valinor

(ii)   Dates in the period from the Valian Year 2900

The year 2900, in which Morgoth sued for pardon, was changed to 2700, following the change in the length of his imprisonment from nine to seven ages (900 to 700 Valian Years) made earlier (note 9). These changes must have been made while the *Annals* were in progress, in view of the second entry for 2900 that follows in the text as written, *During two more ages Valinor abode yet in bliss*, i.e. two more ages from the *emended* date, 2700, when Morgoth sued for pardon and was released.

For the shifting of the date 2950 see note 16.

Almost all the dates from 2990–1 to the end were emended in pencil, and the results are best set out in a table. (The dates given in the text as 2992 to 2995 are themselves emendations in ink, apparently in each case advancing the date by one year from that originally written.)

The sentence *Thus about 2992 of Valian Years* (p. 266) was changed to *Thus in the dread Year of the Valar 2999 (29991 S.Y.)*, where S.Y. = Sun Year; cf. the opening of the *Annals*, where it is explained that a Valian Year was equal to ten years 'now', i.e. of the Sun.

It will be seen that the effect of the later pencilled changes given in the table below was to speed up events from the Battle of Alqualondë to the landing of Fingolfin in Middle-earth, so that they extend over only a single Valian Year. In the passage giving the reckoning of the First Ages of the World (p. 269), over *nine* in *Two Thousand save nine were Years of the Trees* my father wrote *one*; this one year is *the dread Year of the Valar 2999*.

In this table, only actual pencilled changes made to the dates are recorded. The change of 2991 to 2998–3000 is intended to cover all that follows, or refers only to the beginning of the entry: *Valinor now lay in great gloom, and darkness . . . fell on all the World.*

Original Annals		After changes	
(Valian Years)		*(Valian Years)*	*(Sun Years)*
2990–1	Destruction of the Trees and escape of Morgoth	2998	
2991	Rebellion of Fëanor	2998–3000	
2992	Preparation for the Flight of the Noldoli	2999	
2992	The Battle of Alqualondë	2999	29991
2993	The Doom of Mandos		29992
2994	The Noldoli in the far North; the burning of the ships		29994

Original Annals		After changes	
(Valian Years)		(Valian Years)	(Sun Years)
2995	The landing of the Fëanorians and the encampment in Mithrim		29995
2996	The Battle under Stars and the death of Fëanor		Date struck out
2997	Capture of Maidros		29996
2998	Maidros hung from Thangorodrim		
3000	Landing of Fingolfin		

Commentary on the *Annals of Valinor*

In the preamble to the *Annals of Valinor* (AV) we meet one Pengolod the Wise of Gondolin, who dwelt at Tavrobel in Tol Eressëa 'after his return unto the West'. Pengolod (or Pengoloð) often appears later, but nothing more is told of his history (the reference to Sirion's Haven shows that he was one of those who escaped from Gondolin with Tuor and Idril). I am much inclined to think that his literary origin is to be found in Gilfanon of the *Lost Tales*, who also lived at Tavrobel (which now first emerges again); there Eriol stayed in his house ('the house of a hundred chimneys'), and Gilfanon bade him write down all that he had heard (II.283), while in the preamble to AV Eriol saw Pengolod's book at Tavrobel and translated it there. Moreover Gilfanon was of the Noldoli, and though in the *Lost Tales* he is not associated with Gondolin he was an Elf of Kôr, 'being indeed one of the oldest of the fairies and the most aged that now dwelt in the isle', and had lived long in the Great Lands (I.175); while Pengolod was also an Elf whose life began in Valinor, since he 'returned' into the West.

It is not clear whether the ascription of both sets of *Annals* to Pengolod of Tavrobel, where Ælfwine/Eriol translated them, is a departure from or is congruent with the title of the *Quenta* (pp. 77–8), in which Eriol is said to have read the Golden Book (*Parma Kuluina*) in Kortirion. In the early notes and outlines there are different conceptions of the Golden Book: see II.287, 290–1, 310. On the explicit equation of *Ælfwine* and *Eriol* in the preamble to AV see p. 206.

On the later addition to AV (note 20) 'Here endeth that which Rúmil wrote' see pp. 292–3. Rúmil re-emerges from the *Lost Tales* also as the author of the *Ambarkanta* (p. 235).

In the opening passage of AV, and in the later alterations made to it, there are some developments in the composition and relations of the

Valar. The Nine Valar are the same as the nine 'chieftains of the Valar' or the 'Nine Gods' of the opening section in Q; and the association of the Valar with their spouses has undergone little change from the *Lost Tales*: Manwë and Varda; Aulë and Yavanna; Oromë and Vana; Tulkas and Nessa; Ossë and Uinen; Mandos and Nienna. But now Estë first appears, the spouse of Lórien (as is implied here by the arrangement of the passage, and as is expressly stated in the Old English version of AV, p. 285).

The 'consanguinity' of the Valar. In the *Lost Tales* Aulë and Yavanna Palúrien were the parents of Oromë (I.67), and Nessa was Oromë's sister (I.75). In the addition to AV given in note 1 Nessa is still the daughter of Yavanna;* as will appear subsequently (p. 293) Oromë was the son of Yavanna, but not of Aulë. In *The Silmarillion* (p. 29) Oromë and Nessa remain brother and sister, though their parentage is not stated.

Varda and Yavanna are said to be sisters in Q, as in AV; in Q Vana is a third sister, though apparently not so in AV, and she remains the younger sister of Yavanna in *The Silmarillion* (*ibid.*).

Manwë and Melko are said in AV to be 'brethren' (cf. *The Silmarillion* p. 26: 'Manwë and Melkor were brethren in the thought of Ilúvatar'), and Nienna is their sister; in *The Silmarillion* (p. 28) she is the sister of the Fëanturi, Mandos and Lórien.

If these sources are combined the fullest extension of the genealogy is therefore:

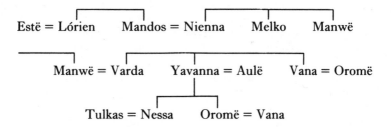

Estë = Lórien   Mandos = Nienna   Melko   Manwë

Manwë = Varda   Yavanna = Aulë   Vana = Oromë

Tulkas = Nessa   Oromë = Vana

Only the sea-gods, Ulmo, and Ossë with Uinen, are not brought in.

By the emendation given in note 2 Vairë appears, and is clearly by the arrangement of the passage the spouse of Mandos, as she remained; and Nienna now becomes solitary, again as she remained. Of course it is altogether unclear what is really meant by the terms 'brother', 'sister', 'mother', 'son', 'children' in the context of the great Valar. The term *Valarindi* has not occurred before; see further p. 293.

In what follows I relate my remarks to the dates of the *Annals*. In most respects this text (as originally written) is in harmony with the *Quenta*,

---

*In Q §6 (p. 99) Nessa is the daughter of Vana, though this statement was struck out (note 2).

and I notice only the relatively few and for the most part minor points in which they are not, or in which the *Annals* offer some detail that is absent from the *Quenta* (a great deal is of course found in the much longer *Quenta* that is omitted in the brief *Annals*).

Valian Year 500   The words 'Morgoth destroyed *by deceit* the Lamps' indicates the story of his devising the pillars out of ice, as in the *Ambarkanta* (see pp. 238, 256).

Valian Year 2000 (later 1900, 1950)   The making of the stars seems still to be thought of as accomplished by Varda at one and the same period, as in Q §2 (see p. 168). A later addition in AV (note 7) makes the Sickle of the Gods the last of Varda's works in the heavens, and thus the Elves awoke when the starmaking was concluded, as in *The Silmarillion* (p. 48); in S and Q they awoke 'at the making of the stars'. The addition given in note 8 telling that the Elves were for this reason called 'the children of the stars' is interesting; but later evidence shows that this was not yet the meaning of the name *Eldar*.

The Elves are said to have awoken 'in the midmost of the World'; in S and Q Cuiviénen is 'in the East', 'far in the East', as in *The Silmarillion*. But I doubt that this is significant, in view of the placing of Kuiviénen on the *Ambarkanta* map IV (p. 249), which could be referred to either as 'in the East' or as 'in the midmost of the World'.

In S and Q there is no mention of the Elves who would not leave the Waters of Awakening (see p. 44); in AV there is at least a suggestion of them in the reference to 'the most part' of the Elves having followed Oromë. But the story of the three original ambassadors of the Elves is still absent (see p. 168).

In S and Q (§ 4) the length of Morgoth's imprisonment in the halls of Mandos was seven ages; in Q 'seven' was emended to 'nine', but this was then rejected (note 1); in AV 'nine' was emended to 'seven' (note 9). In *The Silmarillion* (p. 65) the number of ages is three.

The rending and sundering of the lands in the war that ended in the captivity of Morgoth is described in the *Ambarkanta* (see pp. 239, 257–9).

The term *Quendi* for the First Kindred is still used in AV as in Q, and as in Q was later changed to *Lindar*. The addition in note 13 makes it explicit that Thingol did not awake from his enchanted sleep until his people had passed over the Sea; so in the *Tale of Tinúviel*, II.9: 'Now when he awoke he thought no more of his people (and indeed it had been vain, for long now had those reached Valinor).' He is now the brother of Elwë Lord of the Teleri (cf. I.120).

Valian Year 2200 (later 2111)   The name *Alqalondë* (not in S and Q, where only the English name, Swanhaven or Haven of the Swans, is used) reappears from *(Kópas) Alqaluntë* of the *Lost Tales*; cf. *Alflon* on the *Ambarkanta* map V (pp. 251, 261).

It is to be noticed that while the changing of the dates (p. 272) greatly reduced the time during which the Teleri dwelt on the coast of Beleriand (from 100 Valian Years to 10), it does not affect the length of their sojourn in Tol Eressëa, 100 Valian Years, equivalent to 1000 Years of the Sun (cf. Q §3: 'Of this long sojourn apart came the sundering of the tongue of the Foamriders and the Elves of Valinor').

Valian Year 2500 Wholly new is the matter of the pencilled addition given in note 14. My father was here working out the chronology at large, for there is no reason for this story to appear in Annals of Valinor.* It agrees with what is told in *The Silmarillion* (p. 54), save that Denethor's father is there Lenwë not Dan, and that these Elves came from the third host, the Teleri, not from the Noldor.

This is the first indication of the origin of the Green-elves, who have hitherto only appeared in association with Beren (see p. 62, and Q §14), and the first appearance of their Elvish names *Laiqi* or *Laiqeldar* (later *Laiquendi*). For earlier forms of Ossiriand see p. 233; the final form occurs also in emendations to Q (§§9, 10, 14). *Eredlindon* appears in a late addition to Q §9, note 3.

Valian Year 2900 (later 2700) In S and Q it is Tulkas and Ulmo who are opposed to the release of Morgoth, as in *The Silmarillion* (p. 66); in AV it is Tulkas and Aulë. In AV appears the intercession of Nienna on Morgoth's behalf, and this was retained in *The Silmarillion* (p. 65), though Nienna is no longer his sister.

Valian Year 2950 'The Dispossessed', the name given to the House of Fëanor, has appeared in the Old English name *Yrfeloran*, p. 212.

I have noticed in my commentary on Q §4 that the later interpolation (note 6), telling that a messenger came to the Gods in council with tidings that Morgoth was in the North of Valinor and journeying to the house of Finwë, is the first hint of the story of Morgoth's going to Formenos and his speech with Fëanor before the doors. In AV also, as originally written, the northward movement of Morgoth was absent (he fled at once into Arvalin after the council of the Gods in which they deposed Fëanor and sent to apprehend Morgoth); but in the pencilled interpolation given in note 16 Morgoth 'hid himself in the North of the land, as was known only to Finwë and Fëanor, who dwelt now apart'. It was then that the Gods sent to apprehend him, though no explanation is given of how they knew where he was; but the story now becomes

---

*It remained in the 'tradition' of these Annals, however, and is still present in the much later *Annals of Aman* (though there with a direction to transfer it to the *Annals of Beleriand*).

structurally the same as that in *The Silmarillion* (p. 72), where it was only when Finwë sent messengers to Valmar saying that Morgoth had come to Formenos that Oromë and Tulkas went after him.

Valian Years 2990–1   The addition given in note 17, 'This reward got Finwë for his friendship', refers, I think, to the relations between Morgoth and the Noldoli before his exposure. This seems much more likely than that Morgoth actually succeeded in cozening the Noldoli in exile in the North of Valinor, that they formed an alliance with him.

It is remarkable that according to the revised dating no less than 48 Valian Years (2950–2998), that is 480 Years of the Sun, elapsed between Morgoth's flight into Arvalin and the destruction of the Trees.

The insertion (in two instalments) given in note 18 introduces further new history of the 'Dark Ages' of Middle-earth. The Havens on the coast of Beleriand were marked in later on the Westward Extension of the first map (p. 228), where they are named *Brithombar* and *Eldorest* (see p. 227). Now appears also the withdrawal of the Elves of Beleriand behind the Girdle of Melian; cf. *The Silmarillion*, pp. 96–7: '[Thingol] withdrew all his people that his summons could reach within the fastness of Neldoreth and Region.' The name *Menegroth* of the Thousand Caves has not occurred before.

The incomplete pencilled addition is the first hint of the battle of the Elves of Beleriand with the Orcs after Morgoth's return ('the first battle in the Wars of Beleriand', *The Silmarillion* p. 96), in which Denethor was slain.

Valian Year 2992 (later 2999)   In the account of the Flight of the Noldoli there is a suggestion, in the words 'The march began, though the Gods forbade (and yet hindered not)', of the speech of the messenger of Manwë as the march began in *The Silmarillion* (p. 85): 'Go not forth! . . . No aid will the Valar lend you in this quest, but neither will they hinder you.'

Valian Year 2993 (later Sun Year 29992)   More is now told of the content of the Prophecy of Mandos, in particular as it concerns the altered fate of the Noldoli who would not turn back from their rebellion. In Q (§5) nothing is said of this, and the curse, as reported, is restricted to the doom of treachery and the fear of treachery among themselves; but in a later passage (§7), which goes back to S and indeed to the *Lost Tales* (see p. 51), it is told that

> Immortal were the Elves, and . . . no sickness or pestilence brought them death. But they could be slain by weapons in those days . . . and some waned and wasted with sorrow till they faded from the earth.

In AV the Doom of Mandos foretells that

a measure of mortality should visit them [the House of Fëanor and those who followed them], that they should be lightly slain with weapons, or torments, or sorrow, and in the end fade and wane before the younger race.

At first sight this seems at odds with the story as it stands, where Finwë and many other Elves had already been slain by Morgoth, who thus 'began slaughter in the world'; 'a measure of mortality' was their fate in any case. But it may be that the word 'lightly' is to be given full weight, and that the meaning is that the Noldoli will be less resistant to death that comes in these ways. In *The Silmarillion* (p. 88) Mandos or his emissary said:

> For though Eru appointed you to die not in Eä, and no sickness may assail you, yet slain ye may be, and slain ye shall be: by weapon and by torment and by grief.

This I take to mean, in effect: 'Do not forget that, though you are immortal in that you cannot die through sickness, you can nonetheless be slain in other ways; and you will indeed now die in such ways abundantly.'

The waning of the Elves now becomes an element in the Doom of Mandos; on this see p. 172.

The statement in AV that when Finrod and many others returned to Valinor and were pardoned by the Gods 'Aulë their ancient friend smiled on them no more' is interesting. It does not appear in *The Silmarillion*, where nothing is said of the reception of Finarfin (Finrod) and those who came with him on their return beyond the fact that 'they received the pardon of the Valar, and Finarfin was set to rule the remnant of the Noldor in the Blessed Realm' (p. 88); but it is to be related to a passage in the old *Tale of the Sun and Moon* (I. 176) in which Aulë's peculiar anger against the Noldoli for their ingratitude and for the Kinslaying is described.

The alliances and friendships between the princes of the Noldoli in the third generation have been touched on in S and Q §5, where Orodreth, Angrod, and Egnor, sons of Finrod, sided with the Fëanorians in the debate in Tûn before the Flight of the Noldoli; in AV this becomes a friendship especially with Celegorm and Curufin, and is no doubt to be related to the evolution of the Nargothrond legend.

Valian Year 2994 (later Sun Year 29994) The friendship of Celegorm and Curufin with Orodreth, Angrod, and Egnor just referred to leads to the remarkable development (in the addition given in note 21) that these three sons of Finrod were actually allowed passage in the ships by the Fëanorians, and that only Felagund came over the Helkaraksë with Fingolfin (note 23). This story if adhered to would presumably have affected the further evolution of the history of the Noldor in Beleriand.

In *The Silmarillion* the only especial relationship of friendship between any of the sons of Fëanor and their cousins (apart from that with Aredhel Fingolfin's daughter) is that between Maedhros and Fingon; and Maedhros, not perceiving that his father meant to burn the ships, proposed that Fingon be among the first of the other Noldor to be brought over in a second journey (p. 90).

Valian Year 2995 (later Sun Year 29995)   Here the firth of *Drengist* is named for the first time in the narrative texts (it occurs in the list of Old English names, p. 210, but is not named on the Westward Extension of the first map); *Eredlómin* has the later sense of the Echoing Mountains (see pp. 192–3, 221); and *Mithrim* is used not only of the Lake but of the region about the Lake, and the *Mountains of Mithrim* are mentioned for the first time (see p. 221, entry *Hithlum*). The encampment of the Fëanorians by Lake Mithrim now precedes the Battle under Stars.

Valian Year 2996 (date later struck out)   The first battle of the returning Noldor with the Orcs is now fought in Mithrim, not on the Northern plain (Q §8), and the plain at last receives an Elvish name, *Bladorion*, referring to the time when it was still grassland (with *Bladorion* perhaps compare *Bladorwen* 'the wide earth', a name of Yavanna given in the old Gnomish dictionary, I.264, entry *Palúrien*). The Orcs are pursued into Bladorion and Fëanor is wounded there, but dies in Mithrim. The name *Battle under Stars* is added in Q §8, note 2, but this is the first occurrence of an Elvish name, *Dagor-os-Giliath* (later *Dagor-nuin-Giliath*). *Eredwethion* replaces, in the text as written, *Eredlómin* as the Elvish name of the Shadowy Mountains (previously it is found only in later alterations, Q II§15, note 1, and on the first map, p. 221).

Valian Year 2997 (later Sun Year 29996)   A new element in AV is the condition which Morgoth proposed for the release of Maidros.

Valian Year 3000   Here is introduced the story that Fingolfin after landing in Middle-earth marched even to Angband and beat on the gates, but (in the emendation given in note 28) being prudent retreated to Mithrim; and although in S and Q §8 it is already told that the two hosts of the Noldor were encamped on opposing shores of Lake Mithrim, it is now added that the Fëanorians removed to the southern shore when Fingolfin came.

On the phrase 'after came measured time into the World' see Q §6 note 6, and pp. 171–2.

With 'the *Pennas* or *Qenta*' cf. the title of Q (p. 77): *Qenta Noldorinwa or Pennas-na-Ngoelaidh*.

APPENDIX

Old English versions of the Annals of Valinor, made by Ælfwine or Eriol

The first version given here is certainly the oldest, and is perhaps earlier than the Modern English *Annals*. A few late pencilled alterations or suggestions are given in the notes.

I

þéos gesegen wearþ ǽrest on bócum gesett of Pengolode þám Úþwitan of Gondoline ǽr þám þe héo abrocen wurde, 7 siþþan æt Sirigeones Hýþe, 7 æt Tafrobele on Toleressean (þæt is Ánetíge), æfter þám þe he eft west cóm; 7 héo wearþ þær gerǽdd and geþíedd of Ælfwine,   5
þám þe ielfe Eriol genemdon.

Frumsceaft Hér ǽrest worhte Ilúfatar, þæt is Ealfæder
oþþe Heofonfæder oþþe Beorhtfæder, eal þing.

D géara þára Falar (þæt is þára Mihta oþþe Goda): án géar
þára Goda bið swá lang swá tíen géar béoð nú on þǽre   10
worolde arímed æfter þǽre sunnan gange. Melco (þæt is
Orgel) oþþe Morgoþ (þæt is Sweart-ós) oferwearp þára
Goda Blácern, 7 þá Godu west gecirdon híe, and híe
þær Valinor þæt is Godéþel geworhton.

M Hér þá Godu awehton þá Twégen Béamas, Laurelin   15
(þæt is Goldléoþ) 7 Silpion (þæt is Glisglóm).

MM Godéðles Middæg oþþe Héahþrymm. Hér bléowon þá
Béamas þúsend géara; ond Varda (héo wæs gydena
æþelust) steorran geworhte; for þám hátte héo
Tinwetári Steorrena Hlǽfdige. Hér onwócon Ielfe on   20
Éastlandum; 7 se Melco wearð gefangen 7 on clústre
gebunden; 7 siððan cómon ielfa sume on Godéðel.

MM oþ MMC Hér wearð Tún, séo hwíte burg, atimbred
on munte Córe. þá Telere gewunodon gíet on þám
weststrandum þára Hiderlanda; ac se Teler þingol   25
wearð on wuda begalen.

MMC oþ MMCC Wunodon þá Telere on Ánetíge.

MMCC Hér cómon þá Telere oþ Godéðel.

MMD   Hér þurh searucræftas apóhton and beworhton þá Nold-ielfe gimmas missenlice, 7 Féanor Noldena   30 hláford worhte þá Silmarillas, Þæt wǽron Eorclanstánas.

MM oþ **MMDCCCC**   Hæftnýd Morgoðes.

MMDCCCC   Hér wearð Morgoþ alýsed, 7 he wunode on Godéðle, 7 lícette þæt he hold wǽre Godum 7 Ielfum.   35

MMDCCCCXCIX   Hér ofslóh Morgoð þá Béamas ond oþfléah, 7 ætferede mid him þára Elfa gimmas 7 þá Eorclanstánas. Siþþan forléton þá Noldelfe hiera hyldo, and éodon on elþéodignes, 7 gefuhton wið þá Telere æt Elfethýðe 7 sige námon 7 ætferedon þa Teleriscan   40 scipu.

Hér wearð micel gesweorc 7 genipu on Godéðle 7 ofer ealne middangeard. þá hwíle edníwede Morgoð his ealde fæsten on þám Norþdǽlum, and getrymede micle, and orcas gegaderode, and þa Eorclanstánas on   45 his irenhelme befæste.

þá fór Féanor mid his seofon sunum and micelre fierde norþ 7 þá siglde on Teleriscum scipum to þám Weststrandum, and þǽr forbǽrndon híe þa scipu ond aswicon hiera geféran þe on lást síðodon.   50

Hér gefeaht Féanores fierd wiþ þam orcum 7 sige námon 7 þá orcas gefliemdon oþ Angband (þæt is Irenhelle); ac Goðmog, Morgoðes þegn, ofslóh Féanor, and Mægdros gewéold siþþan Féanores folc. þis gefeoht hátte Tungolgúð.   55

NOTES

Textual Notes to Version I

All the following changes, except that in line 9, were made very quickly in pencil and without striking out the original forms; they belong to a much later period, as is shown by the fact that *Melkor* for *Melko* was not introduced until 1951.

1   *Pengolode* > *Pengoloðe*
2   *Gondoline* > *Gondolinde*
3   *Tafrobele* > (probably) *Taprobele* (see p. 288 note to line 7, and p. 291 note to line 7).

6 *Eriol* > *Ereol*
9 *Falar* is an emendation in ink of *Valar*.
11 *Melco* > *Melcor* (but not at line 21)
13 *Blácern* > *Léohtfatu*
14 *Godéþel* > *Ésa-eard* (*ésa* genitive plural of *ós*, see p. 208)

Old English Names in Version I

Far less use is made of Old English equivalents than is provided for in the lists given on pp. 208–13; so we have *Gondoline* with an Old English inflectional ending (not *Stángaldorburg*, etc.), *Nold(i)elfe*, also genitive plural *Noldena* (not *Déopelfe*, etc.), *Féanor*, *Mægdros*, *Goðmog*, *on munte Córe*. Old English equivalents, used or only mentioned, are mostly actual translations. Thus *Melco* is *Orgel* ('Pride'); *Morgoð* is *Sweart-ós* ('Black God', 'Dark God', see II.67); *Laurelin* is *Goldléoþ* ('Gold-song', 'Song of Gold' – cf. the translation 'singing-gold' in the name-list to *The Fall of Gondolin*, II.216, and contrast *Glengold* imitating *Glingol*, p. 210); *Silpion* is *Glisglóm* (of which the elements are evidently the stem *glis-* seen in the verbs *glisian*, *glisnian* 'shine, glitter', and *glóm* 'twilight'); *Alqalondë* is *Elfethýð* ('Swan-haven')*; *Tol Eressëa* is *Ánetíg* ('Solitary Isle'); the Battle-under-Stars is *Tungolgúð* ('Star-battle'). *Irenhell* for *Angband* and *Godéðel* ('Land of the Gods') for *Valinor* are found in the list of Old English names.

The Silmarils are *Eorclanstánas* (also treated as an Old English noun with plural *Silmarillas*). There are several different forms of this Old English word: *eorclan-*, *eorcnan-*, *earcnan-*, and *eorcan-* from which is derived the 'Arkenstone' of the Lonely Mountain. The first element may be related to Gothic *airkns* 'holy'. With *middangeard* line 37 cf. my father's note in *Guide to the Names in The Lord of the Rings*, in *A Tolkien Compass*, p. 189: 'The sense is "the inhabited lands of (Elves and) Men", envisaged as lying between the Western Sea and that of the Far East (only known in the West by rumour). *Middle-earth* is a modern alteration of medieval *middel-erde* from Old English *middan-geard*.'

Varda's name *Tinwetári*, Queen of the Stars, goes back to the tale of *The Chaining of Melko* (I.100), and is found also in Q §2.

Dates in Version I

The date MMDCCCCXCIX (written with M for MM, as also the two occurrences of MMDCCCC, but these are obviously mere slips without significance), 2999, does not agree with that in the Modern English version for the destruction of the Two Trees and the rape of the Silmarils, which are there given under 2990–1.

---

*This Old English name (with variant initial vowel, *Ielfethýþ*) is found long before in a marginal note to *Kópas Alqaluntë* in the tale of *The Flight of the Noldoli*, I.164, footnote.

II

This text relates very closely indeed to the Modern English version. There are slight differences of substance between them here and there, and some of the emendations made to the modern version are embodied in the Old English text; these points are mentioned in the notes, as also are some details concerning the dates and some features of the names. The text was lightly emended in pencil, but these changes are almost without exception modifications of word-order or other slight syntactical changes, and all such I take into the text silently. It breaks off abruptly at the beginning of the annal entry equivalent to 2991 with the words 'Valinor lay now'; these are not at the foot of a page, and none of the text has been lost.

At first sight it is puzzling that in the preamble the *Annals of Valinor* are called *Pennas*, since the *Pennas* or *Quenta* (see pp. 205-6) is clearly intended to represent a different literary tradition from the *Annals*, or at least a different mode of presenting the material. The preamble goes on to say, however, that this book *Pennas* is divided into three parts: the first part is *Valinórelúmien*, that is *Godéðles géargetæl* (i.e. Annals of Valinor); the second is *Beleriandes géargetæl* (i.e. Annals of Beleriand); and the third is *Quenta Noldorinwa* or *Pennas nan Goelið*, that is *Noldelfaracu* (the History of the Noldorin Elves). Thus, here at any rate, *Pennas* (*Quenta*) is used in both a stricter and a wider sense: the whole opus that Ælfwine translated in Tol Eressëa is the *Pennas* (*Quenta*), 'the History', but the term is also used more narrowly of the *Pennas nan Goelið* or *Quenta Noldorinwa*, which may be thought of as 'the Silmarillion proper', as opposed to the 'Annals'. In fact, in an addition to the very brief Old English version III of the *Annals of Valinor* (p. 291, note to line 5) it is expressly said: 'This third part is also called *Silmarillion*, that is the history of the *Eorclanstánas* [*Silmarils*].'

Her onginneð séo bóc þe man *Pennas* nemneð, 7 héo is on þréo gedæled; se forma dæl is *Valinórelúmien* þæt is Godéðles géargetæl, 7 se óþer is Beleriandes géargetæl, 7 se þridda *Quenta Noldorinwa* oþþe *Pennas nan Goelið* þæt is Noldelfaracu. þás ærest awrát Pengolod se   5
Úþwita of Gondoline, ær þám þe héo abrocen wurde, 7 siþþan æt Siriones hýþe 7 æt Tavrobele in Toleressean (þæt is Ánetége), þá he eft west cóm. And þás béc Ælfwine of Angelcynne geseah on Ánetége, þá þá he æt sumum cerre funde híe; 7 he geleornode híe swa he   10
betst mihte 7 eft geþéodde 7 on Englisc ásette.

I

Hér onginneð Godéðles géargetæl.

On frumsceafte Ilúuvatar, þæt is Ealfæder, gescóp
eal þing, 7 þá Valar, þæt is þá Mihtigan (þe sume menn
siþþan for godu héoldon) cómon on þás worolde. Híe
sindon nigon: Manwe, Ulmo, Aule, Orome, Tulkas,   15
Mandos, Lórien, Melko. þára wǽron Manwe 7 Melko
his bróþor ealra mihtigoste, ac Manwe wæs se yldra, 7
wæs Vala-hláford 7 hálig, 7 Melko béah to firenlustum
and úpahæfennesse and oferméttum and wearþ yfel and
unmǽðlic, and his nama is awergod and unasprecenlic,   20
ac man nemneð hine Morgoð in Noldelfisc-gereorde.
þa Valacwéne hátton swá: Varda 7 Geauanna, þe
gesweostor wǽron, Manwes cwén 7 Aules cwén; 7 Vana
Oromes cwén; 7 Nessa Tulkases cwén (séo wæs
Oromes sweostor); 7 Uinen, merecwén, Osses wíf; 7   25
Vaire Mandosses cwén, 7 Este Lóriendes cwén. Ac
Ulmo 7 Melko næfdon cwéne, 7 Nienna séo geómore
næfde wer.

Mid þissum geférum cómon micel héap lǽsra
gesceafta, Valabearn, oþþe gǽstas Valacynnes þe lǽsse   30
mægen hæfdon. þás wǽron Valarindi.

And þá Valar ǽr þám þe Móna 7 Sunne wurden
gerímdon tíde be langfirstum oþþe ymbrynum, þe
wǽron hund Valagéara on geteald; 7 án Valagéar wæs
efne swá lang swá tén géar sindon nú on worolde.   35

D   On þám Valagéare D mid searucræfte fordyde
Morgoþ þa blácern, þe Aule smiþode, þætte séo weorold
mid sceolde onleohted weorðan; 7 þá Valar, búton
Morgoþe ánum, gecerdon híe West, and þær
getimbredon Valinor (þæt is Godéðel) be sǽm   40
twéonum (þæt is betwuh Útgársecge þe ealle eorðan
bebúgeð, and séo micle Westsǽ, þæt is Gársecg, oþþe
Ingársecg, oþþe Belegar on Noldelfisce; 7 on Westsǽs
strandum gehéapodon hie micle beorgas. And
middangear[d]es rihtgesceap wearþ on þám dagum   45
ǽrest of Morgoðe onhwerfed.

M   Hér, æfter þám þe Valinor wearð getimbrod, 7
Valmar þæt is Godaburg, gescópon 7 onwehton þá
Valar þá Twégen Béamas, óþerne of seolfre óþerne of
golde geworhtne, þe hira léoma onléohte Valinor. Ac   50
Morgoþ búde on middangearde and geworhte him þǽr

micel fæsten on norþdælum; and on þǽre tíde forbrǽc
he and forsceóp he micle eorðan 7 land. Siþþan wearþ
þúsend géara blǽd 7 bliss on Godéþle, ac on
middangearde þá wæstmas, þe be þára blácerna   55
ontendnesse ǽr ongunnon úpaspringan, amerde
wurdon. To middangearde cóm þára Vala nán bútan
Orome, þe oft wolde huntian on þǽre firnan eorðan be
deorcum wealdum, 7 Iauannan þe hwílum fór þider.

MM   þis géar biþ Valaríces Middæg oþþe Heahþrymm   60
geteald, 7 þá wæs Goda myrgþu gefullod. þá geworhte
Varda steorran 7 sette híe on lyfte (7 þý hátte héo
Tinwetári, þæt is Tungolcwén), and sóna æfter þám of
Godéþle wandrodon Valarindi sume 7 cómon on
middangeard, and þára gefrǽgost wearð Melian, þe   65
wæs ǽr Lóriendes híredes, 7 hire stefn wæs mǽre mid
Godum: ac héo ne cóm eft to Godabyrig ǽr þon þe fela
géara oferéodon and fela wundra gelumpon, ac
nihtegalan wǽron hire geféran 7 sungon ymb híe be
þám deorcum wudum on westdǽlum.   70

þá þá þæt tungol, þe gefyrn Godasicol oþþe
Brynebrér hátte, líxte ǽrest forþ on heofonum, for þám
þe Varda hit asette Morgoþe on andan him his hryre to
bodianne, þá onwócon þá yldran Ealfæderes bearn on
middan worolde: þæt sindon Elfe. Híe funde Orome   75
and wearþ him fréondhald, and þára se mǽsta dǽl
siþþan West fóron him on láste and mid his
latteowdóme sóhton Beleriandes weststrand, for þám
þe Godu híe laþodon on Valinor.

þá wearþ Morgoþ ǽr mid micle heregange forhergod   80
and gebunden and siþþan æt Mandosse on cwearterne
gedón. þǽr wearð he wítefæst seofon firstmearce (þæt is
seofon hund Valagéara) oþ þæt he dǽdbétte and him
forgifennesse bǽde. On þám gefeohtum éac wurdon
eorðan land eft forbrocen swíðe 7 forscapen.   85

þá Cwendi (þæt wǽron Léohtelfe) and þá Noldelfe
sóhton ǽrest to lande on Valinor, 7 on þám grénan hylle
Córe þám sǽriman néah getimbrodon híe Tún þá hwítan
Elfaburg; ac þá Teleri, þe síþ cómon on Beleriand,
gebidon áne firstmearce þǽr be strande, and sume híe   90
ne fóron þanon siþþan nǽfre. þára wæs þingol gefrǽgost,
Elwes bróðor, Teleria hláfordes: hine Melian begól.

Híe hæfde he siþþan to wífe, and cyning wearð on
Beleriande; ac þæt gelamp æfter þám þe Ulmo oflǽdde
Teleria þone mǽstan dǽl on Ánetíge, and bróhte híe   95
swá to Valinore. þás þing wurdon on þám Valagéarum
MM oþ **MMC.**

Of **MMC** oþ **MMCC** wunodon þá Teleri on
Toleressean onmiddum Ingársecge, þanon híe mihton
Valinor feorran ofséon; on **MMCC** cómon híe mid   100
micelre scipferde to Valinore, and þǽr gewunodon on
éastsǽriman Valinores, and geworhton þǽr burg and
hýþe, and nemdon híe Alqualonde, þæt is Elfethýþ, for
þǽm þe hie þǽr hira scipu befæston, 7 þá wǽron
ielfetum gelíc.   105

þæs ymb þréo hund sumera, oþþe má oþþe lǽs,
apóhton þá Noldelfe gimmas and ongunnon híe
asmiþian, and siþþan Féanor se smiþ, Finwes yldesta
sunu Nol[d]elfa hláfordes, apóhte and geworhte þá
felamǽran Silmarillas, þe þéos gesǽgen fela áh to   110
secganne be hira wyrdum. Híe lixton mid hira ágenum
léohte, for þám þe híe wǽron gefylde þára twégra
Béama léomum, þe wurdon þǽroninnan geblanden and
to hálgum and wundorfyllum fýre gescapen.

MMDCC Hér Morgoþ dǽdbétte and him forgefennesse 115
bæd; ond be Niennan þingunga his sweostor him
Manwe his bróðor áre getéah, Tulkases unþance and
Aules, and hine gelésde; 7 he lícette þæt he hréowsode 7
éaðmód wǽre, and þám Valum gehérsum and þám
elfum swíþe hold; ac he léah, and swíþost he bepǽhte þá 120
Noldelfe, for þám þe he cúþe fela uncúþra þinga lǽran;
he gítsode swáþéah hira gimma and hine langode þá
Silmarillas.

MMCM þurh twá firstmearce wunode þá gíet Valinor on
blisse, ac twéo 7 inca awéox swáþéah manigum on   125
heortan swulce nihtsceadu náthwylc, for þám þe Morgoþ
fór mid dernum rúnungum and searolicum lygum, and
yfelsóþ is to secganne, swíþost he onbryrde þá Noldelfe
and unsibbe awehte betwux Finwes sunum, Féanor
and Fingolfin and Finrod, and ungeþwǽrnes betwux   130
Godum 7 elfum.

MMCMD   Be Goda dóme wearþ Féanor, Finwes yldesta sunu, mid his hírede 7 folgoþe adón of Noldelfa ealdordóme – þý hátte siþþan Féanores cynn þá Erfeloran, for þám dóme 7 for þý þe Morgoþ beréafode 135 híe hira máþma – 7 þá Godu ofsendon Morgoþ to démanne hine; ac he ætfléah 7 darode on Arualine and beþóhte hine yfel.

MMCMD –   Hér Morgoþ fullfremede his searowrencas
MMCMDI   sóhte Ungoliante on Arualine and bæd híe 140 fultumes. Þa bestǽlon híe eft on Valinor 7 þá Béamas forspildon, and siþþan ætburston under þám weaxendum sceadum and fóron norþ and þǽr hergodon Féanores eardunge and ætbǽron gimma unrím and þá Silmarillas mid ealle, 7 Morgoþ ofslóh Þǽr Finwe 7 145 manige his elfe mid him and awídlode swá Valinor ǽrest mid blódgyte and morþor astealde on worolde. He þá fléame generede his feorh, þéah þe þá Godu his éhton wíde landes, siþþan becóm he on middangeardes norþdǽlas and geedstaðelode þǽr his fæsten, and fédde 150 and samnode on níwe his yfele þéowas, ge Balrogas ge orcas. Þá cóm micel ege on Beleriand, 7 Þingol his burgfæsten getrymede on Menegroþ þæt is þúsend þéostru, and Melian séo cwén mid Vala-gealdrum begól þæt land Doriaþ and bewand hit ymbútan, and siþþan 155 sóhton se mǽsta dǽl þára deorc-elfa of Beleriande Þingoles munde.

MMCMI   Hér læg Valinor on

NOTES TO VERSION II

5   *Noldelfaracu* emended in ink from *Noldelfagesægen*.

7   *Tavrobele* > (probably) *Tafrobele*, in pencil. In version I *Tafrobele* probably > *Taþrobele*, and in version III *Taþrobele* as written, but in this case the emendation seems clearly to be to *f*; this would be a mere spelling-correction (*f* being the Old English spelling for the voiced consonant [v] in this position).

13–14   This phrase (*þe sume menn siþþan for godu héoldon*) is not in the Modern English version, but cf. the opening section of Q (p. 78): 'These spirits the Elves named the Valar, which is the Powers, though Men have often called them Gods.'

15 Ossë has been inadvertently omitted.

17 It is not said in the Modern English version that Manwë was the elder.

22 *Geauanna*: this spelling would represent 'Yavanna' in Old English. At line 59 the name is spelt *Iauanna(n)*, and in the Old English version of the *Quenta* (p. 207) *Yavanna*; in version III *Geafanna* (p. 291).

26–8 The text here embodies the sense of the pencilled emendation to the Modern English version (p. 270 note 2) whereby Vairë enters as the spouse of Mandos and Nienna becomes solitary. At line 28, after *næfde wer*, was added in pencil: *Séo wæs Manwes sweostor 7 Morgoðes*; this is stated in the Modern English version as written.

41–3 *Útgársecg, Gársecg, Ingársecg*: see pp. 208, 210. – *Belegar*: see pp. 210, 249–51.

45 *middangeardes*: see p. 283.

48 Valmar is *Godaburg* in the list of Old English names, p. 211.

60–2 The changes made to the text of the Modern English version, in order to date the Starmaking and the Awakening of the Elves before 2000 (see p. 270, notes 6 and 10), are not embodied in the Old English.

65–6 The statement that Melian was of Lórien's people is not in the Modern English version, but is found in S and Q (§2) and goes back to the *Tale of Tinúviel* (II. 8): '[Wendelin] was a sprite that escaped from Lórien's gardens before even Kôr was built.'

72 *Brynebrér* ('Burning Briar'): this name for the Great Bear, not found in the Modern English version, occurs in Q (§2) and in the *Lay of Leithian*.

82 *seofon firstmearce*, not 'nine ages' as first written in the Modern English version (p. 270 note 9). *firstmearce* ('spaces of time') is an emendation made at the time of writing from *langfirstas* (one of the words used for Valian 'ages' earlier, line 33).

86 *Cwendi* emended in pencil first to *Eldar* and then to *Lindar*; *Quendi* > *Lindar* also in Q (§2 and subsequently) and in the modern version. – *Léohtelfe* is not one of the Old English names of the First Kindred given in the list on p. 212, but they are called *Light-elves* in S and Q (§2; see p. 44).

95 *Ánetíge* spelt thus, as in version I line 4; *Ánetége* lines 8 and 9.

99 *Ingársecge* < *Gársecge* (see lines 42–3).

115 For the date 2700 see note to line 82 above, and the note on dates, p. 273.

135 *Erfeloran* ('the Dispossessed'), with variant initial vowel *Yrfeloran*, is found in the list of Old English names of the Fëanorians, p. 212.

139 These dates are presumably to be interpreted as 2950–1: in the

previous entry (line 132) MMCMD corresponds to 2950 in the Modern English version. My father was here using D = 50, not 500. But 2950–1 does not correspond to the Modern English version, which has 2990–1. The discrepancy is perhaps no more than a mere error of writing (though version I is also discrepant in this date, having 2999); the date of the next entry, MMCMI (2901), is obviously an error, from its place in the chronological series.

152–7 This sentence represents part of the passage added to the Modern English version (p. 271 note 18), but omits the reference to the Elves who remained in Brithombar and Eglorest.

III

This version, on a single manuscript page, gives a slightly different form of the first twenty-odd lines of version II. It is much later than II, as is shown by *Melkor*, not *Melko* (see p. 282), but was nonetheless taken directly from it, as is shown by the continued absence of Ossë from the list of the Valar (see note to line 15 in version II). Later changes pencilled on version I are here embodied in the text (*Pengoloð* for *Pengolod*, *Taþrobele* for *Tafrobele*, *Melkor* for *Melko*).

Version III is cast in a different form of Old English, that of ninth century Mercia (some of the forms are peculiarly characteristic of the Mercian dialect represented by the interlinear glosses on the Vespasian Psalter). A few pencilled emendations are not included in the text, but recorded in the notes that follow.

Hér onginneð séo bóc þe man *Pennas* nemneð on ælfisc, 7 hío is on þréo gedǽled: se forma dǽl is *Ualinórelúmien* þæt is Godoeðles gérgetæl; 7 se óðer dǽl is Beleriandes gérgetæl; 7 se þridda *Quenta Noldorinwa* oððe *Pennas na Ngoeloeð*, þæt is Noldælfaracu. Þás bóc ǽrest awrát Pengoloð se úðwita on   5
Gondoline ǽr þám þe héo abrocen wurde 7 seoððan æt Siriones hýðe 7 æt Taþrobele on Tol-eressean (þæt is Ánetége), þá he eft west cóm. And þás béc Ælfwine of Ongulcynne gesæh on Ánetége ða ða he æt sumum cerre þæt land funde; 7 he ðær liornode híe swá he betst mæhte 7 eft   10
geþéodde 7 on englisc gereord ásette.

Hér onginneð Godoeðles gérgetæl, 7 spriceð ǽrest of weorulde gescefte. On frumscefte gescóp Ilúuatar þæt is

Allfeder all þing, 7 þá þá séo weoruld ærest weorðan ongon þá
cómun hider on eorðan þá Ualar (þæt is þá Mehtigan þe sume   15
men seoððan for godu héoldun). Hí earun nigun on ríme:
Manwe, Ulmo, Aule, Orome, Tulcas, Mandos, Lórien,
Melkor. þeara wérun Manwe 7 Melcor his bróður alra
mehtigoste, ac Manwe wes se ældra 7 is Uala-hláfard 7 hálig,
7 Melcor béh to firenlustum 7 to úpahefennisse 7 ofer-   20
moettum 7 wearð yfel 7 unméðlic, 7 his noma is awergod 7
unasproecenlic, for þám man nemneð hine Morgoþ on Nold-
ælfiscgereorde. Orome 7 Tulcas wérun gingran on Alfeadur
geþóhte acende ær þere weorulde gescepennisse þonne óðre
fífe. þá Uala-cwéne háttun swé: Uarda Manwes cwén, 7   25
Geafanna Aules cwén (þá þá he and híe wurdon to sinhíwan
æfter þám þe Ualar hider cómon on weorulde).

NOTES TO VERSION III

2–4 *Ualinórelúmien þæt is* and *Quenta Noldorinwa oððe* are circled
in pencil as if for exclusion.

5 Added in pencil here: 'and þes þridda dǽl man éac nemneð
Silmarillion þæt is Eorclanstána gewyrd.' See p. 284.

5–6 *on Gondoline* is an emendation in ink from *of Gondoline*, i.e.
Pengoloð began the work in Gondolin; but this is implied in the
preambles to versions I and II, which have *of Gondoline* here. –
Gondoline > *Gondolinde* in pencil, as in version I (note to
line 2).

7 *Taþrobele* is very clearly written with þ; see p. 288 note to line 7.

17 Ossë is left out following version II.

18 *Melkor* > *Melcor* in ink at the second occurrence, no doubt at the
time of writing, since *Melcor* is written at line 20.

23–5 The statement that Oromë and Tulkas 'were younger in the
thought of Ilúvatar' is absent from the other versions (cf. *The
Silmarillion* p. 26: 'Manwë and Melkor were brethren in the
thought of Ilúvatar'). – *óðre fífe*: i.e. the other Valar with the
exclusion of Manwë and Melkor. See p. 293, Old English text
lines 1–4.

26 *Geafanna*: see p. 289, note to line 22.

26–7 It is very notable that Aulë and Yavanna are here (alone) said to
have become husband and wife (*wurdon to sinhíwan*) after the
Valar came into the world. In *The Silmarillion* the only union
among the Valar that is said to have taken place after the entry
into Arda is that of Tulkas and Nessa; and Tulkas came late to
Arda (pp. 35–6). See further p. 293.

IV

This is not a version, but a single page of manuscript with, first, a different beginning to the *Annals of Valinor* in Modern English, and then ten lines, written very rapidly, in Old English. Both contain interesting features. The first reads as follows:

Annals of Valinor

These were written first by Rúmil the Elfsage of Valinor, and after by Pengolod the Wise of Gondolin, who made also the Annals of Beleriand, and the *Pennas* that are set forth below. These also did Ælfwine of the Angelcynn turn into speech of his land.

Here beginneth the Annals of Valinor and the foundations of the world.

Of the Valar and their kindred

At the beginning Ilúvatar, that is Allfather, made all things, and the Valar, or Powers, came into the world. These are nine: Manwë, Ulmo, Aulë, Oromë, Tulkas, Ossë, Lórien, Mandos, and Melko.

Pennas is here used in the narrow sense of 'The History of the Gnomes' (*Quenta Noldorinwa, Silmarillion*): see p. 284. Here Rúmil appears as author, and in view of the interpolation in AV (note 20) 'Here endeth that which Rúmil wrote' it is clear that the words of this preamble 'These were written first by Rúmil . . . and after by Pengolod' mean that Pengolod completed what Rúmil began. The next version of the *Annals of Valinor* in fact makes this explicit, for after 'Here endeth that which Rúmil wrote' the later text has 'Here followeth the continuation of Pengolod'; and the two interpolations in AV (notes 14 and 18) concerning events in Middle-earth before the Return of the Noldoli are embodied in the second version as additions by Pengolod: 'This have I, Pengolod, added here, *for it was not known unto Rúmil.*'

In the original tale of *The Music of the Ainur* (I.47–8) Rúmil was a Noldo of Kôr,* but he also spoke to Eriol of his 'thraldom under Melko'. From the reference here to Rúmil as 'the Elfsage of Valinor', however, and from his ignorance of events in Middle-earth, it seems clear that in the later conception he never left Valinor. It might be suggested that his part in the *Annals* ends where it does (p. 267 and note 20) because he was

---

*As he remained; cf. *The Silmarillion* p. 63: 'Then it was that the Noldor first bethought them of letters, and Rúmil of Tirion was the name of the loremaster who first achieved fitting signs for the recording of speech and song.'

one of those who returned to Valinor with Finrod after hearing the Doom of Mandos. This is admittedly pure speculation, but it is perhaps significant that in the next version of the *Annals* the end of Rúmil's part in the work was moved on to the end of the entry for the Valian Year 2993, after the words 'But Aulë their ancient friend smiled on them no more, and the Teleri were estranged'; thus his part ends with the actual record of Finrod's return, and of the reception that he and those with him received.

The passage in Old English that follows begins with virtually the same phrase, concerning Oromë and Tulkas, as that in version III lines 23–5; but this manuscript has a curious, uninterpretable sign between *Orome* and the plural verb *wǽron*, which in view of the other text I expand to mean *7 Tulkas*.

> Orome [7 Tulkas] wǽron gingran on Ealfæderes geþóhtum acende ǽr þǽre worolde gescepennisse þonne óþre fífe, 7 Orome wearð Iafannan geboren, séo þe wyrð æfter nemned, ac he nis Aules sunu.
>
> Mid þissum mihtigum cómon manige lǽssan gǽstaþ æs ilcan cynnes 7 cnéorisse, þéah lǽssan mægnes. þás sindon þá Vanimor, þá Fægran. Mid him éac þon wurdon getealde hira bearn, on worolde acende, þá wǽron manige and swíþe fægre. Swylc wæs Fionwe Manwes sunu

There follow a few more words that are too uncertain to reproduce. Here Oromë, younger in the thought of Ilúvatar than the other great Valar 'born before the making of the world', is declared to be the son of Yavanna but not of Aulë, and this must be connected with the statement in the Old English version III that Yavanna and Aulë became *sinhíwan* after the entry of the Valar into the world (see p. 291, note to lines 26–7).

In what is said here concerning the lesser spirits of Valarin race there are differences from AV (p. 263) and the Old English version II (p. 285). In this present fragment these spirits are not called *Valarindi* but *Vanimor*, 'the Fair'.* The Children of the Valar, 'who were many and very beautiful', are counted among the *Vanimor*, but, in contradiction to AV, they were *on worolde acende*, 'born in the world'. At this time, it seems, my father was tending to emphasize the generative powers of the great Valar, though afterwards all trace of the conception disappeared.

---

*The word *Vanimor* has not occurred before, but its negative *Úvanimor* is defined in the tale of *The Coming of the Valar* (I.75) as 'monsters, giants, and ogres', and elsewhere in the *Lost Tales* Úvanimor are creatures bred by Morgoth (I.236–7), and even Dwarves (II.136).

VII
THE EARLIEST ANNALS
OF BELERIAND

As with the *Annals of Valinor*, these are the 'earliest' *Annals of Beleriand* because they were followed by others, the last being called the *Grey Annals*, companion to the *Annals of Aman* and belonging to the same time (p. 262). But unlike the *Annals of Aman*, the *Grey Annals* were left unfinished at the end of the story of Túrin Turambar; and both as prose narrative and still more as definitive history of the end of the Elder Days from the time of *The Lord of the Rings* their abandonment is grievous.

The earliest *Annals of Beleriand* ('AB') are themselves found in two versions, which I shall call AB I and AB II. AB I is a complete text to the end of the First Age; AB II is quite brief, and though it begins as a fair copy of the much-emended opening of I it soon becomes strongly divergent. In this chapter I give both texts separately and in their entirety, and in what follows I refer only to the earlier, AB I.

This is a good, clear manuscript, but the style suggests very rapid composition. For much of its length the entries are in the present tense and often staccato, even with such expressions as 'the Orcs got between them' (annal 172), though by subsequent small expansions and alterations here and there my father slightly modified this character. I think that his primary intention at this time was the consolidation of the historical structure in its internal relations and chronology – the *Annals* began, perhaps, in parallel with the *Quenta* as a convenient way of driving abreast, and keeping track of, the different elements in the ever more complex narrative web. Nonetheless major new developments enter here.

The manuscript was fairly heavily emended, though much less so towards the end, and from the nature of the changes, largely concerned with dating, it has become a complicated document. To present it in its original form, with all the later changes recorded in notes, would make it quite unnecessarily difficult to follow, and indeed would be scarcely possible, since many alterations were made either at the time of writing or in its immediate context. A later 'layer' of pencilled emendation, very largely concerned with names, is easily separable. The text given here, therefore, is that of the manuscript *after all the earlier changes and additions (in ink) had been made to it*, and these are only recorded in the notes in certain cases. The later pencilled alterations are fully registered.

That AB I is earlier than the comparable portion of AV is easily shown. Thus in AB I, as in Q (§8), there is no mention of Fingolfin's march to

Angband immediately on his arrival, whereas it appears in AV (p. 269); again as in Q and in contrast to AV (p. 268) the Battle under Stars was fought, and Fëanor died, before the encampment in Mithrim. Further, the names *Dagor-os-Giliath* and *Eredwethion* are added in pencil in AB I, whereas in AV they appear in the text as first written, and *Erydlómin* still means the Shadowy Mountains (see p. 280). That AB I is later than Q is shown by a multiplicity of features, as will be seen from the Commentary. There follows the text of AB I.

ANNALS OF BELERIAND

Morgoth flees from Valinor with the Silmarils, the magic gems of Fëanor, and returns into the Northern World and rebuilds his fortress of Angband beneath the Black Mountain, Thangorodrim. He devises the Balrogs and the Orcs. The Silmarils are set in Morgoth's iron crown.

The Gnomes of the eldest house, the Dispossessed, come into the North under Fëanor and his seven sons, with their friends Orodreth, Angrod, and Egnor, sons of Finrod.[1] They burn the Telerian ships.

First of the Battles with Morgoth,[2] the Battle under Stars. Fëanor defeats the Orcs, but is mortally wounded by Gothmog captain of Balrogs, and dies. Maidros, his eldest son, is ambushed and captured and hung on Thangorodrim. The sons of Fëanor camp about Lake Mithrim in the North-west, behind the Shadowy Mountains.[3]

Year 1 Here Sun and Moon, made by the Gods after the death of the Two Trees of Valinor, appear. Thus measured time came into the Hither Lands. Fingolfin leads the second house of the Gnomes over the straits of Grinding Ice into the Hither Lands. With him came the son of Finrod, Felagund,[4] and part of the third or youngest house. They march from the North as the Sun rises, and unfurl their banners; and they come to Mithrim, but there is feud[5] between them and the sons of Fëanor. Morgoth at coming of Light retreats into his deepest dungeons, but smithies in secret, and sends forth black clouds.

2 Fingon son of Fingolfin heals the feud by rescuing Maidros.

1–100   The Gnomes explore and settle Beleriand, and all the vale of Sirion from[6] the Great Sea to the Blue Mountains,[7] except for Doriath in the centre where Thingol and Melian reign.

20   Feast and Games of Reuniting were held in Nan Tathrin, the Land of Willows, near the delta of Sirion, between the Elves of Valinor returning and the Dark-elves, both those of the Western Havens (Brithombar and Eldorest)[8] and the scattered Wood-elves of the West, and ambassadors of Thingol. A time of peace followed.[9]

50   Morgoth's might begins to move once more. Earthquakes in the North. Orc-raids begin. Turgon son of Fingolfin is great in friendship with Felagund son of Finrod; but Orodreth, Angrod, and Egnor, sons of Finrod, are friends of the sons of Fëanor, especially Celegorm and Curufin.

50   Turgon and Felagund are troubled by dreams and forebodings. Felagund finds the caves of Narog and established his armouries there.[10] Turgon alone discovers the hidden vale of Gondolin. Being still troubled in heart he gathers folk about him and departs from Hithlum, the Land of Mist about Mithrim, where his brother Fingon remains.

51   The Gnomes drive back the Orcs again, and the Siege of Angband is laid. The North has great peace and quiet again. Fingolfin holds the North-west and all Hithlum, and is overlord of the Dark-elves west of Narog. His might is gathered on the slopes of Erydlómin[11] the Shadowy Mountains and thence watches and traverses the great plains of Bladorion up to the walls of Morgoth's mountains in the North. Felagund holds the vale of Sirion save Doriath, and has his seat[12] beside Narog in the South, but his might is gathered in the North guarding the access to Sirion's vale between Erydlómin and the mountainous region of Taur-na-Danion, the forest of pines. He has a fortress on a rocky isle in the midst of Sirion, Tolsirion. His brothers dwell in the centre about Taur-na-Danion and scour Bladorion thence, and join in the East with the sons of Fëanor. The fortress of the sons of Fëanor is upon Himling, but they roam and hunt all the woods of East Beleriand even up to the Blue Mountains. Thither at times many of the Elf-lords go for hunting. But none get tidings of Turgon and his folk.

70   Bëor born in the East.

88. 90   Haleth, and Hádor the Goldenhaired, born in the East.

100   Felagund hunting in the East comes upon Bëor the mortal and his Men who have wandered into Beleriand. Bëor becomes a vassal of Felagund and goes west with him. Bregolas son of Bëor born.

102   Barahir son of Bëor born.

120   Haleth comes into Beleriand; also Hádor the Golden-haired and his great companies of Men. Haleth remains in Sirion's vale, but Hádor becomes a vassal of Fingolfin and strengthens his armies and is given lands in Hithlum.

113 Hundor son of Haleth born. **117** Gundor son of Hádor born. **119** Gumlin son of Hádor born.[13]

122   The strength of Men being added to the Gnomes, Morgoth is straitly enclosed. The Gnomes deem the siege of Angband cannot be broken, but Morgoth ponders new devices, and bethinks him of Dragons. The Men of the three houses grow and multiply, and are gladly subject to the Elf-lords, and learn many crafts of the Gnomes. The Men of Bëor were dark or brown of hair but fair of face, with grey eyes; of shapely form, of great courage and endurance, but little greater than the Elves of that day. The folk of Hádor were yellow-haired and blue-eyed and of great stature and strength. Like unto them but somewhat shorter and more broad were the folk of Haleth.

124. 128   Baragund and Belegund, sons of Bregolas son of Bëor, born.

132   Beren, after named the Ermabwed[14] or One-handed,[15] son of Barahir, born.

141   Húrin the Steadfast, son of Gumlin, born. Handir son of Hundor son of Haleth born.

144   Huor Húrin's brother born.

145   Morwen Elfsheen, daughter of Baragund, born.

150   Rían daughter of Belegund, mother of Tuor, born.[16] Bëor the Old, Father of Men, dies of old age in Beleriand. The Elves see for the first time the death of weariness, and sorrow over the short span allotted to Men. Bregolas rules the house of Bëor.

★ **155**   Morgoth unlooses his might, and seeks to break into Beleriand. The Battle begins on a sudden on a night of mid-winter and falls first most heavily on the sons of Finrod and their folk. This is the Battle of Sudden Fire.[17] Rivers of fire flow from Thangorodrim. Glómund the golden, Father of Dragons, appears.[18] The plains of Bladorion are turned into a great desert without green, and called after Dor-na-Fauglith, Land of Gasping Thirst.

   Here were Bregolas slain, and the greater part of the warriors of Bëor's house. Angrod and Egnor sons of Finrod fell. Barahir and his chosen champions saved Felagund and Orodreth, and Felagund swore a great oath of friendship to his kin and seed. Barahir rules the remnant of the house of Bëor.

155   Fingolfin and Fingon marched to the aid of their kin, but were driven back with great loss. Hádor, now aged, fell defending his lord Fingolfin, and with him Gundor his son. Gumlin took the lordship of Hádor's house.

   The sons of Fëanor were not slain, but Celegorm and Curufin were defeated and fled with Orodreth son of Finrod. Maidros the left-handed did deeds of great prowess, and Morgoth did not take Himling as yet, but he broke into the passes east of Himling and ravaged into East Beleriand and scattered the Gnomes of Fëanor's house.

   Turgon was not at that battle, nor Haleth or any but few of his folk. It is said that Húrin was at foster with Haleth, and that Haleth and Húrin hunting in Sirion's vale came upon some of Turgon's folk, and were brought into the secret vale of Gondolin, whereof of those outside none yet knew save Thorndor King of Eagles; for Turgon had messages and dreams sent by the God Ulmo, Lord of Waters, up Sirion warning him that help of Men was necessary for him. But Haleth and Húrin swore oaths of secrecy and never revealed Gondolin, but Haleth learned something of the counsels of Turgon, and told them after to Húrin. Great liking had Turgon for the boy Húrin, and would keep him in Gondolin, but the grievous tidings of the great battle came and they departed. Turgon sends secret messengers to Sirion's mouths and begins a building of ships. Many set sail for Valinor, but none return.[19]

Fingolfin seeing the ruin of [the] Gnomes and the defeat of all their houses was filled with wrath and despair, and rode alone to the gates of Angband and challenged Morgoth to single combat. Fingolfin was slain, but Thorndor rescued his body, and set it in a cairn on the mountains north of Gondolin to guard that valley, and so came the tidings thither. Fingon ruled the royal house of [the] Gnomes.

157   Morgoth took Tolsirion and pierced the passes into West Beleriand. There he set Thû the wizard, and Tolsirion became a place of evil.[20] Felagund and Orodreth, together with Celegorm and Curufin, retreated to Nargothrond, and made there a great hidden palace after the fashion of Thingol in[21] the Thousand Caves in Doriath.

Barahir will not retreat and holds out still in Taur-na-Danion. Morgoth hunts them down and turns Taur-na-Danion into a region of great dread, so that it was after called Taur-na-Fuin, the Forest of Night, or Math-Fuin-delos[22] Deadly Nightshade. Only Barahir and his son Beren, and his nephews Baragund and Belegund sons of Bregolas and a few men remain.[23] The wives of Baragund and Belegund and their young daughters Morwen and Rían were sent[24] into Hithlum to the keeping of Gumlin.

158   Haleth and his folk lead a woodland life in the woods about Sirion on the west marches of Doriath and harry the Orc-bands.[25]

160   Barahir was betrayed by Gorlim, and all his company is slain by the Orcs save Beren who was hunting alone. Beren pursues the Orcs and slays his father's slayer and retakes the ring which Felagund gave to Barahir. Beren becomes a solitary outlaw.

162   Renewed assaults of Morgoth. The Orc-raids encompass Doriath, protected by the magic of Melian the divine, west down Sirion and east beyond Himling. Beren is driven south and comes hardly into Doriath. Gumlin slain in an assault upon the fortress of Fingon at Sirion's Well[26] in the west of Erydlómin.[27] Húrin his son is mighty in strength. He is summoned to Hithlum and comes there hardly. He rules the house of Hádor and serves Fingon.

163   The Swarthy Men first come into East Beleriand. They were short, broad, long and strong in the arm, growing much hair on face and breast, and this was dark as were their eyes; their skins were sallow or dark, but most were not uncomely. Their houses were many, and many had liking rather for the[28] Dwarves of the mountains, of Nogrod and Belegost, than for the Elves. Of the Dwarves the Elves first learned in these days, and their friendship was small. It is not known whence they are, save that they are not of Elf-kin, nor of mortal, nor of Morgoth.[29] But Maidros seeing the weakness of the Gnomes and the waxing power of the armies of Morgoth made alliance with the new-come Men, and with the houses of Bor and of Ulfand.[30] The sons of Ulfand were Uldor, after called the Accursed, and Ulfast, and Ulwar; and by Cranthir son of Fëanor were they most beloved, and they swore fealty to him.

163–4   The great geste of Beren and Lúthien.[31] King Felagund of Nargothrond dies in Tolsirion[32] in the dungeons of Thû. Orodreth rules Nargothrond and breaks friendship with Celegorm and Curufin who are expelled.[33] Lúthien and Huan overthrow Thû. Beren and Lúthien go to Angband and recover a Silmaril. Carcharoth the great wolf of Angband with the Silmaril in his belly bursts into Doriath. Beren and the hound Huan are slain by Carcaroth, but Huan slays Carcharoth and the Silmaril is regained.

Beren was recalled from the dead by Lúthien and dwelt with her[34] in the Land of Seven Rivers, Ossiriand, out of the knowledge of Men and Elves.[35]

164   Húrin weds Morwen.

165   Túrin son of Húrin born in winter with sad omens.[36]

165–70   *The Union of Maidros.* Maidros enheartened by the deeds of Beren and Lúthien plans a reuniting of forces for the driving back of Morgoth. But because of the deeds of Celegorm and Curufin he receives no help from Thingol, and only small support from Nargothrond, where the Gnomes attempt to guard themselves by stealth and secrecy. He gathers and arms all the Gnomes of Fëanor's house, and multitudes of the Dark-elves, and of Men, in East Beleriand. He gets help in smithying of the Dwarves, and summons yet more Men over the mountains out of the East.

Tidings come to Turgon the hidden king and he prepares in secret for war, for his people who were not at the Second Battle will not be restrained.

167   Dior the Beautiful born to Beren and Lúthien in Ossiriand.

168   Haleth, last of the Fathers of Men, dies. Hundor rules his folk. The Orcs are slowly driven back out of Beleriand.

171   Isfin daughter of Turgon strays out of Gondolin and is taken to wife by Eöl a Dark-elf.

★   **172**   *The year of sorrow.* Maidros plans an assault upon Angband, from West and East. Fingon is to march forth as soon as Maidros' main host gives the signal in the East of Dor-na-Fauglith. Huor son of Hádor[37] weds Rían daughter of Belegund on the eve of battle and marches with Húrin his brother in the army of Fingon.

The Battle of Unnumbered Tears,[38] the third battle of the Gnomes and Morgoth, was fought upon the plains of Dor-na-Fauglith before the pass in which the young waters of Sirion enter Beleriand between Erydlómin[39] and Taur-na-Fuin. The place was long marked by a great hill in which the slain, Elves and Men, were piled. Grass grew there alone in Dor-na-Fauglith. The Elves and Men were utterly defeated and their ruin accomplished.

Maidros was hindered on the road by the machinations of Uldor the Accursed whom Morgoth's spies had bought. Fingon attacked without waiting and drove in Morgoth's feinted attack, even to Angband. The companies from Nargothrond burst into his gates, but they and their leader Flinding son of Fuilin[40] were all taken; and Morgoth now released a countless army and drove the Gnomes back with terrible slaughter. Hundor son of Haleth and the Men of the wood were slain in the retreat across the sands. The Orcs got between them and the passes into Hithlum, and they retreated towards Tolsirion.

Turgon and the army of Gondolin sound their horns and issue out of Taur-na-Fuin. Fortune wavers and the Gnomes begin to gain ground. Glad meeting of Húrin and Turgon.

The trumpets of Maidros heard in the East, and the Gnomes take heart. The Elves say victory might have been theirs yet but for Uldor. But Morgoth now sent forth all the folk of Angband and Hell was emptied. There came afresh a hundred thousand Orcs and a thousand Balrogs, and in the forefront came Glómund the Dragon, and Elves and Men withered before him. Thus the union of the hosts of Fingon and Maidros was broken. But Uldor went over to Morgoth and fell on the right flank of the sons of Fëanor.

Cranthir slew Uldor, but Ulfast and Ulwar slew Bor and his three sons and many Men who were faithful, and the host of Maidros was scattered to the winds and fled far into hiding into East Beleriand and the mountains there.

Fingon fell in the West, and it is said flame sprang from his helm as he was smitten down by the Balrogs. Húrin and the Men of Hithlum of Hádor's house, and Huor his brother, stood firm, and the Orcs could not pass into Beleriand. The stand of Húrin is the most renowned deed of Men among the Elves. He held the rear while Turgon with part of his battle, and some of the remnant of Fingon's host, escaped into the dales and mountains. They vanished and were not again found by Elf or by spy of Morgoth until Tuor's day. Thus was Morgoth's victory marred and he was greatly angered.

Húrin fought on after Huor fell pierced with a venomed arrow, and until he alone was left. He threw away his shield and fought with an axe and slew a hundred Orcs.

Húrin was taken alive by Morgoth's command and dragged to Angband where Morgoth cursed him and his kin, and because he would not reveal where Turgon was gone chained him with enchanted sight on Thangorodrim to see the evil that befell his wife and children. His son Túrin was nigh three years old,[41] and his wife Morwen was again with child.

The Orcs piled the slain and entered Beleriand to ravage. Rían sought for Huor, for no tidings came to Hithlum of the battle, and her child Tuor son of Huor was born to her in the wild. He was taken to nurture by Dark-elves, but Rían went to the Mound of Slain[42] and laid her down to die there.[43]

173 Morgoth took all Beleriand or filled it with roving bands of Orcs and wolves, but there held still Doriath. Of Nargothrond he heard little, of Gondolin he could discover nothing. In Beleriand outside these three places only scattered Elves and Men lived in outlawry, and among them the remnant of Haleth's folk under Handir, son of Hundor, son of Haleth.[44]

Morgoth broke his pledges to the sons of Ulfand,[45] and drove the evil Men into Hithlum, without reward, save that they there ill-treated and enslaved the remnants of Hádor's house, the old men and the women and children. The remnants of the Elves of Hithlum also he mostly enslaved and took to the mines of Angband, and others he forbade to leave Hithlum, and they were slain if Orcs found them east or south of the Shadowy Mountains.[46] Nienor the sorrowful, daughter of Húrin and Morwen, born in Hithlum in the beginning of the year.

Tuor grew up wild in the woods among fugitive Elves nigh the shores of Mithrim;[47] but Morwen sent Túrin to Doriath begging for Thingol's fostering and aid, for she was of Beren's kindred. They have a desperate journey, the boy of seven and his two guides.[48]

181   The power of Morgoth waxes and Doriath is cut off and no tidings of the outer world reach it. Túrin though not fully grown takes to war on the marches in company of Beleg.

184   Túrin slays Orgof, kinsman of the royal house, and flees from Thingol's court.

184–7   Túrin an outlaw in the woods. He gathers a desperate band, and plunders on the marches of Doriath and beyond.

187   Túrin's companions capture Beleg. But Túrin releases him and they renew their fellowship, and make war on the Orcs, adventuring far beyond Doriath.[49]

189   Blodrin Ban's son betrays their hiding place, and Túrin is taken alive. Beleg healed of his wounds follows in pursuit. He comes upon Flinding son of Fuilin,[50] who escaped from Morgoth's mines; together they rescue Túrin from the Orcs. Túrin slays Beleg by misadventure.

190   Túrin healed of his madness by Ivrin's well,[51] and is brought at last by Flinding to Nargothrond. They are admitted on the prayer of Finduilas daughter of Orodreth, who had before loved Flinding.

190–5   The sojourn of Túrin in Nargothrond. Beleg's sword is reforged and Túrin rejects his ancient name and is renowned as Mormegil (Mormakil)[52] 'Black-Sword'. He calls his sword Gurtholfin 'Wand of Death'. Finduilas forgets her love of Flinding, and is beloved of Túrin, who will not reveal his love out of faithfulness to Flinding; nonetheless Flinding is embittered. Túrin becomes a great captain. He leads the Gnomes of Nargothrond to victory and their ancient secrecy is broken. Morgoth learns of the growing strength of the stronghold,[53] but the Orcs are driven out of all the land between Narog and Sirion and Doriath to the East, and West to the Sea, and North to Erydlómin.[54] A bridge is built over Narog. The Gnomes ally them with Haleth's folk under Handir.

192 Meglin comes to Gondolin and is received by Turgon as his sister's child.

194 In this time of betterment Morwen and Nienor leave Hithlum and seek tidings of Túrin in Doriath. There many speak of the prowess of Mormakil,[55] but of Túrin none know tidings.

195 Glómund with a host of Orcs comes over Erydlómin and defeats the Gnomes between Narog and Taiglin. Handir is slain. Flinding dies refusing succour of Túrin. Túrin hastens back to Nargothrond but it is sacked ere his coming. He is deceived and spellbound by Glómund. Finduilas and the women of Nargothrond are taken as thralls, but Túrin deceived by Glómund goes to Hithlum to seek Morwen.

News comes to Doriath that Nargothrond is taken and Mormakil is Túrin.

Tuor was led out of Hithlum by a secret way under Ulmo's guidance, and journeyed along the coast past the ruined havens of Brithombar and Eldorest[56] and reached Sirion's mouth.[57]

195–6 Túrin goes to Hithlum and finds his mother gone. He slays Brodda and escapes. He joins the Woodmen and becomes their lord, since Brandir son of Handir is lame from childhood. He takes name of Turambar (Turumarth)[58] 'Conqueror of Fate'.

196 Here Tuor meets Bronweg at Sirion's mouth. Ulmo himself appears to him in Nan-tathrin; and Tuor and Bronweg guided by Ulmo find Gondolin. They are received after questioning, and Tuor speaks the embassy of Ulmo. Turgon does not now harken to it, partly because of the urging of Meglin. But Tuor for his kindred's sake is held in great honour.

Morwen goes to Nargothrond, whither Glómund has returned and lies on the treasure of Felagund. She seeks for tidings of Túrin. Nienor against her bidding rides in disguise with her escort of Elves of the folk of Thingol.

Glómund lays a spell on the company and disperses it. Morwen vanishes in the woods; and a great darkness of mind comes on Nienor.

Túrin found Nienor hunted by the Orcs. He names her Níniel, the tearful, since she knew not her name, and himself Turambar.

197–8 Nienor Níniel dwells with the Woodfolk and is beloved by Túrin Turambar and Brandir the lame.

198 Túrin weds Nienor.

199 Glómund seeks out the dwellings of Túrin. Túrin slays him with Gurtholfin his sword; but falls aswoon beside him. Nienor finds him, but Glómund ere death releases her from the spell and declares her kindred. Nienor casts herself away over the waterfall in that place.[59] Brandir reveals the truth to Túrin and is slain by him. Túrin bids Gurtholfin slay him, and he dies. So ended the worst of Morgoth's evil; but Húrin was released from Angband, bowed as with age, and sought for Morwen.

Tuor weds Idril Celebrindal daughter of [Turgon of] Gondolin, and earns the secret hate of Meglin.

200 Here was born Eärendel the Bright, the star of the Two Kindreds, unto Tuor and Idril in Gondolin. Here was born also Elwing the White, fairest of women save Lúthien, unto Dior in Ossiriand.

Húrin gathers men unto him. They find the treasure of Nargothrond and slay Mîm the Dwarf who had taken it to himself. The treasure is cursed. The treasure is brought to Thingol. But Húrin departs from Doriath with bitter words, but of his fate and of Morwen's after no certain tidings are known.

201 Thingol employs the Dwarves to smithy his gold and silver and the treasure of Narog, and they make the renowned Nauglafring,[60] the Dwarf-necklace, whereon is hung the Silmaril. Enmity awakes[61] between the Elves and Dwarves, and the Dwarves are driven away.

202 Here the Dwarves invaded Doriath aided by treachery, for many Elves were smitten with the accursed lust of the treasure. Thingol was slain and the Thousand Caves sacked. But Melian the divine could not be taken and departed to Ossiriand.

Beren[62] summoned by Melian overthrew the Dwarves at Sarn-Athra[63] and cast the gold into the River Asgar, which afterwards was called Rathlorion[64] the Golden-bed; but the Nauglafring and the Silmaril he took. Lúthien wore the necklace and the Silmaril on her breast. Here Beren and Lúthien depart out of men's knowledge and their deathday is not known; save that at night a messenger brought the necklace unto Dior in Doriath, and the Elves said: 'Lúthien and Beren are dead as Mandos doomed.'

Dior son of Lúthien and Beren, Thingol's heir, returned unto Doriath and for a while re-established it, but Melian went back to Valinor and he had no longer her protection.

203 The necklace came to Dior; he wore it on his breast.

205 The sons of Fëanor hear tidings of the Silmaril in the East, and gather from wandering and hold council. They summon Dior to give up the jewel.

206 Here Dior fought the sons of Fëanor on the east marches of Doriath, but he was slain. Celegorm and Curufin and Cranthir fell in battle. The young sons of Dior, Elboron and Elbereth, were slain by the evil men of Maidros' host, and Maidros bewailed the foul deed. The maiden Elwing was saved by faithful Elves and taken to Sirion's mouth, and with them they took the jewel and the necklace.

Meglin was taken in the hills and betrayed Gondolin to Morgoth.

207 Here Morgoth loosed a host of dragons over the mountains from the North and Gondolin's vale was taken and the city besieged. The Orcs sacked Gondolin and destroyed the king and most of his people; but Ecthelion of the Fountain slew there Gothmog lord of Balrogs ere he fell.

Tuor slew Meglin. Tuor, Idril, and Eärendel

escaped by a secret way devised by Idril and came to Cristhorn, Eagles' Cleft, a high pass beneath Fingolfin's cairn in the North. Glorfindel was there slain in an ambush, but Thorndor saved the remnant of Gondolin, and they escaped at last into the vale of Sirion.

The ruin of the Elves was now well-nigh complete, and no refuge or strong place or realm remained to them.

208 Here the wanderers from Gondolin reached the mouths of Sirion and joined with the slender company of Elwing. The Silmaril brings blessing upon them and they multiply, and build ships and a haven, and dwell upon the delta amid the waters. Fugitives gather to them.

210 Maidros hears of the upspringing of Sirion's Haven and that a Silmaril is there, but he forswears his oath.

224 The unquiet of Ulmo comes upon Tuor and he builds the ship Eárámë, Eagle's Pinion, and departs with Idril into the West and is heard of no more. Eärendel weds Elwing and is lord of the folk of Sirion.

225 Torment of Maidros and his brothers because of their oath. Damrod and Díriel resolve to win the Silmaril if Eärendel will not yield it.

Here unquiet came upon Eärendel and he voyaged the seas afar seeking Tuor, and seeking Valinor, but he found neither. The marvels that he did and saw were very many and renowned. Elrond Half-elfin, son of Eärendel, was born.

The folk of Sirion refused to give up the Silmaril in Eärendel's absence, and they thought their joy and prosperity came of it.

229 Here Damrod and Díriel ravaged Sirion, and were slain. Maidros and Maglor gave reluctant aid. Sirion's folk were slain or taken into the company of Maidros. Elrond was taken to nurture by Maglor. Elwing cast herself with the Silmaril into the sea, but by Ulmo's aid in the shape of a bird flew to Eärendel and found him returning.

230   Eärendel binds the Silmaril on his brow and with Elwing sails in search of Valinor.

233   Eärendel comes unto Valinor and speaks on behalf of both races.

240   Maglor, Maidros, and Elrond with few free Elves, the last of the Gnomes, live[65] in hiding from Morgoth, who rules all Beleriand and the North, and thrusts ever East and South.

233–43   The sons of the Gods[66] under Fionwë son of Manwë prepare for war. The Light-elves arm, but the Teleri do not leave Valinor, though they built a countless host of ships.

247   Fionwë's host draws nigh to the Hither Lands and his trumpets from the sea ring in the western woods. Here was fought the Battle of Eldorest,[67] where Ingwil[68] son of Ingwë made a landing. Great war comes into Beleriand, and Fionwë summons all Elves, and Dwarves, and Men, and beasts, and birds to his standards, who do not elect to fight for Morgoth. But the power and dread of Morgoth was very great, and many did not obey.

★ 250   Here Fionwë fought the last battle of the ancient North, the Great or Terrible Battle. Morgoth came forth, and the hosts were arrayed on either side of Sirion. But the host of Morgoth were driven as leaves and the Balrogs destroyed utterly, and Morgoth fled to Angband pursued by the hosts of Fionwë.

He loosed thence all the winged Dragons, and Fionwë was driven back upon Dor-na-Fauglith, but Eärendel came in the sky and overthrew Ancalagon the Black Dragon, and in his fall Thangorodrim was broken.[69]

The sons of the Gods wrestled with Morgoth in his dungeons and the earth shook and all Beleriand was shattered and changed and many perished, but Morgoth was bound.

Fionwë departed to Valinor with the Light-elves and many of the Gnomes and the other Elves of the Hither Lands, but Elrond Half-elfin remained and ruled in the

West of the world. Maidros and Maglor perished in [70] a last endeavour to seize the Silmarils which Fionwë took from Morgoth's crown.[71] So ended the First Age of the World and Beleriand was no more.

NOTES

1   This sentence, *with their friends Orodreth, Angrod, and Egnor, sons of Finrod*, was an early addition; cf. the addition made to AV, note 21.

2   Later addition: *Dagor-os-Giliath*, which is found in AV as first written, entry Valian Year 2996.

3   Later addition: *(Eredwethion)*, which is found in AV as first written, entry Valian Year 2996. – Pencilled in the margin against this passage, but then struck out, is: *The passage of the Gnomes into Mithrim occupied equivalent of 10 years of later time or 1 Valinorian year*. Cf. AV, p. 268.

4   This is an early alteration, going with that given in note 1, of *With him come the sons of Finrod*; cf. the alteration made to AV, note 23.

5   An early alteration from: *They march to Mithrim as the Sun rises, and unfurl their banners; but there is feud* . . .

6   Later addition: *Belegar*. This name occurs in the Old English version II of AV, p. 285 line 43.

7   Later addition: *Eredlindon*. This name occurs in late additions to Q (§9 note 3) and AV (note 14).

8   *Eldorest > Eglarest > Eglorest* (cf. notes 56, 67). On the Westward extension of the first map (see pp. 227–8) the name is *Eldorest*; in an interpolation to AV (note 18) it is *Eglorest*; in *The Silmarillion* it is *Eglarest*.

9   The conclusion of this annal (very probably changed at the time of composition) was originally: *A time of peace and growth. Before the Sun were only the pines and firs and dark* . . . . .

10   Later addition: *at Nargothrond*.

11   *Erydlómin > Eredwethion* (twice; later changes). See note 3, and pp. 192–3, 221.

12   Later addition: *at Nargothrond*.

13   These three annals are placed here and written thus in the manuscript, and enclosed in square brackets. The brackets perhaps only indicate that the annals are an addition (Gumlin's birth was first placed in the annal 122, but struck out probably at the time of writing, and the mention of the birth of Handir son of Hundor was an early addition to annal 141).

14   Later change: *Ermabwed > Ermabuin*. *Ermabwed* is the form in the *Lay of the Children of Húrin* and in Q (§10).

15 Later addition: *or Mablosgen the Empty-handed*.

16 Most of the birth-dates from 124 to 150 were changed by a year or two, but since the figures were overwritten the underlying dates cannot all be made out with certainty. The entry for the birth of Rían was first given a separate entry under the year 152: *Rían the sorrowful, daughter of Belegund, born*.

17 Later addition: *Dagor Hurbreged*.

18 Later addition: *in full might*.

19 These two sentences were an addition, though a very early one: hence the change of tense.

20 Later addition: *Tol-na-Gaurhoth, Isle of Werewolves*.

21 Later addition: *Menegroth*. This name occurs in an interpolation to AV (note 18) and in the Old English version II, p. 288 line 153.

22 *Math-Fuin-delos* > *Gwath-Fuin-daidelos* (late change). On *delos*, *daidelos* see p. 259 third footnote and p. 272 note 27.

23 Later addition: *Gorlim, Radros, Dengar, & 7 others*. Above *Dengar* is written (later) *Dagnir*.

24 This sentence was struck through in pencil and the following replacement written in: *Their wives and children were captured or slain by Morgoth, save Morwen Eledwen Elfsheen (daughter of Baragund) and Rían (daughter of Belegund), who were sent*, &c.

25 Following this the original text had: *Haleth, last of the Fathers of Men, dies in the woods. Hundor his son rules his folk*. This was struck out while the *Annals* were in course of composition, for it reappears later, and not as an insertion (year 168).

26 *Sirion's Well* > *Eithyl Sirion* (later change). *Eithyl* (of which the *y* is uncertain) replaces an earlier form, probably *Eothlin*.

27 *Erydlómin* > *Eredwethion* (later change; cf. note 11).

28 Later addition: *nauglar or* (i.e. *for the nauglar or Dwarves*). *nauglar* seems to have been changed from *nauglir*, the form in Q.

29 These two sentences, from *Of the Dwarves* ..., bracketed in pencil; see pp. 335–6.

30 *Ulfand* is an early emendation from *Ulband*, and so also in the next sentence.

31 Later addition: *Tinúviel, daughter of Thingol of Doriath*. – For the word *geste* see III. 154.

32 *Tolsirion* > *Tol-na-Gaurhoth* (later change; cf. note 20).

33 Later addition: *Nargothrond is hidden*.

34 Later addition: *among the Green-elves*.

35 *Elves* > *Gnomes* (later change, depending on that given in note 34).

36 These two entries, for the years 164 and 165, are early replacements of essentially the same entries originally placed under 169 and 170: *Húrin son of Hádor weds Morwen Elfsheen daughter of Baragund son of Bëor*, and *Túrin son of Húrin born*. The first of these contains two errors, which cannot be other than the merest slips in rapid

composition, for *son of Gumlin son of Hádor* and *son of Bregolas son of Bëor*. Similarly in the entry for 172 Huor is called *son of Hádor*.

37   *Huor son of Hádor:* an error; see note 36.

38   Later addition: *Nirnaith Irnoth*, changed to *Nirnaith Dirnoth*. In the *Lay of the Children of Húrin* there are many different forms of the Elvish name of the Battle of Unnumbered Tears, one replacing another: the last are *Nirnaith Únoth* replaced by *Nirnaith Ornoth* (the final form *Nirnaith Arnediad* is also found in the poem, written in at a later period, as in Q §11, note 16).

39   *Erydlómin* > *Erydwethion* (later change; cf. notes 11, 27).

40   *Flinding* first > *Findor*; then *Flinding son of Fuilin* > *Gwindor son of Guilin* (later changes).

41   *Túrin was nigh three years old* depends on the earlier date of his birth in the year 170: see note 36.

42   Later addition: *Cûm-na-Dengin*. The name *Amon Dengin* is found in a late rewriting of a passage in Q §16, note 3.

43   This passage replaced, at the time of writing, the original: *Rían sought for Huor and died beside his body*. See note 46.

44   The date 173 was added subsequently, though early, to this passage. It remains in its original place, not struck out though not included here, at the beginning of the next passage, *Morgoth broke his pledges . . .*

45   *Ulfand* early < *Ulband*, as previously (note 30).

46   The original text had here: *Tuor son of Huor was born in sorrow*, which was struck out at the time of writing when the additional passage concerning Tuor at the end of annal 172 was written in (note 43). The sentence concerning Nienor that follows was an early addition.

47   This sentence is roughly marked for transference to between the annals 184 and 184–7.

48   This paragraph, from *Tuor grew up . . .*, was dated 177, but the date was struck out. As the *Annals* were first written, Túrin's birth was placed in the year 170, but this entry was rejected and replaced under 165 (note 36). When the present passage was dated 177, therefore, Túrin was 7 when he went to Doriath; but with the striking out of this date the passage belongs under 173, and the years of Túrin's life in Hithlum become 165–73, which may or may not signify a change in his age when he went to Doriath. In *The Silmarillion* (p. 198) he was eight; but the statement here that he was seven is left unchanged.

49   After this annal another was inserted in the later, pencilled layer of emendation: *188. Halmir son of Orodreth trapped and hung to a tree by Orcs*.

50   *Flinding son of Fuilin* > *Gwindor son of Guilin* (later change; cf. note 40). *Flinding* > *Gwindor* at all occurrences of the name in annals 190, 190–5, 195.

51   *Ivrin's well > the well of Ivrineithil* (later change).
52   *Mormegil (Mormakil) > Mormael (Q. Mormakil)* (later change).
     This is the first occurrence of the form *Mormegil*; for earlier forms
     see p. 184.
53   *Morgoth learns of the growing strength of the stronghold* is an early
     change from *Morgoth learns of the stronghold*.
54   *Erydlómin > Erydwethion*, as previously (later change); again in
     annal 195.
55   *Mormakil > Mormael (Mormakil)* (later change; cf. note 52).
56   *Eldorest > Eglorest* (later change; cf. note 8).
57   This entry, from *Tuor was led out of Hithlum* . . ., originally dated
     196, was changed (early) to 195, but left where it was, with its date,
     after that for 195–6. A pencilled direction places it in the position in
     which it is printed here.
58   The *h* of *Turumarth* circled in pencil for deletion. The sentence is
     an early addition.
59   Later addition: *Silver Bowl (Celebrindon)*. This was struck out and
     the following substituted: *which was called Celebros Silver Foam,
     but after Nen Girith Shuddering Water.*
60   *Nauglafring > Nauglamír* (later change); again in annal 202.
61   *Enmity awakes* is an early change from *War ensues.*
62   Later addition: *and the Green-elves* (cf. note 34).
63   *Sarn-Athra > Sarn-Athrad* (later change). The same change is
     made in Q (§14, note 8).
64   *Rathlorion > Rathloriel* (later change). The same change is made in
     Q (§14, note 11).
65   Later addition: *upon Amon Ereb the Lonely Hill in East Beleriand.*
     Above *East Beleriand* is written *in the South.*
66   *the Gods > the Valar that is the Gods* (later change).
67   *Eldorest > Eglarest > Eglorest* (later changes; cf. notes 8, 56).
68   *Ingwil > Ingwiel* (later change). *Ingwiel* is the form in an addition to
     Q (Q II, §17, note 19).
69   Written hastily in the margin against this paragraph: *This great war
     lasted 50 years.*
70   *perished in > made* (later change).
71   Later addition: *but Maidros perished and his Silmaril went into the
     bosom of the earth, and Maglor cast his into the sea, and wandered
     for ever on the shores of the world.*

Commentary on the *Annals of Beleriand* (text AB I)

This commentary follows the annal-sections of the text (in some cases
groups of annals).

Opening section (before the rising of the Sun). Morgoth 'rebuilds his
fortress of Angband'. This is as in S and Q, before *Utumna* reappeared,

as it does in the *Ambarkanta* (see pp. 257, 259–60); AV is not explicit, merely saying (p. 266) that he 're-established his stronghold'. Angband is 'beneath the Black Mountain, Thangorodrim'; on this see pp. 220, 260.

There is here the remarkable statement that Morgoth 'devises the Balrogs and the Orcs', implying that it was only now that they came into being. In Q (§2), following S, they originated (if the Balrogs were not already in existence) in the ancient darkness after the overthrow of the Lamps, and when Morgoth returned to Angband 'countless became the number of the hosts of his Orcs and demons' (§4); similarly in AV (p. 266) he 'bred and gathered *once more* his evil servants, Orcs and Balrogs'. A note written against the passage in Q §4 directs, however, that the making of the Orcs should be brought in here rather than earlier (note 8); and in the version of 'The Silmarillion' that followed Q (later than these *Annals*) this was in fact done: when Morgoth returned,

> countless became the hosts of his beasts and demons; and *he brought into being the race of the Orcs*, and they grew and multiplied in the bowels of the earth.

(The subsequent elaboration of the origin of the Orcs is extremely complex and cannot be entered into here.) It is clear, therefore, that these words in AB I, despite the fact of its being evidently earlier than AV, look forward to the later idea (itself impermanent) that the Orcs were not made until after Morgoth's return from Valinor.

According to AV Morgoth escaped in the course of the Valian Years 2990–1; some century and a half of later time elapsed, then, between the first making of the Orcs and the beginning of their raids, referred to under the first of the annals dated 50.

On the addition (notes 1 and 4) that Orodreth, Angrod, and Egnor came to Middle-earth in the ships with the Fëanorians, while Felagund crossed the Grinding Ice with Fingolfin, see the commentary on AV, p. 279.

Annal 1   The reason for the alteration in note 5 is not clear to me; unless the purpose was to emphasize that the second host of the Noldoli came 'from the North', i.e. from the Grinding Ice, not from Drengist.

Annals 20 to 51   The 'Feast of Reuniting' is the later name, as in *The Silmarillion* (p. 113); in Q (§9) it is the 'Feast of Meeting'. But it is still held in the Land of Willows (see p. 175). Now appear at the Feast ambassadors out of Doriath, and Elves from the Western Havens Brithombar and Eldorest (> Eglorest); for the growth of the idea of the Havens see p. 227, entry *Brithombar*. Whereas in Q the Feast took place within the period of the Siege of Angband, it now preceded the laying of the Siege, which in the later story began after the Glorious Battle (*Dagor Aglareb*) – of which the earthquakes and the Orc-raids of the years 50–51 are the first suggestion.

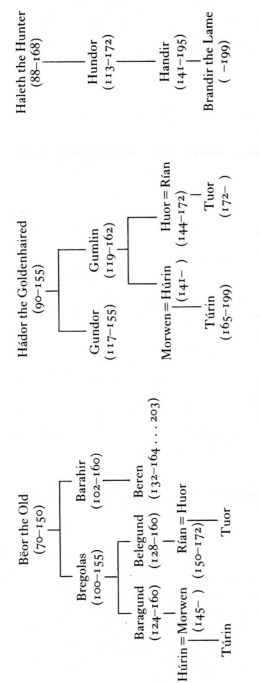

Haleth the Hunter
(88–168)

Hundor
(113–172)

Handir
(141–195)

Brandir the Lame
(–199)

Hádor the Goldenhaired
(90–155)

Gundor
(117–155)

Gumlin
(119–162)

Morwen = Húrin
(141–)

Huor = Rían
(144–172)

Túrin
(165–199)

Tuor
(172–)

Bëor the Old
(70–150)

Bregolas
(100–155)

Barahir
(102–160)

Baragund
(124–160)

Belegund
(128–160)

Beren
(132–164 . . . 203)

Rían = Huor
(150–172)

Húrin = Morwen
(145–)

Túrin

Tuor

Bregolas, Hádor, and Gundor were slain in the Battle of Sudden Fire (155); Barahir, Baragund, and Belegund were slain as outlaws on Taur-na-Danion (160); Gumlin was slain at the fortress of Sirion's Well (162); Huor and Hundor were slain in the Battle of Unnumbered Tears (172); Handir was slain at the Fall of Nargothrond (195).

(See p. 317)

In the second annal dated 50 a major new feature emerges: the story of the dreams and forebodings of Turgon and Felagund, leading to the foundation of Nargothrond and Gondolin. (A later note in Q refers to 'the Foreboding of the Kings', §9 note 15.) In Q Nargothrond was founded after the escape of Felagund from the Battle of Sudden Flame (p. 106), and the hidden valley of Gondolin was never known until Turgon's scouts, in the flight from the Battle of Unnumbered Tears, climbed the heights above the vale of Sirion and saw it beneath them (§15, p. 136; later rewritings to Q alter the story: notes 1 and 2). But in AB I Turgon's departure with his people from Hithlum to Gondolin took place immediately on his finding of the secret valley, whereas in the later story he remained still in Vinyamar (of which there is as yet no sign) for long years after his discovery (*The Silmarillion* pp. 115, 125–6).

The definition of Hithlum as 'the Land of Mist about Mithrim' may imply that *Mithrim* was still only the name of the Lake: see AV, entry 2995, and commentary p. 280.

Fingon is now so named in the text as written, not Finweg > Fingon as in Q.

Fingolfin is now named as the overlord of all the 'Dark-elves' west of Narog, and his power is gathered in the northward range of the Shadowy Mountains, whence he can watch the plain of Bladorion (which is named in AV, entry 2996). The island on which the tower of Felagund stood is now named *Tolsirion*, and Felagund is alone associated with it (cf. Q §9 'A tower they [the sons of Finrod] had on an island in the river Sirion', but also §10 'Felagund they buried on the top of his own island hill'); the pre-eminence of Felagund among his brothers is firmly established, and his isolation from them.

In Q §9, note 1, the name of the great pineclad highland before it was turned to a place of evil first appears, in the form *Taur Danin*; *Taur-na-Danion* occurs in the list of Old English names (p. 211). It is said of the sons of Fëanor in Q (§9) that 'their watchtower was the high hill of Himling, and their hiding place the Gorge of Aglon'.

Annals 70 to 150   In the entries giving the birth-dates of the Bëorians is seen the emergence of an elder line of descent from Bëor the Old beside Barahir and Beren: Barahir now has a brother Bregolas, whose sons are Baragund and Belegund (in this History all three have been named in rewriting of the *Lay of Leithian*, III. 335, but that belongs to a much later time). In this line Morwen and Rían are genealogically placed, and as the daughters of Baragund and Belegund become cousins. But though nothing has been said before of Rían's kindred, the idea that Morwen was related to Beren goes right back to the *Tale of Turambar*, where (as that text was first written, when Beren was a Man) Mavwin was akin to Egnor, Beren's father (see II. 71, 139).

The Bëorian house is thus now in its final form in the last and most important generations, though Barahir and Bregolas were later to be removed by many steps from Bëor with the lengthening of the years of Beleriand from the rising of the Sun.

By this genealogical development, too, Túrin and Tuor are descended both from the house of Bëor and from the house of Hador; and they become cousins on both sides.

Haleth, who in Q was the son of Hador, now becomes independent, a 'Father of Men'; cf. the pencilled alterations to Q §9 (note 11 and p. 175), where Haleth 'the Hunter' enters Beleriand shortly before Hador – as is implied also in AB I. The account of the physical characters of the Men of the Three Houses of the Elf-friends is the origin of that in *The Silmarillion* (p. 148); but at this stage the people of Haleth are likened to those of Hador rather than to the Bëorians, and this is undoubtedly a reflection of the fact that the 'Hadorian' and 'Halethian' houses had only just been divided (see pp. 175–6).

In Q (§13, p. 129), Brandir the Lame was the son of Handir, son of Haleth; but now in AB I a new generation is introduced in the person of Hundor, by early addition to the text (see note 13).

In the house of Hador the removal of Haleth as Hador's elder son leads to the appearance of Gundor, as seen already in the later alteration to Q §9 (note 11 and pp. 175–6). In AB I *Hador* is spelt both *Hádor* and *Hador*, and on the assumption that the accent must be intended whereas its absence may not I have extended the form *Hádor* throughout.

The genealogies of the Three Houses of the Elf-friends, together with their dates as given in AB I (after revision), are now therefore as shown on p. 315.

That Hádor became a vassal of Fingolfin (annal 120) is extended from the statement in Q §9, 'the sons of Hador were allied to the house of Fingolfin', with the addition that he was given lands in Hithlum. That his grandson Húrin had his house in Hithlum is of course an ancient feature of the legends.

Beren's name *Mablosgen*, the Empty-handed (note 15) first appears here (*Camlost* in *The Silmarillion*).

The sadness of the Elves who witnessed it at Bëor's death 'of weariness' (annal 150) foreshadows the passage in *The Silmarillion*, p. 149.

Annals 155 to 157   In these annals (to be compared with Q §9) are many new details and one major development. In a later addition (note 17) the Battle of Sudden Fire (itself appearing, as the Battle of Sudden Flame, in a later addition to Q, note 19) receives the Elvish name *Dagor Hurbreged*; and Glómund is present at the battle – by another later addition (note 18) now in his 'full might'. At each stage, in addition to S, in Q, in addition to Q, in AB, and in addition to AB, the history of Glómund is pushed further back; for the details see pp. 181–2. In *The Silmarillion* p. 151 the same expression 'in his full might' is used of Glaurung at the Battle of Sudden Flame, where the statement has the point that at his first appearance (p. 116) he was not yet full-grown; see pp. 336–7.

The death of Bregolas and the greater part of the warriors of Bëor's house is recorded (cf. *The Silmarillion* pp. 151–2), as also is the death of Hádor 'now aged' and his son Gundor, defending Fingolfin (in *The Silmarillion* they fell at Eithel Sirion). Orodreth as well as Felagund is said to have been rescued by Barahir: this is not at all suggested in Q, where he came to Nargothrond with Celegorm and Curufin only 'after a time of breathless flight and perilous wanderings', and it seems natural to suppose that he had escaped from Taur-na-Danion (Taur-na-Fuin) when his brothers Angrod and Egnor were slain. On this matter see further below, annal 157.

Whereas in Q Himling is said to have been 'fortified' by the sons of Fëanor at this time (p. 106; previously it was their 'watchtower', p. 103), in AB it has been said earlier (annal 51) that Himling was their 'fortress', and it is now told that through the prowess of Maidros it was not lost to them. The passage of Orcs through 'the passes east of Himling' into East Beleriand, and the scattering of 'the Gnomes of Fëanor's house', are now first mentioned: in *The Silmarillion* (p. 153) this is much amplified.

Much the most important and interesting development in these annals is the sojourn of Húrin in Gondolin, of which there has been no hint hitherto; but there are many differences from the story in *The Silmarillion* (p. 158). In AB it was Haleth and his fosterling Húrin (a boy of fourteen) who were brought to Gondolin, having been found by some of Turgon's people in the vale of Sirion; and it is suggested that this was done because Turgon had been warned by messages from Ulmo that 'the help of Men was necessary for him' – this being an element in Ulmo's message to Turgon by the mouth of Tuor at a much later time in Q: 'without Men the Elves shall not prevail against the Orcs and Balrogs' (pp. 142, 146–7). In this earliest version of the story Haleth and Húrin left Gondolin because of the tidings of the Battle of Sudden Fire. In the later legend, on the other hand, it was Húrin and his brother Huor who were brought (by the Eagles) to Gondolin, and this happened during the battle itself; they left the city because they desired to return to the world outside, and they were permitted to go (despite Maeglin) because, having been brought by the Eagles, they did not know the way. This was an important element in the later story, since Húrin could not reveal the secret of Gondolin whether he would or no. The messages and dreams sent by Ulmo, which caused Turgon to receive Húrin and Huor well when he found them in his city, counselled him expressly 'to deal kindly with the sons of the house of Hador, from whom help should come to him at need'. Of course the essential element of Turgon's leaving arms at Vinyamar on Ulmo's command was not yet present. The story in AB has however the liking of Turgon for Húrin and his desire to keep him in Gondolin, the oath of secrecy, and the fostering of Húrin among the people of Haleth (with whom, however, the 'Hadorians' were not yet allied by intermarriage). Now too appears Turgon's sending of messages to Sirion's mouths and the building of ships for vain embassage to Valinor (*The Silmarillion* p. 159).

The annal 157 introduces the interval of two years between the Battle of Sudden Fire and the taking of Tolsirion, which thenceforward was the Isle of Werewolves (and by the later addition given in note 20 receives the Elvish name *Tol-na-Gaurhoth*); cf. *The Silmarillion* p. 155. But in this annal it is said that not only Orodreth and Celegorm and Curufin retreated to Nargothrond at this time, but Felagund also, and that they made there a great hidden palace. It is difficult to know what to make of this, since in the entry for the year 50 it is said that Felagund 'established his armouries' in the caves of Narog, and in that for 51 'he has his seat beside Narog in the South' (though his power is centred on Tolsirion). Possibly the meaning is that though Nargothrond had existed for more than a hundred years as a Gnomish stronghold it was not until the Battle of Sudden Fire that it was made into a great subterranean dwelling or 'palace', and the centre of Felagund's power. Even so, the story still seems very confused. In annal 155 'Barahir and his chosen champions saved Felagund and Orodreth', but also 'Celegorm and Curufin were defeated and fled with Orodreth'; while two years later, in 157, 'Felagund and Orodreth, together with Celegorm and Curufin, retreated to Nargothrond'.

The implication of the last two of these statements is surely that Celegorm and Curufin fled west with Orodreth after Taur-na-Danion was overrun and took refuge with Felagund on Tolsirion; and when Tolsirion was taken two years later all four went south to Narog. If this is so, it seems to contradict the first statement, that Barahir saved Felagund and Orodreth at the Battle of Sudden Fire in 155. Perhaps the fact that the annal heading 155 is written twice hints at an explanation. The second heading is written at the top of a manuscript page (which finishes at the end of the entry for 157); and it may be that this page is a revision which was not properly integrated into the narrative.

In the second paragraph of 157 various new elements appear: the sending of Morwen and Rían to Hithlum (cf. *The Silmarillion* p. 155); Morwen's name *Eledwen* (note 24; she is called 'Elfsheen' in Q §9 and in annal 145); the presence of Baragund and Belegund in Barahir's band, and (by later addition, note 23) the names of two others (in addition to Gorlim): Radros and Dengar (> Dagnir). Dagnir remains in *The Silmarillion*; Radros became Radhruin.

It may be noticed here that while my father subsequently greatly expanded the duration of Beleriand from the rising of the Sun to the end of the Elder Days, this expansion was not achieved by a general, proportionate enlargement of the intervals between major events. Rather, he increased (in successive versions of the *Annals*) the lapse of time in the earlier part of the period, the Siege of Angband being enormously extended; and the relative dating of the later events remained little affected. Thus in AB I the Battle of Sudden Fire took place in the year 155, the attack on the fortress of Sirion's Well in 162, and the Fall of Nargothrond in 195; in *The Silmarillion* the dates are 455 (p. 150), 462 (p. 160), and 495 (p. 211).

Annal 162   The renewed assault of Morgoth seven years after the Battle of Sudden Fire, and the death of Gumlin at Sirion's Well, are referred to in *The Silmarillion*, p. 160 (with Galdor for Gumlin). Sirion's Well is referred to in the *Lay of the Children of Húrin* (line 1460) and marked on the map (p. 222): but 'in the west of (the Shadowy Mountains)' in this annal must be a slip for 'east'. The Elvish name *Eithyl Sirion* (note 26) here first occurs.

Húrin was 'summoned to Hithlum', clearly, because he was at that time still with his fosterfather Haleth in the vale of Sirion.

Annal 163   The Swarthy Men were referred to somewhat obliquely in Q §11, as first written: 'Men from East and South' came to Maidros' banner (p. 117), and 'the swart Men, whom Uldor the Accursed led, went over to the foe' (p. 118). In a later interpolation (note 14) the Men from the East are 'the Swarthy Men' and 'the Easterlings', and 'the sons of Bor and Ulfang' are referred to, Uldor the Accursed being the son of Ulfang. It is not made clear in Q when these Men came out of the East. In AB they entered Beleriand in the year following the attack on Eithel Sirion, while in *The Silmarillion* their coming is put somewhat earlier (p. 157); but the description of them in AB is preserved closely in *The Silmarillion*, with the mention of their liking (clearly boding no good) for the Dwarves of the mountains. The interpolation in Q has the final form *Ulfang*, whereas in AB he is *Ulfand* (< *Ulband*, notes 30, 45);* his sons are *Uldor*, *Ulfast*, whose names were not afterwards changed, and *Ulwar*, who became *Ulwarth*. The association of Cranthir (Caranthir) with these Men also now appears. With the words of AB concerning the Dwarves cf. Q §9, p. 104.

Annal 163–4   On the Green-elves of Ossiriand, appearing in a later interpolation (note 34, and again subsequently, note 62), see AV note 14, and p. 277.

Annal 165–70   There is some slight difference in the accounts in Q §11 and in AB: thus the deeds of Celegorm and Curufin are here made the reason for Thingol's refusal to join the Union of Maidros, and the reluctance of the Elves of Nargothrond is due to their strategy of stealth and secrecy, whereas in Q (as in *The Silmarillion*, pp. 188–9) Thingol's

---

*My father doubtless had both Q and AB in front of him as working texts for a considerable time, and some emendations to Q are later than some emendations to AB.

motive is the demand made on him by the Fëanorians for the return of the Silmaril, and it is the deeds of Celegorm and Curufin that determine Orodreth's policy. There is possibly a suggestion in the words 'for his people will not be restrained' that the emergence of the host of Gondolin was against Turgon's wisdom; in Q §11 as rewritten (in note 7, where the story of the much earlier foundation of Gondolin had entered) Turgon 'deemed that the hour of deliverance was at hand'.

Annal 168 'The Orcs are slowly driven back out of Beleriand': cf. the rewritten passage in Q §11, note 14, 'Now for a while the Gnomes had victory, and the Orcs were driven out of Beleriand.' But this comes *after* 'Having gathered at last all the strength that he might Maidros appointed a day': as I noted (p. 179), the two phases of the war are not clearly distinguished – or else it is only with the *Annals* that the first successes against the Orcs are moved back, with the concomitant idea that Maidros 'made trial of his strength too soon, ere his plans were full-wrought' (*The Silmarillion* p. 189).

Annal 171 In Q §15 Isfin was lost *after* the Battle of Unnumbered Tears, and Eöl 'had deserted the hosts ere the battle'.

Annal 172 In this account of the Battle of Unnumbered Tears, with which is to be compared that in Q §11, the *Annals* introduce many new details that were to endure. Thus it is now told that Huor wedded Rían 'on the eve of battle'; and that there was to be a visible signal from Maidros to the hosts waiting in the West. The doubt concerning the part of the people of Haleth (see pp. 180–1) is now resolved, and 'Hundor son of Haleth and the Men of the wood were slain in the retreat across the sands'; the 'glad meeting of Húrin and Turgon' now arises out of the story first told in annal 155; Balrogs smote down Fingon, though Gothmog is not yet named as his slayer; Turgon took with him in his retreat a remnant of Fingon's host (so in *The Silmarillion* p. 194); Huor died of a venomed arrow (*ibid.*); Húrin threw away his shield (*ibid.* p. 195).

The change of *Flinding son of Fuilin* to *Gwindor son of Guilin* (note 40), which is made also in Q, clearly occurs for the first time in AB, since *Flinding* here became *Findor* before he became *Gwindor*.

In a few points AB differs from the later story. Here, Turgon's host descended out of Taur-na-Fuin, whereas in Q (as rewritten, note 7) 'they encamped before the West Pass in sight of the walls of Hithlum', just as in *The Silmarillion* (p. 192) the host of Gondolin 'had been stationed southward guarding the Pass of Sirion'. The loyalty of Bór and his sons, not mentioned in Q, now appears, but whereas in the later story Maglor slew Uldor, and the sons of Bór slew Ulfast and Ulwarth 'ere they themselves were slain', in AB Cranthir slew Uldor, and Ulfast and Ulwar slew Bór and his three sons. The number of a thousand Balrogs who came from Angband when 'Hell was emptied' shows once again (see II.212–13 and p. 173), and more clearly than ever, that Morgoth's demons of fire were not conceived as rare or peculiarly terrible – unlike the Dragon.

The passage at the end of annal 172 concerning Rían and Tuor, with the further reference to Tuor in annal 173, follows the rewriting of Q §16, note 3; and here as there there is no mention of Tuor's slavery among the Easterlings, which was however referred to in Q as first written.

Annal 173   The words 'others [Morgoth] forbade to leave Hithlum, and they were slain if Orcs found them east or south of the Shadowy Mountains' must refer to those Elves who were not enslaved in Angband; but this is surprising. Cf. Q §12, where it is told that Morgoth penned the Easterlings behind the Shadowy Mountains in Hithlum 'and slew them if they wandered to Broseliand or beyond'; similarly in *The Silmarillion* (p. 195) it was the Easterlings that Morgoth would not permit to leave.

In Q §12, as in S, and as in *The Silmarillion* (pp. 198–9), Túrin left his home before his sister Nienor was born (see p. 59). The entry in AB for Nienor's birth is an early addition and certainly belongs with the revised dating of Túrin's birth (i.e. in the year 165, not 170, see note 36) and of his journey to Doriath (i.e. in 173 not 177, see note 48); thus Túrin left *after* his sister's birth.

Annals 181 to 199   In the legend of the Children of Húrin there is virtually no development from its form in the *Quenta*, from which the *Annals* doubtless derive it direct. The compression is very great, and AB was obviously not intended as an independent composition – thus Túrin's slaying of Brodda is recorded in the annal 195–6 without any indication of the cause, and Brodda has not even been mentioned. The passage in the entry for 196: 'Glómund lays a spell on the company and disperses it. Morwen vanishes in the woods; and a great darkness of mind comes on Nienor' is hardly recognisable as an account of the events known from the *Tale*, S, Q, and *The Silmarillion*; but the general concurrence of all these other versions shows that the wording of AB is the result of severe compression of the narrative, composed very rapidly (see p. 294). It is here, however, that the only development in the story appears: Morwen 'vanishes in the woods', and is not, as in Q §13, led back in safety to Doriath.

The dates in these annals are of much interest as indicating my father's conception of the duration and intervals of time in the legend, concerning which the other early texts give very little idea. Thus Túrin's life as an outlaw after his flight from Doriath and until the capture of Beleg lasted three years, and a further two until the band was betrayed by Blodrin; he spent five years in Nargothrond, and was thirty years old at the time of its fall. Nienor dwelt among the Woodmen for some three years; she was twenty-six years old when she died, and Túrin Turambar was thirty-four.

Annal 181   The first sentence of this annal refers to the time when tidings of Morwen ceased – seven years after Túrin's arrival in Doriath according to the *Tale of Turambar* (II.90) and the first version of the *Lay of the Children of Húrin* (line 333), nine according to the second version of the Lay (line 693) and in *The Silmarillion* (p. 199). In AB it is eight years since his coming to Doriath.

Annal 184   Túrin, born in 165, was thus nineteen when he slew Orgof, as in the *Tale of Turambar* and the *Lay of the Children of Húrin*; see II.142.

Annal 188   In the entry for this year added later in pencil (note 49) the story of the slaying of Orodreth's son Halmir by Orcs re-emerges from the *Lay of the Children of Húrin*, lines 2137–8, where Orodreth's hatred for 'the broods of Hell' is explained:

> his son had they slain,   the swift-footed
> Halmir the hunter   of hart and boar.

This disappeared again later, and the name *Halmir* came to be borne by one of the Lords of Brethil, when that line was much changed and extended. (In the list of Old English names of the Noldorin princes (p. 213) Orodreth has two sons, *Ordhelm* and *Ordlaf*, without Elvish equivalents given.)

Annal 190   The added Elvish name *Ivrineithil* (note 51) first occurs here (*Eithel Ivrin* in *The Silmarillion*).
'They are admitted on the prayer of Finduilas' is a reminiscence of the Lay (lines 1950ff.).

Annal 190–195   In this annal is the first occurrence of the form *Mormegil* (*Mormaglir* in Q), though here corrected later (notes 52, 55) to *Mormael*.
The early emendation given in note 53 is curious: from 'Morgoth learns of the stronghold' to 'Morgoth learns of the growing strength of the stronghold'. It looks as if this change was made in order to get rid of the idea that the loss of the 'ancient secrecy' of the Elves of Nargothrond in Túrin's time led to Morgoth's discovery of its site. I have said in my commentary on Q §13 (p. 184) that while there is no suggestion that Túrin's policy of open war revealed Nargothrond to Morgoth, this element goes back to the *Tale of Turambar* and its absence from Q must be due to compression (earlier in Q, at the end of §11, it is said that after the Battle of Unnumbered Tears Morgoth paid little heed to Doriath and Nargothrond 'maybe because he knew little of them'). In *The Silmaril-*

lion it is said (p. 211) 'Thus Nargothrond was revealed to the wrath and hatred of Morgoth', and this is an important element in the contention over policy between Túrin and Gwindor in a late passage that was not fully assimilated to the *Narn i Hîn Húrin* (*Unfinished Tales* p. 156):

> You speak of secrecy, and say that therein lies the only hope; but could you ambush and waylay every scout and spy of Morgoth to the last and least, so that none came ever back with tidings to Angband, yet from that he would learn that you lived and guess where.

The alliance of the Gnomes of Nargothrond with the people of Handir (Haleth's grandson) is not found in *The Silmarillion*. In AB (annal 195) Handir was slain in the battle of the fall of Nargothrond; in *The Silmarillion* (p. 212) he was slain in the year of the fall, but before it, when Orcs invaded his land.

Annal 192   Cf. the beginning of Q §16, and note 1.

Annal 195   'Glómund with a host of Orcs comes over Erydlómin (> Erydwethion, note 54) and defeats the Gnomes between Narog and Taiglin' shows that, as in Q, the battle before the sack of Nargothrond was not fought at the later site, between Ginglith and Narog; see p. 184.

That Glómund passed over the Shadowy Mountains implies that he came from Angband by way of Hithlum, and it seems strange that he should not have entered Beleriand by the Pass of Sirion; but in the next major version of the *Annals of Beleriand* it is said expressly that he 'passed into Hithlum and did great evil' before moving south over the mountains. There is no indication of why Morgoth commanded, or permitted, this.

In the redating of the entry (196 > 195, see note 57) concerning Tuor's journey from Hithlum to the sea and along the coast to the mouths of Sirion there is a foreshadowing of the situation in *The Silmarillion*, where (p. 238) 'Tuor dwelt in Nevrast alone, and the summer of that year passed, and the doom of Nargothrond drew near'; thus it was that Tuor and Voronwë on their journey to Gondolin saw at Ivrin, defiled by the passage of Glaurung on his way to Nargothrond, a tall man hastening northwards and bearing a black sword, though 'they knew not who he was, nor anything of what had befallen in the south' (p. 239).

Why were the havens of Brithombar and Eldorest (> Eglorest) 'ruined'? Nothing has been said anywhere of the destruction of the Havens. In the next version of the *Annals of Beleriand* the same remains true, and the Havens are again said, in the corresponding passage, to be in ruins. Later, the Havens were besieged and destroyed in the year after the Battle of Unnumbered Tears (*The Silmarillion* p. 296), and I have suggested (p. 229) that the statement on the Westward extension of the first map 'Here Morgoth reaches the shores' may be a reference to this story: it seems then that it was present, though my father neglected to refer to it until much later.

Annal 195–6   If the *h* of *Turumarth* was to be deleted (note 58) this was a reversion to the form in the *Tale of Turambar* (II. 70, 86). In Q §13 *Turumarth* was later changed to *Turamarth* (note 12).

Annal 199   The addition *Silver Bowl (Celebrindon)* (note 59) is another case, like that of *Flinding* > *Gwindor* in annal 172, where the alteration to AB preceded that made to Q. This is shown by the first, rejected form *Celebrindon*, whereas in the addition to Q (§13, note 14) there is only *Celebros* (translated, as here, 'Foam-silver').

Tuor entered Gondolin in 196, and thus dwelt there for three years before he wedded Idril. This agrees with S (§16, see p. 67); in Q nothing is said on the subject.

Annal 200   Húrin's band is now composed of Men, not Elves (see II. 137; in Q §14 they are only described as 'outlaws of the woods'); but the story as very briefly given in AB does not advance matters at this difficult point (see my discussion, p. 188). Húrin's fate, and Morwen's, is now unknown; in Q 'some have said that he cast himself at last into the western sea', and (at the end of §13) 'some have said that Morwen, wandering woefully from Thingol's halls . . . came on a time to that stone and read it, and there died'.

Annals 201 and 202   In the story of the Nauglafring (> Nauglamír, note 60) there is very little narrative development from Q (§14); but the change from 'War ensues between the Elves and Dwarves' to 'Enmity awakes' (note 61) suggests that my father was revising the story at this point. The 'war' is the fighting in the Thousand Caves which first enters the narrative in Q, and of which the slain were buried in Cûm-nan-Arasaith, the Mound of Avarice.

The name of the river in which the gold was drowned, *Asgar*, is found also in the list of Old English names (p. 209); in Q, and on the Eastward extension of the map, as in *The Silmarillion*, the form is *Ascar*.

It is made clear that Lúthien died as a mortal (see pp. 190–1), and the suggestion is that she and Beren died at the same time. It is seen from the dates that they lived on only a very brief while after the coming of the Silmaril to Ossiriand; cf. Q 'the brief hour of the loveliness of the land of Rathlorion departed'. Here is first mentioned the bringing of the Silmaril to Dior in Doriath by night.

Annal 206   A minor addition to the story in Q (§14) is that the battle between the Elves of the renewed Doriath and the Fëanorians took place on the eastern marches of the realm; and the young sons of Dior were slain 'by the evil men of Maidros' host' – which does not necessarily mean that the Fëanorians came upon Doriath with mortal allies, since 'men' is used in the sense 'male Elves'. The sons of Dior, named Eldûn and Elrûn in an addition to Q (note 14), here bear the names Elboron and Elbereth;

the latter must be the first occurrence of *Elbereth* in my father's writings. It is seen from the next version of the *Annals of Beleriand* that the names *Eldûn* and *Elrûn* replaced those given here.

Annal 207   As with the legend of the Necklace of the Dwarves, the extremely abbreviated account of the Fall of Gondolin in AB shows no change from that in Q §16.

Annals 208 to 233   In annal 210 it is said that Maidros actually forswore his oath (although in the final annal he still strives to fulfil it); and this is clearly to be related to his revulsion at the killing of Dior's sons in the annal for 206. Damrod and Díriel now emerge as the most ferocious of the surviving sons of Fëanor, and it is on them that the blame for the assault on the people of Sirion is primarily laid: Maidros and Maglor only 'gave reluctant aid'. This develops further an increasing emphasis in these texts on the weariness and loathing felt by Maidros and Maglor for the duty they felt bound to.

In annal 229 Maglor, rather than Maidros as in Q §17, becomes the saviour of Elrond; this change is made also in a late rewriting of Q II (§17 note 10), where however Elrond's brother Elros also emerges, as is not the case in AB.

The story of Elwing and Eärendel follows that in Q II: Elwing bearing the Silmaril is borne up out of the sea by Ulmo in the form of a bird and comes to Eärendel as he returns in his ship, and they voyage together in search of Valinor; and it is Eärendel's 'embassy of the two kindreds' that leads to the assault on Morgoth (see p. 196).

Annal 240   This is the first mention of any kind of the life of the few surviving Gnomes who remained free after the destruction of the people of Sirion; and in a later addition (note 65) is the first appearance of Amon Ereb, the Lonely Hill in East Beleriand, where they lurked.

Annal 233–43   The refusal of the Teleri to leave Valinor at all (though they built a great number of ships) seems to be a reversion to the story in Q I §17 (p. 149); in Q II (p. 154) 'they went not forth save very few', and those that did manned the fleet that bore the hosts of Valinor. But AB may here be simply very compressed.

Annals 247 and 250   In the account of the assault on Morgoth from the West there are some additions to the narrative in Q (§17): the Battle of Eldorest (> Eglorest), where Ingwil (> Ingwiel) landed in Middle-earth (*Ingwiel* is the form in an addition to Q II, note 19; the form *Ingwil* in AB preceded this), the summons of Fionwë to all Elves, Dwarves, Men, beasts and birds to come to his banners, and the array of the hosts of West and North on either side of Sirion.

The statement (subsequently corrected, notes 70–1) that both Maglor and Maidros 'perished in a last endeavour to seize the Silmarils' seems to suggest a passing movement to yet another formulation of the story (see the table on p. 202); but may well have been a slip due to hasty composition and compression.

It remains to notice the chronology of the last years of Beleriand that now emerges. Tuor wedded Idril in the year (199) of the deaths of Túrin and Nienor; and both Eärendel and Elwing were born in the following year, five years after the Fall of Nargothrond (195). Dior's re-establishment of Thingol's realm lasted no more than four years (202–6), and the Fall of Gondolin followed only one year after the final ruin of Doriath (in the old *Tale of the Nauglafring*, II.242, the two events took place on the very same day), and one year after the capture of Meglin in the hills. Eärendel was seven years old at the Fall of Gondolin (as stated in Q §16), and thirty-three years old when he came to Valinor. The settlement at the delta of Sirion lasted twenty-three years from Elwing's coming there.

The shortness of the time as my father at this period conceived it is very remarkable, the more so in comparison with the later lavish millennia of the Second and Third Ages, not to mention the aeons allowed to the ages before the rising of the Sun and Moon. The history of Men in Beleriand is comprised in 150 years before the beginning of the Great Battle; Nargothrond, Doriath, and Gondolin were all destroyed within thirteen years; and the entire history from the rising of the Sun and Moon and the coming of the exiled Noldoli to the destruction of Beleriand and the end of the Elder Days covers two and half centuries (or three according to the addition given in note 69: 'This great war lasted fifty years').

The second version of the earliest Annals of Beleriand

This brief text, 'AB II', is in the first annals closely based on AB I, with some minor developments, but from the entry for the year 51 becomes a new work, and an important step in the evolution of the legendary history. The text was lightly emended in pencil, and these few changes are given in the notes, apart from one or two small alterations of wording or sentence-order that are taken up silently. As to its date, it was later than AV if one judges from the fact that the crossing to Middle-earth of Orodreth, Angrod, and Egnor in the ships with the Fëanorians is embodied in the text, whereas in AV it is an insertion (note 21).

ANNALS OF BELERIAND

Translation of Ælfwine

Before the Uprising of the Sun Morgoth fled from Valinor with the Silmarils the magic gems of Fëanor, and returned into the Northern regions and rebuilt his fortress of Angband beneath the

Black Mountains, where is their highest peak Thangorodrim. He devised the Balrogs and the Orcs; and he set the Silmarils in his iron crown.

The Gnomes of the eldest house, the Dispossessed, came into the North under Fëanor and his seven sons, with their friends Orodreth, Angrod, and Egnor, sons of Finrod. They burned the Telerian ships. They fought soon after the First Battle with Morgoth, that is Dagor-os-Giliath, or the 'Battle-under-Stars'; and Fëanor defeated the Orcs, but was mortally wounded by Gothmog, captain of Balrogs, and died after in Mithrim.

Maidros, his eldest son, was ambushed and captured by Morgoth, and hung on Thangorodrim; but the other sons of Fëanor camped about Lake Mithrim behind Eredwethion, that is the 'Shadowy Mountains'.

Years of the Sun

1   Here the Moon and Sun, made by the Gods after the death of the Two Trees of Valinor, first appeared. Thus measured time came into the Hither Lands.[1] Fingolfin (and with him came Felagund son of Finrod) led the second house of the Gnomes over the straits of Grinding Ice into the Hither Lands. They came into the North even with the first Moonrise, and the first dawn shone upon their march and their unfurled banners. And Morgoth at the coming of Light withdrew dismayed into his deepest dungeons, but there he smithied in secret, and sent forth black smokes. But Fingolfin blew his trumpets in defiance before the gates of Angband, and came south to Mithrim; but the sons of Fëanor withdrew to its south shores, and there was feud between the houses, because of the burning of the ships, and the lake lay between them.

2   Here Fingon son of Fingolfin healed the feud, by rescuing Maidros with the help of Thorndor, king of Eagles.

1–50   Here the Gnomes wandered far and wide over Beleriand exploring it, and settling it in many places, from the Great Sea, Belegar, to the Eredlindon, that is the 'Blue Mountains', and all Sirion's vale, save Doriath in the middle, which Thingol and Melian held.

20   Here the 'Feast and Games of Reuniting' (that is in

Gnomish Mereth Aderthad) were held in Nan Tathrin, the 'Land of Willows', near the delta of Sirion, and there were the Elves of Valinor, of the three houses of the Gnomes, and the Dark-elves, both those of the Western Havens, Brithombar and Eglorest,[2] and the scattered Wood-elves of the West, and ambassadors of Thingol. But Thingol would not open his kingdom, or remove the magic that fenced it, and trusted not in the restraint of Morgoth to last long. Yet a time of peace, of growth and blossoming, and of prosperous mirth followed.

50 Here unquiet and troubled dreams came upon Turgon son of Fingolfin and Felagund, his friend, son of Finrod, and they sought for places of refuge, lest Morgoth burst from Angband as their dreams foreboded. And Felagund found the caves of Narog and began there to establish a strong place and armouries, after the fashion of Thingol's abode at Menegroth; and he called it Nargothrond. But Turgon journeying alone discovered by the grace of Ulmo the hidden vale of Gondolin, and he told no man as yet.

51 Now Morgoth's might began suddenly to move once more; there were earthquakes in the North, and fire came from the mountains, and the Orcs raided into Beleriand. But Fingolfin and Maidros gathered their forces, and many of the Dark-elves, and they destroyed all the Orcs that were without Angband, and they fell upon an army that gathered upon Bladorion, and before it could retreat to Morgoth's walls they destroyed it utterly; and this was the 'Second Battle', Dagor Aglareb, 'the Glorious Battle'. And afterward they laid the Siege of Angband which lasted more than two[3] hundred years; and Fingolfin boasted that Morgoth could never burst from his leaguer, though neither could they take Angband nor recover the Silmarils. But war never ceased utterly in all this time, for Morgoth was secretly arming, and ever and anon would try the strength and watchfulness of his foes.[4]

But Turgon being still troubled in heart took a third part of the Gnomes of Fingolfin's house, and their goods, and their womenfolk, and departed south and vanished, and none knew whither he was gone; but he came to Gondolin and built a city and fortified the surrounding hills.

But the rest beleaguered Angband in this wise. In the West, were Fingolfin and Fingon, and they dwelt in Hithlum, and their chief fort was at 'Sirion's Well' (Eithel Sirion), on the east of Eredwethion, and all Eredwethion they manned, and watched Bladorion thence and rode often upon that plain, even to the feet of the mountains of Morgoth; and their horses multiplied for the grass was good. Of those horses many of the sires came from Valinor. But the sons of Finrod held the land from Eredwethion to the eastern end of Taur-na-Danion the Forest of Pines, from whose northern slopes also they guarded Bladorion. But Fingolfin was overlord of the Dark-elves as far south as Eglorest[5] and west of Eglor; and he was King of Hithlum, and Lord of the Falas or Western Shore; and Felagund was King of Narog, and his brothers were the Lords of Taur-na-Danion, and his vassals; and Felagund was lord of the lands east and west of Narog as far south as Sirion's mouths, from Eglor to Sirion, save for part of Doriath that lay west of Sirion between Taiglin and Umboth-Muilin. But between Sirion and Mindeb no man dwelt; and in Gondolin, south-west of Taur-na-Danion, was Turgon, but that was not known.

And King Felagund had his seat at Nargothrond far to the South, but his fort and strong place was in the North, in the pass into Beleriand between Eredwethion and Taur-na-Danion, and it was upon an isle in the waters of Sirion, that was called Tolsirion. South of Taur-na-Danion was a wide space untenanted between the fences of Melian and the regions of Finrod's sons, who held most to the northern borders of the wooded mountains. Easternmost dwelt Orodreth, nighest to his friends the sons of Fëanor. And of these Celegorm and Curufin held the land between Aros and Celon even from the borders of Doriath to the Pass of Aglon between Taur-na-Danion and the Hill of Himling, and this pass and the plains beyond they guarded. But Maidros had a strong place upon the Hill of Himling, and the lower hills that lie from the Forest even to

Eredlindon were called the Marches of Maidros, and he was much in the plains to the North, but held also the woods south between Celon and Gelion; and to the East Maglor held the land even as far as Eredlindon; but Cranthir ranged in the wide lands between Gelion and the Blue Mountains; and all East Beleriand behind was wild and little tenanted save by scattered Dark-elves, but it was under the overlordship of Maidros from Sirion's mouths to Gelion (where it joins with Brilthor), and Damrod and Díriel were there, and came not much to war in the North. But Ossiriand was not subject to Maidros or his brethren, and there dwelt the Green-elves between Gelion and Ascar and Adurant, and the mountains. Into East Beleriand many of the Elf-lords even from afar came at times for hunting in the wild woods.

51–255[6] This time is called the Siege of Angband and was a time of bliss, and the world had peace and light, and Beleriand became exceedingly fair, and Men waxed and multiplied and spread, and had converse with the Dark-elves of the East, and learned much of them, and they heard rumours of the Blessed Realms of the West and of the Powers that dwelt there, and many in their wanderings moved slowly thither.

In this time Brithombar and Eglorest were builded to fair towns and the Tower of Tindobel was set up upon the cape west of Eglorest to watch the Western Seas; and some went forth and dwelt upon the great isle of Balar that lieth in the Bay of Balar into which Sirion flows. And in the East the Gnomes clomb Eredlindon and gazed afar, but came not into the lands beyond; but in those mountains they met the Dwarves, and there was yet no enmity between them and nonetheless little love. For it is not known whence the Dwarves came, save that they are not of Elf-kin or mortal kind or of Morgoth's breed. But in those regions the Dwarves dwelt in great mines and cities in the East of Eredlindon and far south of Beleriand, and the chief of these were Nogrod and Belegost.

102 About this time the building of Nargothrond and of Gondolin was wellnigh complete.

104 About this time Cranthir's folk first met the Dwarves as is told above; for the Dwarves had of old a road into the West that came up along Eredlindon to the East and passed westward in the passes south of Mount Dolm and down the course of [the] R[iver] Ascar and over Gelion at the ford Sarn Athrad and so to Aros.[7]

105 Morgoth endeavoured to take Fingolfin at unawares and an army, but a small one, marched south, west of Eredlómin, but were destroyed and passed not into Hithlum, but the most were driven into the sea in the firth at Drengist; and this is not reckoned among the great battles, though the slaughter of Orcs was great.

After this was peace a long while, save that Glómund the first of Dragons came forth from Angband's gate at night in 155 and he was yet young. And the Elves fled to Eredwethion and Taur-na-Danion, but Fingon with his horsed archers rode up and Glómund could not yet withstand their darts, and fled back and came not forth again for a long time.

170 Here Bëor was born east of Eredlindon.

188 Here Haleth was born east of Eredlindon.

190 Here Hádor the Goldenhaired was born east of Eredlindon.

200 Meeting of Felagund and Bëor. Bregolas born.

202 War on east marches. Bëor and Felagund there. Barahir born.

220 Unfriendliness of sons of Fëanor to Men – because of lies of Morgoth: – hence tragedy of their treaty in end of need to the worst Men, and their betrayal by them.[8]

NOTES

1 Added in pencil: *At this time Men first awoke in the midst* [emended to *east*] *of the world. In the meantime (Fingolfin,* &c.) In the second sentence *led* was changed to *had led*.

2 *Eglorest* is an early change in ink from *Eglarest*; cf. AB I, notes 8, 67.

3 *two* was changed from *one* while these *Annals* were in process of composition; see note 6.

4   This sentence was an early addition, probably made when my father
    was writing the annal for 105.
5   *Eglorest* < *Eglarest*, as in note 2. At the occurrences of the name in
    the annal 51–255 it was written *Eglorest*.
6   255 is a change in pencil from 155, but it obviously belongs with the
    change given in note 3, made while the *Annals* were being written, as
    can be seen from the reference in annal 105 to Glómund's emergence
    in 155, which took place during the Siege. My father must have
    overlooked the need to change the date, and put it in later when he
    noticed it.
7   Added in pencil: *But they came not into Beleriand after the coming of
    the Gnomes, until the power of Maidros and Fingon fell in the Third
    (Fourth) Battle.*
8   At the end the text was written at increasing speed and the last few
    lines are a scrawl. The unfilled annal 220 was to be the entry of Haleth
    and Hádor into Beleriand. In the final sentence 'tragedy' replaced
    'justice' at the time of writing.

Commentary on the *Annals of Beleriand* (text AB II)

The revised dates. The period of the Siege of Angband is extended by a
hundred years, and now lasts from 51 (as in AB I) to 255 (notes 3 and 6).
The birth dates of Bëor, Haleth, Hádor, Bregolas, and Barahir, and the
meeting of Felagund with Bëor, are all increased pari passu with the
lengthening of the Siege by a hundred years from AB I.

This commentary again follows the annal-sections of the text. The
many cases where names pencilled on the AB I manuscript are embodied
in the text of AB II can be noticed together: *Dagor-os-Giliath, Eredwethion, Belegar, Eredlindon, Eglorest (< Eglarest), Eithel Sirion,
Sarn Athrad* (for *Sarn Athra*). *Menegroth* in annal 50 occurs in an
addition to AV (note 18) and in the Old English version II (p. 288).

Opening section and Annals 1 to 51   As I have said, while AB II is
here closely based on AB I, there are some minor developments. Where
in AB I Thangorodrim is called 'the Black Mountain', it is now the
highest peak of 'the Black Mountains'. Whether the story of the Battle-
under-Stars had yet shifted is not clear; the statement that the sons of
Fëanor encamped about Lake Mithrim *after* the capture of Maidros
belongs to the older story (see p. 295), whereas Fëanor's death 'in
Mithrim' (which shows that Mithrim was a region and not only the name
of the lake) suggests the later. Fingolfin's defiance before Angband is
now present, and the removal of the Fëanorians to the southern shores of
the lake when Fingolfin's people arrived, as they are in AV (pp. 269–70).
    In annal 20 the Elvish name *Mereth Aderthad* for the Feast
of Reuniting now appears for the first time; and a little more is

said of Thingol's policies at this time (a passage that reappears in *The Silmarillion*, p. 111), though nothing of his hostility to the Gnomes.

In AB I Turgon's departure to Gondolin is given under the year 50, but in AB II it was in this year that he discovered it ('by the grace of Ulmo'), and in 51 he departed from Hithlum (with a third of the Gnomes of the second house: so also in *The Silmarillion*, p. 126). Under 102 it is stated that the building of Gondolin was 'wellnigh complete'; and this (relative) dating survived into *The Silmarillion* (p. 125), where Gondolin was 'full-wrought after two and fifty years of secret toil' – though in the final story it was only then that Turgon himself abandoned his halls of Vinyamar.

Annal 51   The Glorious Battle, of which there is only a suggestion in AB I (under the years 50–51), now becomes a determinate event with a name (and the Elvish *Dagor Aglareb* appears), and the driving back of the Orcs becomes the destruction of an Orc-host on Bladorion; cf. *The Silmarillion* p. 115. Fingolfin's boast that Morgoth could never break the Siege goes back to Q §9: 'The Gnomes boasted that never could he break their leaguer.'

In AB II the passage concerning the disposition of the Gnomish princes during the years of the Siege is greatly expanded, with much new detail (later appearing in *The Silmarillion* in chapter 14, *Of Beleriand and its Realms*). It was clearly composed very rapidly.

We now hear of the horses of the Lords of Hithlum that pastured on Bladorion, many of whose sires came from Valinor (cf. *The Silmarillion* p. 119). In AB I Fingolfin was overlord of 'the Dark-elves west of Narog' (which no doubt implies the relatively small importance of Nargothrond before the Battle of Sudden Flame), but here his authority is over the Dark-elves west of the river Eglor (*Eldor* on the Westward extension of the first map, pp. 227–8), and he is 'Lord of the Falas' (cf. *Falassë* on the *Ambarkanta* map IV, pp. 249, 257); while Felagund is lord of the whole territory between Eglor and Sirion except for Doriath-beyond-Sirion. In *The Silmarillion* (p. 120) Felagund (there called Finrod) likewise 'became the overlord of all the Elves of Beleriand between Sirion and the sea, save only in the Falas'; but the Falas were ruled by Círdan the Shipwright, of whom there is still no trace. Felagund's brothers have now become his vassals, as they are in *The Silmarillion* (p. 120).

Between Sirion and Mindeb (see p. 222) is a land where 'no man dwelt', but it is not named; in *The Silmarillion* (p. 121) it is 'the empty land of Dimbar'. 'A wide space untenanted' lay between the Girdle of Melian in the North and Taur-na-Danion, but Nan Dungorthin (see p. 222) is not named. Orodreth's land is now specifically in the east of the great pine-forested highlands, where he is near to his friends Celegorm and Curufin, whose territory between Aros and Celon (afterwards called

Himlad) and extending up through the Pass of Aglon is now made definite, and as it was to remain.

The territories of the other sons of Fëanor are also given clearer bounds, with mention for the first time of the Marches of Maidros, of Maglor's land in the East 'even as far as Eredlindon' (afterwards 'Maglor's Gap'), of Cranthir's (not yet called Thargelion) between Gelion and the mountains, and of the territory of Damrod and Díriel in the South of East Beleriand. I do not know why Maidros' overlordship is said to extend from Sirion's mouths to Gelion 'where it joins with Brilthor'. At this time Brilthor was the fifth (not as later the fourth) of the tributaries of Gelion coming down from the mountains, the sixth and most southerly being Adurant (pp. 230–1).

Annal 51–255　With the opening paragraph of this annal cf. Q §6:

The Dark-elves they met and were aided by them, and were taught by them speech and many things beside, and became the friends of the children of the Eldalië who had never found the paths to Valinor, and knew of the Valar but as a rumour and a distant name.

The reference to the building of Brithombar and Eglorest 'to fair towns' is found in *The Silmarillion* (p. 120), but there with the addition of the word 'anew'; this is because in the later narrative the Havens of the Falas had long existed under the lordship of Círdan, and were rebuilt with the aid and skill of the Noldor of Felagund's following. In the same passage it is said that Felagund 'raised the tower of Barad Nimras to watch the western sea', and also that some of the Elves of Nargothrond 'went forth and explored the great Isle of Balar', though 'it was not their fate that they should ever dwell there'. The present annal is the first occurrence of the Isle and Bay of Balar. The Tower of Tindobel, forerunner of Barad Nimras, is marked on the Westward extension of the first map, p. 228.

The climbing of Eredlindon by the Gnomes and their meeting with the Dwarves is in *The Silmarillion* (pp. 112–13) ascribed specifically to Caranthir's people settled in Thargelion. The Dwarf-cities are in AB II still placed 'far south of Beleriand', as on the Eastward extension of the map (pp. 231–2). The view of the Gnomes' relations with the Dwarves, and of the Dwarves themselves, though very briefly expressed, is much as in the passage of Q §9 on the subject – as emended (note 4) from 'There they made war upon the Dwarves of Nogrod and Belegost' to 'There they had converse with' them: there is no suggestion here that there was fighting between the peoples, though there is also no mention of traffic between them, which is much emphasized in the passage that 'structurally' corresponds in *The Silmarillion* (p. 113).

Annal 104　In AB I it is not until annal 163 that the Elves' first encounter with the Dwarves is mentioned; this passage was bracketed (note 29), obviously because the matter was to be introduced earlier. The description of the Dwarf-road agrees precisely with the later course of the road on the Eastward extension of the map (see pp. 231–2). Mount Dolm, which is marked on the map, is here first named in the narrative texts. It is notable that the Dwarves are here said to have had this road 'of old'; and the pencilled interpolation given in note 7 certainly means that they *no longer* came into Beleriand after the return of the Noldoli. In Q §14 it is recorded that 'Dwarves first spread west from Eryd-luin, the Blue Mountains, into Beleriand after the Battle of Unnumbered Tears'. In *The Silmarillion* (p. 91) Dwarves entered Beleriand and its history very long before: 'It came to pass during the second age of the captivity of Melkor that Dwarves came over the Blue Mountains of Ered Luin into Beleriand', and it was Dwarves of Belegost who devised the mansions of Thingol, the Thousand Caves. 'And when the building of Menegroth was achieved . . . the Naugrim yet came ever and anon over the mountains and went in traffic about the lands.' Annal 104 in AB II must be the first sign of this important structural change in the history; and it is probably significant that the reference is to the first encounter of the Gnomes (not of Elves in general) with the Dwarves.

The next version of the *Annals of Beleriand* makes it clear that the reference in the interpolated passage (note 7) to 'the Third (Fourth) Battle' is to the Battle of Sudden Flame, despite the naming of Fingon rather than Fingolfin. In AB II the first battle is Dagor-os-Giliath, the second Dagor Aglareb, and the third (though AB II did not reach it) the Battle of Sudden Flame. This interpolation shows my father already thinking of what became the First Battle of Beleriand, in which Denethor of the Green-elves was slain, and which is first hinted at in a pencilled addition to AV (note 18); after the inclusion of this battle in the great Battles of Beleriand, that of Sudden Flame became the fourth.

Annal 105   In this annal are described for the first time Morgoth's tests of the strength and watchfulness of the besiegers, referred to in annal 51, and which remain in *The Silmarillion* (p. 116). The first of these is there said to have taken place nearly a hundred years since Dagor Aglareb, not as here fifty-four; but the route taken by Morgoth's host is the same in both accounts, southwards down the coast between Ered Lómin and the sea to the Firth of Drengist. The story of the emergence of Glómund, not yet full-grown, from the gates of Angband by night, the flight of the Elves to Eredwethion and Taur-na-Danion, and the rout of Glómund by Fingon's horsed archers, is very close to the account in *The Silmarillion*, where however it took place a hundred years after the attack that ended at Drengist: in AB II, again, the time was only half as long. These differences are associated with further great lengthening of the duration of the Siege.

The addition 'in full might' (of Glómund at the Battle of Sudden Flame) made to AB I (note 18) clearly depends on this final stage in the backward movement of Glómund's entries into the history: see pp. 317–18. Some lines of Old English verse accompanying the lists of Old English names refer to Fingon's victory over the Dragon:

> þá cóm of Mistóran   méare rídan
> Finbrand felahrór   flánas scéotan;
> Glómundes gryre   grimmum strǽlum
> forþ áflíemde.

Finbrand is given as Ælfwine's rendering of Fingon (p. 213); *Mistóra* is Mithrim (p. 210).

The concluding, hastily scrawled, sentence of AB II is interesting. In *The Silmarillion* the Haladin (the 'People of Haleth') dwelt in the south of Thargelion after crossing the Blue Mountains, and there 'the people of Caranthir paid little heed to them' (p. 143); after their brave defence of their homes Caranthir 'looked kindly upon Men', and 'seeing, over late, what valour there was in the Edain' offered them free lands to dwell in further North under the protection of the Eldar: an offer which was refused. This is the only reference in *The Silmarillion* to 'unfriendliness' on the part of the Fëanorians towards Men (though one could well imagine it); but it is noteworthy, in respect of the last words of these *Annals*, that it was to Cranthir (Caranthir) that the treacherous sons of Ulfang were allied (AB I annal 163, *The Silmarillion* p. 157).

★

APPENDIX

Old English version of the Annals of Beleriand made by Ælfwine or Eriol

This is the only further fragment of Ælfwine's work in Tol Eressëa in his own language. Its relation to the Modern English version is puzzling, since, though it largely corresponds closely to AB II, it also has features of the AB I text. For instance, the defiance of Fingolfin before Angband and the withdrawal of the Fëanorians to the southern shore of the lake is absent from annal I; the date 'I–C' follows AB I; while *Mereth Aderthad* in annal XX agrees with AB II the annal is otherwise as AB I; and annal L is a confused mixture. The simple explanation that my father made the Old English version after AB I but before AB II (and hence the headnote to AB II 'Translation of Ælfwine') comes up against the difficulty that in the Old English the Siege of Angband lasted *tú hund géara oððe má* (line 81), whereas AB II has 'one hundred' emended to 'two hundred'. But the matter is not of importance.

Like version II of the Old English *Annals of Valinor*, the text breaks off in mid-sentence. My father composed these annals, like the others, fluently and rapidly (hence such variations as *Mægdros*, *Mægedros*, *Maidros*); but he was interrupted, no doubt, and never took them up again. I suspect that Ælfwine's version of the *Annals of Beleriand* was the last.

Beleriandes Géargesægen

Fore sunnan úpgange: Morgoþ gefléah Godéðel þæt is Falinor, ond genóm þá eorclanstánas Féanóres, and þa cóm he eft on Norþdǽlas ond getimbrode þǽr on níwan his fæsten Angband (þæt is Irenhell) under þám Sweartbeorgum. He of searucræfte gescóp þá Balrogas   5 ond þá orcas; ond þá eorclanstánas sette he on his isernan helme. Þá cómon þá Noldielfe þǽre yldestan mǽgþe, þe Ierfeloran hátton, ond sóhton to lande, and gelǽdde híe Féanor and his seofon suna. Þǽr forbǽrndon híe þá Teleriscan scipu; and híe gefuhton   10 siþþan wiþ Morgoþes here and geflíemde hine: þæt wæs þæt ǽreste gefeoht, and hátte on noldisce Dagor-os-Giliað, þæt is on Englisc gefeoht under steorrum oþþe Tungolgúþ. Þær Féanor gewéold wælstówe ond adrǽfde þá orcas, ac wearð self forwundod þearle of   15 Goþmoge Balroga heretoga, Morgoþes þegne, and swealt siþþan on Miþrime. Þá wearð Mægdros his yldesta sunu of Morgoþe beswicen, and wearð gefangen, and Morgoþ hét hine ahón be þǽre rihthande on þangorodrim. Þá gedydon þá óþere suna Féanóres   20 ymb Miþrim þone mere on Northwestweardum landum, behindan Scúgebeorge (Eredweþion).

Æfter sunnan úpgange

Sunnan géar I Hér ætíewdon on ǽrest se móna 7 séo   25 sunne, and þa Godu scópon híe æfter þám þe Morgoþ fordyde þá Béamas, for þon þe híe næfdon léoht. Swá cóm gemeten Tíd on middangeard. Fingolfin gelǽdde þá óþere mægþe þára Noldielfa on Norþdǽlas ofer Ísgegrind oþþe Helcarakse on þá Hiderland; ond þá fór   30 Felagund mid sume þǽre þriddan mægþe. Þá fóron híe ealle norþan mid þám þe séo sunne arás, and þá onbrugdon híe hira gúþfanan, and cómon siþþan mid micle þrymme on Miþrim. Þǽr wæs þá gíet him fǽhþ betwux þǽre mægþe Féanóres ond þám óþrum.   35

Morgoþ mid þý þe léoht ætíewde béah on his déopestan
gedelf, ac siþþan smiþode þǽr fela þinga dearnunga and
sende forþ sweartne smíc.

II Hér Fingon Fingolfines sunu sibbe geníwode betwux
þám mǽgþum for þám þe he áhredde Mǽgedros.   40

I–C Hér geondférdon and gescéawodon þá Noldelfe
Beleriand and gesǽton hit missenlice ond eal Sirigeones
dene of Gársecge (þe Noldelfe Belegar hátaδ) oþ
Hǽwengebeorg (þæt sind Eredlindon), butan Doriaδe
on middan þám lande þe þingol and Melian áhton.   45

XX Hér wearδ se gebéorscipe and se fréolsdæg and se plega
þe Noldelfe Mereþ Aderþad nemnaδ (þæt is
Sibbegemótes fréols) on Wiligwangas gehealden, þe
Noldielfe Nantaþrin hátaδ, néah Sirigeones múþum,
and þǽr wurdon gesamnode ge elfe of Godéδle ge   50
deorcelfe ge éac sume á elfe of þám Westhýþum and of
Doriaδe of þingole gesende. þá wearδ long sibbtíd.

L Hér wearþ eft unfriδu aweht of Morgoþe, ond wurdon
micle eorþdynas on Norδdǽlum, ond þá orcas
hergodon floccmǽlum on Beleriand ond þé elfe híe   55
fuhton wi ͘.

Hér wurdon Turgon Fingolfines sunu 7 Inglor Felagund Finrodes sunu his fréond 7 mǽg yfelum swefnum
geswencte, 7 híe fæsten 7 friþstówa gesóhton ǽr þon þe
Morgoþ ætburste swá hira swefn him manodon. þá   60
funde Felagund þá déopan scrafu be Naroge stréame,
7 he þǽr ongann burg gestaδelian and wǽpenhord
samnian, æfter þǽre wísan þe þingol búde Menegroþ, 7
he þæt heald Nargoþrond nemnde. Ac Turgon ána
férde 7 be Ulmoes láre funde Gondoelin þá díeglan   65
dene, ne sægde nánum menn þá gíet.

Hér ongann Morgoþ eft his mægen styrian; 7 wearþ
oft unfriδu aweht on Beleriandes gemǽrum. Micle
eorδdynas wurdon on norδdǽlum, 7 þá orcas hergodon
floccmǽlum on Beleriand, ac þá elfe fuhton híe wiδ 7   70
híe geflíemdon.

LI Hér gegaderode Morgoδ medmicelne here, and fýr
ábærst of þám norδernum beorgum; ac Fingolfin 7
Maidros fierda gesamnodon and manige þára deorcelfa

mid, 7 híe fordydon þone orchere to nahte, and áslógon   75
ealle þe híe útan Angbande gemétton, and híe éhton þæs
heriges geond þone feld Bladorion, þæt nán eft to
Angbandes durum cómon. Þis gefeoht hátte siððan
Dagor Aglareb, æt is Hréþgúþ on Englisc. Siþþan
gesetton híe 'Angbandes Ymbsetl', and þæt gelǽston   80
híe tú hund géara oððe má, 7 Fingolfin béotode þæt
Morgoþ nǽfre from þám ymbhagan ætberstan mihte.
He ne mihte self swáþéah Angband ábrecan ne þá
Silmarillan áhreddan. Unfriðu wearð nǽfre eallunga
áswefed on þisse langan tíde, for þǽm þe Morgoþ   85
d. . .lice hine gewæpnode 7 ǽfre ymbe stunde wolde
fandian þǽre strengu and þǽre wæcene his gefána.
      Turgon cyning swáþéah

NOTES

1–17   Another, earlier, Old English account of these events is found at
       the end of version I of the *Annals of Valinor*, p. 282.

2   *eorclanstánas*: see p. 283. As in the Old English version I of AV
    the name *Silmaril* is also treated as an Old English noun, with
    plural *Silmarillan* (line 84) (in the AV version *Silmarillas*).

8   *Ierfeloran*: with variant vowels *Erfeloran, Yrfeloran* in the Old
    English version II of AV (line 135), and in the list of Old English
    names, p. 212.

14   *Tungolgúþ* occurs also in the Old English version I of AV,
     line 55.

32   *sunne*: *sunnan* MS.

48   *Wiligwangas* is a pencilled correction from *Wiligléagas*.

51   *þám*: *þá* MS.

53–71   The text of this annal is confused. The first paragraph follows
        the beginning of the first entry numbered 50 in AB I; the second
        paragraph corresponds closely to AB II annal 50; and the third
        repeats the first.

65   *Gondoelin* is clearly written thus.

86   The illegible word is not *dirnlice* 'secretly'.

New Old English names in this text are:

Sweartbeorgas (line 5) 'Black Mountains' (O.E. *sweart* 'black,
    dark');

Scúgebeorg (line 22) = *Eredwethion* (O.E. *scúa* 'shadow');

Ísgegrind (line 30) = *Helcaraksë* (O.E. *gegrind* 'grinding
    together, clashing');

Hǽwengebeorg (line 44) = *Eredlindon* (O.E. *hǽwen* 'blue');
Wiligwangas (line 48) = *Nan Tathrin* (O.E. *wilig* 'willow';
wang 'meadow, flat place' (cf. *Wetwang* in *The Lord of the Rings*); the rejected name *Wiligléagas* contains *léah*, Modern English *lea*).
Westhýpum (line 51, dative plural) = Western Havens (cf. *Elfethýð* = Swanhaven, p. 283; Modern English *hithe*).
Hréþgúþ (line 79) = *Dagor Aglareb* (O.E. *hréþ* 'glory').

The most notable name here is *Inglor Felagund* (line 57). This is the first occurrence of *Inglor*, which remained his 'true' name for many years, though its existence is indicated by the Old English equivalent *Ingláf Felahrór* (p. 213).

INDEX

This Index, like those of the previous volumes, attempts both to provide an almost complete register and to give some indication of the interrelations of names for the same places, persons, and events; but from the nature of this book the range of such variation is here particularly large, and some names appear in complicated relations (and several languages), so that inconsistency in the arrangement of the material has been hard to avoid.

In general, Modern English names are not given separate entries when they occur solely in association with an Elvish name, but are included under the latter.

Page-references include the occurrences of names in Ælfwine's works in Old English ('O.E.'), but these are not distinguished as such unless the name has a distinctive Old English form; and in such cases the Old English name is not given a separate entry, but included under the original name (as *Elfethýð* under *Alqualondë*).

Names that occur on the first 'Silmarillion' map and its Eastward and Westward extensions are not referenced to the reproductions themselves, but those on the *Ambarkanta* maps and diagrams are (including the emended names that are noticed on the facing pages, as *Silma > Ilma > Ilmen*): all these references are preceded by an asterisk.

References to the published *Silmarillion* are not included, and those to the individual tales of *The Book of Lost Tales* are collected under the entry *Lost Tales*.

So many variant arrangements of capitalisation and hyphenation are found in compound names in the texts (as *Sarn-athrad*, *Sarn-Athrad*, *Sarn Athrad*) that I have adopted a single form for the purposes of the Index.

306–7, 325; *the geste of Beren and Lúthien* 300; the destiny of Lúthien 63–4, 190–1, 325. See *Lay of Leithian, Tinúviel.*

Mablon the Ilkorin 58

Mablosgen 'Empty-handed', name of Beren. 311, 317. (Replaced by *Camlost.*)

Mablung Called 'Heavyhand' (113). 113–14, 117, 179, 185, 187 ('with weighted hand').

Maedhros See *Maidros.*

Maeglin See *Meglin.*

Magic Isles 20, 38, 69, 98, 150, 153, 155, 198, *249, 257. See *Enchanted Isles.*

Maglor (1) = Beren. 5. (2) Son of Fëanor. 15, 22, 26–7, 33, 35, 38–40, 64, 69–71, 74, 88, 113, 115, 150, 152, 154–6, 158–9, 161–2, 170, 196, 201–2, 212, 308–10, 313, 321, 326, 331, 335; O.E. *Dægmund Swinsere* 212; *Maglor's Gap* 259, 335

Maidros Eldest son of Fëanor; called 'the Tall' and 'the Left-handed' (298). 15, 22–3, 26–7, 38–41, 52–3, 57, 69–71, 88, 101–2, 116–18, 120–1, 135, 150, 152–4, 156, 158, 161–2, 172–3, 179, 181–2, 195–6, 201–2, 204–5, 212, 268–9, 274, 280, 282–3, 295, 298, 300–2, 307–10, 313, 318, 320–1, 325–31, 333, 335, 338–9; O.E. *Dægred Winsterhand* 212, in the texts *Maegdros* etc.; *Marches of Maidros* 331, 335. Later form *Maedhros* 180, 182, 212, 280. See *Russandol, Union of Maidros.*

Mailgond The elder of Túrin's guardians on the journey to Doriath. 28, 58, 183; later form *Mailrond* 58. (Replaced *Gumlin* (1).)

Makar Warrior Vala. 7–8

Mandos (both the Vala and his abode) 13–16, 18, 21–2, 25–6, 33, 43, 45, 48, 51–2, 54–5, 63–4, 70, 78–9, 84, 87, 89, 91, 96, 100, 115, 134, 166, 170, 172, 179, 190, 205, 207–8, 263–4, 267, 273, 275–6, 279, 285–6, 289, 291–2, 307; O.E. *Néfréa* 166, 208, but *Mandos* (gen. *Mandosses*) in the texts, also called *neocerna hláford* and *wælcyriga* 207. See *Nefantur, Vefántur; Prophecy, Doom, of Mandos.*

Manwë 5, 10, 12–14, 17, 19–20, 23, 44, 47, 50, 52, 68, 72–3, 78–81, 85, 87–90, 92, 94, 97–8, 102, 151, 153–4, 159, 162, 166, 173, 196, 198, 202, 206, 208, 236, 263, 265, 270, 275, 278, 285, 287, 289, 291–2, 294, 309; O.E. *Wolcenfréa* 208, but *Manwë* in the texts.

Marach Leader of the third host of Men to enter Beleriand. 175

Marches of Maidros See *Maidros.*

Marching Forth See *Union of Maidros.*

March of the Elves (1) The Great Journey from Kuiviénen. *249, 256, 264, 271–2; see *Great March.* (2) The expedition from Valinor. 68, 70, 72, 74, 168

Martalmar The roots of the Earth. 241, *242–5, 255. See *Earthroots, Talmar Ambaren.*

Qenya 9, 78

Qerkaringa The Chill Gulf, between the Icefang and the Great Lands. 170

Quendi (In the 'Sketch' spelt also *Qendi*) (1) In the *Lost Tales*, the original name of all Elves, becoming distinct from *Eldar*. 44. (2) The First Kindred (replaced by *Lindar*). 13–15, 17, 37, 40, 44, 72, 85–7, 89–90, 93–6, 149, 151, 153–4, 159, 168, 196, 202, 264, 270, 272, 276, 289; O.E. *Cwendi* 286, 289. (3) (Final sense) The original name of all Elves. 86, 168. See *First Kindred*.

Quenta Noldorinwa (Also *Qenta*) 77, 205–6, 270, 280, 284, 290–2. See especially 206, 284, and see *Pennas, Noldoli*.

Quenya 174, 255, 313

Radhruin Companion of Barahir on Taur-na-Danion. 319. (Replaced *Radros*.)

Radros Earlier name of Radhruin. 311, 319

Ragnarök 207

Rainbow Cleft 5, 141, 193. See *Glorfalc, Cris Ilbranteloth, Cris-Ilfing, Kirith Helvin, Cirith Ninniach*.

Rána Name of the Moon given by the Gods. 97, 170

Rathlorion, River 'Golden-Bed', name given to Ascar after the drowning in it of the treasure of Doriath. 134–5, 189–90, 234, 307, 313, 325; later form *Rathloriel* 135, 189, 234, 313

Red Mountains 239, *249, 255–6. See *Orocarni*.

Region The forest forming the southern part of Doriath. 278

Reynolds, R. W. 11, 41

Rían Mother of Tuor. 35, 67, 122, 141, 146, 183, 193, 298–9, 301, 303, 311–12, 315–16, 319, 321–2

Ringil (1) Originally the pillar of the Northern Lamp, 256; in the *Ambarkanta* the Southern Lamp, which became the Sea of Ringil, (238), 239, *249, 256, 258. See *East(ern) Sea*. (2) Fingolfin's sword. 106–7

Ring of Doom The council-place of the Valar. 81, 167

Rodothlim Precursors of the Gnomes of Nargothrond. 60, 180, 223

Rog Lord of the people of the Hammer of Wrath in Gondolin. 144, 194

Rómen East. *243, *249, 255

Roos 215

Rúmil 235, 271, 274, 292–3; called *the Elfsage of Valinor* 292

Russandol Name of Maedhros. 212

Salmar Companion of Ulmo, called also Noldorin. 68

Sári Name of the Sun given by the Gods. 170

Sarn Athra(d) The Stony Ford, Ford of Stones. Original form *Sarnathrod* 190, 223, replaced by *Athrasarn* 223–4 and *Sarn Athra* 133, 135, 232–3, 307, 313, 333; final form *Sarn Athrad* 135, 233, 313, 332–3. For the site see 232.